# THE
# BOY WHO
# NEVER
# GREW UP

ALSO BY DAVID HANDLER:

*The Woman Who Fell From Grace*
*The Man Who Would be F. Scott Fitzgerald*
*The Man Who Lived by Night*
*The Man Who Died Laughing*
*Boss*
*Kiddo*

# THE
# BOY WHO
# NEVER
# GREW UP

*A Stewart Hoag Novel*

# David Handler

A PERFECT CRIME BOOK
DOUBLEDAY
NEW YORK   LONDON   TORONTO   SYDNEY   AUCKLAND

A Perfect Crime Book
Published by Doubleday
a division of Bantam Doubleday Dell
Publishing Group, Inc.
666 Fifth Avenue,
New York, New York 10103

Doubleday is a trademark of Doubleday,
a division of Bantam Doubleday Dell
Publishing Group, Inc.

*Book design by Tasha Hall*

Library of Congress Cataloging-in-Publication Data

Handler, David, 1952–
The boy who never grew up: a Stewart Hoag novel
/ by David Handler.
p.  cm.
"Perfect crime."
I. Title.
PS3558.A4637B69   1992
813'.54—dc20                                        92-6360
                                                        CIP

ISBN 0-385-42159-1
Copyright © 1992 by David Handler
Printed in the United States of America
September 1992

1  3  5  7  9  10  8  6  4  2

*First Edition*

*For the Bartuccas,*
*who found us a home*

*You can't run away from true love, Debbie. Just like you can't run away from God or your country or your family. It's a part of you, and you're a part of it. That's why you and me, aw heck, we've just gotta get married when we grow up. We'll have a mess of kids together. We'll get old and gray together. It'll be really neat. You'll see.*

—Badger Hayes to Debbie Dale
in *Badger Hayes, All-American Boy,*
a film by Matthew Wax

# THE
# BOY WHO
# NEVER
# GREW UP

# Chapter One

Matthew Wax's very own little movie studio, Bedford Falls, kept its very own little suite of rooms all year around on the eighteenth floor of the Waldorf Towers, the major-bucks wing of the Waldorf-Astoria Hotel. The Towers comes with its own special entrance around on Fiftieth Street off Park, its own doorman, its own desk, its own elevator, and its own style, or lack of it. Understated elegance is what they aim for. Stodgy is about as close as they get. Still, the security isn't terrible. Ronnie and Nancy used to stay there when they hit town from the White House. The Bushes still do. On this crisp autumn morning the place was a madhouse and there wasn't even a single politician in town. Unless you count the mayor, and not many people do.

The street outside was mobbed with reporters and photographers and television news crews. There was local TV, national TV, tabloid TV. *A Current Affair* was there. *Inside Edition* was there. *Hard Copy, Entertainment Tonight*, everybody was there. The police had set up blue barricades to contain all of them, but it was no use. They spilled out into the street, blocking traffic and exchanging graphic taunts with the cab drivers who were trying to get by. Limo drivers who were parked there gulped hot coffee from take-out cups and enjoyed the free show. And the divorce war between Matthew Wax, the most successful director in the history of Hollywood, and Pennyroyal Brim, his breathtakingly adorable leading lady, was indeed a show. The press hadn't pursued a bedtime story with such lunatic zeal since Donald and Ivana split. Every morning brought fresh hot scoops, each more lurid and venal than the last. Just this morning alone *The National Enquirer* had Pennyroyal claiming that Matthew had forced her to make love to her costar, Johnny Forget, in a bathtub while he sat there watching them do it. *The Star*, not to be outdone, was contending that Pennyroyal was secretly pregnant. The identity of her love child's father was being kept under wraps, they revealed, though Pennyroyal's current boyfriend, actor Trace Washburn, certainly had to be the lead candidate. I doubted that. My own money was on Elvis.

I stood there on the edge of the crowd for a moment, collecting myself, much like a diver up on the high board. The only difference is he dives into clear blue water, and I was diving into a sewer. I took a deep breath and plunged right in, elbows flying. It gets a little easier every time I do it.

At the door I was halted by a phalanx of gruff, beefy cops in uniform. I gave one of them my name and assured him I was expected. He looked me over top to bottom. I wore the glen plaid double-breasted cashmere suit I'd had made for me in London by Stricklands. There was a fresh white carnation in my lapel. The white cotton broadcloth shirt and burgundy-and-yellow silk bow tie were from Turnbull and Asser, the silver cuff links from Grandfather, the cordovan brogans from Maxwell's. My trench coat was over my arm. My borsalino, freshly blocked for the fall, was on my head. I did not look like any of the others. This he couldn't deny. Grudgingly, he gave my name to the doorman, who gave it to the desk. He called up. After a moment, they let me inside. I still had to wait in the lobby for a security guard to come down and get me. I did, watching the commotion outside.

It was no surprise that this one was so hot, given the principal players and their images and the millions of dollars involved. In one corner we had Matthew Wax, the gentle giant with his gee-whiz films and gee-whiz life-style. The man was straight out of *Ozzie and Harriet*. He didn't smoke or drink or take drugs. He liked his mom, milkshakes, and his privacy. Matthew Wax was only nineteen years old when he directed his first TV series. He had gone on from there to helm five of the ten top grossing films in Hollywood history, including *Yeti*, *Yeti II* and the highest grosser of them all, *Dennis the Dinosaur*. Estimates of his personal worth ran somewhere between $250 and $400 million, depending on who you talked to, and he wasn't forty yet. In the other corner we had Pennyroyal Brim, the goody-goody star of his last three movies, the perky, dimply little twenty-five-year-old blonde who was so squeaky clean she made Lady Di look dirty. And so impossibly cute the public had fallen for her just as Matthew Wax had. She was Pretty Penny, America's sweetie pie and *People* magazine's most popular cover girl. Her adorable dimples were even insured by Lloyds of London for two million dollars—one million per dimple. Two years ago, she and Matthew Wax had tied the knot. For each it was their first. Six months ago, she had given birth to their first child, a healthy baby boy they named George Bailey Wax. "Little Georgie," America's cutest little mother called him. It was all right out of a storybook or, more appropriately, a Matthew Wax movie. Until the marriage abruptly fell apart a few weeks ago. Penny had filed for divorce citing irreconcilable differences, most notably Matthew's "personal and professional tyranny." She wanted sole custody of Little Georgie and—given that they lived in California, land of golden sunshine and community property—one half of Matthew Wax's entire fortune, including Bedford Falls, the independent movie studio he had purchased a few years before. Matthew's counteroffer: joint custody of Little Georgie, the deed to their Pacific Palisades mansion, an undisclosed cash settlement believed to be around ten million dollars, and *no* share of Bedford Falls. That's when it turned ugly.

She hired herself Abel Zorch, the meanest, most ballistic divorce attorney in Los Angeles, a flamboyantly gay bad-ass who loved the limelight so much he had his own full-time publicist. In an earlier life, Abel Zorch had been a hand-picked Nixon thug, a high-ranking young official in the Committee to Re-Elect the President. Unlike so many of the others, he'd been smart enough to leave no fingerprints behind when Watergate hit the fan. In fact, a number of well-informed people believed it was he who was Deep Throat. He quickly relocated in Hollywood. It proved to be a natural fit. A gifted go-between, deal maker, dispenser of favors, and trader of inside information, Zorch was now one of the most powerful men in the movie business, and certainly one of its most ruthless. Out there he was known as the Iguana—because of his personality and because he happened to look like one. No one liked to go up against him. To do so was to get Zorched. And that's what was happening right now to Matthew Wax. Pretty Penny's lawyer was destroying him. Day after day, nasty little items about Matthew's carefully guarded private life were finding their way into the tabloids. Items about how he kept Penny a virtual prisoner in her own home. About how he was a Howard Hughes-like recluse who spent hundreds of hours at a stretch in a darkened room eating Fig Newtons and watching tapes of old movies and TV shows. About how he hated to bathe and refused to cut his toenails. And how he suffered from chronic premature ejaculation. And was hung up on his mother. And insisted on sleeping in twin beds because Beaver Cleaver's parents had. On and on it went. And it would keep on going until Matthew backed down. But he wouldn't. Instead, he had sued Pretty Penny for defamation of character. And withdrawn his settlement offer. He now wanted sole custody of Georgie, claiming Penny was an unfit mother. His basis for this: the very public affair she was carrying on with Trace Washburn, the fiftyish, ruggedly handsome leading man who had starred in a number of Matthew's biggest hits and whose reputation as a filmland hound rivaled that of Warren Beatty. "Best sex I've ever had," America's sweetie pie had boasted to the world on page one of the *New York Post.* "It's great to be with a real man for a change."

The press was calling it the House of Wax.

The public couldn't get enough of it.

For me, it was just another day at the office.

The security guard was big and blond and bulked up. He carried an old copy of the first novel, *Our Family Enterprise*, the one that prompted the *Times* to label me "the first major new literary voice of the eighties." The one that won me every award in existence, including Merilee Nash. I still have the awards someplace. Merilee is another story. My picture is on the back of the dust jacket. I'm standing on the roof of my brownstone looking awful goddamned sure of myself, and about nineteen.

He peered at it, then at me. "You're Stewart Hoag?"

"I am."

"I don't know," he said unsurely. "You look awful different here."

"You would, too."

"I guess this was taken a long time ago, huh?"

"Why don't you take out your gun and finish the job?"

"No need to be touchy, mister. Just being careful. This way, please." He started for the elevator, then stopped. He had noticed Lulu, my basset hound, for the first time. She was traveling incognito that season in the wraparound shades she'd taken to wearing when she picked up a dose of pinkeye while summering at Merilee's farm. Her eyes were perfectly fine now. She'd kept on wearing the shades because she thought they made her look sexy. I thought they made her look like George Shearing.

"Is she with you?" the guard wanted to know.

"She is," I replied. "But we still haven't made any serious commitment to each other. If you want to take a crack at her, I won't stand in your way."

He started to say something. Nothing came out except for an exasperated grunt. I get a lot of those. The three of us got into the elevator and he punched eighteen. Then the doors closed and up we went.

To be honest, this wasn't where I really wanted to be right now. Fiji was my first choice. Merilee was shooting a movie there with Michelle Pfeiffer. It's a dirty job, but somebody's got to do it. I had stayed behind to work on novel number three. It's a dirty job, but nobody's got to do it. She also hadn't invited me to come along with her. The two of them were playing turn-of-the-century Catholic nuns who fall in love with each other. Merilee didn't think she could stay in character if I were there. Or so she'd said. The fact is we hadn't been getting along too well lately. She'd been snappish, moody, distant. Something was troubling her. What, I didn't know. She had left six weeks ago. For good, according to Liz Smith, who reported the very next day in *Newsday* that we were no longer an item. Merilee and me, that is. I'd been dumped, said Liz. I didn't know where she'd heard that. I didn't know if it was true. Merilee wouldn't answer any of my letters. I hadn't heard one word from her since she left. Not even a postcard. I had kept good and busy though. So far I had generated a whopping seventy-five pages of tumid, overheated gibberish. Presently I was lost in a jungle of my own delusions with no compass and only a dull pocket knife to hack my way out with. That takes time, and time takes money. That's why I was here to see Matthew Wax's brother-in-law, Sheldon Selden, the president of Bedford Falls. My agent said he answered to Shelley. She didn't say if he could also roll over and play dead, but she did say he was housebroken—a rarity among studio executives. She thought he sounded nice. They always do, when they want something from you.

When we got to the eighteenth floor my escort got out first and looked both ways down the long, carpeted corridor. Then we proceeded. There was another guard just like him parked outside the suite.

"Expecting a Libyan hit squad?" I asked.

"The Seldens always travel with security," the one on the door replied.

"Do they need it?"

He rapped twice on the door and told me to go in. I went in. They stayed outside.

The living room was large and charmless. There was a fireplace, a terrace, and a lot of toys scattered about. Also two midget human life forms, one female, one male. The girl was about five, tanned and dark-haired. She wore a Bedford Falls sweatshirt, jeans, and hot pink nail polish, chipped. The boy wore a Dodgers warm-up suit. He was younger, maybe three, chubby and fair-haired. He squealed with delight at the sight of Lulu. Both of them made right for her. Lulu let out a low, unhappy moan. Something she picked up from me. Not that I mean to sound churlish. I don't mind kids. I like them just fine—as long as they're properly stuffed.

Mommy stopped them short. "Sarah? Benjamin? Don't you go running up to her! She may not like it!" She turned to me and asked, "Is she friendly?"

"Many people actually consider her the personality of the outfit," I replied.

Sarah went nose to nose with her. Benjamin tried to climb up on her back. Lulu suffered this in silence. At least neither of them was yanking on her ears. She hates that.

"I'm Shelley Selden, Mr. Hoag," Mommy said, offering me her hand.

"My mistake," I said, taking it. "I was told you were a man."

"Oh, Shelley *is*," she exclaimed. "Sheldon Selden is my husband. He's Shelley, I'm Shelley. They call us the Two Shelleys. Just one of those things." She chuckled merrily. "Matthew Wax is my little brother."

Big Sis was in her early forties, and she didn't look very much like baby brother. She was a tiny woman, not more than five feet tall, plump and pretty, with lustrous dark eyes, a wide, full mouth, and olive skin. Her hair was a frizzy shock of black streaked with silver. She wore a white cashmere turtleneck with a well-tailored pair of gray flannel slacks and Bally slip-ons. She was a warm, comfortable woman. Matronly, almost. "I'm afraid Shelley's on the phone," she said. "He's always on it. Most little boys like to imitate their daddy shaving. Benjamin imitates his daddy yelling into a cordless phone. Show him, sweetie. Show him how you do Daddy."

Benjamin held a chubby little fist up to his ear and screamed, "Deal's dead! Deal's dead! Deal's dead!"

"Isn't he cute?" Shelley asked, beaming proudly.

"As a bug's ear."

Lulu had had enough of him and his sister both. I know this because she unveiled her secret weapon—she yawned in Sarah's face.

"Ugh," cried Sarah, recoiling in disgust. "Her breath  . . ."

"She has rather strange eating habits," I explained.

"Mommy, let's go," commanded Sarah. "I wanna go."

"In a minute, button," Shelley said. To me she said, "We're going shopping."

"Mommy, come *on!*" Sarah insisted, stamping her foot.

"In a minute!"

Benjamin, meanwhile, waddled over to a miniature rubber football and picked it up and brought it to me. It was wet and rather sticky. I didn't know from what, and I didn't want to know. He stood there, clapping his hands together eagerly. I tossed it to him, underhanded, from about three feet away. It bounded softly off his chest and was halfway to the floor before he finally clapped his hands together to catch it.

"Chip off the old block," proclaimed Sheldon Selden, gazing at his son proudly from the bedroom doorway. "Poor kid even got my lightning quick reflexes. Hey, real glad you could make it, guy," he said genially, limping over to me on a heavily wrapped ankle.

"Get bit by an agent?" I asked.

"Naw. Tripped rounding first in our studio softball game."

"Shelley isn't exactly Mr. Coordination," Mrs. Shelley explained. "I call him Twinkle. Short for Twinkletoes."

"We had to move into a one-story house because I kept falling down the damned stairs," he confessed jovially.

Mr. Shelley was a chubby, sheepish, panda bear of a guy

with thinning strawberry blond hair and pink skin. He was sort of soft and round all over, like one of those rubber toys that squeak if you squeeze them. His eyes were set unusually close together, so close they almost seemed to be on the same side of his nose, like a cartoon character's. He wore a chunky, geometrically patterned sweater and wide-wale corduroy slacks. He seemed, at first glance, like a bit of a cream puff to be someone who ran a studio. Oafish almost. I doubted this was the case. Oafs do run studios, but they are never cream puffs.

"What do your friends call you?" he asked, as he shook my hand.

"Any number of vile things. Make it Hoagy."

"As in Carmichael?"

"As in the cheese steak."

"I'm a major fan of your work, Hoagy. Merilee's, too. How's she liking Fiji?"

Mrs. Shelley elbowed him sharply in the ribs and glared at him.

"Oops," he said, reddening. "Sorry. I forgot that you two—"

"No need to be sorry," I assured him. "Merilee's fine, I'm fine, we're both fine." This was me putting on my happy face. It's not one of the things I'm best at.

"Glad to hear it," he said, and he seemed to be. "Oh, hey, sorry about all that security downstairs. We need it when we travel."

"Because of the press?"

"The nuts," Mrs. Shelley replied.

"Which ones?" I asked.

"Kidnappers," he replied grimly. "Sarah and Benjamin are major targets. Shelley, too. All these stories in the papers about how many hundreds of millions of dollars we're worth. The numbers aren't even close to true, but people get ideas, you know? There are just so many crazies out there, and all it takes is one. We stay prepared at all times."

I nodded. Hollywood celebrities live in utter terror of loons these days. Some of it is paranoia, but not all of it. Not even maybe.

He held his arms out to his side and spun slowly around. "How do I look to you?"

"Terrific. Don't change a thing."

"I'm wearing bullet-proof body armor. Guy said it wouldn't show. Cost me two thousand bucks."

I turned to his wife. "And you?"

"You should see this little lady on the target range," he said. "Dead solid perfect."

She lowered her eyes demurely. "Now, Twinkle . . ."

"I'm serious," he said. "She's won all kinds of badges. Sure as hell beats the pants off of me."

"He's just being modest, Hoagy," she said.

"And the other wives can't even begin to touch her."

"A lot of us shoot," she explained. "We want to be able to defend ourselves if we have to."

"What do you use?" I asked her.

"Well, I started out with a Smith and Wesson Chief Special," she replied. "But now I prefer the Glock nine-millimeter semiautomatic pistol. The other ladies seem to like it, too. There's less recoil. The trigger's lighter, don't you think?"

"I wouldn't know," I replied. "I try to get by on my wits."

"Some people you just can't reason with," Mr. Shelley pointed out.

"In that case, I have my protector," I said, indicating Lulu, who was sniffing delicately at a vase of yellow mums on the coffee table.

"I go to the range with my mother every Saturday," Mrs. Shelley said. "Pennyroyal used to come with us, but not anymore."

"And Matthew?"

"He hates guns," said Mr. Shelley.

"Is he here at the hotel with you?" I asked.

"No, he's home in L.A.," he replied. "Press downstairs all think he's here because we used the studio jet. They have informers who tip them off about stuff like that. Only this time they're way off."

"They usually are."

"Mommy, let's go!" whined Sarah. "C'monnn . . ."

"Okay, okay, button. We'll be back after lunch," she said to her husband, as she gathered up her purse.

"Take Frank with you, Cookie," he said. "And don't go out the Tower entrance. The chauffeur's waiting for you around the corner outside of the Bull and Bear."

"We'll be fine, Twinkle."

He kissed both kids, then kissed his wife, gazing at her adoringly. "Love you," he cooed.

"Love you back," she murmured. "Nice meeting you, Hoagy. Let's go, troops!"

And out the door they went. It seemed uncommonly silent now.

"God, I love my kids," he confessed. "They make it all worthwhile. All the lies. All the bullshit. You got any?"

"Not that I know of."

"When I see Matthew and Pennyroyal fighting over little Georgie this way . . ." His eyes filled with tears. "The sweetest, sunniest baby you ever saw, Hoagy. Matthew adores him. Would you believe he had a fucking *circus* waiting there in the front yard when she brought him home from the hospital? Elephants, clowns, chimpanzees . . ." The tears began streaming down his face. He was a very emotional guy. I couldn't imagine what he was like at a Shirley Temple movie. "It's tearing him apart, Hoagy. Me, too. Because, Christ, we *love* Pennyroyal. She's *family*. There are no villains here. Just two people who can't stop hurting each other. She's a mixed-up kid. An actress, and you know what they're like."

"Intimately."

He dabbed at his eyes with a napkin. "That was her on the phone just now. She was crying, she's so upset about this shit in today's paper. It's totally one hundred percent false. She's absolutely *not* pregnant."

"There goes my bet."

"Which bet?"

"Never mind."

"Seems she went to see her gynecologist yesterday. Routine checkup. Somebody must have spotted her in the parking lot, followed her up there, and seen the guy's name on the door. One thing leads to another and—"

The phone rang.

"Sorry. It never stops." He limped over to the desk by the window and picked it up. "Yeah? . . . Yeah? . . . No, absolutely not. We will not give Johnny Forget gross profit participation. What do you mean, don't we love him? We're offering him a job, aren't we? Name one other studio that is. He hasn't worked in a year. He's been in jail for attempted murder. He's been in

Betty Ford for drugs. In spite of all of that we want him—*because* we love him. And because the public thinks of him as Badger," he added quickly. "But if he holds out for gross points, we'll just get somebody else . . . I am *not* threatening you. I'm stating our final position. Take it or leave it . . ." No cream puff indeed. This doughboy was solid muscle inside. "Fine! Deal's dead! Deal's dead!" Not a bad imitation by Benjamin, either. Maybe the kid had a future in mimicry. He certainly didn't have one in sports. "Fine! We'll be happy to forget it! . . . *You're* sick of 'Forget' jokes? Hey, I knew Johnny long before you did, pal. I knew him when he still pronounced it For-jay. He happened to be a nice, sweet French Canadian kid then. And he didn't have a greedy scumbag like you for an agent!" He slammed down the phone and grinned at me sheepishly. "Now you know what I do all day —I'm the Abominable No Man."

"Ever say yes?"

"Somebody has to be the adult."

"And that's you?"

"That's me. Just between us, I can't stand Johnny. The little turd's a train wreck waiting to happen. But Matthew has to have him."

"His new picture is a fourth Badger Hayes?"

"Yes," he replied curtly. He phoned downstairs and stopped all of his calls for an hour. Then he limped out onto the terrace.

There was a table and chairs out there, and a not terrible view of the cabs playing bumper car up and down Park Avenue. A room service cart with coffee, pastries, and fresh strawberries awaited us. Lulu followed us out and curled up under my chair. Shelley poured us coffee and snatched a Danish.

"Don't tell my wife," he said, gobbling it hungrily. "She's always on me about my weight."

"Not to worry. Keeping secrets is my specialty."

"I hope it is, Hoagy," he said, turning serious. "I hope it is. Now, where were we?"

"Pennyroyal."

"Oh, right. All this crap in the papers. Half of it is nothing more than the tabloids playing their usual tricks. Like this bit about Matthew forcing her to make love to Johnny in a bathtub while he watched them."

"Did he?"

"Of course he did. That was the big love scene in *Badger*

*Goes to College*, when Badger tries to change Debbie Dale's tire and gets all covered with mud, remember? It was in the movie. He was directing the two of them."

I nodded, though I hadn't actually seen Matthew Wax's last picture. The critics had massacred it. Most everyone had stayed away. Matthew Wax, it seemed, could do nothing right these days.

"And the rest of it?" I asked.

"A mean-spirited smear campaign on the part of Zorch. He's trying to get Matthew to cave in."

"Will he?"

"His attorney is advising him not to."

"Who's his attorney?"

"I am," Shelley replied, grinning.

I tugged at my ear. "All in the family, huh?"

"It won't work, Hoagy. We won't give her half of the studio. I don't care if the Iguana smells the record or not."

"Which record is that?"

"Biggest Hollywood divorce settlement of all time," he replied. "The record right now is the $112 million Frances Lear got from Norman. Amy Irving supposedly got a hundred mil from Steve Spielberg. Zorch won't be satisfied unless he can top both of them."

"Can he?"

"Not without one hell of a court fight from us."

"There was no prenuptial agreement?"

"None. They just ran off to Vegas like a couple of crazy kids and got married. I just wish I could get the two of them in a room together. Get them communicating again. But Zorch won't allow it. As far as he's concerned, this is war. It's criminal, the way he's using her. That's his specialty—preying upon confused, vulnerable women. He doesn't care what happens to her or the baby. All he cares about is headlines. She swears she gave him all of that personal stuff about Matthew in the absolute strictest confidence. He promised her it was for his ears only. As soon as he got hold of it, he ran right to the papers with it." He shook his head, disgusted. "I mean, really, whose business is it how often Matthew Wax cuts his toenails?"

"Not mine."

"He's even got detectives following Matthew around, hoping to catch him with another woman."

"Will he?"

"No way. There's nobody else. Doesn't stop the scumbag, though. We had to kick one off the lot the other day, passing himself off as an electrician." He reached for another Danish and bit into it. "I've tried to set her straight. The poor kid's as much a victim here as Matthew is. She's hurting. I told her, hey, sweetie pie, Zorch works for you. You turned him loose. You want to cool things off, fire him. You know what she said to me? She said 'You've never respected me, Shelley.' Can you imagine?"

"Is she really having an affair with Trace Washburn?"

He nodded. "Another prime user of vulnerable women. They've been seen together all over town, hugging and kissing. A man Matthew once looked up to. God, what a mess."

"How is he holding up under all of it?"

"He's tearing his hair out."

"And where do I come in?"

"It seems Zorch has put Pennyroyal together with a publisher," he said. "They're giving her over a million bucks to tell all about her life with Matthew. The dirtier the better."

"Who's writing it for her?"

"A woman named Cassandra Dee."

I winced.

He noticed. "You know her?"

"I've scraped her off the bottom of my shoes a couple of times."

"She's not reputable?"

"Cassandra and reputable are not two words I would put together in the same sentence. Or novella. Cassandra D'Amico is her full name. She's a bare-knuckle fighter from Bensonhurst. Got her start stringing for Page Six of the *Post*, then moved up— or down—to the *Enquirer*, depending on how you look at it. She's now considered the mistress of the slash and burn. Did that sleazy Rock Hudson book, the unauthorized Julia Roberts bio. She works the low road. She'll do anything to get a scoop, and I do mean anything."

"So I've been told," he acknowledged sourly. "You can imagine how Matthew feels about it. All he keeps saying is 'Why can't they leave me alone?'"

"I'm afraid that's not possible anymore. Once this kind of thing starts . . ."

"I know, I know. That's why I contacted you."

"Dueling memoirs?"

"Exactly. Only ours will be tasteful. The self-portrait of a Hollywood genius. I'm here to talk to publishers. Can I trust any of them?"

"No."

He laughed. "Then I should feel right at home. I wanted your input before I sat down with any of them."

"I'm flattered."

"We're flattered that a writer of your caliber would even be interested."

The stroking. It's what they give you out there, in exchange for your self-respect. Hardly necessary in this case. We were talking guaranteed best-seller. And my self-respect was long gone.

"We want class," he claimed grandly. "We want depth, taste, humanity. We want *you*. You're the only writer Matthew would even consider."

I lapped this all up in silence. I never said I didn't like the stroking.

"And we'll pay you whatever you want," he promised. "Just name your price. We won't even dicker."

I sipped my coffee. "You realize, of course, that Pennyroyal may not go through with it. This may be just a scare tactic."

"She'll have to go through with it," he snarled, turning tough on me. "Because we don't scare. We fight back. And believe me, Pennyroyal Brim has a lot more to hide than Matthew Wax does."

"What have you got on her?"

"Why?"

"I'll have to know."

He hesitated. His close-set eyes met and held mine. Then he reached for another Danish, either his third or his fourth. I'd lost count. "She had an abortion her senior year of high school," he said, gobbling.

"Who was the father?"

"Some kid she knew. High school boyfriend. The point is, Hoagy, she's never been the goody-goody that the public thinks she is. That's strictly image. We created it. We nurtured it. Very carefully."

"What else?"

"What makes you think there's anything else?"

I didn't bother to answer. At my feet, Lulu began to snore softly. She thinks that's sexy, too. Trust me, it isn't.

Shelley cleared his throat uncomfortably. "Before Matthew discovered her, she had, well, modeled in the nude—under another name. Carla Pettibone. We own the negatives. Bought 'em outright from the shakedown artist who took 'em. I was afraid he'd try to sell them to *Penthouse* or somebody. I keep them locked away in my office. Sure, I know exactly what you're thinking—I ought to leak them to the press now and smear her. But I won't do it."

"That's not what I was thinking."

"What were you . . . ?"

"I was wondering why you didn't just destroy them."

"Hey, I run a studio," he reasoned. "You never know when you might need some leverage."

"Like now, for instance."

Shelley shook his head vehemently. "She's the mother of Matthew's child. I won't destroy her. I won't stoop to Zorch's level. No way."

"Any chance this photographer will resurface with another set of negatives?"

"Zero chance. He's dead. Somebody shot him a few weeks after I bought him off. Small wonder, the kind of business he was in. Shambazza was his name. Rajhib Shambazza. Black dude. Convinced Penny he was getting her into show business, apparently. What the hell, she was seventeen. We've all been victimized. We've all done things we're not proud of. I didn't care. Strictly damage control, from my point of view."

"And from Matthew's?"

"As far as he's concerned, Pennyroyal Brim was born on the day she met him. She has zero past of her own." He puffed out his cheeks. "And to think I was the one who encouraged them. She was a sweet kid. I thought she'd make him happy. I thought she really loved him. Not like all of the others."

"Others?"

"The women out there. They've pursued him for years, relentlessly. He was never interested. Not even just for fucking. He was always waiting for the right girl. True love. And with Pennyroyal, he found it. Or so he thought. Now she says she needs to be free. I don't know. Maybe she was never the girl he thought she was. Maybe . . . maybe he saw in her only what he wanted to see."

"That's as good a definition of love as any."

He drained his coffee and limped over to the railing and gazed thoughtfully out at the skyline. Or maybe he was searching the windows for a sniper. "Let me tell you about Matthew Wax, Hoagy. I've known him since he was thirteen years old, back when I first started dating Shelley. Matthew is a *child*, Hoagy, a gifted, special child who just happens to be thirty-eight years old. I say this in all seriousness. I'm not overselling you. Matthew is the exact same person he was when I first met him twenty-five years ago—a meek, sensitive, trusting, nutty kid who lives in a nutty kid's world of make-believe. It's a fact of human nature that people never grow up if they're constantly being rewarded for *not* growing up. Well, that's Matthew. He became such a huge success at such a young age that he never had to. He didn't want to. And, frankly, no one else wanted him to. Let's face it—his childlike innocence is his greatest gift as a director. Matthew is *genuine*. He *is* that little kid sitting in the front row with a box of popcorn. He *believes* in that happy, wonderful, cornball world he puts on the screen. He's at his best when he's on the set. He's got all of his new toys to play with, and everyone does just what he tells them to. They have to—he's the director. And he's a real pro. He always knows what he wants. Off the set, he has the social and emotional maturity of a thirteen-year-old. Would you believe he still eats a cheeseburger, fries, and a chocolate shake for lunch every single day?"

"Has he had his cholesterol checked lately?"

"His idea of a fun night is eating take-out pizza and playing video games. He owns the largest private library of old TV shows in America. Has tapes of every series you've heard of, and a lot you haven't. He doesn't travel. Doesn't entertain. Doesn't go to parties. Doesn't have the slightest interest in the movie business, or in playing the game. That's why he's never won an Oscar. He's never even been to the Awards. Mostly, he spends his time with us and with his mom, Bunny. It drove Pennyroyal crazy after a while. She said she felt like a shut-in." He hobbled over to the coffee pot and refilled his cup. "Don't get me wrong—I love the big goon. Took him under my wing right from the very start. I don't know why. I guess because I never had a kid brother, and because he needed somebody to watch out for him. That's what

I've done. Watch out for him." He reached for another Danish. "People in this business, they exploit talent like his. They devour it, they destroy it, and they enjoy doing it."

"Tell me something I don't already know."

"I made it clear from the start that they had to go through me to get at him. That's how it's always been. I'm his human shield. When he needed someone to negotiate his contracts, I did that. When he needed someone to produce his movies, I did that. When he needed someone to run Bedford Falls, I did that, too. I stand between him and the scum. He never gets involved in any contract squabbles. Never talks to agents. The politics, the egos, the power plays, the lying, the cheating, the back-stabbing—I handle all of that. All he's ever wanted was the freedom to be that little boy playing with his toys. I've made sure he got it. I've devoted my life to that. Not just me—all of us have. Shelley, Bunny, Sarge . . ."

"Sarge?"

"She's his assistant. Matthew'd be totally lost without her. We've all made sure he could keep on telling those sweet, wonderful stories that make so many millions of people around the world feel so good. All along, I've felt I was doing the right thing. He was so happy, so productive . . ." He sat back down heavily. "Now, I'm not so sure. Because I've left him totally unprepared for all of this shit. He can't deal with any of it. What she's doing to him. What the industry is doing to him. He honestly doesn't understand what's happening to him."

"Everyone has to grow up some time," I pointed out.

"That they do," he acknowledged readily. "Matthew is finally going through puberty. And it's not pretty."

"It seldom is. I take it he's working?"

Up went the shield. "That's correct," Shelley Selden replied briskly. "He just finished writing the script for *Badger Four* last week. He's casting it now, scouting locations. Goes into production in a few weeks."

"How's the script?"

"Great!" he exclaimed.

I tugged at my ear. "Let's try that again—how is the script?"

"I try to stay out of the creative end," he replied tactfully. "I know my limitations. I'm just the numbers man. So I'm really the wrong person to ask."

"I'm asking."

He hesitated. "Okay, sure . . . My feeling is he needs to do a big, noisy, fun, Matthew Wax kind of picture right now. Something with maybe some nice, fuzzy aliens in it . . ." He trailed off. And, slowly, began to deflate before my eyes. I could almost hear the air hissing out of him. "Instead, he wants to do an adult drama—in black and white. It's a Badger, only this one's darker and much more personal than anything he's ever done before. I —I think the script still needs a little work. I don't think it hangs together yet. But it's what Matthew wants to do next. He keeps saying he wants to be taken . . . seriously."

"Tell him to start wearing glasses. That's what Daryl Hannah did."

"He already wears glasses," Shelley said miserably.

There, he was good and deflated now, like a beanbag chair. I could have lounged atop the man if I cared to.

"Does he know how you feel?" I asked.

"Not totally."

"Is he happy with the script?"

"Not totally." He brightened a little. "That's why he wants you."

"I'm not a screenwriter."

"He knows. But, see, this is the first movie that Matthew's ever done that's about *him*. He's not used to introspection. In fact, he's avoided it his whole life. Writing this book, he hopes, will help him to examine his life. Which will in turn help the script. This is a major step for Matthew, Hoagy. For him, it's like going into therapy."

"I'm not a therapist."

"But you do possess a certain . . ."

"Effortless style?"

"Knack," he said.

I shrugged. "Everybody ought to be good at something."

"Go to work on him, Hoagy. Draw him out. He'll give you as much of his time as you need. This isn't just a book to him. Or a movie. This is him becoming a man."

I sampled a Danish. There was only one left, and I didn't think he'd leave it there for long. "Exactly how much of this is because of Pennyroyal?"

"It has everything to do with Pennyroyal, and it has nothing to do with Pennyroyal," he replied. "It has to do with real life.

He's face to face with it for the first time, and he's finding it pretty ugly."

"Only because it is. Are you actually trying to tell me the man's never been fucked over before? Not once?"

"Oh, he has been," Shelley conceded. "Sure he has. Schlom's done it to him in every imaginable way, and then some." That would be Norbert Schlom, the president of Panorama City Studios. "He's the one who discovered Matthew, and first put him to work. Became like a father to him. And cheated him every single step of the way. Cheated him out of millions. This is a man with no sense of morality, Hoagy. A man who lies on spec. You know he actually claims that *Yeti*, which only happens to be the fourth highest grossing movie in Hollywood history, still hasn't netted a profit? Matthew only made his salary on that picture. Not a penny more on the back end. It wasn't until he did the sequel that he had enough clout to demand, and get, gross points. And then when he did *Dennis the Dinosaur* I made sure he retained all of the licensing rights to his characters. That's where the gold was. Schlom knew it, too, but I said take it or leave it. So he took it."

"I'm surprised you stayed at all."

"Don't be. You know what they call the Disney Studio under Jeff Katzenberg's rule? Mouschwitz. Better the devil you know. Fewer surprises that way." Shelley shook his head, disgusted. "Schlom's clever though. He still figured a way to force Matthew into that *Three Stooges* disaster. Matthew, he was deeply, deeply hurt by that experience. But it didn't set him straight about the business. No way. See, Matthew had a real shitty relationship with his father, who was a major scumbag. To Matthew, Schlom was simply his father being shitty to him all over again. That's the only way he was able to comprehend it. I had to get him out of there after that. That's what Bedford Falls is about. It's a home. A safe environment where he can feel comfortable and not have to associate with the Schloms of the world. He named it after the town Jimmy Stewart lived in in *It's A Wonderful Life*, the Frank Capra movie. Matthew's favorite. He watches it at least once a week. That's where the name Georgie came from, too—Stewart's name in the movie was George Bailey. He even owns the 'George Lassos the Moon' needlepoint that Donna Reed made for Stewart in the movie. Bedford Falls is a dream come true, Hoagy. An old-fashioned Hollywood studio, like out of the thirties. Eight sound-stages, a back lot, office buildings—all ours. We've created an alternative to the madness. A place where talented young people can come and do good work and know we're not out to screw them. We won't tack on millions in bogus overhead. We won't cheat them out of their back end. We're *nice*. They can't get over it. Coppola tried doing it years ago with American Zoetrope, only he fell on his face because he wasn't a sound businessman. The major studios, they want us to fail, too. We're a threat to them. But we won't. We're bottom-line oriented and we're realistic. We make a small, select slate of maybe eight Bedford Falls films a year. Romances, family comedies, the kind of movies Matthew likes. A lot of them are directed by kids who used to work for him. Strictly moderate budgets. We draw the line at twenty million and we won't go over it. We won't work with crazed stars who demand ten million and gross points and then disappear in their trailer all day because somebody looks at 'em funny. We won't work with egomaniacal directors who demand we take out a full-page ad in *Variety* calling them geniuses. We won't work with coked-up producers who demand we build them their own three-million-dollar kingdom out in our parking lot. We work with decent, enthusiastic, hard-working professionals who enjoy their work." He paused, glancing hungrily at the empty Danish plate. He'd really wanted that last one. "We also have something else Coppola didn't have. We have Matthew Wax. He's an industry unto himself."

"Sounds wonderful," I observed.

"It is wonderful," he enthused.

"So what's your problem?"

He stared at me. I stared back at him. That's one of the things I am best at. He sipped his coffee. He cleared his throat. "If Pennyroyal gets half of Bedford Falls in her divorce settlement, she's made it clear she intends to sell out immediately—to Panorama City. Schlom again. I hear he's offering her $150 million. A sweetheart deal—she'll get her own unit there and everything. And Schlom will own half of our studio."

"Making him your partner."

"Not for long, if he can help it. Once Schlom gets half of Bedford Falls he'll stop at nothing to get the other half. He wants to gobble us up. Desperately."

"Does Pennyroyal realize this?"

"I've tried to explain it to her, but it doesn't seem to sink in. She's in over her head."

"You can't convince her to accept cash in lieu of half the studio?"

"There is no cash, Hoagy. At least not that kind. Matthew sank his entire fortune into Bedford Falls. Other than his house, it's all he owns. He and the bank. And the overhead is huge. The bank loan, the payroll, insurance, taxes. We rent out the sound stages, but that barely dents it. Matthew keeps it afloat himself. He's our cash flow machine. Channels all of the profits from his movies and merchandising back into the studio. Twenty-eight million last year alone."

"And this year?"

"This year he didn't do quite so well," Shelley replied tactfully.

"I see." Now I understood why he wanted Matthew to make a movie with fuzzy aliens.

"Someday soon, we'll be able to stand on our own," Shelley vowed bravely. "I'm sure of it. We'll make it. But right now he's personally keeping us afloat."

"You don't own a piece of the studio yourself?"

"It belongs to him," he said, with no trace of bitterness. "I earn a nice salary, and I've already made all the money my family will ever need. We're also taken care of in case anything should happen to him. Half of Bedford Falls goes to Shelley and me, half to Georgie. Pennyroyal was to control Georgie's half until he turned twenty-one, but I changed Matthew's will the day she walked out. Shelley and I control it now."

"Why is Schlom so interested in Bedford Falls? Because you pose a threat to him?"

"Because we're an asset. If he takes us over, he makes Panorama City Communications even more attractive than it already is."

"To whom?"

He raised an eyebrow at me. "Who do you think?"

I poured myself more coffee and sat back in my chair. "Are we talking foreign investors, here? Pacific Rim, perhaps?"

"We are," he informed me, gravely.

The selling of America. The business pages had been full of

little else lately. One of the news magazines had gone so far as to run a picture of the Statue of Liberty on its cover adorned with a For Sale sign. This was no mere gossip column war I was walking into. This was bigger. Much bigger.

I said, "You'd better tell me the rest."

"It's getting harder and harder to make a movie," he began. "The average cost has tripled in the last ten years—up to thirty million. That's the *average.* Pictures like *Dick Tracy* and *Terminator 2* actually ended up costing a *hundred* mil by the time they finished marketing them. Revenues, meanwhile, have flattened out. All of the studios, no matter how big they are, are in desperate need of fresh capital. That means globalization. Four of the seven majors have already been bought up by foreign corporations. They're suckers for the Hollywood mystique. They love it. Rupert Murdoch, who's Australian, has bought Fox. Pathé, an Italian company, has bought MGM-UA. And the Japanese electronics giants are squabbling among themselves over the rest. Sony buys Columbia for $5 billion, so Matsushita turns right around and buys MCA for $6.6. And now their third biggest hardware empire, Murakami, wants to take over Panorama for who knows how much—that means Panorama City Studios *and* their theme park in Orlando, their TV production company, record company, cable system, publishing house . . . If Schlom can deliver them Bedford Falls on top of all that—even better. They'll own the rights to all of Matthew's movies then. They love Matthew in Japan. I hear Murakami wants to build a *Yeti* theme park in Osaka. It'll be a major draw for them. Big time."

"What's Schlom's stake in this?"

"He's Panorama's single largest shareholder. He personally stands to pull down $350 million on the deal in stock. Plus get a megacontract to keep on running the studio. He'll swing the biggest dick in town, no question. So will the guy who's brokering the deal. And guess who that is? Guess who is serving as the go-between?"

"Abel Zorch?"

"Doink—Penny's lawyer. Who happens to be very tight with Schlom. And also happens to speak fluent Japanese. See how all the pieces fit together now?"

"Neatly."

"So you can appreciate the position we're in."

"I can—you're fucked."

He puffed out his cheeks again. "It's true. We are. Unless . . ."

"Unless what?"

"Unless Matthew and Pennyroyal somehow get back together." He looked across the table at me pleadingly. "They have to patch things up, Hoagy. They just have to."

"You're not asking me to write his book for him. You're asking me to save his marriage."

"And his studio," he admitted. "And all of the people who depend on it." He sighed and ran a chubby hand over his face. "Maybe I'm asking too much."

"You can drop the maybe."

"It's just that . . . there are no secrets in the film business. Everyone in town knows exactly what's happening to us. No one's bringing us any new projects—their agents are advising them not to. And the banks won't finance any of our go projects. Not until this thing is settled. Matthew's new movie is the only thing we've got going, and that's coming out of his own pocket. All I can do is sit around, waiting for the ax to fall. I feel so totally helpless." His eyes welled up. Again with the waterworks. He swiped at them with his napkin. "Maybe . . . maybe it is too late for us. Maybe we're history. Whatever happens, it's not your problem. I didn't mean to lay it on you. I'm sorry. Really, I am. You write books. Good books. Write Matthew one. That's all I ask." He wadded up the napkin and laid it in the ashtray. "Will you do it? Please?"

I got to my feet, rousing Lulu. "Anything else I should know?"

His whole face lit up. He looked like Benjamin when it did. "Yeah. It was a hundred and seven in L.A. yesterday. The Santa Ana winds are blowing."

"How nice of them." I picked up my trench coat and hat and started inside.

"One other thing, Hoagy," Shelley said nervously.

I stopped. There was always one other thing. I waited.

"Do you know how to duck?" he asked.

"Why?"

"Because you may get caught in the cross fire."

"Oh, that." I put on my hat and grinned at him. "Not to worry. I can see them just fine, but they can't see me at all. I'm a ghost, remember?"

• • •

Not that I ever thought I would be.

Then again, I don't suppose anyone purposely sets out to become an invisible man. Let's face it—on the human dignity scale, ghosting ranks somewhere between mud wrestling and writing speeches for Dan Quayle. But it does finance my fiction, which is how I get my true, unbridaled jollies. And I am ideally suited for it. In fact, I happen to be the best. Three bestselling celebrity memoirs to my noncredit, as well as someone else's bestselling novel. Not that the three memoirs weren't what you'd call fiction, too. A memoir, after all, is an exercise in self-deception and self-glorification. People remember things the way they want to remember them. And celebrities are by nature fictitious creations. "Everyone wants to be Cary Grant," the great star once acknowledged. "*I* want to be Cary Grant." My background as a world-class novelist comes in real handy. So does my own former celebrity. I know how to handle stars. The lunch pail ghosts don't. They treat them like rational, intelligent human beings. I know better.

There is, however, a pitfall to my second career. Pretty big one, too. As a novelist, the greatest hazard I face is being called a no-talent bozo in the *New York Times Book Review*. Ghosting is a good deal scarier. Memoirs are about secrets, past and present. My job is to dig them up. The problem is there's usually someone around who wants those dirty little secrets to stay buried, and will go to great lengths to see that they do. As a consequence, I've been shot at a number of times, punched, kicked, drugged, and suffocated—almost. And I can't even begin to tell you what's happened to Lulu. I haven't been killed yet, but a lot of people around me have. This part of the job I'm not suited for. But I can't seem to avoid it. Trouble has this way of following me around. I think it's my personality. I figured I should warn you about it in case you're an aging film star who is thinking of hiring me. Think again. Or in case you're a young, ambitious writer who figures ghosting might be an easy way to make a shitload of money. It isn't. Not even maybe.

I also don't need the competition. So back off. I mean it.

# Chapter Two

I flew out two days later on Bedford Falls' own Boeing 727 jet. Most studios have their own. Part of the image. The most important thing to remember about the movie business, an old-time director once told me, is that superficiality is everything. The family Selden wasn't with me. Mr. Shelley still had more business in New York. But I was not alone. Several others had booked seats on the flight. The usual collection you get on a studio jet. A couple of record company executives. A VJ from MTV, who had just gotten her own sitcom, and who wore very little clothing. Peter Weller, the actor. Ed Bradley from *60 Minutes*. The agent who represents three-fifths of the Lakers' starting lineup, and who spent four-fifths of the flight on the phone. I seemed to be the only one on board who wasn't wearing cowboy boots, and that included our stewardess, Jennifer. I had on my white-and-brown spectator balmorals with my unlined suit of blue-and-cream cotton seersucker and my white straw boater. Lulu stuck with her shades.

Jennifer was very friendly and helpful, and she made an enemy of me for life before we'd even taken off. Just as soon as she got done fussing over Lulu. "Are you her trainer?" she asked me.

I stiffened. "Her what?"

"Isn't she a movie dog? What did I see her in?"

"I'm afraid you're mistaken."

Nonetheless, Lulu snuffled with glee and was a giant pain in the ass from that moment on. Even more so than usual. She has this problem with her head, you see. It swells even more easily than mine does.

Lunch was a salad of assorted field greens topped with grilled chicken. Free-range, of course. I had pineapple for dessert, and a Bass ale. Lulu had the fresh linguine with red clam sauce, minus the fresh linguine. There was an extensive library of videocassettes aboard. Lulu spent much of the flight watching *Turner and Hootch* with Tom Hanks for the eighth time. It's one of her favorites, though she's always thought Beasley was a little over the top with that saliva thing. I spent my time plowing through the fat manila envelope the Bedford Falls publicity people had sent me. In it were the major magazine articles that had been written about Matthew Wax through the years. Profiles in *Rolling Stone*, *Esquire*, the *New York Times Sunday Magazine*, *American Film*. If you could call them profiles. They were really about his movies, not him. What he did on the screen. Not who he was. An enigma, several writers called him. What else could you call a director who didn't grant interviews, didn't promote his films, didn't appear in public, period. About the only time he had was during the Film Colorization hearings in Washington, D.C., when he testified before a Senate committee in a halting, emotional voice that colorization was "like spray painting graffiti on the Liberty Bell."

The biographical details were sketchy. Matthew Wax had grown up in the middle-class Sepulveda section of Los Angeles' San Fernando Valley. He started writing and directing his own 8mm films when he was still in high school, and went on from there to USC film school. His first 16mm student short, *Bugged*, was the story of an unpopular teenager who awakens one morning to find himself transformed into a large, distasteful insect. It so impressed Norbert Schlom, then vice president of television production at Panorama Studios, that he immediately hired the nineteen-year-old to direct *Rick Brant, Adventurer*, a new CBS Saturday morning serial in the tradition of the Hardy Boys and Tom Swift. Within weeks of its premiere, *Rick Brant* was the most popular kids' show in a decade. Matthew Wax never looked back. At age twenty-one he wrote and directed his first feature film, *The Boy Who Cried Wolf*, a low-budget Hitchcockian thriller about a lonely little boy who happens to witness the friendly couple next door committing a murder. *The Boy Who Cried Wolf* was a viscerally terrifying film right out of a kid's worst nightmares. It made a vivid impression on filmgoers. So did its seven-year-old star, a wide-eyed little Canadian boy named Jean Forget. It also made $20 million. His second, *I Was Invisible*, a giddy spoof about an invisible teenager, became the sleeper box office hit of 1976. America's most influential film critic, Pauline Kael of *The New Yorker*, breathlessly stamped young Matthew Wax with greatness when she wrote: "An adroit, look-ma-no-hands screwball farce by a young master who already knows more than Howard Hawks ever learned."

That was the end of low-budget filmmaking for Matthew Wax. From then on he cranked out an unprecedented string of blockbusters, transforming his own childhood fears, fantasies, and fascinations into spirited special-effects extravaganzas that everyone simply had to see. It was uncanny how he kept topping himself. Even more uncanny was his impact. Because if there was one man who was responsible for the infantilization of American mass entertainment, it was Matthew Wax. It was due to his astonishing success that Hollywood virtually gave itself over to the making and marketing of huge, dumb, kid-oriented blockbusters. It was because of him that George Lucas and Steven Spielberg found film careers, stepping forward to direct comic book megasuccesses of their own, one after another after another.

But there was only one Matthew Wax.

The young master's first blockbuster was *To the Moon*, his lavish 1978 homage to those schlocky space flight movies of the 1950s. The story of a moon launch set off course by a meteorite storm, it broke box office records nationwide for fourteen straight weeks. And made an international star of Trace Washburn, the lean, rugged former USC quarterback and movie stuntman who played Rip O'Keefe, the fearless astronaut who single-handedly battles a race of demented, slavering Martian mutants. Its sequel, *Back to the Moon*, in which Rip discovers the moon to be populated by demented, slavering Nazi scientists, became the first movie in the history of Hollywood to gross more than *Gone with the Wind*. That particular record would not stand for long. Lucas would break it with *Star Wars*, Spielberg with *E.T.* Wax would go on to break it himself three more times. He broke it in 1982 with *Yeti*, his $40 million monster epic based on

*The Abominable Snowman of the Himalayas*, a 1957 B-movie starring Peter Cushing and Forrest Tucker. Filmed on location in the Himalayas, *Yeti* featured both the greatest avalanche in movie history and Lord Laurence Olivier as the Dalai Lama. Trace Washburn returned to action in the role of Duke Jardine, fearless adventurer. Pro football's John Matuszak shot to stardom, briefly, as the hairy behemoth with the heart of gold and the fatal weakness for Baby Ruths. *Yeti* would spawn *Yeti II*, which featured a surprisingly scary Glenn Close as the snowman's revenge-crazed mate. The sequel did even better.

But the biggest was yet to come. Exhausted by two years of rigorous location filming, Wax turned next to a heartwarming animated fable about a young brontosaurus named Dennis who becomes separated from his family and encounters all sorts of strange, magical creatures as he tries to find his way back to them. Jean Forget, the child star of Matthew's first film, provided the voice of Dennis. A roster of notable actors joined him, including Meryl Streep as Dennis's mother. *Dennis the Dinosaur* was an unabashed homage to *Bambi* and *Dumbo* and the other Disney classics of Matthew Wax's own childhood. And it was a phenomenon. Audiences of all ages went back to see it again and again. Within four months of its 1985 summer release it had become the top grossing film of all time. (It still is—to date, it has grossed $367 million.) Before long, there was a top-rated *Dennis* prime-time TV show, a *Dennis* Ice Capades show, a series of children's books featuring all-new *Dennis* adventures. There were *Dennis* dolls, *Dennis* shower curtains, beach towels, sheets, pillowcases, pajamas, calendars, notebooks, puzzles, hats, sneakers, shoelaces, lunch boxes. There was no escaping *Dennis*. *Dennis* was everywhere. *Dennis* was loved.

And so was Matthew Wax. His movies were a tonic. "High priest of the New Optimism" was what *Time* called him when they put him on their cover at the height of the *Dennis* craze. Looking back, they could just as easily have labeled him the unofficial voice of the Reagan years. Just like the President, he reminded people of the good old days before Vietnam and Watergate. He put smiles on their faces. He made them believe again in that America of spunk and determination, that America where Good triumphed over Evil, and Love triumphed over all. That America we all wanted to believe in—the America of happy endings.

He did stumble. Even a master can stub his toe. And Matthew Wax did with *The Three Stooges in Orbit*, the unfortunate 1986 remake starring Chevy Chase, Bill Murray, and Steve Martin as Larry, Curly, and Moe. "A thirty-million dollar wind-up gadget that lurches from one dim-witted idea to the next," sniffed Kael in *The New Yorker*. "Staggeringly unfunny," agreed Siskel and Ebert, who gave it two thumbs down. So did Wax himself. He clashed repeatedly with the stars and with the studio. He disavowed the final cut that Panorama released into the theaters, where it barely broke even. Through his spokesman, Sheldon Selden, he announced he would never make another film for Panorama City. Or anyone else for that matter. He took his toys and went home.

Home to Bedford Falls, formerly Lucerne Studios, which he bought with the vast fortune he'd earned from *Dennis*. Here, as lord of his own realm, he immediately made *Badger Hayes, All-American Boy*, his most nostalgic and evocative work. *Badger* was a misty-eyed look back at growing up in a small American town called Homewood in the fifties. Homewood was the America that never was, except perhaps in a Norman Rockwell painting. It was ham radios, soap box derbies, and malt shops. It was sturdy, fresh-scrubbed boys and neat, pretty girls. There was no such thing as orthodonture or acne in Homewood. There was no teen pregnancy, no drug abuse, no divorce, rape, suicide, poverty, or racial injustice. Homewood was everyone's fantasy hometown. It was Carvel, where Andy Hardy was from. And Badger Hayes was another Andy Hardy—eager, irrepressible, good-natured, and utterly confused. Little Jean Forget, who was now eighteen and going by the Americanized Johnny Forget, soared to teen stardom as Badger. Pennyroyal Brim, the complete unknown who played Badger's girl-next-door, Debbie Dale, captivated audiences, too. She was so fantastically cute. Trace Washburn returned from a rather long screen absence in the role of Badger's dad. Teri Garr played his mom. The movie was immensely popular. Wax made a sequel, *Badger Hayes and His Chemistry Set*, which scored again. He also married Pennyroyal Brim. His world was complete now. It was time to live happily ever after.

Only he hadn't. His latest movie, *Badger Goes to College*, had been a colossal flop. His first. It was a typical Wax job, a warmhearted bit of nostalgic fluff about Badger and Debbie's up and downs at Homewood U in the midsixties. Only this time, audiences stayed away. And the critics sneered. Laughed at its portrayal of a sixties college campus totally devoid of long-hairs and blacks and even the slightest awareness of Vietnam. They called it a pathetic joke. They didn't just attack it—they went after the director himself. "What Matthew Wax doesn't seem to realize," wrote David Denby in *New York Magazine*, "is that he isn't nine years old anymore, and neither are we."

Times had changed. Reagan had ridden off into the sunset. The stock market had crashed. Donald Trump was broke. Mike Milken was in jail. The eighties were over and out, and Matthew Wax was over and out with them. The public turns fast when you're on top. They had turned on Matthew Wax. Suddenly they saw something inherently false about his dogged determination to make everything over into a feel-good experience. Suddenly his movies weren't sweet anymore. They were saccharine. A sham. If anyone needed proof, all they had to do was pick up a newspaper. Johnny Forget, all-American boy, got himself busted in Los Angeles for coke possession one week after the movie opened. A few weeks later he was arrested for attempting to murder his manager, who also happened to be his mother. And now there was this business, the House of Wax. Matthew's storybook marriage to Pretty Penny had gone boom. And it looked like Bedford Falls would be next to have a great fall. And all the king's horses and all the king's men . . .

I sat back in my plush club chair, stared out the window at the clouds covering the Midwest, and thought about my own storybook marriage. My sunshine days, I called them. When I was that tall, dashing, fabulously successful author of that fabulously successful first novel. When Merilee was Joe Papp's newest, loveliest darling. New York was ours then. The red 1958 Jaguar XK-150 was ours. Lulu was ours. We had it all. God, we were something. Until I lost it. Lost my voice, my juices, my touch. Lost Merilee. She got the Tony for the Mamet play, the Oscar for the Woody Allen movie. I got Lulu, my drafty fifth-floor walk-up on West 93rd Street, and my ego, which requires its own room and bath, with kitchen privileges.

My sunshine days were gone, and they don't ever return.

My juices did come back. There was a second novel, *Such Sweet Sorrow*, which the critics hated. Readers merely ignored it. Merilee came back, too. We were still something. We just didn't know what. Somehow, we stuck it out. Or at least we had. I wasn't sure what was happening between us right now. All I knew was that something was wrong and that she wouldn't talk about it. And that she was in Fiji and out of my life for the next three months. Part of me understood. Part of me didn't. All of me felt alone.

Los Angeles isn't terrible to fly into by night. The lights spread out beneath you like jewels, a hundred miles in every direction. Pretty, almost. We began our descent in the middle of the afternoon. Not so pretty. Just a vast, arid expanse of tar and concrete shrouded under a thick blanket of saffron-colored smog. The end of so-called civilization as we know it.

Our bags were waiting for us in the air-conditioned charter terminal, along with a row of limo drivers and four or five dozen members of the House of Wax press corps. It was me they were waiting for. Our mutual publisher had already commenced banging the drum over Matthew's million-dollar book deal, and my association with it. He was fond of drum banging. Almost as fond as he was of telling you that he knew more about publishing than anyone else in publishing. I wouldn't know. I do know you can always count on him to overpay.

I was assaulted the second they spotted me. Microphones were shoved at me. TV lights blinded me. Shouts deafened me.

*"TELL US ABOUT THE BOOK!"*

*"GONNA NAIL HER?!"*

*"WHAT'S PRETTY PENNY SAY?"*

Me, I had nothing to say. Blinking, I pulled my boater down low over my eyes and began fighting my way through the reporters. Of course, that would have been a lot easier if Lulu hadn't stayed behind to vogue it up for the cameras like Jayne Mansfield arriving for her latest star-studded premiere. All she needed was a mink stole and false eyelashes. I wasn't kidding about how her head swells. Cursing, I fought my way back toward her, so as to strangle her. Only now I was being carried along by the crowd—jostled, buffeted, helpless. Until a rampaging wild woman came bursting through the crowd, grabbed me, grabbed Lulu, and spirited us toward the door, ramming, roaring, elbowing, shoving at anyone who got in our way. She was a black woman, and quite some woman. A good three inches over six feet tall, broad-shouldered, high-rumped, long-legged, *big*. And as sleekly muscled as a thoroughbred racehorse. A redcap waited by the glass doors with my bags and the carton of the only canned food Lulu will eat, Nine Lives mackerel for cats and very weird dogs. My rescuer grabbed the whole load from him and stormed out into the bright sunshine, moving very fast. Lulu and I followed her, the pack in pursuit.

I was unprepared for just how searingly hot it was. Well over a hundred. Dry hot. My skin tightened, my hair crackled, my throat constricted. This was no heat wave. This was the earth moving closer to the sun. Black limos were baking at the curb. Press vans were parked everywhere. We made for a tan Toyota Land Cruiser that was double-parked, engine running, tailgate open. My rescuer threw my stuff in and slammed it shut. I reached for the passenger door.

"Don't touch!" she warned, her voice deep and straight up from the diaphragm. "Handle'll burn you!"

I used my linen handkerchief on it. Then I jumped in, Lulu on the floor at my feet. The air-conditioning was on but it wasn't what you'd call cool inside. My rescuer jumped in behind the wheel and pulled away with a screech, working her way through the snarled airport traffic with total mastery. She gripped the wheel and gear shift tightly in her powerful hands, cords of muscle standing out on her neck and forearms.

"Nice weather if you happen to be a lizard," I observed.

"They been saying it'll break tomorrow," she boomed. "Of course, they been saying that for, like, three days. Otherwise people'll start murdering each other in the streets, y'know what I'm saying?"

We were clear now, zipping out of the airport onto Century Boulevard. She let out a breath of relief and smiled. Big smile. Everything about her was big. "Charmaine Harris, Mr. Hoag."

"Make it Hoagy."

"In that case, make it Sarge."

The woman who ran Matthew Wax's life was in her midthirties, totally fit and totally no-nonsense. She wore no makeup and no jewelry, other than the *Dennis the Dinosaur* watch on her wrist. Her hair was cut short in a flattop fade. She had on a pink polo shirt with the sleeves turned up, khaki shorts, and running shoes. She exuded readiness, capability, and efficiency. I would have been perfectly happy to have her run my life. Also to have her on my side in a fight. She was as imposing a woman as I'd ever seen. Next to her, Merilee, the woman who Frank Rich once called the Connecticut Yankee Amazon, looked like Annie Potts.

"Shoot, smell like something died in here," she said, making a face.

"That's Lulu." She lay there under the dashboard, panting miserably. She doesn't do well in the heat, being covered with hair. I wasn't feeling too sorry for her though. "Pull another stunt like that," I warned her, "and you'll spend the rest of this assignment in a carrier—eating *steak!*" She grumbled at me and dripped some doggy saliva on my shoes. Fiji. I should have sent her to Fiji, C.O.D.

"Y'all meet the two Shelleys?" Sarge asked.

I said I had.

"He's a real rarity in this business," she said. "A human being. Not a whole lotta them running studios. He gives you his word, he means it. The rest of 'em are just trying to give you some kind of lower body root canal job, y'know what I'm saying?"

"And Matthew?"

"Matthew is a spoiled little boy who wakes up in the middle of the night screaming 'Zeppelins! Zeppelins! I wanna do a battle between two zeppelins!' It's my job to find out who can pull it off and how much it'll cost. Shelley's his go-between with the suits. I'm his go-between with the troops." She glanced over at me. "Not that I *know* what Matthew says when he wakes up in the middle of the night," she added carefully. "Or at any other time."

She pulled off Century onto the San Diego Freeway, heading north toward the west side. The traffic was at a standstill, five lanes of cars stacked up end to end. More than a few drivers rode their horns as they sat there in anguish, broiling under the midafternoon sun.

I sat back and relaxed. "It certainly is nice to be back in paradise."

"Hey, any fool back East still thinks of this as El Lay, land of quiche-eating volleyball players, is living in the seventies," Sarge declared flatly. "Ain't nobody smiles and says have a nice day around here no more. Too afraid they'll get their head blown off. We got it all, man—high crime, bad air, lousy schools, too many people, not enough water. Lot of folks are moving on. Finding some new place to mess with. Portland, Seattle . . . Well, lookie, lookie . . ." Her eyes were on her rearview mirror. "We got us some company."

"Who?" I asked, turning around for a look.

"Dude in the red Porsche."

It was two cars back and a lane over, a whale-tailed 911 Turbo, brand-new, which would run you just a little more than a three-bedroom ranch home in Indianapolis. The driver wore sunglasses, and kept stalling it.

"Looks like he needs a tune-up," she observed.

"Just driving lessons. Is he one of the reporters from the airport?"

"One of Zorch's detectives. Been tailing me since I left Bedford Falls to come get you."

"Kind of a conspicuous car for a detective, isn't it?"

"Not for one who's hanging around the lot. It's all flash there. Honda would be what sticks out. By the way, I got something for you." Sarge opened the glove compartment and pulled out a blue plastic three-ring binder with Bedford Falls stamped on it. She had a gun stashed in there, too, a Glock semiautomatic pistol. More new-wave Hollywood security. I suppose it beat body armor, what with the heat and all. "Studio directory," she said, handing it to me. "Tell you everything you need to know. Your gate pass is in there, too."

Her pocket phone bleated.

"That'll be the man. Excuse me." She answered it. "Yeah, darling, I got him . . ." She glanced over at me. "Looks *plenty* okay if you like tall, skinny white boys." She laughed. "Taking him to his hotel, we ever get there." I was billeted at the Four Seasons in Beverly Hills. Lulu always likes to be within walking distance of the Ralph Lauren Polo Shop if possible. "That's true," Sarge said. "Uh-huh. Okay . . ." To me she said, "Studio's on our way there. He wants us to stop by now. You can get acquainted, get the tour . . ."

"I'd rather get settled in first."

Her eyes flickered at me. "He says he wants to get settled first," she said into the phone. "Uh-huh . . ." To me she said: "He really wants you to stop by now. We may as well, traffic being so bad. Okay?"

"No, it's not okay."

"The thing is," she persisted, "it's really more convenient for him to do it now."

"It's not more convenient for me."

"What, you having a bad day?"

"I'm having a great day. I'm just having a bad life."

She stared at me curiously. I get a lot of that. "He says no," she said into the phone, reluctantly. "That's right. I don't know why. He just does . . . Okay . . ." She hung up.

We inched forward in silence, the air conditioner struggling to keep up with the heat and Lulu's fish breath.

Sarge narrowed her eyes at me. "What you doing on him?" she wondered.

"My job."

"Your job?"

"It's what they pay me for."

"They pay you to disrespect people?"

"Vast sums. Why, don't you ever say no to him?"

She didn't care for that one. "You jammin' me, man?" she demanded fiercely, a panther ready to pounce.

"Wouldn't dream of it. Just wondered."

She relaxed, somewhat. "Not my job to be gas-facing him. Director always gets his way. He's like a general. I'm just his associate producer."

"I hear you're a lot more than that."

"I care about him, if that's what you mean. He been nothing but good to me. And he's hurting right now. You gonna help him?"

"I'm just a former writer."

"I hear you're a lot more than that," she said, her face breaking into a smile.

"Been with him long?" I asked, smiling back at her.

"Ever since I got out of UCLA."

"Film school?"

She erupted into laughter. "Get outta here, man!" she whooped. "My major was the four hundred meters. Finished third in the NCAA's my junior year. Made the '80 Olympic team as an alternate, only we didn't go that year."

"Well, I was close. I was guessing high hurdles. You've got a hurdler's legs." I gave them an admiring once over. "No offense."

"None taken, believe it. I ran those, too, only not as good. You know track?"

"I threw the javelin in college."

"Spear-chucker, huh?" This seemed to amuse her greatly. "You any good?"

"Only for the Ivy League. You've stayed in shape."

"Gets harder every year. Work out two hours every morning before work. Weights, Stairmaster . . ." She checked me out. "You have, too."

"Appearances can be deceiving. How did you get together with Matthew?"

"He was a big fan of my honey, Sugar Bear. Started me out as a gofer on account of him. Sugar Bear Davis. He backed up Bill Walton at center when he was at UCLA, then Jabbar for three seasons for the Lakers. Until he blew out his knee. We been together since college."

"What's he doing now?"

"Three to five in San Quentin for armed robbery," she replied matter-of-factly. "He's had some adjustment problems since he stopped playing. Got used to living large, y'know what I'm saying? His old Crenshaw High posse got him into some bad shit. But he's up for parole next year. Shelley's promised him a job on the lot."

We inched our way along. We were near the Culver Boulevard off-ramp now.

I glanced at Grandfather's Rolex. "Okay, you can call him. I've changed my mind."

"What, now it's okay to stop there first?" she asked, baffled.

"I think he's sweated long enough." I swiped at the back of my neck with my handkerchief. "I certainly have."

I stared out at the traffic while she phoned him. When she was done she turned and looked at me, utterly mystified. Then she turned back to the road.

"You a strange dude, Stewart Hoag," she said quietly.

"Tell me something I don't already know."

The red Porsche got off with us at Culver Boulevard. He stalled it at the bottom of the off-ramp. Sarge took a right and guided us through the Culver City commercial district, which isn't much, unless you happen to be looking for a dozen doughnuts or a discount muffler. At Overland we passed the old MGM lot, which had been Lorimar the last time I was in town, and then Columbia, by way of the Sony buy-out. Now it was Sony Studios. Just past there Culver angled into Washington Boulevard, and we were at Bedford Falls. The main office building faced right onto the street. It was quite old and had been designed to look like a colonial mansion, most distinguished. A baron might live there. But the giant soundstages looming behind it gave away its real purpose. Baldwin Hills formed a backdrop behind them. There were still a few old oil towers up there, poking up into the smog.

"Studio goes all the way back to people like Hal Roach and Cecil B. de Mille," Sarge informed me, slowing up before it. "There was one soundstage built in 1913 that was still standing. We had to tear it down. Didn't pass the new earthquake laws. Whole lotta history in this place. You into history?"

"I *am* history, category semiliving."

"What, you mean like Count Dracula?"

"Except he gets out more at night."

There was a guard in a booth at the main gate to stop people there, and a twelve-foot-high chain link fence topped with razor wire to stop them everywhere else. The red Porsche made a U-turn and parked across the street from the gate, where a few sweaty photographers were keeping up their House of Wax vigil in the shade of a catering truck. They were too hot to pay me any notice.

"Remember them old cavalry movies?" Sarge asked. "Where the soldiers lived in those forts with them big high walls? Only place they felt safe? Every time I drive in here I feel that same way."

"Fort Bedford," I said.

"You got that right."

The uniformed guard on the gate was a thickly built black man in his fifties. He had a big belly and heavy, familiar features. Very familiar. He flashed Sarge a gold-toothed grin. She grinned back as we passed on through, and noticed me studying him.

"Recognize him?"

"I'm sure I do. . . ."

She stopped the car, backed up, and rolled down her window. "Got yourself another one, baby," she called out. "Bust a move."

He let out a husky laugh and stepped out of the booth, moved slowly around to the front of our car, and stood there, his back to us. He was armed with a Glock and a nightstick. He took out the nightstick and gripped it with both hands like a baseball bat. Then he went into a right-handed batter's stance, a typical stance, bat cocked to swing. Until just before he got himself settled, when he did something unexpected. He wiggled his big butt once, twice, three times. Only one batter in history had ever done that. It was his trademark.

"Shadow Williams," I declared. "Played outfield for the Dodgers in Brooklyn, then a few more seasons after they moved out here. No one stepped into the box like he did."

"The ladies sure never forgot him," Sarge chuckled.

She introduced us. He gently squeezed my hand with his huge one and told me to call him Shadow. I said I would. Then someone pulled in behind us and honked, and we drove on in.

"Matthew, you'll discover, hasn't much good to say about his dad," Sarge told me, as we passed the visitors' parking lot. "About the only positive memory he's got is when he took him to a Dodger game one time when he was little. Shadow pinch-hit a grand salami with two out in the bottom of the ninth to win it. Matthew never forgot it. A few years back he read that the man was having some trouble finding work. So he got him a security job at Panorama City. When we took over Bedford Falls, he came over with us. He's chief of security now."

"Happy ending, huh?"

"Only kind there is. You'll get off on Shadow—he's deep."

"That makes one of us."

Ahead was a cluster of giant soundstages. We eased slowly along the shaded canyon between them. There were speed bumps to keep people from going too fast. Lulu climbed up in my lap, planted her rear paws firmly in my groin, and stuck her large black nose against the window so as to see. Not that there was really much to see. A studio is a factory like any other. Beer-bellied workmen in shorts and heavy boots wheeled cameras and sound equipment along. Many were shirtless in the heat, and wore do-rags over their heads. Young, tanned production assistants wearing Bedford Falls golf visors zipped along on bikes and golf carts with pouches of mail, scripts, tapes. A few waved at Sarge. She waved back. One of the stages had a row of makeup trailers parked outside it. A big sign said "Coven High."

"ABC is taping a new midseason sitcom here," Sarge said. "Something about a bunch of teenagers who're all witches. I hear it's real stupid."

"Imagine that."

Two dozen dwarfs in red silk underwear came spilling out of another stage, smoking huge cigars.

"New David Lee Roth video," she explained, as we passed them.

Well, maybe not a factory exactly like any other.

We cruised past a prop warehouse, carpentry shop, machine shop. Then another parking lot. There were names on the curb-stones here, and little or nothing resembling basic transporta-tion. Vintage English ragtops seemed to be in that season. I spot-ted a couple of MGAs, a Triumph Spitfire, an Austin Healey 3000. Seeing them made me miss the Jag. We arrived next at the gift shop and commissary, then found ourselves in a bungalow col-ony. Dozens of snug pink stucco cottages with tile roofs were situated neatly around a chain of courtyards with fountains and benches.

"Most of our own offices are up in the main building," Sarge informed me. "We rent a lot of these out to people who have development deals around town. Producers, directors, lots and lots of writers. Gives 'em a place to go every day. Gets 'em out of the house. I can get you one if you want."

"No, thanks."

"Don't like being in an office?"

"Don't like being around writers."

She nodded wisely. That one she got right away. "Want to check out our back lot?"

Lulu snuffled excitedly in my lap.

"I guess we do," I said.

Movie studios nowadays are mostly complexes of offices and soundstages. The old back lots, with their dusty Western streets, their medieval villages and rows of Brooklyn tenements have been sold off. The land was too valuable. Exteriors are generally shot on location now. Universal and Panorama still keep a few acres set aside in case someone wants the vintage Hollywood feeling, but their so-called back lots are largely tourist attractions now.

The Bedford Falls back lot was a different story. A different world—Homewood, the Anytown, U.S.A., of Badger Hayes's boy-hood. It was all here. The quaint old town square with its court-house and town hall. The town green, the ornate bandstand, the steepled white church with its bell tower, where Badger first kissed Debbie Dale. Main Street—the Tivoli Theater, the malt shop, Mr. Hayes's hardware store, where Badger worked after school. Elm Street, with its row of solid, comfortable houses, including the white cape where Badger lived. Debbie's red brick colonial right next door. It was all here in living color, big as real life. And even more fake.

At the end of Elm, Sarge made a sharp left and we were right back among the soundstages. Only these stages were idle, grim evidence of the shaky ground Bedford Falls stood on. She pulled up at Stage One, and parked there next to a bike rack filled with shiny 1950s Western Flyer Springers. A white Jaguar XJ-6 was also parked there. Beyond was a courtyard that led up to the main office building.

It was cold inside Stage One and dark after the brightness of outside. I bent down and removed Lulu's shades so she could see. A soundstage is a strange, disorienting place. There's the vastness, of course. This one was big enough to hold four jumbo jets with a good-sized chunk of ancient Rome on the side. But the size isn't the strange part. The sensory deprivation is. You can't see or hear or smell anything from the outside world. Time and place cease to exist. It could be day. It could be night. You could be here. You could be anywhere. A soundstage is the hall closet you locked yourself in when you were a little kid, just to see what the utter blackness and silence would do to your head. And how long you could take it.

There were some bins just inside the door filled with sound and light equipment. Beyond them an empty expanse of pavement until we arrived at the back of some standing sets. The overheads were on here. Sarge slipped through a gap between the sets into the brightness. I followed. We were in Badger Hayes's living room. There was the big fireplace with the American eagle hanging over it. The two easy chairs, the sofa, the bookcases. There was the stairway leading upstairs to the bedrooms. The entry hall, where Badger's dad always hung up his coat when he got home from the store, often hollering for Badger. Of course, it didn't look like it did in the movies. It was smaller, and the stairway led to nowhere, and one wall was missing. That modern, big-screen TV and VCR certainly weren't the property of the Hayes family. The place was also a complete mess. The coffee table was heaped with video games and candy wrappers and soda cans. A man's sneakers and dirty socks were strewn around the floor.

The swinging doors into the kitchen didn't go to the kitchen.

The kitchen was across the stage with the other sets, all of them laid out in a big U like a cul-de-sac. The cheerful kitchen with its gleaming white appliances, where Badger's mom gaily mopped the floor in her crisp housedress and pearls, hair perfectly coiffed. The garage door with the basketball hoop over it, where Badger and his pals played Horse. The master bedroom, its twin beds separated by the nightstand. And Badger's own bedroom, with the bunk beds, Homewood High banner, framed photo of President Eisenhower, elaborate chemistry set. His guinea pig cages weren't there, but a short, chubby woman in her late sixties was, busily picking up the dirty laundry that was heaped about.

"Now that there's Bunny," Sarge murmured to me under her breath. "She's a real pistol. And she don't take too well to outsiders. So tread lightly, if you know how."

"I don't."

"I noticed." She started over toward Matthew's mother, calling out "How's my Bunny-honey?!"

Bunny's face lit up. "Charmaine!" She came over and hugged her tightly, her face disappearing into Sarge's stomach. "How was the traffic?"

"Murder," Sarge replied. "Say hey to Hoagy. He's the writer helping Matthew with his book."

Bunny peered up at me, eyes narrowed behind the oversized black spectacles she wore. "Hello," she said, her voice guarded.

"Pleased to meet you, Mrs. Wax," I said.

Bunny Wax was cute and cuddly and well under five feet tall in her white Reeboks. Daughter Shelley had inherited her size and shape, also her features and coloring, though Bunny's hair was mostly white now. And she looked a lot feistier. Her chin was worn thrust forward. Her eyes were alert and shrewd. She wore a purple silk camp shirt, white sweatpants, and a ton of jewelry. Her earrings and two of her rings were jade. Her watch and her other rings were gold, as was her charm bracelet, a big, heavy affair made up of as many bunny rabbit charms as could possibly exist in the world. Whenever she moved it clanged around on her wrist like wind chimes.

She looked me over, her chubby little fists on her hips. She took her time doing it. "What's with this 'Mrs. Wax' business?" she huffed. "You make me sound like some old lady. I'm Bunny."

"Okay, Bunny."

"That's better." She was starting to thaw a couple of degrees
—until she caught sight of Lulu ambling over from the dining
room. "All right, who let that mutt in here?"

Lulu let out a low moan. I assured her I could handle it.
Then I turned to Bunny and said, "Lulu's with me. And she is not
a mutt."

"Why is she with you?" Bunny demanded.

"We're a team. We always work together."

"I don't understand that at all," she fumed, dismissing the
whole idea with a wave of her clanging wrist. "What kind of
grown man takes his doggy with him to work?"

I tried again. "Ever see *Hondo*, the John Wayne movie? He
played the tough, brooding loner with the savage dog, Sam,
whom he refused to feed because he didn't want Sam to ever
become dependent on him."

Bunny frowned. "Yes . . . ?"

"Well, we're not like that."

"What are you, mister, a wisenheimer?" she snapped, glaring at me.

"I am not."

"Better not be. I got no use for them. Never have." She shot
a glance at Sarge, then down at Lulu. "Is she at least paper
trained?"

Lulu snuffled indignantly. She definitely wanted a piece of
the old biddy now. I shrugged and let her have her. I'd done all I
could.

Slowly, Lulu stalked over to her, Bunny watching her every
move disapprovingly. When she arrived at Bunny's Reeboks she
gave her The Treatment. First, the look—her saddest, most
mournful face. A definite ten on the hankie meter. Second, a
slight whimper, more a catch in the throat really. Third, her
knockout punch—she rolled over onto her back, landing directly
on Bunny's feet with a soft plop, paws in the air, tail thumping.
The little ham overplayed it this time, if you ask me. Possibly it
was the surroundings. No matter. The Treatment never fails.

Bunny fell to her knees immediately. "Aw, I'm sorry, sweetheart. Bunny's sorry, okay? She's sorry." She knelt there rubbing
Lulu's belly. To Lulu she said, "Such a little sweetheart." To me
she said, "Oy, yoy. What does she eat, dead fish?"

"Exclusively," I replied. "They flop around if they're still
alive."

"Have you thought about Milk Bones?" she asked. "I understand they're very good for this sort of thing."

"She won't eat them."

"Why not?"

"They're for dogs."

Bunny got up and finished tidying Badger's room. "Sorry about all of this mess, Hoagy. I didn't know we were having company until five minutes ago. At the last minute Matty tells me. Look at all of this, will you?" She scooped up a huge load of dirty T-shirts. "I'll be up half the night washing it." She carried it off to the living room and deposited it next to the front door to nowhere. Her purse was there.

I followed her. "You do his laundry?"

"You never stop being a mother," she replied. "Not if your baby needs you." She bustled over to the coffee table and started picking up the shoes and socks, humming.

I stood there a moment watching her. Then I turned to Sarge and said, "This is where he lives? He actually sleeps in Badger's bed?"

She looked away uncomfortably. "I thought you knew."

"I knew he was staying on the lot. I thought he had a suite of rooms or something."

"He does, sort of." She looked around at the sets. "Kind of strange though, I reckon."

"You can forget the kind of. This is not good." This was far from good. This was Dysfunction Junction. And welcome to it.

"He likes it here," Sarge insisted. "Feels safe. The man's hurting, like I told you."

"You didn't tell me how much. Nor did Shelley."

"What did Shelley tell you?"

"That he's tearing his hair out."

"He is," she affirmed. "Lookie, I got to leave you now. Shit to do. He's in casting—be down in a minute. Just yell when you're ready to leave for the hotel, okay?"

"Thanks for the lift—and the tour." I looked around at the sets. "I think."

She grinned at me. "No problem." Then she yelled good-bye to Bunny and strode off into the darkness out beyond the lights, rump high, calf muscles rippling. A moment later the stage door slammed shut.

"Such a lovely girl," observed Bunny, scooping wadded-up

candy wrappers into a wastebasket. "Strong, smart, big-hearted. And carrying a torch for that bum. That convict. Poo." She finished clearing the coffee table and wiped it off with a damp rag. "I usually make Matty a snack now. I'll make you one, too. But you have to come help."

"It's a deal."

The fridge in the Hayes's kitchen was hooked up. Bunny pulled a carton of milk and a jar of Welch's grape jelly from it. The Wonder bread and Skippy peanut butter, the chunky kind, were in the cupboard.

"You like crusts?" she asked. "Matt won't eat his."

"I will."

"Good boy."

"That's what I tried to tell you."

"Mothers have their own ways of finding these things out," she said, going to work on the sandwiches.

Lulu ambled in after us and curled up under the kitchen table.

"Do you live here, too, Bunny?"

"Oh, heavens no. I have a place of my own."

This I was glad to hear. "Whereabouts?"

"Bungalow C. The old writers' court."

"Oh." Not that glad.

"I fixed it up real nice. Got my own Nordic Track, a washer-dryer combination. You'll have to come visit me." She cut my sandwich in half and put it on a plate and handed it to me. "Sit," she commanded. I did. "You want Bosco in your milk?"

"No, thanks." I bit into my sandwich. I hadn't tasted Welch's grape jelly since I was ten. It was so sweet I could practically feel the sugar dissolving my teeth.

She handed me my milk and sat across from me, watching me eat. "So you and Lulu go everywhere together, huh?"

"Like I said, we're a team. For better or worse."

"Have you considered an alternative form of companionship?"

"Such as?"

"A nice girl."

"Tried it."

She shook her index finger at me, her charm bracelet gonging. "You're the one who's always mixed up with Merilee Nash. Sure, I was just reading about you at the beauty parlor."

"That's me, all right."

"So has she really dumped you for good this time?"

I sighed inwardly. "I'm really more interested in talking about Matthew and Pennyroyal."

She wrinkled her nose. "Feh."

"Feh?"

"I never liked her. Not from the get-go. It had nothing to do with her not being a Jewish girl, either. Religion has never been a big deal in our family. Not like with some families," she added darkly, so darkly I couldn't help but wonder about it. "I didn't like her because she deceived him."

"There's deception in any relationship," I observed. "Deception holds it together."

"Trust holds it together," Bunny argued, smacking the table with her little fist. "Marriage is a partnership. A man and a woman sharing together, building together. Matty and Penny, they never had that. She put a spell on him, is what she did. And poor Matty, he was helpless. He simply could not believe that someone that blond, that lovely—a cheerleader yet—would go out with him. And why shouldn't she? Who wouldn't go out with a nice Jewish boy who is bright and personable and worth four hundred million dollars?"

"Sounds good to me."

"Not that I ever said anything. He deserved to be happy. And she made him happy, while it suited her. Made him a lovely home, a beautiful child. But all along she was deceiving him. As soon as she got what she wanted, she took off. Stole his child. Broke his heart. A snake, that's what she is."

"Your son-in-law would like to see them patch it up."

She shrugged her shoulders. "Sheldon's worried about what'll happen to the studio. That's his job. Mine is to worry about Matty. And for what she's doing to him—the publicity, the sleeping around, the ugliness—she should be punished, not welcomed back. She should be made to suffer like he is."

"You don't think she's suffering?"

"I think she's having the time of her little life," Bunny snapped angrily. "Believe me—Pennyroyal Brim is not the person she pretends to be."

"Who among us is?"

"But she'll get hers," Bunny vowed. "You'll see. She'll get it. She'll do it to herself or someone will do it to her."

"Which would you prefer?"

"All I want is to see my Matty happy again." She peered across the table at me. "And you, Hoagy? What is it you want?"

"I'd like to learn as much as I can about his boyhood," I replied. "About his father—"

"What about him?" she demanded.

"Their relationship. I gather it wasn't so terrific."

She stuck out her lower lip, weighing this. "And what good will this do?"

"A lot of Matthew's movies are about childhood. Yet audiences know very little about his own. They're curious." I sipped my milk. "It may also be good for him right now to do some looking back."

She nodded, her eyes glinting at me. "If it means helping him, I'm all for it. But if it doesn't . . ." She reached across the table and grabbed me by the wrist. She had a grip of iron. "You don't want Bunny Wax for an enemy, mister. Believe me."

"I believe you," I assured her, watching the color drain from my hand.

She relaxed her grip. "Just so we understand each other," she said, smiling.

"We do."

"About what, Ma?"

We both looked up. Matthew was standing, or I should say lurking, there in the doorway.

One look at him and I knew just what Shelley and Sarge meant when they said that Matthew Wax was tearing his hair out.

# Chapter Three

---

I t was quite some bald patch. It started where his forelock should have been and it wandered all the way over behind his right ear. He was down to bare white scalp in many spots. A few thin, reddish brown tufts still clung to life in others. The rest of his hair was shaggy and unkempt. He looked like a kid who'd used his haircut money to buy comic books and then tried doing it himself—with his mom's pinking shears.

"Just so you understand each other about what, Ma?" he repeated, tugging nervously at his ravaged forelock with his fingers.

"Nothing, sweetheart," she replied, gazing up at him with a mixture of pride and awe. And maybe some fear. "Here's your friend. Say hello."

He loped over to me and stuck out his hand. "Glad you could make it," he exclaimed, as we shook. "Stewart, right?"

"Make it Hoagy."

"As in Carmichael?"

"As in the cheese steak."

"Hey, I love cheese steaks!" He grinned at me happily. "Especially with tons of onions and hot peppers. Man, they're great!"

"That they are."

If this was Matthew Wax down, I didn't think I wanted to be around him when he was up. He was a bundle of energy—an eager, boisterous, overgrown kid. He was uncommonly tall, seven or eight inches over six feet, and gawky of build, like a teenager who hasn't filled in yet. His shoulders were narrow, his arms skinny and unusually long, so long that his hands hung nearly down to his knees. They were surprisingly small, delicate hands, and the backs were covered with freckles. So was his face. His skin was fair, almost pasty. He had a rabbit nose, pink and busy, and a jaw you could shovel snow with. He had shaved recently but not well. He wore glasses, thick ones with wire frames that had broken at the hinge and been Scotch-taped together. The eyes behind them were earnest and bright. He wore a faded Bedford Falls T-shirt, old jeans that were three inches too short for him, and a new pair of Air Jordans. He had huge feet. They made him look like a Great Dane puppy. It really was hard to believe he was thirty-eight. So much of him was kid. I would have said happy kid, too, if it weren't for his hair. His hair made him look positively haunted.

"Okay, okay, you're *Meat*," he announced.

"Am I?"

"That's what I'm gonna call you—Meat."

"I've been called worse things."

"Can we have 'em for dinner tonight, Ma?" His fingers went up to his scalp again, worrying it like a gardener trying to pull out crabgrass.

"Have what, sweetheart?" she wondered.

Before he could answer, Lulu came out from under the table and yawned. She was feeling ignored.

Matthew wrinkled his rabbit nose at me, mystified.

"That aroma of the San Pedro docks at low tide is Lulu," I explained.

He looked down. "Oh, wow! You have a basset hound!" He flopped to his knees and petted her, thrilled. "I love basset hounds! *Love* 'em!"

"She's very sensitive," Bunny informed her son. "So be nice."

"Know who she looks just like?" he said, peering at her.

I nodded. "Streisand. Everyone says so."

"Cleo. Remember *The People's Choice?*"

"Vaguely," I replied, not liking where this was going.

"It was a sitcom in the fifties, with Jackie Cooper. Cleo was his dog. She used to make comments about everything that was going on. She didn't actually *talk*. It was more like we heard her thoughts. Lulu looks just like her."

"How nice," I said, watching her head swell even more.

"Mary Jane Croft was the actress who did her voice," he added quickly, as if that was going to be my next question. "She played Clara Randolph on *Ozzie and Harriet* and Joan's friend Helen on *I Married Joan* and Chester Riley's sister, Cissy, on *The Life of Riley*. You into trivia?"

"These days, I'm happy just to remember my own name," I confessed.

He sat back on his haunches, chuckling with delight over Lulu. "Hey, can she do any tricks?"

"I wouldn't exactly call them tricks."

Lulu threw back her head and started moaning loudly. She needs very little encouragement.

"Oy, yoy, what's that?" asked Bunny, aghast.

"Her imitation of Roseanne Barr singing the *National Anthem*," I replied. "Good girl, Lulu. You can stop now."

She wasn't done though. Not with a world-famous director as her captive audience. She covered her eyes with her paws now, hamming shamelessly.

Matthew frowned. "And that?"

"That would be Asta, whenever Nick and Nora started to get mushy. Okay, Lulu. You can—"

"Can she flap her ears straight up in the air like Cleo?" asked Matthew.

"Only if she's in the process of falling from a very tall building. Which she may soon be, if she doesn't behave herself."

She grunted at me and went back under the table, peeved.

"What is it you wanted to have tonight, sweetheart?" Bunny asked Matthew.

"Cheese steaks," he replied. "With lots of onions and hot peppers. Can we, Ma?"

"I'm making salmon patties," she replied firmly. "And those Tater Tots you like. Now go eat your sandwich."

"Sure, Ma."

It was on the counter by the sink. She'd cut the crusts off for him. He loped over to it and began chomping, slumped there against the sink.

She watched him eat, crinkling her nose at every bite. I think she'd have chewed his food for him if she could have. "Don't slouch," she reminded him.

"Sure, Ma." He stood straighter, grinning down at her fondly.

"And how many days have you been wearing that T-shirt?" she demanded, scowling up at him fiercely.

"Dunno," he mumbled, reddening.

"I want you to take a bath, tonight," Bunny ordered, shaking a finger at her towering manchild. "And change those jeans, too. You've been wearing them so long they could stand up by themselves."

"Right, Ma."

"Look at your nice friend here." She glanced at me approvingly. "With his nice seersucker suit. Why, he's fresh as a daisy."

"I wouldn't go quite that far," I said.

"All right, I'm going," she announced abruptly. "You two boys have business to discuss." She went over to Matthew and held her face up to him. He bent over and kissed her on the forehead. "I'll be back at six. Will you be joining us for dinner, Hoagy?" she asked, scurrying off toward the living room.

"Thanks, but I have to get settled in," I replied. We followed her. Matthew immediately flopped onto the sofa, his big sneakered feet up on the coffee table.

Bunny whirled and barked, "Get those gunboats off the coffee table!" He obeyed. "I have to watch him like a hawk," she clucked at me. "A hawk!" Then she gathered up his dirty clothes and went bustling off into the darkness.

The second she was gone he put his feet right back up. And grabbed the radio controls for a toy car, a Lamborghini Countach that was parked on the floor by the TV. He flicked it on and sent it speeding around the set, watching it intently. I sat, watching him. He reminded me of a kid who has just been left with his new babysitter.

"It's a prototype," he explained, his eyes never leaving it. "I know the guy who makes 'em. He sends 'em to me."

He sent it under the easy chair where I sat, then over toward the fireplace, where Lulu was. She didn't like that. She thought it was an alien chasing her. She scampered over to me and crouched between my legs, trembling.

"Don't mind Ma, Meat," Matthew said, his eyes still on the car. "She means well."

"I'm sure she does."

We both sat there watching the car zip around, its high-pitched whine the only sound in that vast, airtight building. It was odd sitting there on that set, surrounded by all of that blackness. It felt as if the cameras were rolling and our dialogue was already scripted for us. It felt as if none of this was quite real. I never lost that feeling the whole time I worked with Matthew Wax. I was always waiting for someone to yell "Cut!"

"So tell me what you need, Meat," Matthew said.

"Your attention, for starters."

"You've got it," he assured me, as the car zipped around the sofa and toward me.

I intercepted it with my foot and picked it up, its wheels spinning in midair.

"Hey, put that back!"

I had other plans. I hurled it as high and as far as I could out into the darkness beyond the set. It clattered on the pavement, then was silent.

"What did you do that for?" he cried, outraged.

"When we work, we work," I said quietly.

He stared at me like I was a madman. I stared right back at him like I was a madman. I'm very good at that. It isn't much of a stretch in my case.

He backed down first. "Okay, okay. I'm sorry. You're right. We work."

"Fine."

Matthew cleared his throat. "I guess I'm just . . ." He lowered his chin to his chest and tugged at a lock of hair, jittery and at a loss for words. "I'm not used to giving interviews, I guess."

"This isn't an interview."

"Right," he acknowledged quickly. "I know that. So . . . what can I tell you?"

"How you are."

"I'm great." He smiled at me easily. "Really great."

I nodded patiently. I'm used to being lied to. People lie to me all the time in my business. Almost as often as they try to use me. "I'm glad to hear that, Matthew. And who, may I ask, does your hair?"

Startled, he dropped his hand to his lap. It flopped around there, like a live animal.

"Let's try that one again," I said. "How are you, Matthew?"

He took his time answering. He shrugged his narrow shoulders, sniffled. Laid his head back on the sofa, gazed up into the overhead lights. He had an unusually short neck for someone so gangly. Actually, the more I looked at him, the more he seemed to have been assembled entirely out of spare parts. "Not so great," he finally said, softly. "I'm trying to stay up for Ma. I don't want her to worry about me."

"No offense, but I don't think you're fooling her."

"I don't think I am either," he admitted. "I feel, I don't know, like a tree that's trying to make it through a hurricane." He sat up, warming to the idea. "The wind is howling . . ." He made a whistling noise through his teeth. The wind. Howling. "My trunk is bent over. My limbs are snapping off, one by one by one . . ." He was turning it all into a scene, the stirring climax of *Matty, the Little Maple Tree Who Could.* Coming soon to a theater near you. "There I am, the wind is building and I'm—"

"Are you bitter?" I broke in.

He frowned. "Bitter? It's not in my nature to be bitter. Why, were you?"

"Me?"

"Wasn't your love life smeared all over the papers, too?"

"Still is, when I'm not looking."

"It's not very much fun," he said, swallowing. His hand went back up to his scalp.

"No, it's not."

"Do you have any advice for me, Meat?" he wondered. "Anything you've learned?"

"You mean hurricane prevention tips?"

He waited for me to answer.

"About all I've learned," I replied, "is that if you want a low-profile personal life, don't fall for an actress."

"You did."

"Couldn't help myself."

"Me neither. Actresses are . . . I don't know, different from other girls."

"That they are."

"Why is that?" he asked suddenly. "What makes them so special, Meat?"

He sounded just like Badger. Innocent. Ingenuous. Endlessly curious. Next he'd be asking me why people have to get old and die. "I'm still working on that one, Matthew," I said.

"Will you let me know when you figure it out?"

"You will be among the first."

"Great." There was a package of Milky Way bars on the coffee table before him. He tore into one and took a bite. "So what do we do now?" he asked, munching.

"Tomorrow I start asking you questions."

"About what?"

"You. Your life, your work, your attitudes. Lots of questions. A million questions. So many I'll start getting on your nerves."

"And then?"

"And then I'll ask you more questions."

"What happens if we disagree on something?"

"We fight."

"Gee, I don't know if that'll work, Meat," he said doubtfully. "I'm used to having total say on everything I do."

"And you will," I assured him. "This is your book. I'm only here to help you. But I have to know you're willing to dig. And keep digging, no matter how much it hurts. Otherwise, you're just wasting your time. And mine."

He thought this over. "I am ready," he said grimly. "I definitely am."

"How come?"

"How come?" he repeated.

"Why do you want to do this book?"

He frowned, confused. "Didn't Shelley tell you what—?"

"I want to hear it from you."

He jumped to his feet and paced around the set. Lulu opened one eye briefly, stirred and went back to sleep. He loped over to the staircase, then back again.

"I think it will help to change how the public sees me," he declared.

"And how do they see you?"

"Like I'm some kind of freak."

"So you're doing this because you want to be understood?"

He flopped back down on the sofa. "Sure."

"As what?"

He shrugged. "A guy who's trying to entertain people. Make

them happy." He stared at me for a second. "Do you go see my movies?"

"Why, is that a prerequisite for this job?"

"No, no. I just . . . I'm not used to being around anyone who doesn't, that's all. Why do *you* think I'm doing this book?"

"Because the critics have blasted you," I replied. "And you're shook. And you think this will somehow help you get your touch back. I think you could care less if anyone understands you."

He thought this over. "That's not true, Meat," he said solemnly. "There is someone who I really wish understood me."

"And who is that, Matthew?"

His eyes met mine. "Me."

I nodded approvingly. "Good answer."

We were both silent a moment. The silence made him uncomfortable. Or maybe his candor had. He wadded up his candy wrapper and tossed it on the floor, fidgeted, drummed the coffee table loudly with his fingers. It was annoying, but it still beat watching him tear out his hair.

"I met Shadow Williams at the gate," I said. "Sarge was telling me about how you saw him hit his home run."

"I knew it was gone the second it hit his bat," Matthew recalled excitedly. "Man, he got *all* of it!"

"That particular story has a happy ending," I said. "I want the ones that don't."

He frowned. "Like which?"

"Like Norbert Schlom."

His face darkened. "What about him?"

"Shelley told me he cheated you out of millions."

Matthew said nothing. His eyes shone behind his battered glasses. The child's hurt was still there.

"What else did he do?"

"Terrible things," he replied, his voice quavering.

"I want to know what they were."

"You want to know what they were?" he said hotly. "Okay, let's put it in the book. Sure. That'll be super. He wanted me to take on this Three Stooges movie, see? And I wasn't interested. The script was somebody else's, and it smelled, and I wanted to make my Badger movie. Only Norbert wouldn't green light me unless I did the Stooges movie first. So Shelley made a deal for me to do Badger for Orion. We were going to leave Panorama. Norbert, he didn't like that idea. So he made sure I couldn't."

"How?"

"He planted a bunch of coke in my bungalow and called the studio cops on me, that's how! Told them I was a major drug dealer! He gave me ten minutes to say yes to the movie or go to jail. And it was no bluff, either. Not with Norbert."

"I take it you agreed to his terms."

He nodded unhappily. "And he called them off. But he swore he'd do it again in a second if I ever tried to walk off the picture. It was like he was holding a loaded gun to my head. I couldn't eat, I couldn't sleep, I couldn't concentrate. Naturally, the movie was no good. Shelley got me out of there right after that. We swore we'd never do business with Norbert again, and we haven't. That's the whole ugly story. Shadow has a featured role in that one, too, come to think of it."

"Oh?"

"He was the studio cop who actually planted the coke. Hid it all over the place, bags and bags of it. He felt awful about it. Still does. But, hey, I don't blame him. He was just doing his job."

"About Pennyroyal . . ."

He stiffened. "No, no, no. Forget that. Just forget it."

"Forget what, Matthew?"

"I won't cream Penny. I won't do that to her. I won't!"

"Relax. That's not what I'm after."

"Good." He was clearly relieved to hear this. But he didn't relax. "Then what do you—?"

"I want to interview her."

"You *what?* No way."

"I need to," I said.

"Uh-uh. Forget it."

"I think it will be helpful to get her side."

"This is *my* book!"

"And it will be a fuller, more mature one if I can sit down with her. Just think about it, will you?"

"All right, but it's still gonna be no." He heaved a huge sigh. Then heaved another, though this one sounded much more like a sob. "C-Can you believe what she's told the papers about me?"

"She's being used. She was crying to Shelley about it on the phone the other day."

"You actually sound like you feel sorry for her."

"I feel sorry for both of you. And for Georgie most of all."

His brow creased at my mention of his baby.

"What do you feel for her?" I asked him.

"I feel nothing. Pennyroyal is from the past. Pennyroyal is history. My life starts now." He chanted this woodenly, as if it were a mantra.

"You're saying you wouldn't take her back?"

He let out a short laugh. "Would you?"

"If I loved her."

"Well, I don't. I don't love her. It's over. We had some good times together. Fixing up the house, having Georgie. We had fun. She showed me how. I'd never really enjoyed anything besides my work until I met her. That part . . . that was good. Like when she showed me around Las Vegas on our honeymoon. She used to party there in college. She likes to party. She likes to go out and do things, be around people. I—I don't. She just never accepted that about me." He stuck his chin out stubbornly. "Look, I know it would be a lot easier for everybody if we just kissed and made up. But that's not going to happen, okay? This isn't . . ."

"This isn't one of your movies?" I suggested.

He grinned at me crookedly. "Then you *have* seen them."

"They're kind of hard to avoid."

"Is that so bad?"

"Don't mind me. I just tend to prefer things that are in short supply."

"It's over, Meat. Penny and me. Don't think of it as anything but over. All I care about now is my studio and my son." He let out another of those sobs. "God, I miss him. It's driving me crazy how much I miss him. I have a mind to drive over there in the night and just snatch him from her."

"And get thrown in jail for it? That's precisely the sort of fool thing Zorch would love you to do."

"But he's *mine!*"

"She was in on it, too," I said coldly.

That one made him mad, so mad he nearly blew. But he didn't. He just glared at me in angry, hurt silence.

"Anything you'd like to ask me?" I said. A peace offering.

"Yeah, there is. Did I piss you off before?"

"When?"

"When I asked you to stop here before you went to your hotel."

"You didn't ask me. You told me."

He chuckled, amused. "Gotcha. I'll remember that."

"See that you do. Anything else you want to know?"

"Yeah. How do you feel about *It's a Wonderful Life?*"

I tugged at my ear. "I understand that's your favorite movie of all time."

"Because it's so uplifting," he said enthusiastically. "I must have seen it two hundred times, and every time I do I sob with joy. It's definitely what I've aspired to with my Badger movies. You've seen it?"

"I hate it."

The color, what little of it there was, drained from his face. "You're kidding."

"I am not."

"B-But how could you?" he sputtered, flabbergasted.

"Because I come from a small town. A real one, not one that's on a back lot in Culver City. It was a mean, narrow-minded place, and no one lived happily ever after. I fled as soon as I could. That movie takes me back there. I find it depressing."

"But it's such a *happy* movie!"

"It's a fake movie."

"No, no, no," he argued vehemently. "It's not fake. It's an *ideal*. We need our ideals, Meat. They're vital. Without them, we'd all be lost. Totally *lost!*"

He got good and worked up. I let him. Because it wasn't Frank Capra he was defending. It was Matthew Wax. He was answering all of those critics who had blasted his last Badger movie. He was also giving me an excellent self-appraisal of his work.

"I can't *believe* you, Meat!" he fumed. "I really can't. I mean, I've *never* met *anyone* who said that before!"

"You never met me before."

He shook his head at me, baffled. "I don't understand you."

"I'm something of an acquired taste, like raw oysters."

"I hate raw oysters," he snapped. "They taste like snot."

Lulu sat up at all of this talk of seafood. I glanced at Grandfather's Rolex. It was past her suppertime back home in New

York, where her stomach's clock was still set. Of course, when it comes to Lulu and seafood, it's always suppertime somewhere in the world.

I got to my feet and smoothed my trousers. "I'd like to go to my hotel now."

"Sure, sure," he said, agreeably. "Hey, you in a hurry?"

"Seldom."

"Then c'mon," he exclaimed, jumping to his feet. "I want to show you something first."

He bounded off of the set into the darkness beyond. I tagged along, Lulu bringing up the rear. The late day sun was almost blinding after being inside the soundstage. Lulu froze there in the doorway, blinking, until I slipped her shades on for her. Matthew pulled a Western Flyer out of the bike rack and climbed on. I did the same. Then we set off, riding slowly. It was a comfortable ride, what with the padded seat and whitewall balloon tires. Also a familiar one. I'd had one just like it when I was a kid, and deep down inside I'd always preferred it to the jazzy, grown-up ten-speeder I gave it up for. Matthew's was somewhat small for him. He rode with his knees stuck out, like a kid using his little sister's bike. But he seemed used to it. Lulu ran up ahead and escorted us, arfing ebulliently. More hamming.

"Definitely a great dog," observed Matthew. "She ever do any acting?"

"Every day of her life."

"I've always loved dog pictures. *Rin Tin Tin, Lassie.* Ever since I was a kid. Lulu would make a perfect star, y'know. She's got looks, personality. Have you ever considered . . . ?" He trailed off when he noticed the look on my face. "Why are you glaring at me like that, Meat?"

"No reason." A conspiracy, that's what this was.

"I'd love to direct one of my own someday," he went on. And on. "I've just never found the right story. Hey, if you come up with an idea, let me know. We could develop it together."

"I don't do screenplays," I said. Because I don't, and because there's no greater way to keep a movie person eating out of your hand than to reject them. I've never understood why that's so, but it is.

"Suit yourself." He seemed disappointed.

But not as disappointed as you-know-who. She slowed up alongside my bike and showed me her teeth. I showed her mine.

The studio was quiet now. It was past five, and many workers had gone home. The few we saw gazed at Matthew with reverence as he rode by. But they didn't wave or call out to him. And he seemed not to notice them at all. We turned off into Homewood and rode our bikes leisurely along Elm. An odd sensation. I felt like I should be tossing the evening paper onto everyone's front porch. My first paying job, a few short decades back.

"Tell me about your new movie," I said, shaking off the memory. "I understand it's to be another Badger."

"That's right," he said. "I'm picking his story up a few years after he's graduated from Homewood State. He's moved out here to L.A. and become a really successful film director—although the critics hated his last picture. Debbie Dale is an actress. The two of them are married, but she's just left him and taken their baby with her."

"Sounds somewhat autobiographical," I observed.

"Yeah, it kind of is," he said sincerely. "I'm calling it either *Badger Goes to Hollywood* or *Badger All Alone*. Which do you like?"

"Neither."

"God, you're so negative!" he cried out, chuckling. Then he turned serious. "See, Badger, he's always had things turn out his way. And now they're not, and he's all alone and—"

"Hence the title."

"Maybe that is a little heavy-handed," he admitted, glancing over at me. "Johnny's coming back in it. This is an important picture for him."

"And what about Pennyroyal?"

"Oh, she'll still be a presence. Debbie's constantly in Badger's thoughts. His dreams, memories. I've got footage of her from the first three movies that I never used. Plenty of stuff. She'll be in it. She has to be."

"And Trace Washburn?"

"Badger doesn't need a dad anymore," he said gruffly. "Badger's on his own now."

And Trace was out on his ear. His affair with Pennyroyal was costing Matthew's one-time leading man plenty.

"And how does it end?" I asked.

"Not happily, Meat," he revealed. "At least it doesn't in my current draft. I'm still not a hundred percent sure though. I guess I'm still trying to find it."

" 'The thing that's important to know,' " I quoted, " 'is that you never know. You're always sort of feeling your way.' "

"Very true," he agreed. "Who said that?"

"Diane Arbus, shortly before her suicide."

The town square was shady, and a bit cooler. Matthew pulled up in front of the courthouse and got off his bike and sat down on the courthouse steps, his long legs stretched out before him. I joined him, the steps feeling warm through my trousers. Lulu stretched out languorously on the sidewalk directly before Matthew, preening like a bikini-clad starlet at a big shot's pool party. It was a truly shameless display. A stern talking-to was definitely called for.

"I really love this place," Matthew said wistfully, gazing out over the town green to the old white church. Its steeple was still brightly lit by the sun. The rest of it was in shadow. "A lot of good times here, Meat. Good memories."

I glanced over at him. There was something creepy about the way he'd said it. As if this were an actual town, not a collection of false fronts.

"I'm gonna use it again in my new movie," he said. "As what it really is—the place where Badger filmed his last hit, before it all went sour for him. He returns here, searching for answers—like Dana Andrews in the bomber junkyard scene in *The Best Years of Our Lives*. I always loved that scene." He turned and looked at me. "You really grew up in a town like this?"

"I grew older. I wouldn't say I grew up."

He held a freckled hand out to Lulu. She quickly scampered up the steps to him and let him scratch her ears. Me she snubbed. I wasn't a big-time director. Hell, I didn't even do screenplays.

"And you?" I asked.

"It wasn't at all like this." He shook his semibald head. "Not my old neighborhood. I've never been back there, y'know. Not since the day we moved away. That was after Dad died. I'd started working at Panorama. Twenty years. That's how long it's been. Not too many good memories of that place. Not any, in fact."

"Well, that settles that," I said.

"Settles what, Meat?"

"What we're doing tomorrow morning, first thing."

"Do we have to?" he blurted out, like a scared, spoiled kid. "I mean, I'd really rather not."

"All the more reason to do it."

His eyes searched my face. "It's important?"

"It is. Trust me."

He hesitated, then sighed with resignation. "Okay, Meat. If you say so. We can drive out there. Sure." He started tearing nervously at his forelock. Abruptly, he stopped himself. "Would you like to read my new script?"

"Yes, I would."

"Great," he said, pleased. "I'm curious to hear what you think."

"Why?"

"Because you'll tell me the truth. Shelley, Sarge and the others—they just tell me what I want to hear. On account of they work for me."

"So do I," I pointed out.

"No, you don't. Not like they do. They depend on me. They'd be lost without me." He paused, groping for the right words. "It can be a real pain sometimes, having so much say over people's lives. Nobody's ever completely straight with me. Not ever." He looked at me pleadingly. "Will you be, Meat? Please?"

"It will be a pleasure," I assured him. I wondered if he really wanted the truth, or if he just wanted me to think he did. I didn't know. I only knew that it would not be a pleasure.

A roar invaded Homewood now. The roar of a motorcycle—a big one, heading our way. It came hard around the corner of Elm, a shiny new Harley Fat Boy, hog of hogs, practically a house on two wheels. A kid with a wild mop of hair was on it. Matthew grinned and waved to him.

The kid grinned back, and pulled up before us with a screech. "Like it?" he called out, revving it.

Matthew gave him two thumbs up.

He revved it again, then shut it off. And then Johnny Forget, Matthew Wax's troubled young star, climbed off and came over to us. Matthew got up and hugged him. He seemed genuinely glad to see him.

"How are you, Johnny?" he asked. He seemed genuinely concerned, too.

"I'm okay," Johnny replied in his soft, little boy's whisper of a voice. "I'm doing okay."

Johnny Forget wasn't a little boy anymore. He was twenty-four. But he still came off like one. He was small, about five feet six, and his body and features still seemed softened by baby fat. His angelic good looks remained. The big, soft brown eyes, the full red lips, the shy innocence that made teenaged girls positively melt. He was the same little Johnny, the Johnny who was, for a couple of years, the most photographed celebrity in America, eclipsing even Johnny Depp, Madonna, and Bart Simpson. Clearly, he didn't want this to be so. He was doing his best to deface himself. His gleaming, matinee idol's blue-black hair was now a wild mop of Rastafarian dreadlocks, dyed to a garish shade of canary yellow. He wore a nose stud in one nostril, an earring in one earlobe, and a two-day growth of beard. Also blue and purple bruises around his throat, as if someone had tried to throttle him. He had on a black leather motorcycle jacket with all sorts of zippers and buckles, no shirt, torn, faded jeans, and black biker boots. But he was still little Johnny, reeking of Patchouli, the old hippie cologne that smells like a cross between marijuana and spoiled pork.

I hadn't realized it before—or cared, frankly—but he was also quite obviously a major league boy toy.

"What happened to your throat?" Matthew wondered, as he looked him over.

Johnny stared at him blankly. He seemed a little slow on the uptake, semiglazed, semi-not all there. That'll happen if you go through a lot of drugs and don't have a lot of extra brains to begin with. "My what?" he finally said, silently mouthing the words a split second before he said them, as if his voicebox were one beat late clicking in.

"You didn't crack up your new bike already, did you?" pressed Matthew.

Johnny fingered the bruises on his throat. "Uh . . . no. Things just got a little rough the other night, y'know?"

"Rough?" Matthew didn't comprehend.

"At a party," Johnny explained, giggling dumbly. "With friends, man."

"Oh, I see," Matthew said, though I don't believe he did. Boys didn't have rough sex with each other in Homewood. Or any other kind of sex with each other. "Say hey to Hoagy. He's working with me on my book."

"I'm Johnny, man," he said, sticking out his hand. "Glad to know you."

"Likewise." His hand was soft and plump, like a girl's. "The vamp over there is Lulu."

She had moved a safe twenty feet away, from where she eyed Johnny witheringly. She has this thing about colognes. She is intensely allergic to Calvin Klein's Obsession, for instance. Patchouli she just flat out hates.

"I've been leaving messages all over for you," Matthew said to him. "Where've you been?"

Johnny shrugged. "Around," he replied vaguely. "I didn't want to hassle you. You got so many hassles."

"You're not a hassle, Johnny," Matthew said, placing his hands on his shoulders. "Stay for dinner, okay? Ma'd love to see you. We can go to Malibu Grand Prix later."

"Can't, man." Johnny glanced back at his bike. "Just wanted you to see it. You really like it?"

It was loaded down with every manner of fender, trim, and ornament there was. A truly gaudy machine. "I really do," Matthew exclaimed, admiring it.

"Go on and take it for a spin," Johnny urged him.

Matthew hopped right on, delighted, and started it up. He revved it a few times, enjoying the roar, then went tearing off down Main Street.

Johnny watched him ride off. Then he fished an unfiltered Camel from his jacket pocket, stuck it between his teeth, and lit it with a Bic lighter. He let the smoke out of his nostrils and tossed his brightly colored mop of hair. "It all seems so stupid," he said, dreamily.

"What does, Johnny?" I asked.

"Life, man. It all seems too stupid."

"Only because it is."

He smiled at me. He liked me now—I understood him. Of course, that wasn't so hard. "Matthew's the only one."

"The only one, Johnny?"

"The only person in this world who cares whether I live or die."

"Your mother doesn't?" I asked gently.

"I got no mother, man," he snarled. "The wicked witch is dead."

I nodded, though I knew this wasn't strictly accurate. He'd only wounded her in the arm when he shot her. She had dropped the charges in exchange for a cash settlement. "What about your friends?"

That got only a short, derisive snort out of him.

"And your fans? Don't they care?"

"Fuck them," he snapped petulantly. He looked down Main. The sound of the Harley was very faint now. "Do you ride?" he asked me.

"Occasionally."

"A few friends and me, we all ride up into Topanga Canyon. Do some beers and smokes and shooting."

"Shooting?"

"Semiautomatics, man. I got this AK47 assault rifle that's major. Totally. I got all kinds of shit—a Colt Sporter, a Tec-9. . . . They're like this real power trip, y'know? Watermelons make the best targets." He imitated the sound of an exploding melon. It wasn't pretty. "Gore, man. Totally."

"Keeping semiautomatics is somewhat frowned upon by the law, isn't it?" Certainly they would frown in the case of this particular puppy.

"Name one fun thing that isn't," he dared me, defiantly.

I let him have that one. "I'd like to interview you for Matthew's book, Johnny. Where do I get in touch with you?"

I got the vacant stare. "He wants me to talk to you?" he finally asked.

"He does."

"It's okay then. If Matthew says so."

I could hear the motorcycle again. Matthew was on his way back.

"Where do I get in touch with you, Johnny?" I repeated.

He tossed his cigarette aside. "I really don't like being tied down to any schedule or place, man."

"I see." He was starting to get on my nerves. Bright, he wasn't. He made Matt Dillon look like John Kenneth Galbraith. Not that he wasn't trying. He was trying real hard—to be tough and nasty and bad. But it was all pose. He was a rebel without a clue, a child star, and if there's a more fucked-up brand of creature on earth, I've yet to come across it. True, he had played Badger convincingly as a wide-eyed kid. But now Matthew was expecting him to play him as an adult—as a famous director who's going through a serious life crisis, no less. Was Johnny capable of this? I wondered. "How do I contact you, Johnny?" I said, trying it a little louder and a lot slower.

He went bratty on me. "Through my agency, man," he sneered. "How do you think?"

"Not as well as I once did," I confessed. "But I try not to let it get me down."

He tossed his hair and stared at me. "Huh?"

"Forget it."

Matthew came roaring back up Main Street. Pulled up in front of us, revved the Fat Boy a couple of times, and shut it off. "I want one," he declared, patting it.

"Take it," Johnny offered. "It's yours."

"I don't want yours, doofus." Matthew laughed. "I'll get my own."

Johnny swiped at his nose with the back of his hand. "Could I maybe talk to you a second, Matthew?"

"Sure, Johnny." Matthew climbed off of the bike. "What's up?"

Johnny glanced over at me uneasily.

"I'll disappear," I suggested.

"No, don't," Matthew said quickly. "C'mon, Johnny. We'll take a walk. Just the two of us." He put his arm around him, and they started off together down the sidewalk. "Something bothering you?"

"I'm going through some weird shit," Johnny said, "and I'm not sure what my attitude's supposed to be . . ."

They were out of earshot after that. I sat back down on the steps and looked at Lulu and patted the step next to me. It was time for our own little heart-to-heart. Sullenly, she ambled over to me and sat with a grunt.

"Now look," I said firmly. "Just because Matthew said you have star potential doesn't mean you do. That's just the way people talk out here. Movie babble. Acting happens to be a horrible life. You'll spend most of your time dragging your tired bones from one audition to the next, getting rejection after rejection. There's thousands of other dogs out there, all of them trying to paw their way to the top. And even if you do make it, it doesn't last. Where is Mike the Dog now, huh? Where is Benji?"

She wasn't listening to me. She had the bug. There's no getting through to them when they do. I wished I could consult her mommy on this. Merilee was a pro. Lulu would listen to her. But I was on my own now. Alone. All I could do was hope she soon returned to her senses, such as they are.

Matthew and Johnny came strolling back. Johnny climbed onto his Fat Boy and started it up.

"Stay in touch, okay?" Matthew urged him. "You always have a home here, Johnny. You know that, don't you?"

"I know that," Johnny said, nodding his canary yellow head. "Thanks, man." Then he sped off.

Matthew watched him go. "Problems with his love life," he volunteered. "He's been seriously involved with somebody lately, and he just found out the guy's seeing somebody else on the side. He doesn't know what to do now. I thought he should confront him. Get it out in the open."

I nodded. Badger's dad would have advised just that.

We got back on our own machines and rode on, Lulu trotting alongside.

"Does he often come to you with his personal problems?" I asked.

"Always has," Matthew replied. "I've been directing Johnny since he was seven years old. He got so used to asking me what his character's attitude should be that he kept right on asking me, even when the cameras weren't rolling. I guess I'm kind of like a father to him. He's pretty messed up, but he's a good kid, really. And he had a terrible time of it when he was little. That mother of his is a horrible, greedy bitch. She never let him be a kid. When he first came in to read for *The Boy Who Cried Wolf* he didn't even know how to throw a baseball or ride a bike. He'd never been to a regular school, never had any pals. He was the family bread-winner, and she drove him beyond belief. Screamed at him, beat him with a hairbrush if he muffed his lines. Got him so upset he'd vomit between takes. It was awful for the poor kid. She's back in Canada now, thank God."

"Who manages him now?" I asked.

"He's with the Harmon Wright Agency," Matthew replied.

I flinched at the name. Inwardly, apparently. He took no note of it.

"Joey Bam Bam is the guy who handles him," he added.

"Joey Bam Bam?"

"Johnny's very happy with him."

We pedaled our way out of Homewood. An alley took us by

some prop warehouses and then to a big garage, where Matthew stopped and got off his bike.

"This is what I wanted to show you," he said. "Come on in."

The sliding garage doors were locked. He used a key to unlock them, then slid one open and went in and flicked on a light. I followed him in.

A dozen or so cars were stored in there. The first one he led me to was a long, low drag racer with chrome pipes. Its body was fashioned out of a coffin, complete with purple velvet upholstery.

"Recognize it?" he asked, grinning at me eagerly.

I shook my head. "Should I?"

"It's Grandpa Munster's Dragula, Meat," he exclaimed. "You know, from *The Munsters*—the TV series. George Barris designed it. He was *the* customizer of the sixties. I bought it at an auction. I've got a bunch of his. Here, here, this one's my pride and joy . . ." He whipped the cover off a low-slung black convertible with tail fins. It looked somewhat like a 1955 Lincoln Futura dream car. "The Batmobile, Meat," he proclaimed with great pride. "Not the fake one from that awful movie, either. This is the one from the TV show. The *real* Batmobile. Cost me plenty," he confided, patting it lovingly. "But how can you put a price tag on something like this?"

"You can't."

"Most of these I got at auctions." He pointed them out, one by one. "That '28 Porter over there's the talking car from *My Mother the Car*. Totally authentic, right down to the license plate: PZR 317."

"Does it—?"

"No, it doesn't talk. And believe me, you're not the first person who's asked that. There's Maxwell Smart's Sunbeam Alpine from *Get Smart*. The motorcycle and sidecar are Colonel Klink's from *Hogan's Heroes* . . ." He stopped, frowning at me. "What are you looking around for, Meat?"

"Mister Ed. I thought perhaps he'd been stuffed and auctioned off as well."

He reddened. "You think I'm silly, don't you? You think I'm totally silly."

"No, not at all."

"I guess it does seem a little bizarre," he admitted. "But, see, I grew up on these shows, Meat. This is my whole childhood, right here. These cars. And now they're actually mine. I can't believe it. It makes my heart pound. Can you understand that?"

"I can, Matthew. Do they run?"

"I have a mechanic who does nothing but keep them running. These aren't museum pieces. They're my cars for getting around town. What are you driving while you're here?"

"I was going to rent something when I got to the hotel."

"What for? Take one of these. Whichever one you want."

"That's extremely generous of you, Matthew, but I really can't see myself zipping around Los Angeles in the Batmobile."

"Why not? C'mon, Meat. Have some fun, will ya?" He froze, a dark shadow crossing his face. "Gee," he said softly. "That's *just* what Penny used to say to me." He swallowed, his eyes shining. No, he wasn't over her. Not even maybe. He shook himself and mustered a smile. "Please, Meat. Take one."

"Matthew, I'll be fine. I'll rent myself something."

"You sure I can't talk you into it?" He really wanted to, it seemed.

"Positive."

He shrugged, disappointed, and we started back outside. As we did my eye caught sight of one car in the back row that I hadn't noticed before. I stood there, staring. Then, slowly, I went over to it.

"Aha!" cried Matthew triumphantly. "I *knew* one of 'em would get to you. I should have guessed it would be this one. You're into machines, not gimmicks."

I was certainly into this machine. How old was I then? Ten? I'd wanted it desperately. It and everything it stood for. And here it was, thirty years later. Factory fresh. "It's the real one?" I asked.

"They actually used several through the years, only none of the others were kept up. Just this one. It's in perfect condition, every inch original—except for the tires, but they're factory spec." Matthew thumped me on the back. "It's all yours, Meat. Sarge'll bring your bags down. Keys are in the ignition. Tank's full. The mileage isn't too hot, but they didn't worry about such things in those days."

"They didn't worry about anything in those days."

He grinned at me, immensely pleased. "This is just great. I feel so much better about you now, Meat."

"Do you?"

"Absolutely. This proves it beyond a shadow of doubt."

"Proves what, Matthew?"

"You *are* human. I was beginning to wonder."

The red Porsche was still waiting there across the street. For me. He fell in behind me the second I pulled out of the gate. I took Washington to Robertson, which jogged under the freeway and then angled north toward Beverly Hills. He stayed with me. He wasn't real steady. Sometimes he was right on my tail. Sometimes he was three or four cars back. Sometimes he stalled it. But he stayed with me. I wasn't easy to lose in a crowd.

The Corvette strained to run. It had a monster under the hood, a 283-cubic-inch V-8 that put out 270 horsepower. This wasn't a car for city traffic. This was a car for the open road—a road like, say, Route 66. It's true. I was behind the wheel of Tod Stiles's Vette, the '59 convertible he and Buz Murdock criss-crossed America in—adventure, opportunity, romance, all up ahead for them around the next bend. It was perfectly tuned, pearl white with red body coves and a red interior. Still had the original AM Wonderbar radio, though I couldn't raise much on it besides talk radio. In Spanish. I rode with the top down. It was dusk now, and the dry air was turning cooler. Lulu rode next to me, nose stuck happily out the window. She didn't remember *Route 66*, but she did approve of the car.

The traffic on Robertson was sluggish, the cramped, aging storefronts south of Pico an ethnic jumble of Jewish, Spanish, Asian, and black. I crossed Pico, still heading north. The Porsche stayed with me. And he was with me when I crossed Olympic into Beverly Hills, where the businesses perked right up. There were trendoid art galleries here, designer showrooms, French bistros. Briefly, I considered trying to lose him. But if he was any good at all he already knew where I was going. So I let him be. Until I got stuck in some gridlock at Wilshire, and got bored. And got out and strolled back to say hello.

He lowered his window as I approached, startled but pleased by my directness. He was young and broad-shouldered. Had on a navy blue suit and one of those flowered silk ties everyone was wearing that season. Wore his hair in a perm of tight, brown curls. He used hairspray on it. A lot of hairspray.

"I'm going to the Four Seasons, in case you lose me," I informed him.

"Why, thanks, Mr. Hoag," he said brightly. "That's ultranice of you to say so. May I buy you a drink when we get there?"

"You may not."

"I really think we should talk," he confided. "I believe you'll find it worth your while."

Not a threat. There was no menace in his voice. Only insistence. And ambition.

I scratched my chin. "I can give you five minutes."

The traffic began to creep forward. So did he, until he stalled it again, cursing.

"Ease that clutch out a little slower," I suggested.

"Thanks, I'll try that, Mr. Hoag. Just took delivery—still haven't got the hang of it."

The Four Seasons is on Doheny and Burton Way. They set an excellent table there, and the staff is efficient and courteous. They happen to smile a little too much for my taste, but that's my own problem.

I pulled the Vette into the wide, circular driveway and ran right smack into another media crush. Reporters and TV cameras everywhere. The doorman had to jog practically out to Doheny to bid me welcome.

"Sorry about all of this, sir," he apologized, opening the Vette's door for me.

"What's this all about?" I asked.

"The writer who's doing the Matthew Wax book is staying with us," he replied. "You know how that goes."

"It happens I do," I said, pulling my boater down low over the eyes. "Can you slip me in the back way?"

His eyes widened. "Sure, sure. I'll take care of it. Just stay put."

He scampered back to the door and used the phone there. Then trotted back to me and got in. Lulu hopped into my lap. The valet parking ramp plunged us straight down to the basement garage.

A security man met me there with my room key and paperwork, and helped me carry my stuff to the elevator. "How come *you* attract such a crowd?" he asked bluntly.

"It's like Billy Wilder once said of the big turnout at Harry Cohn's funeral," I replied. " 'Give the people what they want and they'll come.' "

I rode straight up to my room, bypassing the lobby. Ah, stardom.

It was on the twelfth floor. Had a king-sized bed and a minisized fridge, a writing desk, a dressing table. Glass doors opened onto a terrace overlooking Century City, which used to be the Twentieth Century-Fox backlot, and beyond that the Pacific, where the sun had dropped, leaving a smudge of lavender on the horizon. I opened the doors wide and shut off the air conditioner, hung up my jacket, undid my bowtie. I unpacked Lulu's bowls and put down mackerel and water for her in the bathroom. I unpacked my fifteen-year-old Glenmorangie and poured myself some. I took it out onto the terrace. I sipped it, looking out at the lights of the city. My phone rang. I answered it.

"I'm here, Mr. Hoag." A man's voice.

"Do I know you?"

"The fellow in the red Porsche."

"Come on up."

He did. When I opened the door, I discovered I'd been fooled by his big shoulders. The man was no taller than Bunny Wax. He must have been sitting on the Yellow Pages to see over the Porsche's steering wheel.

"You're quite some event, Mr. Hoag," he declared briskly as he came scurrying in, the trousers of his dark blue suit scuffing along the carpet, picking up lint.

"That I am."

He looked around at the room. "I'll come right to the point." He went over to the chair by the bed, sat, bounced right back up, like a rubber ball. "You're hot, Mr. Hoag. Hotter than you've ever been."

"I don't know if I'd go that far."

"I would," he claimed. "I would indeed. You're poised, Mr. Hoag. On the brink. This is your moment—if you're smart, and I think you are."

Lulu wandered in from the bathroom, her supper completed, and gave him the once-over. Unimpressed, she ambled out onto the terrace and flopped down.

"The opportunities are out there for you, Mr. Hoag," he plowed on. "It's time to capitalize. It's time to maximize. We can do that for you like no one else, and that's no bullshit. I honestly think we—"

"Time out," I broke in. "Who and what are you?"

"I'm with the Harmon Wright Agency, Mr. Hoag. Before you consider anyone else for representation, I hope you'll consider us. And I hope you'll consider me. I'm enterprising, I'm creative, I'm hungry. I'll work my fingers to the bone for you. I never sleep. My name is Joseph Bamber, although everybody calls me—"

"Joey Bam Bam."

His face broke into a smile of pure pleasure. "You've heard of me?"

"Hasn't everyone?"

One thing you should know about Hollywood agents is that the old stereotype is absolutely, positively, one-hundred-percent true. They really *are* short, wired, desperate, and relentless. They can't take no for an answer, can't be insulted, can't be knocked down, can't be killed.

"You followed me from the airport," I said, sipping my drink.

"I'll do anything to get a client," he assured me. "And to keep him happy."

"When did you say you got your new car?"

"This morning."

That explained why Sarge had mistaken him for a detective. She probably would have recognized him otherwise. If a detective really was tailing me, he was a lot more skillful. "You represent Johnny Forget."

Joey Bam Bam sat back down. And stayed down this time, though his knee did begin to shake. "That's right, Mr. Hoag. I'm helping him make the big transish. He's going to be a major adult star. He's poised. He's—"

"On the brink?"

"Just like you are," Bam Bam said confidently. "I'm telling you, you're *the* hottest ghost in the business right now. HWA is *the* place for you. Think of all the celebrity clients we can package you with. Think of the film sale, the TV miniseries. I'm talking synergy. I'm talking total vertical integration. This House of Wax thing is a perfect example. We represent not only Pennyroyal Brim but also her writer, Cassandra Dee. We brought the two of them together." He bounced back up again. It was only a matter of time. "You have to come up and meet our new team. I know you'll be impressed. Sure, sure—we used to be known for divisiveness, for back-stabbing, for boning each other's clients. Not anymore. We're all pulling in the same direction now. We're all out there—getting involved, making it happen. We're coming back, Mr. Hoag."

"You were never gone. And you can give it a rest, Bam Bam. My HWA days are behind me."

That caught him short. "You're a former client?"

"I am."

"As a ghost?"

"As a novelist."

"You write novels?"

"I do."

He frowned. "Under your own name?"

I sighed. "That's correct. And it's a name which still happens to be mud around the senior levels of the Harmon Wright Agency. Which suits me just fine."

"I don't get it," he said, shaking his perm. "What happened?"

"I had a slight run-in with Harmon Wright."

His eyes widened. "You *knew* him?"

"I knew him."

It had happened on my first ghostwriting gig, the memoirs of Sonny Day, the comic. Perhaps you read them. Or about them. That's when I went up against Harmon Wright, the former Heshie Roth, juice man for Bugsy Siegel in Los Angeles during World War II. I came upon some skeletons. He tried to hide them. I tried to unhide them. I won. I also lost. My career was never the same after tangling with Wright. I was no longer considered a major novelist. Some of that was my doing. A lot of it was his. I'll never know how much.

"They all say he was the best," said Bam Bam with hushed reverence. "They say nobody could touch him as a deal maker."

Nobody had. Under his leadership, HWA had been as big as all of the other major agencies put together. He had ruled the town, deciding which movies got made, by whom, with whom, and for whom. The studio bosses were merely his own hand-picked protégés. His favorite: none other than Norbert Schlom. Harmon Wright was dead now. Had been for three years. And no one today swung as big a dick as he had, although Schlom clearly wanted to, with an assist by Abel Zorch. I couldn't help but feel I'd have something to say about that. I also couldn't help but feel

I was right back in the same ring, fighting Harmon Wright all over again.

"There is something you can do for me, Bam Bam," I conceded.

"Anything, Mr. Hoag. Just name it."

"Help me set up an interview with Johnny."

"I'd be thrilled to." And he honestly sounded like he would be. "I'll call you soon as I have the particulars. In fact, you can do it at my office. You'll come up, meet the gang, I'll show you around the place—"

"I've seen it," I said, steering him in the general direction of the door.

"You've seen the old place. We have brand-new offices. New offices, new regime. You had problems with the old HWA, not the new, I assure you."

I opened the door for him. "Can't wait to see it."

"Say, I also happen to represent Romola, the swimsuit model. Just landed her a major speaking role over at Disney in *Ernest Goes to Tampa*. Would you care to have dinner with her some evening while you're out here? Don't get me wrong—I'm not suggesting she'll give you a blow job out in the parking lot. She's just a really fascinating lady. Maybe a group of us could attend a screening together one—"

"I'm afraid I'll be pretty busy."

"Sure, sure," he said, as I politely shoved him out the door. "Oh, hey, you were right about my clutch. I was letting it out too fast."

"You're not going to keep following me, are you?"

"I will if you want me to," he offered.

"Night-night, Bam Bam," I said, closing the door on him.

I unpacked. My clothes I hung in the closet. My beloved late-fifties Olympia solid steel manual portable, the Mercedes 300SL Gull Wing of typewriters, went on the writing desk along with my notes, my notepads, my personal stereo, my Erroll Garner tapes. My reading matter I placed on the nightstand by the bed. I was working my way through a collection of autobiographical essays by M.F.K. Fisher that season, which is something I do every couple of years to remind myself what good writing is. I tend to forget if I've only been reading my own stuff. When I was done unpacking I stripped off my clothes and went into the bathroom. There was a deluxe dressing area in there, outfitted with a televi-

sion set, telephone, and full-length three-way mirror, which I
don't recommend using if you happen to be naked and over the
age of twenty-one. There was an immense tub, a stall shower. I
used the shower, scrubbing myself with the Crabtree and Evelyn
avocado oil soap I'd brought along to remind me of the way
Merilee smelled. The phone rang while I was showering. I didn't
answer it. I was too busy thinking about the plate of chiles rellenos I was going to eat that evening at Chuy's, a little neighborhood place on Sawtelle and National where they keep the bottles
of Dos Equis in a wooden barrel of ice, and where Chuy's ancient
mother makes the soft corn tortillas by hand over an open hearth
and serves them to you fresh off the griddle, hot and crisp around
the edges. After I'd dried off I stropped Grandfather's razor and
shaved and doused myself with Floris. Then I threw open the
bathroom door and padded naked out into the room so as to be
cooled by the breeze coming in through the terrace doors. Only
there was no breeze coming in. The terrace doors were closed
now. And I was not alone.

# Chapter Four

S he was rifling through my notes on the desk, pausing only to scribble choice finds on the back of her left hand and wrist with my gold-tipped Waterman. There was no sign of Lulu, my fierce protector.

"You won't find much," I apologized, standing there in my Floris. "At least it doesn't mean much to me."

She gasped and jumped away from the desk, startled. Of course, Cassandra Dee always looked startled, chiefly because of her eyes, which were goggly, and her brows, which she penciled into a high, exaggerated arch. Her complexion was a vivid milk white, her lips a garish shade of red. Her abundant black hair was swept back and held that way with a black headband, worn low behind the ears, forties style. She came off looking somewhat like a mime done up as Betty Boop. She had on one of those skin-tight black unitards that they used to call catsuits back in Julie Newmar's heyday. Maybe they still do. Whatever you call them, you have to be long and lean to wear one, and she was. She was a tall woman, willowy, about thirty. A ragged denim jacket was tied around her waist, either as an accent or to hide her hips.

"Geez, Hoagy, I—I tried calling ya—I knocked even," she blurted out in a burst of Brooklynese. Her voice was irritatingly nasal. It sounded like a table saw whining its way through a length of knotty pine. "Ya didn't answer, so's I just let myself in."

"How?"

She gaped at me. "Ya mean how did I get in? I'm kinda resourceful that way, is how. Yeah, yeah, shewa—nobody can keep me out if I want in. I'm staying here at the hotel myself, seventh floor, and . . ." She came up for air. "Geez, I hope ya don't mind."

"Would it matter if I did?"

"Yeah, yeah, shewa. But it wouldn't stop me. I'm compulsively nosy. I know that about myself. Can't help it."

She continued to gape at me. My Floris does have that effect on some women. I continued to stand there.

"I thought we oughta talk," she explained. "What with us kinda being in this together and all."

"All right. Have a seat."

She hesitated. "Ya wanna put something on, honey, or ya want me to take something off?"

"Which would you prefer?"

"Makes no difference to me," she fired back. "But one of us oughta do something, don'tcha think?"

I went to the closet and put on my silk target-dot dressing gown from Turnbull and Asser. She untied her denim jacket and tossed it on a chair, then sat on the edge of the bed. There was nothing wrong with her hips, by the way.

"Just out of curiosity," I said, tightening the belt on my dressing gown, "what did you do with Lulu?"

"Your dog? It kept growling at me, scared me shitless. I thought it was gonna bite me."

"And?"

"I locked it out on the terrace."

I groaned. "Oh, dear."

"Gawd, it wouldn't jump off, would it?"

"Nothing quite so simple."

I opened the terrace doors. Lulu was sitting right there, giving me her pained look, but good. It's got a lot packed into it— suffering, humiliation, wounded pride, anger and, most of all, the promise of cold-blooded revenge. This one was a doozy, even worse than the time that churlish Amtrak conductor made her ride in a carrier all the way from New York to Washington. I apologized profusely, vowed I would make it up to her. She grumbled. She groused. I assured her I was sorry. She assured me I didn't even know the meaning of the word. Then she followed me back inside.

"Geez, there ya are," remarked Cassandra. "I thought maybe *you* jumped."

"The thought did cross my mind."

Lulu went over and sniffed at her with disdain.

Cassandra watched her nervously. "It still looks like it's gonna bite me."

"She won't," I said. "She just gets a little protective around other women, particularly if there's a bed nearby. She's rather partial to my ex-wife."

"I hear Merilee dumped ya," Cassandra said, with keen interest.

"You hear wrong."

The Glenmorangie was over by the minifridge. I poured myself two more fingers of it.

"Then how come she's in Fiji and you're not?"

"I'm having Scotch, Cassandra," I said. "May I pour you one?"

"Yeah, yeah, shewa."

"How do you take it?"

"Ya got any diet Coke?"

I opened the fridge and poked around inside. "I have."

"Just dump half a can in with the Scotch."

"I'm sorry, I can't do that."

"Ya can't do what, honey?" she wondered.

"I can't pour diet Coke on top of fifteen-year-old single malt. I'll be happy to give you another glass if you—"

"Nah, nah, nah. Just gimme the diet Coke. Lotsa ice."

I gave it to her, lotsa ice. She gulped it down and punctuated it with a loud belch, key of D-minor. She had a number of things going for her, Cassandra Dee did, but class was not one of them. We had last met up when that infamous Marilyn Monroe diary surfaced. The reputable publisher who plunked down $3.5 million on it wanted me to clean it up and annotate it. Cassandra, who was working for the *Enquirer* then, wanted me to slip it to her. The diary, that is. Just a peek. One teeny peek. I didn't give her one. I didn't clean up the diary either—it turned out to be a major hoax.

I sat in the chair by the bed and sipped my drink. She was

still gaping at me, goggle-eyed. Apparently it wasn't my Floris after all. "My feeding time is two o'clock," I informed her. "Generally, they toss me some raw meat."

"Geez," she gulped, covering her mouth with her hand. "I was staring, huh?"

"You were."

"It's just that to us ghosts . . . I mean, you're the man with the golden touch. Mister Bestseller. And you're kinda my idol. And I still can't believe we're actually woiking together."

"We're not."

"We're on the same story, ain't we?"

"On different sides."

"We can still trade, can't we?"

"That all depends—what have you got?"

She crossed her legs and flared her nostrils at me. "Zorch's detectives found out yesterday that you'd be staying here," she revealed. "His publicist tipped off the media. That's how come they were all waiting here for ya."

"Is Zorch having me followed?"

"I could find out for ya," she offered. "If you'll tell me who Matthew Wax is dicking." She leaned forward anxiously.

"I don't believe there's anyone," I said.

"I don't believe that," she scoffed.

"You don't believe that I don't believe there's anyone, or you don't believe there isn't someone?"

"Either, both, whatever." She rolled her eyes. "Ya always talk that way?"

"What way?"

She got up and went over to the desk, poked around at my notepads. "Ya don't got a computer or a fax machine. How do ya function?"

"I often ask myself the same question."

She moved over to the terrace doors, gazed out at the lights of the city. I don't know if she was more interested in them or in showing me her ass. I do know we both got a fine view.

"I love it out here," she declared grandly, nasally, her arms spread wide. "How about you?"

"I'm just out here to not have a good time."

"What I like about movie people is that they're so *genuine.*"

It was my turn to stare. "Genuine?"

"Yeah, yeah, shewa. Let's face it, Hoagy, all anybody wants

out of life is to reach out and fuck someone. Here, they make no bones about it. They don't pretend to give a fuck about loyalty or friendship or morality. Money, sex, power—that's all anybody cares about. Here, they're honest enough to admit it. I just find that so refreshing. I do, I really do."

"Somewhat dark view of mankind, isn't it?"

"What, ya don't agree?"

"I didn't say that. I simply said it's a somewhat dark view."

She flopped back down on the bed. Lulu growled at her menacingly. Frightened, she settled for the desk chair. Lulu snuffled happily. She doesn't find someone who's afraid of her very often.

"I meant what I said before," she said to me, eyeing Lulu warily. "We oughta help each other out. Compare notes, pool information. Bottom line, we both want the same thing out of this."

"Which is what, Cassandra?"

"A bestseller, of course."

"If that's all you're after, I don't think you have to worry."

"That's not *awl* I'm after, honey."

"What else do you want?"

"You really wanna know? Okay, shewa, here it is: I wanna be the biggest, baddest, scariest mother-fucking celebrity biographer there is. I wanna be Kitty Kelley. I want people to shit in their pants when they hear me coming."

"That's not an ambition. That's a disease."

"And you?" she asked tartly. "Whatta you want?"

"I'm always the last to know."

She laughed, a playful shriek that made the hairs on the back of my neck stand up.

I drained my whiskey. I was getting hungry. "Anything else you wanted to share with me?"

She hesitated, chewing on her lower lip. "Pennyroyal's thing with Trace is history. Or will be, soon."

"She tell you that?"

"She didn't have to."

"Then how do you know?"

"Because Trace hasn't changed his wicked, wicked ways and she ain't the type to put up with 'em. The man is a heat-seeking missile, twenty-four hours a day. I ain't kidding—he fucks every woman he meets. Let me give ya a f'r instance—I'm interviewing him down at his love shack in Trancas, see? A real dump, incidentally. Anyways, I'm trying to get some personal insights, that kinda shit, and I'm getting zilch. I mean, he ain't exactly voibal. All he does is sit there eyeballing my legs. I'm wearing my leather skirt. It's flattering, okay? I'm not boasting. I'm just painting ya a pictcha, okay? So I excuse myself, go into his powder room and I'm sitting there on the toidy taking a pee and, wham, he comes flying through the bathroom door. Breaks the fucking lock. He's real upset and apologetic about it, too. Keeps saying, 'I'm sorry, I'm sorry. I just gotta have you. I gotta. Right now. I'm sorry.' Then he scoops me up off the toidy, carries me into the dining room, and takes me right there on the table. It was unreal," she recalled, shaking her head. "I came three times."

"You didn't have to tell me that part. In fact, you didn't have to tell me any of it."

"You know he has a name for it?"

"For what?"

"His dick. He calls it Big Steve. And he talks to it—just like you talk to your dog."

"I don't think I want to dwell on that one for too long."

"Wait, there's more—afterward, he spilled to me plenty. About her. She's killing his career. The door to Bedford Falls is shut, nobody else in town'll hire him. There's a part he's desperate for at Panorama in the new Mel Gibson but Schlom won't even let him on the lot. Hates his guts. Has for years. Anyways, he's not working and he's bummed and he hates this whole media hassle with her. He so much as told me it's over. He likes her fine, but it ain't like true love or nuttin'. In fact, he thinks she's a total mess."

"What do you think?"

"Me? I think Penny's a very sweet person, you wanna know the truth, who happens to be dazed and confused right now. She's used to Matthew and his people making her decisions. She don't know what hit her. And she don't know who to turn to. She'd never admit it in a million years, but ya know what she'd happily do right now if she got the chance? You'll shit when you hear this—"

"Go back to him," I stated.

"How did ya know that?" she wondered, shocked.

"It's only natural for her to be having second thoughts. This is an ugly scene. I imagine that whatever life she had before doesn't look so bad."

Cassandra sat back in her chair and glanced out at the view. "Would he ever take her back?" she asked, way too casually.

At last—the real purpose of her visit. I didn't answer her right away. I liked watching her work, in a sick sort of way.

"Hey, c'mon. I shared with you," she protested.

"And it was uncommonly generous of you," I conceded. "All right—I don't know if he would. He says no. I do know it would be hard for him. There are a lot of wounds that would have to heal. I suppose it's possible. Stranger things have happened."

She was waiting for me to go on. When I didn't she said, "That's it?"

"That's all I can tell you. You already know much more than I do."

"Impressed?" she asked hopefully.

"I'm not unimpressed."

"We're not so different, y'know," she pointed out proudly. "We both believe in stretching the envelope. You do it your way, I do it my way. I'm so jazzed. It's gonna be so great, watching ya in action. This is such a breakthrough for me. It's gonna be so . . ." She froze, goggle-eyed. "Geez, I just had a shitty thought—what if they really *do* patch it up? We're fucked. Our projects are *dead.*"

"Mine goes ahead either way. His book is about his career, not her."

"But all the heat'll go out of it."

"Some of it will," I conceded.

"Me, I'll be totally screwed," she said miserably. "Penny goes back to him, I'll have zip. The opportunity of a lifetime, right down the toidy."

"Does that mean what I think it means?" I asked.

She frowned. "Dunno. Whattaya think it means?"

"That you're prepared to play the role of agent provocateur."

"The what?"

"The spoiler."

"Hey, no way I'd do that to somebody," she claimed, deeply offended—or giving a superb imitation of it.

"You're sure about that?"

"Positive. I wouldn't fuck over two people who—"

"Three, counting Georgie. And then, of course, there's all of Bedford Falls to consider."

"I wouldn't do it," she insisted. "I wouldn't."

"Okay, you wouldn't." I smiled at her, not believing her for one second.

She smiled right back at me, knowing I didn't. "Hey, I thought we could go eat some Japanese. Whattaya say?"

"I have dinner plans, thanks."

She shrugged. "Yeah, yeah, shewa."

My phone rang. I picked it up.

"Is this Mr. Hoag? Mr. Stewart Hoag?" A male voice, crisp and businesslike.

"It is."

"Please hold."

There was a click. Followed by: "Mr. Hoag? This is Abel Zorch. I wanted to welcome you to town personally." His voice was smooth and sure. The voice of a seducer.

"How very kind of you."

"I wondered if you'd care to join a few of us for supper this evening. Quite informal. Norbert Schlom is as anxious to meet you as I am."

"Love to. Where and when?"

"Spago. Eight-thirty."

"Eight-thirty?" I glanced at Grandfather's Rolex. "I'll be there." I hung up.

Cassandra looked insulted in spite of herself. "Ya didn't have no plans at all," she whined. "Ya were just waiting for a better offer."

"And I got one."

"Hey, I understand," she said, turning cheerful. "Business comes first. I'm the same way—ain't it amazing how alike we are?"

"Amazing. If you'll excuse me, Cassandra, I have to dress."

She grabbed her jacket and sashayed over and ran her finger along my chin. "You woulda had a lot more fun with me, y'know," she purred intimately.

This drew a growl from Lulu.

"Actually, I'm not expecting to have any fun at all," I said.

But I was wrong about that. I had lots of fun. Tons of it.

Spago sits on a little hill overlooking the giant movie billboards on the Sunset Strip and the twinkling lights of West Hollywood below. It had been the favored celebrity eating spot the last time I was in town. And still was, surprisingly. An ebullient fellow named Wolfgang Puck owns it, and you have to know him, or someone who does, to get a table. Bernard, the French maître d', greeted me warmly as I made my way through the bar. He did not, happily, hug me. But he did escort me personally to my table. A lot of names were there that evening. The Walter Matthaus, the Michael Caines, Michael and Diandra Douglas. Swifty Lazar was there with that actress who looks like Margot Kidder but isn't Margot Kidder. Sherry Lansing was there with Henry Kissinger. There was a dusting of literati types—John Gregory Dunne, one of the world's great gasbags, and his wife, Joan Didion, pound for pound one of its great nontalents. Mostly there was a lot of power there—Mike and Jane Eisner, Mike and Judy Ovitz, the Jeff Katzenbergs, the Peter Gubers, David Geffen, Barry Diller. In place of busboys there were HWA agents hopping from table to table, carrying rumors, confirming rumors, denying rumors. Everybody in the place seemed to be dressed in black, which was very in that season. I rather stood out as I made my way through them in my double-breasted white Italian linen suit, my lavender broadcloth shirt, and my blue silk foulard. But I generally do.

The table over by the windows was set for five. I was the last to arrive. I was forty-five minutes late—by design. It's vital to keep movie people waiting for you. If you don't, they know you need them.

Abel Zorch jumped to his feet at my arrival, the genial host. "Ah, Mr. Hoag, you made it!" he exclaimed with great pleasure as he pumped my hand. "I'm so pleased. I've been so looking forward to this."

The Iguana was in his late forties, trimly built, charming, effeminate, cunning, and so oily I half expected to find a puddle forming under his chair. The iguana resemblance was in his eyes, which were hooded, and his complexion, which was deeply tanned and uncommonly reptilian in texture. He was mostly bald. The leathery dome of his skull reminded me of the skin around a ripe avocado. What hair he still had in back he wore long and tied up in a ponytail. He had on a black Armani suit with a black silk shirt and one of the two or three ugliest ties I'd ever seen, iridescent lime green silk adorned with bright orange wedges.

"Now then, let's get acquainted, shall we?" he said, rubbing his hands together. "May I present Toy Schlom, Norbert's lovely wife?"

"How do you do, Mr. Hoag," she said, smiling at me radiantly. Cat suits were officially in. Toy's was black velvet, worn with a diamond choker collar. She was a slender, taut blonde of the Nordic high cheekbone variety, about forty, with slanted, rather exotic violet eyes. She looked like she exercised hard three hours a day and then got rubbed down by a masseuse for two hours more. Her complexion had a strangely smooth, shiny quality, as if she used sandpaper on it and then sealed it over with polyurethane. "My, what a perfectly adorable little dog you have," she observed, her inflection high-toned Park Avenue, with a hint of Locust Valley lockjaw. She wouldn't fool a soul in either of those places, but she wasn't in either of those places.

"Lulu doesn't care for that word," I said, though in fact she wasn't even listening—too busy rubbernecking at all of the heavy hitters about the place. For a would-be starlet, Spago was heaven.

"Adorable?" Toy frowned prettily.

"Dog," I replied.

"Oh, I see." She went back to the smile. "I must tell you—I admire Merilee Nash's work tremendously."

"We all do," Zorch chimed in effusively. "How is—?"

"Merilee's fine," I said, my happy face glued on. "She's fine. I'm fine. We're both fine."

"So glad to hear it," said Zorch. "I don't believe you've met my close friend Norbert Schlom."

Norbert Schlom nodded sourly and didn't offer to shake my hand. The president of Panorama was a gruff, thick-necked bull in his early sixties with too little chin, too many jowls, and a thick, loose underlip that was the color of fresh, moist liver. His eyes were yellow and malevolent. The only other time I'd seen eyes like them was when I once saw a Norway rat scrabbling up through a grate on Amsterdam Avenue. Schlom worked at his grooming. His white hair was carefully layered and combed, his stubby fingers manicured, his teeth capped, his pitted face tanned. There was a ten-thousand-dollar Philippe Patek gold watch on his wrist. His gray flannel double-breasted suit looked custom made, as did his white broadcloth shirt. But none of it helped. He still looked like a thug. He *was* a thug. His first job in

show business had been bouncer at a mob-owned strip joint in
Detroit. From there he graduated to strong-arming for a Chicago
loan shark. Harmon Wright brought him out to L.A. in the midfif-
ties to chauffeur around some of the agency's unsteadier talent.
He moved over to Panorama during a labor dispute and gradually worked his way up from enforcer to hatchet man to mogul.
He was a throwback to the old days of Hollywood—an unedu-
cated bully who ruled by intimidation. He and Abel Zorch made
an odd pair, but Hollywood is full of just such odd partnerships.

Rounding out our party was Zorch's date, a sculpted young
male model done up like a harem boy in shirt and trousers of
billowing purple silk. His name was Geoffrey, with a G, and he
was there to look attractive and to not make a sound.

"Now please," Zorch urged me, "do sit."

I sat. Lulu didn't. She hesitated. For one awful moment, I
was afraid that she was about to go table-hopping, sucking up to
all of those rich, powerful movie people. But she didn't. She was
better raised than that. She curled up under me, content to wait
for her opportunity to come to her.

A waiter appeared at my elbow.

"We're sampling a cabernet sauvignon that Wolf keeps here
for me," Zorch informed me. "It's from my own small winery in
the Napa Valley. Would you care to try it?"

"I would."

The waiter poured. I tasted it, Zorch watching me anxiously.

"Excellent," I declared. And it was excellent—for removing
the shellac from a nightstand.

Pleased, Zorch sent the waiter off for two more bottles of it.

An agent seized the moment to swoop in on Schlom. "Did
you get a chance to read it, Norb?"

"Pass," growled Schlom, staring straight ahead.

"You read it?" he pressed.

"Don't have to," Schlom replied. "Pasadena."

"But it's a slam-dunk script, Norb," the agent protested. "If
you'd only take a look at it."

Schlom pulled a Bottega Veneta leather-bound notepad from
the inner pocket of his jacket and tore off a sheet of crisp, white
notepaper. He rolled this between his thumb and forefinger until
it was a ball, then stuck it in his mouth. Norbert Schlom ate
paper. It was what he did instead of chewing gum or smoking. "I
been making movies for thirty years," he argued, chewing on the

paper until he swallowed it. "I don't have to read a script to know whether or not I want to do it." He waved his hand to indicate the subject was closed. The agent fled.

Zorch smiled at me apologetically. "Have you heard the latest agent joke? Two agents are walking down the street and they pass a gorgeous woman, and one says to the other, 'How would you like to fuck *her?*' And the other says, 'Out of what?'"

I've never been an easy laugh. Geoffrey with a G didn't laugh either, since that would have involved making a sound. Nor did Schlom. I doubt he'd laughed in thirty years, and then only when he was working somebody over. Toy laughed. She was amused, and in no way offended by the coarseness. Toy was, after all, a former call girl—one of three women currently married to film studio bosses who could make such a claim. The happy couples were quite open about this. In fact the husbands, all of them older men on their second marriages, were proud of it, as if being married to an ex-pro served as testimony to their sexual prowess. All three wives were poised, attractive, gracious, and well known for their excellent parties and their tireless good works on the charity circuit. One already had a society ball named after her, and there was even talk of a telethon.

"You can't get through a meal here without at least ten agents stopping by to talk business," Zorch complained airily. "But if you *don't* eat here then you go crazy wondering what you might be missing out on."

"And we can't have that," I said. "Can we?"

"We can't indeed," Zorch said with utmost conviction. "This is where the game is played—the principal players are all here." He looked around the room at them with greedy fascination. "There are three types of movie people, Mr. Hoag. Players, nonplayers, and nonentities. Which type are you?"

"I prefer to think of myself as a conscientious objector."

Toy laughed again. "I believe I like this man already."

"Well, well, you've made yourself a fan, Mr. Hoag," Zorch observed happily.

"My wife creams for clever," growled Schlom.

I raised my glass to her and she and I drank to clever, her exotic violet eyes locking onto mine and lingering a moment. Her husband watched the two of us balefully. Possibly the lady got out nights. Clever was not a commodity she was likely to find in abundance chez Schlom.

Zorch requested, and was granted, liberty to order our first course for us, an assortment of pizzas covered with things like lamb sausage, goat cheese, and smoked salmon. Then an invisible signal passed—Toy suddenly had something she desperately needed to say to Diandra Douglas and Geoffrey with a G was suddenly out of cigarettes. I was now alone at the table with the two amigos. Lulu stayed put under me. The promise of smoked salmon pizza was enough to keep her there for a long while.

Zorch reached under his chair and produced a slender black leather briefcase. Inside was a manila envelope. He handed it across the table to me. I took it. Schlom watched me. Inside was a stock certificate made out for a thousand shares of Panorama City Communications. In my name.

"For your information, Panorama City closed at sixty-five and a quarter today," Zorch said, lighting a cigarette. "And will go up dramatically when the merger with Murakami goes through in the coming weeks. Way up. Way more than you're paying for it."

"And how am I paying for it?" I asked, returning it to the envelope. Schlom watched that, too. Schlom watched everything.

"With your cooperation," Zorch replied.

"I am very cooperative," I said. "Ask anyone."

Schlom ripped another piece of paper off of his little pad and chewed on it. I watched him, wondering how many trees he'd eaten in his lifetime, and what it had done to his digestion.

Zorch took a sip of his awful wine. "We're in the midst of a multibillion-dollar international merger, Mr. Hoag. That's big stuff. Bigger than the three of us at this table. Bigger than Matthew Wax and Pennyroyal Brim and their marital hassles. *Big.* Our absolute, number one priority is to make certain that this deal goes through. Nothing must get in the way of that. Absolutely nothing. Can you understand me so far?"

"I can. I can also count to ten and tie my own shoes."

Zorch's tongue darted out of his mouth, then retreated just as quickly. That was another reason why they called him the Iguana. He smiled faintly. "These sleazy House of Wax headlines, this ugly publicity about their battle over who gets little Georgie and who gets Bedford Falls—"

"Most of which is coming from you," I pointed out.

"It scares the Murakami people," Zorch continued, deftly

slipping my jab. "It shouldn't. It has nothing to do with them directly. But they're extremely sensitive about bad press. They don't wish to find themselves caught in that whole Japan-bashing thing that happened over Rockefeller Center and Yosemite. These are low-profile people. They dislike the way all of this is heating up."

"Because *you're* heating it up," I pointed out.

Schlom glowered at me.

Zorch puffed calmly on his cigarette, refusing to be baited. "And now they're—"

"They're leaning on you," I broke in. "They don't like your gutter tactics. They don't like any of it. They may even pull out of the whole deal."

Zorch smiled at me. "Then you do understand me."

"I understand you perfectly," I said. "I just don't like you."

A low, menacing rumble came from Schlom's throat. Zorch cautioned him with a quick shake of his head, then turned back to me, still smiling. The tongue darted in and out. "We'd like you to help us quiet it down, Mr. Hoag. We're anxious to see things proceed with dignity from here on in."

"It's a little late for that, don't you think?"

"It's never too late for a little well-targeted spin control," he suggested, glancing at the envelope.

I handed it back to him across the table. "I only work for one employer at a time, thanks."

The two of them exchanged an unhappy look.

"Perhaps you'd like to think it over," Zorch offered.

"I would not. No perhaps about it."

"I'm very serious about this, Mr. Hoag." There was a well-oiled edge to his voice now. "I mean business."

"If you do, then why are you wearing that tie?"

"Aw, Christ," growled Schlom. "We're getting nowhere with this coconut. Look, Hoag, my wife, she likes clever. I don't. I like meat and potatoes. Know what I'm talking about?"

"So far, you're talking about meat and potatoes."

"We want you protecting our interests," he raged, stabbing the table with a stubby index finger. "You don't want stock, fine. Tell us what you do want. Cash? A development deal? Just say it plain. And let's get it done with."

I tugged at my ear. "Okay—leave Bedford Falls alone."

"Impossible," grunted Schlom. "Never happen."

"Why not? Why can't you let Shelley Selden find another buyer for Pennyroyal's half of the studio—if she gets it."

"She'll get it," Zorch promised me. "That's a lock."

"We gotta have Bedford Falls," Schlom explained. "We got this *Dennis the Dinosaur* prehistoric planet attraction on the drawing boards for our studio tour. It's gonna be huge, and Murakami is very excited about it. Only, it means tearing out a half-dozen more soundstages. We *need* their soundstages."

"There are other soundstages around town."

"Bedford Falls is part of the deal," Schlom insisted, sticking out his thick, wet underlip. "I already made a verbal commitment to deliver it."

"So your ass is in something of a sling."

"We're not here to talk about my ass."

"Okay, then let's talk about Matthew's book. What don't you want him saying in it?"

Schlom frowned. "I don't follow you."

"I'm here to deliver a book. And you seem very anxious to buy my cooperation. That generally means silent approval of the manuscript. What don't you want him talking about? Is it the *Three Stooges* episode?"

"Whatta you know about that?" Schlom's face turned purple.

"Enough to know I wouldn't want it made public if I were you."

"Damned right I don't!" he roared, pounding the table with his heavy fist. Heads turned at neighboring tables. "And don't you try to do it, you skinny, wise-ass New York *pencil head!*"

"I use a Waterman exclusively."

Zorch tried to step in. "Come on now, Norb. Let's not—"

"Don't *fuck* with me, Hoag!" Schlom spat, ignoring him. "I'll break you! Hear me? I'll *break* you!"

"You're too late. I'm already broken."

He called me a few more cuddly names, then drained his wine in a gulp and slammed down his glass. We sat there in charged silence.

"You interest me, Mr. Hoag," Zorch remarked, a mischievous glint in his eye.

"Why?"

"You obviously don't care what anyone else thinks of you.

That makes you unpredictable. And potentially dangerous. Are you?"

A waiter appeared at my elbow. "More wine, sir?"

"If you insist," I said.

The waiter didn't pour. Just stood there, cackling. I finally looked up at him. I didn't have to crane my neck very far. It was Joey Bam Bam, rocking back and forth on his heels like a hobby-horse with a perm.

"I thought you were going to stop following me, Bam Bam," I said.

"I did stop following you," he said, grinning at me. *"You're following me."*

"My mistake."

"Romola is dying to meet you," he said, indicating a table across the room where four other miniagents in dark suits sat with the latest in a never-ending series of six-feet-tall, ninety-pound teenagers with silicone breasts and collagen lips. "Great bunch of guys for you to meet, too. Come on over and say hello."

"We're discussing business right now."

"Sure, sure. Sorry to interrupt." He lingered there next to me, begging with his eyes like a hungry stray.

I sighed inwardly. "Joseph Bamber of the Harmon Wright Agency, say hello to Abel Zorch and Norbert Schlom."

He shook their hands, beaming. "Mr. Zorch—a pleasure. Mr. Schlom—an ultrathrill, sir. I happen to represent Johnny Forget."

"Oh, yeah?" said Schlom, his jaw working on a piece of paper. "How'd you get stuck with that little fuckhead?"

"I'll be in touch with you, sir, if you don't mind. I have a number of exciting ideas to discuss. Are you a fan of Romola? She happens to be—"

"Disappear," commanded Schlom.

"Yessir."

And he did.

Our pizzas arrived. Toy Schlom and Geoffrey with a G returned with them. We made small talk about the heat wave while we ate, Toy eating with great appetite and pleasure. She swallowed nothing. Each time she finished chewing a mouthful of food she raised her napkin to her mouth and coughed discreetly into it. That season's newest diet. Several other women at Spago, including Romola, were also spitting their designer cuisine into their napkins.

We were discussing our main course selection—Lulu and I were leaning toward the grilled tuna—when Pennyroyal Brim and Trace Washburn walked in. That's the wonderful thing about Spago. You just never know who you'll run into there.

Trace led the way, moving through the room with the self-assured ease of someone who was used to being a star. He limped slightly. Four years of calling the signals at USC followed by ten more of stunt work will leave you slightly battered. But even at fifty he was still very much the Malibu beach boy he'd always been—tall and rangy and narrow-waisted, his shaggy blond hair only slightly tinged with gray, his chiseled face weathered by the sun and handsome as ever. He grinned easily. A big, sleepy grin, his deep-set eyes twinkling roguishly. He wore an old denim shirt, faded jeans with patches on them, and elkskin cowboy boots. He carried his bottle of beer loosely by the neck, and was somewhat drunk.

America's sweetie pie trailed after him, done up like the world's cutest little business executive in a double-breasted gray pin-striped pantsuit with padded shoulders, peaked lapels, and no blouse—no nothing—under it. A very sexy look. Pennyroyal Brim happened to be very sexy. She was about five feet five, slim and curvy, and she knew how to move. True, there were probably three or four women around town who had nicer bodies. But there were none who had her face. There weren't faces like hers anywhere. She had the clear, porcelain blue eyes of a baby—sweet, innocent, and trusting. Her nose was a little girl's snub, her mouth a pink, perfect rosebud, her complexion so flawless it glowed. She wore her long, golden hair parted down the middle and brushed loose. She had on no makeup of any kind. None was needed. The woman already sparkled, especially when she smiled. It wasn't because of her famous dimples. It wasn't because of her shiny white teeth. It was *her*. She was the girl-next-door of every man's dreams. Young and clean and oh, so sweet. She was pure magic.

"Pretty Penny, dear child," Zorch called out to her. "Come join us."

She stiffened at the sound of her attorney's voice, then murmured something to Trace, steeled herself, and marched over, Trace now tagging along.

"I'm glad you're here, Abel," she said, in that unexpectedly deep, hoarse voice of hers. "We have to—"

"We were just about to order, dear," he said brightly. "Sit and eat with us." Our table seated six—there was one empty chair. "I'll have Bernard bring us over another chair."

"Don't bother," muttered Schlom, glaring up at Trace with his yellow rat's eyes. "We're fine just like we are." Clearly, the actor was not welcome at either Norbert Schlom's studio or his dinner table. I wondered why.

In response, Trace launched into his heavy breathing thing. "Well, shit, Norb . . ." he panted. Trace Washburn was a distinguished graduate of what Merilee called the Clu Gulager School of Acting, in honor of the fifties TV Western performer who patented the heavy breathing technique. First take a deep breath. Then pause. Then speak on the exhale. Result: you always sound as if you've just ridden in off the dusty trail, parched and weary. Other noted alumni included Kris Kristofferson and Gary Busey. I can't tell you if they did it even when the cameras weren't rolling. Trace did. "You almost make a . . ." Pant, pant. "Make a guy feel . . . unwelcome."

Schlom refused to look at him. Just stared straight ahead. Toy sipped her wine, coloring slightly.

Trace took a swig of his beer, then squinted at me. "I know you, Buck?"

"I don't believe so."

Zorch made the introductions. Trace's hand was leathery and strong. I got no handshake from Pennyroyal, or smile. Just a grim nod.

"Abel, we have to talk," she said urgently.

"Of course, dear. Have a seat."

She shot a nervous glance up at Trace.

He held up his hands in a gesture of surrender. "Hey, darlin' . . . don't mind me. I'll do some . . . mingling." He looked around, caught sight of Romola seated with the young guns of HWA. "Down, Big Steve!" he exclaimed to his nether region. "Whoa, boy! Down, Steve!" Cassandra wasn't exaggerating—he definitely talked to it. Grinning, he started off in Romola's direction.

"Trace?" said Pennyroyal, stopping him with a hand on his arm. "Behave yourself, okay?"

He took her small hand in his and kissed it affectionately. "I always behave, darlin'. Always." And off he limped.

She sat, reached for one of Zorch's cigarettes, and lit it. "Look, Abel, this sucks," she said, pulling on it tensely. Her hands were shaking.

"What does, dear?" asked Zorch mildly.

"I have fifty photographers parked outside my house day and night, climbing my fence, following me everywhere I go, calling me a whore, lying about me."

Zorch shrugged. "If you're mediocre, people will leave you alone your whole life."

"And where did this 'best sex I ever had' shit come from?" she demanded. "I never said it. Any of it!"

"I honestly don't know, dear," he replied with oily sincerity. It was a wonder the man didn't slide right off his chair onto the floor.

"Abel, I can't stand this anymore!" There was desperation in her voice. The lady was stressed out, no question. "You're turning me into *Madonna!*"

"*I'm* turning you?" he responded coldly. "You're a big girl now, Penny. Too big to play blame games. I am merely your legal advisor. I work for you. If you wish for this to stop, then say so."

"I want it to stop," she declared. "I want it to stop *now!*"

"As it happens," Zorch said graciously, "Norb and I were just discussing that very notion with Mr. Hoag."

"Unsuccessfully," I pointed out.

She shot a quick look over at Trace, who was busy hitting on Romola with the easy confidence of a Hall of Fame slugger. Then she turned to me. "You're the one who's working for Matthew?"

"I am."

"How is he?" she asked.

"I wouldn't exactly call him great."

"Tell him hello, will you?" She swallowed, her pink, perfect lower lip quivering slightly. "Tell him Georgie is fine."

"Why don't you tell him yourself?"

She glanced at Zorch, who shook his head. "No," she said hoarsely. "I can't." To him she said: "I'm really, really unhappy, Abel. I mean it."

"Not to worry, dear," he said soothingly. "It's normal to feel that way at this stage. Just leave everything to me."

"I have," she said miserably. "And everything sucks."

"Of course it sucks, darlin'," Trace broke in as he returned to us. "What'd you expect from the Iguana? C'mon . . . our table's ready."

"In a second, Trace," she said.

"You're wasting your time," Trace insisted, panting. "You won't ever get a straight answer out of him—he's incapable of one. He and Norb both . . . Isn't that right, Norb?" Schlom glowered at him in angry silence. Undaunted, Trace turned and eyeballed the man's wife. "You're looking mighty foxy tonight, Toy," he said with easy familiarity. "Mighty foxy, indeed."

"Thank you, Trace," she said quietly.

Schlom could take no more. He threw down his napkin and galumphed off to the men's room. Two agents popped up and raced off after him. Whoever said it's lonely at the top didn't know the movie business. Studio chiefs don't even pee alone.

"When are you going to grow up, Trace?" Toy scolded.

Trace drained his beer and wiped his mouth with the back of his big, brown hand. "Never, I hope."

"It isn't so, Trace," Zorch fumed. "What you said. And I resent it. I'm being totally straight with Penny. I'm totally straight with everyone. I happen to be a man of my word."

Trace laughed harshly. "Oh, yeah? Then tell me this, man of your word . . . how come I can't get in the door at Panorama?"

"You know why," Zorch replied, under his breath.

"So I was a bad boy," Trace admitted easily. "Big fucking deal. All the bad boys are working. Dennis works. Ryan works . . . Why can't I work?"

"You know why," Zorch repeated.

"You could fix it with him," Trace suggested.

"Oh, I highly doubt that," countered Zorch, his cup spilling over with false modesty.

"He's right, Abel," Penny said. "You could."

"Hey, you want me to beg, I'm begging," Trace persisted. "Put in the word for me, man. I'm starving."

Zorch smirked. He was enjoying this.

Frustrated, Trace grabbed him by his ugly green necktie and pulled. Hard. "Damn it, why won't you let me work, you weasel!?"

Zorch sputtered, arms flailing helplessly. The actor had cut off his air supply.

Pennyroyal rushed over and threw herself between them. "Trace, let him go," she commanded.

Trace did. He was pretty obedient. And she was pretty gutty.

"C'mon, let's go eat," she said to him softly.

She led him off to their table. He went willingly. No one in the place paid much attention to the outburst. They were used to emotional scenes at Spago.

Zorch fingered his throat, shaken. "I hate that man," he said bitterly.

"He doesn't seem particularly fond of you either," I observed.

"I've hated him for thirty years."

"That's a lot of hate."

"I could not be happier that he's on his ass," he added, sneering at him. "Fuck him. Fuck *him.*"

"Why *can't* he work for Panorama?" I asked.

Zorch and Toy exchanged a look.

"That's a long, sad story," Toy replied. She got no further— somebody was approaching our table. Not her husband. Not Trace.

It was Johnny Forget.

He was weeping uncontrollably. His black leather motorcycle jacket was half off one bare shoulder. His nose was bleeding. He was a mess. "*Why*, Abel?!" he wailed, his hairless chest heaving. "Why are you *doing* this to me?!"

"Doing what, John?" Zorch asked him calmly and patiently, as one would a child.

"You *know* what!" Johnny's little boy voice was choked with emotion and rage. He sounded like a five-year-old who'd just learned the truth about Santa Claus. "You're dicking me! You're f-fucking that bimbo behind my back!"

He meant Geoffrey with a G, who took offense. And started to his feet. Zorch stopped him.

Johnny certainly took direction, I'll say that for him. Matthew had suggested he confront his two-timing lover, and that's what he was doing. It just so happened that the two-timer was Abel Zorch. Small town. Always has been.

"I am not dicking you," Zorch assured Johnny. "I am having dinner with some business associates."

"When are you gonna stop *lying* to me?!" Johnny cried at the top of his lungs.

That one drew a reaction from Trace across the room. "Give him hell, Badger!" he called out approvingly.

And brought Joey Bam Bam rushing over.

"May we discuss this later, John?" said Zorch irritably. Schlom was returning to our table from the men's room.

"No! I wanna have it out *now!*" cried Johnny.

"Later," Zorch said sharply.

"Now!"

"C'mon, pal, now's not a good time," Bam Bam advised, putting an arm around his troubled young client. "Man's having dinner, talking business with Mr. Schlom. Right, Mr. Schlom?" He started steering Johnny away. "C'mon, John-John. Let's hit the road."

"Get your hands off me," snapped Johnny.

Joey pulled back instantly. "Okay, okay, they're off. See? They're off."

Johnny stood there gazing at Zorch, his eyes red and swollen, tears streaming down his cheeks. Zorch stared back at him. His own hooded eyes betrayed nothing.

"You'll be sorry," Johnny vowed, his voice quavering. "You'll be sorry you did this to me." Then he stormed out, Bam Bam on his tail.

"What the fuck was that all about?" Schlom muttered to his wife.

Toy shook her head in reply.

Zorch went back to discussing our main course, unfazed.

Ten seconds later there was gunfire. It came from outside. Several shots fired in rapid succession by a semiautomatic. It got very quiet in Spago. They were used to emotional scenes. They were not used to gunfire. Lulu moaned from under my chair. She hates guns. Then there was a screech of tires and Johnny's Fat Boy went roaring off down Sunset.

Bam Bam returned a moment later, very pale. Bernard, the maître d', was with him, also pale.

"It's your Corniche, Mr. Zorch," said Bernard, with a pained expression. "Johnny, he shot out all of the windows and headlights."

"Ah, me," sighed Zorch. "Anyone hurt?"

"No, sir," the maître d' replied. "One other car was hit. A red Porsche."

"My baby," moaned Bam Bam, distraught. "One day old and already it's got bullet holes in it."

"Shall we call the police?" Bernard asked Zorch.

"Don't bother, Bernard," Zorch said coolly. "Boys will be boys. Still, I suppose we should go take a look." He and Geoffrey got up from the table. So did I. "Want to have a look, Norb?"

"I wanna eat," growled Schlom. "I don't know what a guy has to do to get a hot meal around here."

"Ultrasorry about all of this, Mr. Schlom," apologized Joey Bam Bam.

"Disappear."

"Yessir."

I followed Zorch and Geoffrey out through the bar. I never made it to the door. Someone stopped me with a tug at my sleeve. It was Pennyroyal.

"Will you do it?" she asked me urgently.

"Will I do what?"

"Will you tell Matthew I said hello?"

"I'll tell him."

She shot a nervous glance at the door, afraid of Zorch seeing us together. Then she raised her chin defiantly and took a seat at the bar. I joined her. The bartender asked her if she wanted anything. She didn't. I had a glass of Dom Perignon to kill the taste of Abel Zorch's wine.

"How is he really?" she asked me.

"He's tearing his hair out."

"I'm serious," she said.

"So am I." My champagne came. I took a sip. It tasted even better than usual. "He says he's over you, if that's what you want to know."

"Good," she said firmly. "I hope he is."

"Do you?"

Her eyes searched mine. I got lost in them a moment. They were easy to get lost in. So clear and blue. So innocent. So trusting. And she was so very, very good at playing this kind of game. She was an actress, after all, a magic mirror in which you see just exactly what you want to see. Whatever you want to read in an actress's eyes—it's in there. That's one of the things that makes them actresses . . . *What makes them so special, Meat?*

I wondered what Merilee was doing right now. I wondered if she was thinking about me. I wondered if she missed me.

"I still care about him," she said, her lower lip starting to quiver again. "I tried so hard to make it work. So damned hard." She tossed her head, sweeping back her golden hair, and looked around at the people. "He refused to eat here. I could never get him to come to this place." She pulled a cigarette out of her purse. I lit it for her. "What's he going to say about me? Is it horrible?"

I didn't answer her. She wasn't expecting an answer.

"Matthew . . . Matthew never understood me. Never knew me. He just created someone in his own head and tried to make me into her. He refused to let me be *me*. Can you see that?"

"I'd like to."

She drew on the cigarette, glancing at the door. "It's like he's turned his whole life into some old Warner Brothers movie. Shelley, the chubby, good-natured best friend. Bunny, the fiercely protective mom with the heart of gold. Sarge, his tough, loyal gal Friday. Shadow, the weird old baseball player. Trace, the football hero—"

"And you?"

"I was Debbie Dale, the mythic golden girl, radiating this bizarre, trembly sort of purity. I'm *not* her. I couldn't take being her anymore. I was wigging out. I'm not a bad person. I'm really not. I just had to get away from all of that. Get back some control over my own life. Do you have any idea what it's like being a figment of someone's imagination?"

"I believe so," I replied. "I'm a figment of my own."

She relaxed a bit, showed me her dimples. "Cassandra told me about you."

"That must have been good for a laugh."

"You're her idol."

"I know. Don't remind me."

"I'm not a bad person," she repeated, more insistently this time.

"And I'm not here to judge you," I said, admiring her bare, lovely throat. There were no lines etched in it. She had no lines anywhere on her face either. No age lines. No laugh lines. No pain. Nothing showed. It was as if she had never lived at all.

"Are you planning to go all the way?" she asked, gazing at me steadily.

"I generally try to stick it out."

"Good, I'm glad to hear it."

"I'm glad you're glad to hear it."

"Aren't you going to ask me the usual question?" she wondered, a bit demurely.

"Which usual question is that?"

"What it's like to be me."

"You get asked that a lot?"

"A lot."

"And how do you usually reply?"

"Usually I say that it hurts—every day, all day long. Only nobody ever believes me. Do *you* believe me?" She squeezed my arm with her small, brown hand. That edge of desperation again.

"Why shouldn't I?"

She released me. "It's really not fair," she complained, stubbing out her cigarette. "I don't deserve any of this. I'm just trying to get on with my life, make a future for my child. All I want is what I'm entitled to. Not a cent more. Is that so bad? But they're all calling me names. Making me out to be this grasping, airhead megabitch. I know why, too. Because I'm a pretty little girl. Pretty little girls aren't supposed to own fifty percent of a movie studio. That's why everyone's freaking out. That's what this whole mess is about. Power. They don't want me to have any. I'm someone to be patted on the head and fucked and fucked over. Not somebody who's supposed to have any clout. I'm telling you, this business hasn't changed since the days of Louis B. Mayer. A woman has to go to extraordinary lengths to get the slightest bit of clout. A woman has to—" She stopped herself. "Sorry," she said skittishly. "I didn't mean to unload on you. It's just that my life happens to be a total fucking mess."

I drained my champagne. "Why should your life be different from anyone else's?"

She laughed. A sad laugh. Sad lady. "I don't even know who I can trust anymore. I mean, I trusted Abel and he told the press *everything*."

"There's always Trace."

"Get real," she scoffed.

"Tried it. Vastly overrated. Look, if you're asking me my advice . . ."

"I am," she said flatly, her eyes searching my face.

"The best rule of thumb in situations like these is to trust nobody."

"Can I trust you?"

"I'm not nobody."

"Can I?" she pressed, anxiously.

Zorch came back inside now. He immediately spotted us there together at the bar. He didn't like it.

"I'm at the house," Pennyroyal whispered to me. "I'm a prisoner there. Call me. Help me—please."

Zorch made his way over to us. "It seems the little laddie boy took out every single bit of glass in the damned car," he reported, trying to sound merry, and failing. "I don't know how you survived three movies with him, Penny. He wears thin so terribly fast."

"You're not exactly being nice to him, Abel," Pennyroyal said disapprovingly.

Zorch showed her a thin smile. "I made him no promises. It's his own fault if he got carried away."

"It's not his fault that he cares about you," she argued.

"I can see I'm not going to win with you tonight," he said lightly.

"That's right, Abel, you're not." She went back to her table.

Zorch turned his hooded eyes on me. He looked like he had plenty he wanted to say, none of it nice. But all he said was, "Come, let's eat."

"By all means," I said. "Let's eat."

I got back to the Four Seasons shortly before midnight. I took the Vette straight down to the garage and the elevator straight up to twelve like I had before, only this time a half-dozen media people were waiting there for me in the twelfth-floor hallway when the elevator doors opened—mikes thrust in my face, lights flashing, videotape rolling.

*"IF YOU COULD JUST TELL US HOW MATTHEW IS DOING."*

*"A STATEMENT—"*

*"HOW WOULD YOU DESCRIBE HIS MOOD?"*

Happily, Lulu was too tired to be up for any pub right now. She barked ferociously at them. She has a mighty big bark for somebody with no legs. It froze them momentarily, and gave us a chance to make a dash down the hall for our room. They followed us. I hurriedly unlocked the door and we slipped inside and I slammed it shut on them. Safe and snug for the night.

Almost.

Cassandra Dee was taking a bubble bath in my tub. "I don't think Zorch is having ya followed, honey," she informed me, nasally, as she turned the page of the script she was reading. "Nobody tailed ya when you left for din-din. I watched. Cute car, by the way." She took a gulp of the diet Coke that was sitting on the edge of the tub, her belch reverberating in the tiled bathroom. Then she tapped the script. "Matthew's new one—it was waiting for ya down at the concierge's desk."

I opened the bathroom door wide. It was uncomfortably steamy in there. "Little warm for a hot bath, isn't it?"

"Not for me. I adore tubs." She set the script aside and stretched out her legs, feet propped up on the faucet. They were long, narrow feet, and she painted the nails red. "So where'd ya eat, huh? Who with? Whatcha pick up?"

The phone rang. I answered it on my bathroom phone. It was a reporter. I hung up on him, called the switchboard, and asked them to hold my calls for the night. They said they'd be happy to. I hung up and said, "I don't mean to be inhospitable, Cassandra, but what are you—?"

"I figured it was my toin," she explained.

"For what?"

She stood up. It's not easy to stand up in a tub without thrashing around like a hippo. Cassandra Dee was no hippo. She was all goil, long and graceful, breasts firm, nipples pink and perky. She looked fine standing there with my complimentary bath foam sliding slowly down her slick, wet flesh. She looked plenty fine. "To get caught with my pants off," she replied coyly.

"I'm not Trace Washburn."

"That's just as well, honey—I don't think my poor little tootsie roll could take it if you was."

I grabbed a bath towel and held it out to her. "You have sixty seconds."

"For what?" she asked.

"To get out. Or I sic Lulu on you."

She shrieked—her brand of laugh. "You're twisted. I like that about ya."

"She'll tear you to pieces," I threatened. "All they'll find of you is teeth and hair. Go on, show her, Lulu."

Lulu bared her fangs, growling menacingly.

"Wait, wait, hold it," cried Cassandra, fully goggle-eyed now. "You're *serious.*"

"Every once in a while."

She frowned, perplexed. "Yeah, yeah, shewa. Okay. Call her off." She snatched the towel from me. "I don't stick around where I'm not wanted. A doormat I ain't. Geez."

I left her in there to get dressed. My phone rang again. Another reporter. I hung up on him, called the switchboard and asked them, again, to hold my calls for the night. They said they'd be happy to.

Cassandra came out a moment later, fully clothed, flushed from her bath, clutching Matthew's script. "I wanna know what's wrong with me," she said, stung by my rejection. "What, I'm not good enough for ya?"

"Like I said—I'm not Trace Washburn."

Her eyes lit up. "Oh, I get it. You're faithful to Merilee, aren't ya? You're true blue."

"Blue, certainly."

"Gawd, that's so fucking sweet. If any guy was that faithful to me, I'd swallow him whole." She shook her head in amazement. "And it don't even matter that she dumped ya, huh?"

"Good night, Cassandra."

"G'night, Hoagy." She went to the door and opened it.

"The script, Cassandra?"

She looked at me innocently. "The what?"

"The script."

She glanced down at it in her hand, and laughed. "Yeah, yeah, shewa." She tossed it to me like a Frisbee.

I caught it. "By the way, how is it?"

"I only got about halfway through it but so far it's shit."

The instant she was gone I called Sarge's home number. Found it in the Bedford Falls directory. All I got was her machine. I tried her at the studio.

She picked up on the first ring. "Sarge talking," she said briskly. "Go."

"I've reconsidered your offer."

"Which offer was that, Hoagy?" she asked cheerfully.

"I do need a bungalow."

"To work in?"

"And live in."

"When you need it?"

"Would now be too soon?"

"Come on over. I'll tell Shadow where to send you."

"Thanks. You ever go home, Sarge?"

"Baby, I *am* home."

It took me ten minutes to pack, Lulu watching me in total dismay from the bed. This was her new turf, and I was already abandoning it. But it was fine with her as soon as she saw me gathering up her bowls. Together, we fled for Fort Bedford.

Robertson was quiet now, except for the occasional knot of people outside of the occasional restaurant. The wind had picked up, the hot, dry desert wind they call the Santa Ana. The air felt charged with electricity and my skin felt crackly, as if it itched on the inside. It would be blazing hot again tomorrow.

A couple of lights were still on in the big white main building. Floodlights illuminated the gate. Shadow Williams sat there in his booth browsing through Thorstein Veblen's *The Place of Science in Modern Civilization*. Just a little light reading.

He slid the window open when I pulled in. "The Shadow do recall this particular gentleman and lady," he said, showing me his gold tooth.

"How are you, Shadow?"

"The Shadow's fine, sir. Just fine."

"You work a rather long day," I noted.

"Pulling a little overtime," he said, nodding. "Got me my vacation coming up. Going to Phoenix to take a look at some very interesting architecture they got there by Mister Frank Lloyd Wright."

"You're into architecture?"

"The Shadow's into many things."

He directed me to the old writers' court. I said good night and eased the Vette slowly along the silent alley between the soundstages, its pipes burbling in the quiet. Sarge was waiting for me outside my pink stucco bungalow, key in hand. I parked in the empty space by the door.

"What changed your mind?" she asked, tossing me the key.

"Let's just say the elbow room at the Four Seasons isn't what it used to be."

She hoisted my bags out of the trunk, muscles rippling, and helped me inside with them. There was a small outer office for a secretary. It had a desk, filing cabinet, fridge, electric coffee maker.

"I brought some stuff down for you for the morning," she said. "Juice, coffee, milk . . ."

"Any diet Coke?"

"Uh . . . no."

"Good."

There was a bathroom with a stall shower, no three-way mirror, no phone, and no TV. The TV was in the inner office, which had a big walnut desk, a couple of armchairs, and a leather chesterfield sofa. The wind was coming in through the open windows, one of which had an air conditioner stuck in it.

"This opens up into a bed," she said, going over to the sofa. "Plenty comfortable. Linens are in the closet. Want me to . . . ?"

"I can handle it. And thanks. We'll be fine here."

"In the old days, before these were writers' bungalows, they were actors' dressing rooms," she informed me, watching Lulu sniff around. "This here one used to belong to Ramon Novarro, who starred in the silent version of *Ben-Hur.*"

"Does he haunt it?"

"Ain't nobody said nothing," she replied, chuckling.

Another door opened onto the manicured courtyard.

"That there's Bunny's place." She pointed to a bungalow across the way, where a TV glowed like blue neon in the window. "She always falls asleep with her set on. I turn it off for her if I'm around."

"How's Matthew doing?"

"Fine. He's bedded down for the night."

"You often spend the night here yourself?"

"Plenty—got me a sofa in my office."

"He insist on it?"

"Naw, ain't nothing like that," she said, offhanded.

I tugged at my ear. "You don't like to leave him, do you, Sarge?"

She gave me a chilly sidelong glance. "I got budgets to work on," she explained stiffly. "Nighttime's only chance I get. I'll get 'em to stencil your name on your parking space in the morning."

"Something I've always dreamed of."

"You jammin' me again, man?" she demanded, tensing up.

"Wouldn't dream of it, Sarge. You're way too tough for me."

"You got that right," she said with a laugh. Then she left.

I unpacked for the second time since I'd come to town, then undressed and made up the bed and climbed into it with *Badger Goes to Hollywood* or *Badger All Alone* or whatever the hell Mat-

thew decided to call it. Lulu immediately dropped off next to me
on her back, paws up, tongue lolling out of the side of her mouth.
One of her more fetching poses.

A typical screenplay is about a hundred pages long. Mostly
dialogue. Very little description. It takes about a half hour to zip
through one. A lot less than that to tell if the writer has gotten
lost. Matthew Wax had—starting right on page one. He was
opening the movie with Badger talking directly to the camera,
like Woody Allen had in *Annie Hall*. And, boy, did he ever talk.
The movie was a nonstop diatribe. On how conniving and slutty
Debbie Dale was. On how cold and cruel the world was. On how
a man who trusts people is doomed to be crapped on by them. On
how nobody loved him or understood him. On and on it went, all
of it awash in self-pity and sanctimony. The plot, what there was
of it, revolved around Debbie starring in a trashy action picture
at a Panorama-like studio for a Schlom-like executive. Badger,
meanwhile, is trying to get backing for an honest, *real* movie.
Only no one will give it to him—no one in Hollywood believes in
*Truth*. Except for Badger, of course. Beaten down, our Messiah
packs up his belongings and heads back to Homewood, where
the truth still counts for something. As for Debbie, she and her
leading man, who is also her new lover, are both decapitated in a
gruesome helicopter accident on the first day of filming. Badger
does not attend her funeral.

Cassandra had chosen the exact right word for Matthew's
new script—shit. No wonder Shelley Selden wanted him to make
something with fuzzy aliens. This one was as close to being a
surefire flop as a movie can be—especially when you remembered who was going to be playing Badger. The script needed
major work, which wasn't my problem. Matthew needed major
work, which was. The man was chewing on his own tail, which,
as I had noted from watching Lulu do it many times, only makes
it itch worse.

I turned off the lamp and lay there in the dark, listening to
the Santa Ana rustle the leaves of the hibiscus and oleander outside my window. It sounded like bats were flapping their wings
out there. I wanted out. I often did right about now, when I'd
waded in just far enough to realize how deep the water was. But
getting out is something I've never been able to do. My ego won't
allow it, and my ego directs this particular production.

I dreamt that night that I was writing a script for Norbert

Schlom about Merilee and me. All about how Lulu brought the two of us back together again. Lulu talked in it. She sounded just like Roseanne Barr. Pennyroyal Brim was playing Merilee. Andrew Dice Clay was playing me. I don't know how the hell he got into it. It was a horrible dream. It had everything in it but earthquakes and giant toads. I woke from it just before dawn drenched in sweat—Lulu was snoring peacefully on my head. I nudged her over onto the pillow next to me, got up and showered, and started the coffee. Then I went to work.

# Chapter Five

"What's this, Meat?"

"For you. I always like to give a gift."

We were sitting in the Vette, top down, engine raring to run.

He tore into the wrapping paper. "Wow, Silly Putty," he exclaimed. "I didn't even know they still made it."

"The classics never go out of style."

"Gee, thanks, Meat." He seemed genuinely pleased. Also genuinely tense.

We were making an early start in hopes of beating the worst of the heat out in the Valley, where it's usually ten degrees hotter than it is on the west side. Matthew wore a T-shirt and jeans and a beeper. He had not shaved. Sheldon Selden pulled onto the lot just as we were leaving. He drove a sparkling blue Mercedes 560SL, and looked plenty perky and fresh for someone who had just flown back overnight from New York on the Bedford Falls jet. He and Matthew jumped out of the cars and hugged each other warmly.

"How have you been, kid?" Shelley asked him, brow furrowed with brotherly concern.

"Okay," replied Matthew, ducking his semibald head. "How about Sis and the kids?"

"All home in bed fast asleep. I sacked out on the plane. Now listen, kid, we're gonna get through this thing. We're in it together, and we'll get through it together. Okay?"

"Sure, Shelley," Matthew replied, his voice ringing hollow.

I joined them, shaking Shelley's hand. He wore a loose-fitting white knit shirt and gray linen slacks. He was getting around better on his ankle, but he was now sporting a fresh ace bandage on his right wrist.

"Tripped getting on the plane," he explained to me sheepishly. "You guys making out all right?"

"Sure thing," Matthew said. "We're on our way to the old neighborhood now."

Shelley looked at me, surprised. "You're kidding."

"Nope," said Matthew. "Meat thinks it's important, so we're going."

"Oh, hey, Matthew, check this out." Shelley reached into his Mercedes and pulled a stuffed lion out of a shopping bag. "I was up at one of the newspaper syndicates yesterday. Their hottest new comic strip—this bratty little kid and his toy lion, who comes to life in his imagination. They've got it in four hundred newspapers already. They thought of us for the movie." He held the stuffed lion out to Matthew. "Make a cute picture, huh?"

Matthew looked at the lion but wouldn't take it from him. Or discuss it. He went back to the Vette and got in.

Shelley sighed. "Oh, well, I try," he said to me under his breath. "Things okay so far?"

"Fine and dandy."

Shelley glanced at Matthew. "He hasn't been back to the old neighborhood in—"

"Twenty years. I know."

"I'm impressed, Hoagy. You live up to your reputation."

"A few of us have to."

"Be gentle with him, okay? He's an open wound."

"We're fine."

He patted me on the back. "Sure you are." Then he hopped back in his Mercedes and sped off toward the main building.

The press people were still camped outside the gate. I had Matthew duck down when we pulled out so they wouldn't follow us. It was just we two. Lulu had decided she'd rather hang out on the lot and watch reruns of *The People's Choice*. Bunny had also mentioned something about leftover salmon patties. I took Culver Boulevard to the freeway and got on. The morning traffic was heavy coming in from the Valley, but not too terrible going out. I worked the Vette up to seventy and let it cruise there.

"Wow, I used to love this stuff," said Matthew, happily kneading his Silly Putty. "You could bounce it off walls. You could flatten it into a pancake. You could make comic book imprints. What neat stuff."

"Keeps your hands good and busy, too."

He reddened, started to reach for his forelock, stopped himself. "Worth a try, I guess," he mumbled, fingers working furiously at his new toy.

We climbed. The freeway cut a wide swath of pavement through the bare, brown foothills of the Santa Monica Mountains. Brentwood was to our left, Bel Air on our right. We topped off at Mulholland, then began our slow descent into the San Fernando Valley, which until the fifties had been nothing but orange groves and now was nothing but suburban sprawl. The smog hung heavy over it—the Santa Susannas were nowhere to be seen across the valley. It felt more than ten degrees hotter.

"I've been thinking about what you said yesterday, Meat," Matthew said, turning serious.

"I said a lot."

"About you interviewing Pennyroyal. I have a real problem with it. In fact, I'd rather you not even talk to her at all."

"I've already talked to her."

"You what?" he demanded, immediately agitated. "When?"

"I bumped into her last night at Spago."

"Who was with her?" he wanted to know.

I left that one alone.

"Did you see Georgie?"

"No, I didn't." My eyes were beginning to sting from the smog. I dabbed at them with my handkerchief, wondering how people could live here. "She said there's nobody she can trust."

"Oh, that's perfect," he snapped, getting good and worked up. "That's just perfect. She's the poor little victim. She's not responsible for any of this. It's all just *happened* around her. She's amazing. Truly amazing."

I tugged at my ear. "Sure you're not just the teeniest bit bitter?"

"I told you—I am *not* bitter." He glared at me. "I don't have any control over you, do I?"

"Do you want it?"

"Let's just say I'm used to it."

"You can get used to lots of things, if you have to."

"Do I?"

I left that one alone, too.

We rode in silence for a while, through Encino and on out toward the vast, sunbaked valley floor.

"I thought about something else you said," he mentioned sullenly. "About my movies. Have you liked *any* of them?"

I glanced over at him. His eyes were searching my face imploringly. I looked back at the road. "I liked your first movie a lot, *The Boy Who Cried Wolf*. It was, I don't know, real. Damned scary, too."

He nodded with quiet satisfaction. "Funny you should say that. It's still my own favorite. I guess because it was the most personal."

"You witnessed a murder when you were a kid?"

"No. Never. I just mean that the boy, Lucas, was so much like I was."

"How so?"

Matthew looked out at the freeway. "His relationship with his father. The way he was always trying to win his approval."

"He ultimately did."

"That part never happened in real life. My father died when I was a freshman at SC. I'm still sorry about that. I'm sorry he never got a chance to . . ." He trailed off, searching for the words.

"To see you become such a big success?" I suggested.

"To tell me why he hated my guts so much," Matthew replied.

We had cleared Van Nuys now and were nearing Reseda, where Panorama City was. I could just make out the studio's outlandish new office tower in the smoggy distance.

"He adored Shelley," Matthew said. "Always made sure she had piano lessons, ballet lessons, nice clothes, a new bicycle. Not me. I got hand-me-downs. Only reason I got to see Shadow hit his grand-slammer was that Shelley had the measles. Otherwise, he'd have gone with her. He loved Shelley. Me, he never had any use for. Mostly, he ignored me. I'd have done anything to please him. But I couldn't. I always wondered why. I always wondered what was wrong with me. It was never anything I did or said. It was just *me*. Still, I always kept coming back for more. He was my dad, and I loved him. Lou was his name. He was a big man, gruff, a cigar smoker. Worked for a kitchenware manufacturer selling to the restaurant supply houses up and down the West Coast. He spent two weeks out of every month on the road, shlepping his big black sample cases from town to town. I remember his car, this '59 Chevy station wagon, blue, with white tail fins. On the day he was due home I'd go and sit there on the corner and watch for it. I'd sit there for hours, waiting. When he finally did show up he'd drive right on past me without even waving. Like I was invisible."

"What did Bunny have to say about all of this?" I asked.

"Not a whole lot," he replied. "To this day all she can say to me is, 'Your father was not a nice man.' Which he wasn't. He was a shit. Nobody liked him. And Ma had no influence over him. She worked full-time herself. They needed the two paychecks to make ends meet. She was a bookkeeper for an accountant named Carlo Ferraro who had a small office on Reseda Boulevard in Northridge. Nice man. Ma worked for him a long time. She was still working for him part-time up until last year, when he finally retired. She insisted on it. Said she'd get bored otherwise. She always worked. Made us dinner in advance and left it for Shelley to heat up. Shelley and me, we spent a lot of our time on our own. When I was real little, it was her job to walk me home from school. She hated doing it. She wanted to play with her friends instead. One time, when I was in kindergarten, she forgot me—or she said she forgot me. I had to find my way home alone. I got lost. I was terrified. To this day she denies she did it on purpose, but I know she did."

"That's the plot of *Dennis the Dinosaur*."

"Uh-huh."

"Did you resent her for being your father's favorite?"

"I never blamed her for that," he said. "It wasn't her fault. It was strictly him. Shelley and me, we got along okay. We weren't real close. She was a girl, and older than me. But we got along. She was real popular. Always had friends in her room, giggling and trying on makeup."

"And you?"

"I never hung around with other kids much," he said quietly.

"Why not?"

He shrugged. "Just liked being by myself, I guess."

"I need a better answer than that."

He gave it some more thought, his hands working the Silly Putty. "Other kids, they always seemed so cruel. Ganging up on each other, taunting, fighting. They weren't fun. Not like the friends I made up in my own head. And the games I played alone. I loved to hide," he recalled fondly. "Small, dark spaces. Under beds. Behind furniture. My safe places, I called them. They were *mine*. Other kids, they just got in my way." Abruptly, his face fell. "This is it, Meat," he said, looking out the window. "Nordhoff's our turnoff. God, this feels weird."

I made a left at the end of the ramp and we were in Sepulveda, home of the drive-thru landscape. Nordhoff was a flat, scorched boulevard lined with minimalls and gas stations and fast food franchises. It was devoid of personality, of uniqueness, of aspiration. It was nowhere. There was very little shade. The sun was blistering.

"This feels weird," Matthew said again, as he stared out at it.

We passed a high school on our right, James Monroe. It resembled a minimum security prison. Matthew stiffened noticeably at the sight of it.

"Yours?" I asked.

He didn't answer.

A sign at the curb announced Friday night's upcoming football game.

"The Taft game," Matthew said, his voice sounding far away. "That was usually a good one."

"Did you play on any teams yourself?" I asked.

"No, never." He fidgeted, scratched at his arms. "Well, basketball briefly. But no, not really."

I nodded. I would come back to that. And to Monroe High.

He instructed me to make a right at Woodley Avenue, where there were some low, dreary apartment houses. A few of the windows had been lined with tin foil to reflect the bright sun. Then I made the first left, Tupper, which plunged us into a cemetery. Our postwar dreams were buried here. Hundreds of acres of tract houses from the Fabulous Fifties, block after block after block of them. Starter homes, they had called them then, hopefully. Small, cheap one-story cracker boxes, vaguely ranch style. All of them plopped down at once. All of them alike. A handful had acquired bits of character through the years. Most had simply bleached out. It was a neighborhood of quiet resignation now. A slum of the not-too-distant future.

Matthew's old street, Sophia, was a cul-de-sac. His house was the second on the left, vaguely mustard-colored. I parked across the street and we sat there, looking at it. The garage had a rusty basketball hoop over it. A dented old Datsun pickup sat in the driveway. A big olive tree grew in the center of the small, dead lawn.

"Seventeen thousand, Meat," he said softly. "That's how much they paid for it. Shelley and me, we each had our own little room. We shared a bathroom. There was a breakfast nook in the kitchen, where we ate all our meals. We never owned a dining table. The TV was in the living room. A big old Packard Bell with tubes." He shook his head in disbelief. "Place hasn't changed one bit."

"I like the olive tree."

"That was my corner." He pointed to where the sidewalk ended at Tupper. "Where I'd wait for my dad to come home. Across the street from there, that was still open fields when I was little. I got in the one and only fight of my childhood there. This kid who lived down the cul-de-sac, Neal Bricker. A real bully. He used to take off his belt and chase me home, whipping me with it. You wonder why I preferred to play alone—he was a big reason. One day he started throwing dirt clods at me from over there. I started throwing 'em back. Hit him right between the eyes with one. Only it wasn't a dirt clod—it was a rock. Blood started streaming down his face. He went running home in tears. I went running home and hid in my closet. I thought I'd blinded him and was gonna to get sent to jail."

"What did happen to you?"

"Nothing," he said proudly. "All Ma said was he's a bully and sometimes you have to stand up to a bully. And she was right —he never bothered me again after that. Gee, I wonder what he's doing now."

"Probably went into politics," I said, noting once again how much Matthew seemed to see his life in cinematic vignettes. This one had a villain, a boffo climax, even a poignant moment with Ma.

"I wonder who lives here now," he said, gazing at his old house.

"Want to knock on their door?"

"God, no," he said, nervously fingering his Silly Putty. "I just wondered, that's all. The backyard was pretty neat. Seven orange trees, lots of bushes. After school I used to play cowboys and Indians. Had all kinds of wild shoot-outs back there—guys diving over bushes, jumping out of trees. Those were my earliest productions. I was writer, director, stunt coordinator, and sole star. Very low budget—all in my own head. I guess I was six or seven. Most of it came from television. I watched TV morning, noon and night. Couldn't get enough of Westerns—*The Lone Ranger*, *Wild Bill Hickock*, *Cheyenne*, *The Rifleman* with Chuck Connors. I guess *The Rifleman* was my favorite. A boy and his dad together in the Old West . . .''

"Because of a boy and his dad *not* together in Sepulveda?''

He looked at me, startled. "Gee, I never thought of it that way before, Meat. I—I was just into his rifle. But I'll bet you're right.'' He nodded enthusiastically. "That's good. Real good.''

The beeper on his belt went off.

"Want to find a phone?'' I asked.

"No, no. This is much more important than whatever Sarge wants. I'll call her later. Go on, keep asking me questions, Meat,'' he urged.

"Were you also drawn to those all-American family shows?''

"You mean like *Leave It to Beaver* and *Father Knows Best?* Totally. I wanted that. Beaver Cleaver's childhood, that's the childhood I wanted. A big brother who was a best friend. A dad who was there for you, teaching you how to fish. A mom who was always home, baking pies. A family where everybody ate dinner together around a dining table with a tablecloth and cloth napkins and water glasses. I still love those shows—*Ozzie and Harriet*, *Donna Reed*, I watch 'em all the time. Penny, she could never understand why. She thought I confused them with the real world. Like I couldn't tell the difference or something. I can. I'm not crazy, like she's making me out to be. I just happen to *like* that world. It's a happy place. Much happier than the real one. The real world's pretty awful. There's poverty, disease, death . . . It's not good to dwell on that stuff. You gotta escape sometimes. That's why people go to see my movies.'' His face darkened. "Or used to, anyway.''

"You had one dud. Don't let it throw you.''

"I'm not,'' he insisted, sticking out his snow shovel jaw stubbornly.

"Okay, you're not.''

"I liked horror movies a lot, too,'' he reflected, his eye on the

house. "The local TV stations had 'em on all day Saturday and
Sunday—*Godzilla, Rodan, The Thing.* My absolute favorite was
*The Abominable Snowman of the Himalayas.* I loved that movie.
Couldn't get enough of it."

"What made it so special?"

"The monster wasn't evil," he replied simply. "Just sad. That
made a real impression on me. And it stayed with me. When I got
the chance, I remade it."

"Did you generally watch TV alone?"

"Shelley watched with me sometimes. What amazed me
about her was she could just get up in the middle of a show and
walk away. There was other stuff she'd rather be doing. Not me.
There was nowhere else I'd rather be. TV sucked me in, and held
me. I shot baskets by myself sometimes if nothing was on. I had
my homework, and chores. Otherwise, I was glued totally to the
set. TV, it made me who I am today," he said, without regret.
"My dreams, my sense of right and wrong—that all comes from
TV. It had much more to do with how I turned out than my folks
did. Or school."

"Does knowing that bother you at all?"

He thought this over, frowning. "I don't want Georgie to
grow up like I did, if that's what you're asking. I'd much rather
see him grow up around people. People who love him and support him." He let out a pained sigh. "Not that he's getting off to a
very good start."

The sun was overhead now, beating straight down on us. I
put the top up to give us some shade, and pulled away from the
curb.

"Where to?" asked Matthew, eyes lingering on his boyhood
home.

"I want to see your schools."

"Leave no stone unturned, huh?"

"I'm afraid there are always stones unturned. I just hope
none of them turn out to be giant boulders."

"Cross over Woodley and keep on going." His beeper went
off again.

"Sure you don't want to phone in?" I asked.

"Positive. I want to concentrate on this. Script ideas are already starting to swirl around inside my head."

"I've read it, by the way."

He stared at me anxiously. "And . . . ?"

"There are a couple of things I didn't like," I said gently. "Badger talking to the camera for one. That kind of device tends to invite self-indulgence."

"Meaning you think it's self-indulgent?" he asked, his pink rabbit nose twitching at me.

"I also think you've shortchanged Debbie," I went on. "We have to care about her. We have to know that she and Badger had a good life together. Otherwise, we won't care that they're now apart."

"You didn't like it at all, did you?" he demanded, rattled. He was tugging at his forelock again, his Silly Putty forgotten. "You hated it. You did. You hated it."

"I didn't say that. It has potential. I just don't think it's finished yet."

"Neither do I," he agreed hastily. "Neither do I." He took a deep breath, recovering his composure. His hand fell to his lap. "Okay. I'll think about it, Meat. And thank you for your honesty. I appreciate it."

"Sure about that?"

"Positive. I need this kind of input. I—I'm just not used to it." He grinned at me. "Sorry if I bit your head off."

"You didn't. It's still attached to the rest of me, big as ever."

There were more cul-de-sacs on the other side of Woodley. After a couple of turns we found ourselves in front of his elementary school, Gledhill, a complex of small, squat concrete buildings connected by covered walkways. Temporary classroom bungalows edged out onto the blacktopped playground. It was recess, and the kids were out playing. Their teachers stood by, watching them.

"I hated recess," Matthew recalled gloomily, as we sat there. "I never knew where to go."

"Where did you?"

"That bench right over there by the fence. Unless one of the teachers made me get up and play."

"Were you a good student?"

"I was a good daydreamer."

Two of the teachers noticed us lingering there in the Vette, staring at their little charges. They eyed us sternly. I moved on. Matthew's junior high, Sepulveda, was a few blocks away. Same design, if you can call it design. Somewhat larger scale.

"I remember very little about this place," he confessed, "except that I spent three years of my life here, my face broke out the whole time, and I grew eight inches in one semester. And girls became a major deal."

"How did you get along with them?"

He shrugged. "Same as I got along with everybody—not at all. I never went to any dances. Never even learned how to dance. I still don't know how."

"No girlfriends?"

"None," he replied crisply.

"Anyone you had a crush on?"

He fidgeted. "No one."

"Sure about that?"

He laughed nervously. "You sound like you know different or something."

"I don't."

"There was no one."

"And no friends? Not a single one?"

"Why are you asking me so many questions?" he asked, peevishly.

"That's my job. I did warn you."

"That's true, you did," he admitted. He took a deep breath, let it out slowly. "I had one friend—Sheldon Selden. He started dating Shelley when they were sixteen. I was thirteen. He was my first friend. My only friend. He watched TV with me. Dragged me along with them to the Monroe High football games. A couple of times he even took me to the Coliseum to see SC play, just him and me. His dad had season tickets. We saw Trace beat UCLA 21–20 his senior year to go to the Rose Bowl. Gee, Trace was something out on the field. Cool, fearless—a real hero." Matthew shifted his long legs, gazed uncomfortably at his old school. "I never understood why Shelley was so nice to me."

"Maybe he liked you."

"Why would he?"

"Why wouldn't he?"

Matthew swallowed. "Nobody else did."

I circled back toward Nordhoff and pulled up outside of James Monroe. A couple of boys' gym classes were out on the field in T-shirts and shorts playing flag football.

"Sometimes, when I was in junior high I'd ride my bike over here after school and watch the varsity team practice in helmets and pads," Matthew recalled. "They were always the most popular guys. The in guys."

"Did you want to be one of them?"

"Who didn't?"

I thought about the way he'd reacted when we drove by here before. "And did you ever try?"

He was silent a moment. "Shelley, he talked me into it. See, him and me used to shoot baskets sometimes when he'd come over to pick up Sis. I practiced at it a lot. Got to be a pretty fair shooter. I was also six feet six when I was in the eleventh grade. He kept telling me I ought to go out for the basketball team. I really didn't want to. I was so clumsy and unsure of myself. But he talked me into it. He was so incredibly enthusiastic and persuasive. And I actually made the varsity team—as a backup center."

"And how was that?"

"Not for me," he replied, offhanded. "I quit the team after the first game."

"How come?"

"Didn't like it."

"How come?"

"No real reason," he said defensively.

"I think there is," I suggested.

"I don't care what you think!" he snapped. "It's my life and it's my book. I quit the team, *period*. Just leave it at that."

I did for a moment. Then I said, "Why can't you tell me about it, Matthew?"

"Can we get out of here now?" Matthew demanded, growing agitated. "Can we get on the freeway and get out of this place?"

"As soon as you tell me why you quit the team."

"I *told* you—it wasn't for me! Now would you please start this damned car?!"

"I'll find out the reason, Matthew. One of the Shelleys will tell me, Bunny will tell me—"

"No one will tell you. They don't know why. *Nobody* knows why."

"So there is a reason."

"There is not! How many times do I have to tell you?! I just *quit*, okay?!"

"Matthew, let's have a small reality check here. You're thirty-eight years old. You're the single most successful director in the history of the planet. What possible difference can it make why you quit your high school basketball team?"

He didn't answer me. Just sat there, breathing quickly in and out. Faster and faster. Until he abruptly bolted from the car and vomited on somebody's front lawn.

When he was done he got back in, and I got us back on the freeway. I pushed him no farther. I was satisfied for now. It wasn't exactly a breakthrough, but it was a start.

We didn't go straight back to Bedford Falls. On the way he had me stop off in Northridge at Malibu Grand Prix, a go-cart race-way. Fairly elaborate one, too. The track had hairpin twists and turns. The go-carts looked just like Formula One race cars. I imagine it was quite the place if you were eleven years old, or Matthew Wax. He bought himself a fistful of tickets, pulled on a helmet, and took off into the bright, hot sun. A few kids who'd cut school were out there, too, but mostly Matthew had the place to himself.

I found myself a shady spot in the bleachers and watched him. He drove his go-cart racer skillfully and hard. After his first lap he waved to me. From then on he stayed totally focused on the course. And his thoughts. He had a lot on his mind. Some people lose themselves in drink when they do. Some in drugs. Some in sexual liaisons. This was Matthew's escape. I jotted down some notes while he drove. What he'd told me about his childhood that morning. What he hadn't told me. I was anxious to talk to his sister. And to Bunny. I was sorry I couldn't talk to Lou Wax about it as well. But probably not as sorry as Matthew was.

Afterwards, we stopped for lunch at a Denny's on Ventura Boulevard. Matthew ordered a cheeseburger, fries, and a choco-late shake from our waitress, who recognized him and stared. He was still lost in thought, eyes watching the traffic on Ventura outside the window next to us, fingers absently working his Silly Putty. I ordered a Denver omelet and hash browns. Then I sat there, waiting him out.

He took a deep gulp of his shake when she brought it. Then he unloaded. "The thing is," he declared forcefully, "if you're an ugly goon when you're fifteen, you're an ugly goon for the rest of your life. Until the day you die. You're always a goon.

Even if lots of years go by, even if you get married and have a kid, even if you're more successful than you ever thought you'd be in your wildest dreams—you're still that same goon who everybody laughed at. It never changes. It's who you are." With that he took another gulp of his shake and sat back in the booth, spent.

I sipped my iced tea. "You're saying you quit the basketball team because people laughed at you?"

He shook his head, exasperated. "Why do you keep asking me about that?"

"Because you won't answer me about that."

"You're missing my whole point, Meat."

"Sorry. I get a bit dense sometimes."

"What I'm saying is that nothing ever changes."

"How can it—if you don't let it?"

He frowned. "What do you mean?"

"I mean that if you keep dwelling on every hurtful adolescent fender bender then yes, you're right. You are your past. But that's your own choice. And your own mistake. Because you're *not* that person anymore, except in your own head. We're living in the present. Whatever happened before doesn't matter anymore. You have to put it behind you."

"I have," he said broodingly.

"Bullshit."

"I have," he insisted. "Here, here, I'll give you a perfect example—an invitation came to me at the studio a few weeks back. My high school graduating class is having its twentieth reunion. A big dinner dance at the Sheraton Panorama City. And it didn't even faze me one bit. I just shrugged it off and tossed it in the trash. Because I'm not that person anymore, just like you said."

"You're going," I informed him.

He instantly turned pale. "I'm what?"

"You're going to your reunion. This is one dance you're not going to miss."

"Forget it. No way."

"You're going," I assured him. "And I'm going with you."

"I am *not* going," he argued, his voice rising. "You can't make me go. I hate those people. The day I graduated I swore I'd never see any of them ever again. I won't go. You hear me? I won't go!"

"You have to go, Matthew. You have to get over this thing—whatever it is."

He went back to watching the cars out on the street again. "I won't go."

"Fine. Then I'll go without you. And I'll find out what happened."

"I refuse to allow it!"

"You can't stop me, Matthew."

"Look, Meat, I have a great idea—let's just forget this whole book, okay? I obviously didn't know what I was getting into, and you obviously are a loose cannon. Really, I can't remember the last time I met such a stubborn, domineering pain in the—"

"Careful," I said demurely. "You're going to make me blush."

"Let's just forget it, okay?"

"Okay, Matthew. If that's how you feel."

He sighed. "It's *not* how I feel. I—I just . . . why is this so important?"

"Because you've made it so important."

He thought this over, nose twitching, eyes blinking repeatedly behind his glasses. Before he could say anything more his beeper went off again. "Damn. That's the third time. I'd better find out what she wants. You mind?"

"Go right ahead."

There was a pay phone outside of the restrooms. He loped off toward it.

The waitress brought our lunch while he was gone. I waited for him to come back before I dove in.

He returned quickly, flopped down in the booth, and stared at his food. "Better hurry up and finish, Meat," he said numbly. "We have to get back."

"What happened?"

"The *Enquirer* got hold of Pennyroyal's nude shots. They're rushing them into print."

"I thought Shelley had the only set of negatives."

"He did. Somebody broke into his office and stole them out of his desk." His eyes filled with tears. "Where does this end, Meat? Can you tell me that? Where does this end?"

• • •

"I have to give the press a statement." Shelley Selden sat slumped behind his desk, distraught. "I have to tell them something, *anything.*"

We were all seated in his paneled office in the executive suite of the big white building. Matthew, Sarge, Bunny, Shadow. Shadow was still half asleep—he'd been on the gate all night and only just gone to bed when Shelley called him. Lulu lay at my feet making low, unhappy sounds and shooting murderous looks at Bunny. One salmon patty too many, evidently.

There was a fireplace in Shelley Selden's office, a leather sofa, armchairs, a long conference table of polished walnut. His desk was also walnut. A fine piece, except for where the bottom drawer had been smashed open. It was a sedate office, the office of a judge or college president. Matthew's office next door looked more like a playroom, with all of the pinball machines and toys he had crammed in there. The executive suite was on the building's second floor, directly across the hall from the screening room. An outer office for secretaries, a waiting area, and Sarge's office made up the rest of the suite.

Sarge sat cross-legged on the floor shooting worried looks at Matthew, who seemed to have withdrawn inside himself. He sat sprawled in an armchair playing with his Silly Putty, gazing off into space and saying not one word. His face was a blank.

"What you gonna tell them?" she asked Shelley.

"I don't have the slightest idea," he replied irritably. "Except that we had nothing to do with it, and we don't know how it happened."

"They won't be satisfied with that," she pointed out.

"Hey, I know that," he acknowledged, helping himself to a handful of jelly beans from a big jar on his desk. "And who can blame them? Everybody's going to think we leaked them ourselves to get back at her."

"Is the *Enquirer* saying how they got them?" I asked.

"Nope," he replied. "Just that they're authentic and that they'll be printing them tomorrow, suitably touched up. *Playboy* and *Penthouse* are already in a major bidding war over who gets the X-rated version." He shook his head ruefully. "Zorch was on the phone screaming bloody murder at me. He's threatening to sue us."

"Why don't he sue *them?*" Sarge wondered. "Get some injunction to stop them from publishing the pictures?"

"That never works," argued Shelley. "All it does is give them more publicity, which is exactly what they want. Besides, Zorch is the very person who did this. Zorch had them stolen. Zorch leaked them. It's Zorch!" he cried, pounding the desk with his fist. His bandaged wrist didn't like that. He massaged it, wincing. "Zorch did this. I know he did."

"Why would he?" I asked. "His client is in the middle of a bitter custody battle. He wants her to look like the good little mother. Why smear her this way?"

"He doesn't care about Pennyroyal," said Shelley. "All he cares about is heat. And he's getting plenty."

I wondered. That wasn't what Zorch had said to me at Spago. He'd said the Japanese wanted him to turn down the heat. Had he and Schlom just been blowing smoke at me?

"Shameful," said Bunny, her lips tightly pursed. "My grandson's mother posing naked in the newspapers. This will never go away. Somebody will always remind Georgie of this. Always."

Matthew shifted restlessly in his chair at the mention of Georgie's name.

"I blame myself for this," said Shelley bitterly. "I should have put the negatives in my safety deposit box at the bank the second Zorch got involved. That's what I should have done. But I thought they were safe here. I mean, shit, my desk is always locked when I'm not here. So is my office. And we have damned good security, don't we, Shadow?"

"Yessir," said Shadow, yawning. "That we do."

"We have a fence topped with razor wire around the entire lot," Shelley said forcefully, as if he were waging an argument with someone. "We have floodlights, three guys patrolling on electric carts, a man on the front gate twenty-four hours a day. We're talking *Mission Impossible* for somebody to get on this lot who doesn't belong here. I don't understand how it happened. I just don't."

"You mentioned to me in New York that Zorch's private detectives were getting onto the lot," I reminded him.

"They were," Shadow acknowledged. "But we've tightened up since then. No visitor gets through the gate without we phone up the department they're visiting to confirm it. They're issued a pass, and they have to return it when they leave so's we can account for everybody. No strays. No stragglers." He turned to Shelley and said, "Be best to let the Culver City Police handle it from here."

"No police," said Shelley sharply. "You let the police in, you're letting the press in—where one goes the other follows. We'll have reporters swarming all over the lot. No way. We keep this thing in the family. It's our mess. We clean it up ourselves."

"Zorch was aware that the negatives existed?" I asked.

"Of course," Shelley said, reaching for more jelly beans. "Pennyroyal warned him all about them. That's how come I'm so sure he's responsible. He must have had one of his detectives do it. Or maybe some sleazy reporter."

I could think of one such reporter right off. Someone who no one could keep out if she wanted in. Someone who would do anything to climb atop the bestseller list.

There was a tapping at the door. Shelley's secretary poked her head in. "Excuse me, we're holding an urgent call for you, Mr. Hoag."

"Take it right here, Hoagy," offered Shelley, pushing his phone toward me. "Put it through, Brenda."

It rang a moment later. I picked it up.

"Mr. Hoag? It's Abel Zorch." He sounded upset. Very upset. "Are you free to talk?"

"I'm afraid not."

"We must talk."

"Okay."

"It's *vital*."

"I said okay."

"Can you make it up to my house this evening? Six-thirty?"

I said that would be fine. He gave me his address. Then I hung up. Shelley was looking up at me expectantly.

"Reporter," I explained. "They'll try anything." I came around his desk to get a better look at the drawer. The wood was dented and splintered, the lock shattered. It looked like a pry bar had been used on it. "Any idea what time this happened?"

"After I got you settled in your bungalow I worked a little longer in my office," Sarge said. "Came in here about one-thirty to leave some budget projections on the desk. It looked fine then."

"How did you get in here?" I asked.

She frowned. "What you mean?"

"Wasn't his door locked?"

"I have keys to everything," she informed me, a bit defensively.

"Who else does?" I asked.

"The Shadow does," said Shadow. "Other guards, custodians . . ."

"What time do they generally clean?"

"Between seven and nine in the evening," he said.

"Did you spend the night here?" I asked Sarge.

She nodded. "On my sofa. Locked up before I went to sleep. The hall door was locked. Shelley's door was locked. Both of 'em. I'm sure of it."

"And you didn't hear anything in the night?" I asked her.

"I heard nothing."

"Pry bar didn't wake you?"

"I heard *nothing*," she repeated, narrowing her eyes at me. "My office door was closed and my air conditioner was on. I'm also a heavy sleeper."

"What time did you get up?"

"Six. I work out at our health club every morning before work."

"Which is where?"

"Next door to the commissary."

"You didn't notice anything unusual when you left?"

"Nothing."

"Did you come in here?"

She drew herself up. "Why you slicin' and dicin' me, man?" she woofed.

"He's not accusing you of anything, Sarge," Shelley said soothingly.

"Of course he's not," said Bunny. She glared at me. "Are you?"

"I am not," I assured her.

Sarge relaxed. "No, I didn't come in here," she said with exaggerated patience.

"Who discovered the break-in?" I asked.

"I did," Shelley replied. "I came up here right after you guys left, about a quarter to eight. I was the first one in. The doors

were locked. I came in, found the desk all busted and the negatives gone."

"So it happened some time between one-thirty in the morning and a quarter to eight," I mused aloud. To Shadow I said,
"None of the doors were forced?"

"No, sir," he replied, looking down at his big feet. "Whoever did it had keys. Or else he picked the locks. Ain't like they be
dead bolts or nothing. Professional could be in and out like a
mouse."

"A professional would have picked the desk lock, too," I
said. "Not smashed the drawer in."

"Maybe he tried to pick it and it wouldn't cooperate," countered Shadow. "Hard telling."

"This was no wild search," I suggested. "Whoever did this
knew exactly where you kept the negatives. Penny knew?"

Shelley froze, eyes widened as if he'd just taken a pair of
scissors in the back. "No way," he said in a stunned half-whisper.
"She didn't know. I'm sure she didn't. She couldn't have. But
then that would . . . that means somebody *else* tipped off
Zorch . . ."

"So it would seem," I said.

It got very quiet in Shelley's office. The only sound was Lulu
burping sourly under my chair. Alka-Seltzer. She needed an
Alka-Seltzer.

"Who else knew?" I asked.

"You may include the Shadow out," the security chief spoke
up promptly. "The Shadow don't know nothing about such executive business."

"That's true, he didn't," Shelley acknowledged. He looked
warily around the room at the others. "Just the family knew. No
one else. Just us." His eyes returned to me. "And you. You knew."

Lulu growled softly. I assured her I could handle it. To Shelley I said, "Care to elaborate on that?"

"I did mention them to you in New York," he pointed out. "I
even told you where I kept them. You show up in town and, bam,
your first night here they disappear. You have to admit—"

"Let's not be bashful about this," I said. "If you think I had
something to do with it come right out and say so."

"No, wait, Meat," Matthew broke in, horrified. Everyone
looked at him in surprise—these were the first words he'd spoken

since we arrived. "Shelley wasn't saying you did it. Tell him you weren't saying that, Shelley. Please tell him."

Shelley didn't say anything for a moment. Just sat there in his high-backed chair, watching me with his close-set eyes. "I wasn't accusing you," he finally confessed, most sincerely. "I'm sorry if that's how it sounded. I'm just kind of upset right now."

"I understand," I said. And I meant it. Because I realized exactly what Shelley realized—somebody in this room was involved. Only who? And why? Was it to get back at Pennyroyal? Maybe so. But there was a heavy downside to such sweet revenge —escalation. The more the war between her and Matthew heated up, the less likely it was that they'd ever patch it up. Which made the future for Bedford Falls look even iffier. Then again, maybe that was the whole idea. Maybe someone in the family *wanted* to see the studio fall. But why? What possible reason could they have? I turned to Shadow and said, "Did anyone come onto the lot after midnight last night?"

"Yessir," he replied. "You did."

"Besides me."

"The Shadow seen nobody," he replied.

"Any messengers? Delivery boys?"

"Nobody."

"Did you leave the gate at any time?"

"Only to conduct some personal business," he replied. "And I had someone else spell me. Nobody came through. It was a quiet night. Damned hot."

"Who else besides the family was here?"

Shadow scratched his chin with a thick finger. "The security men. The Shadow can vouch for all of them . . . A comedy team writing late on that witch sitcom. They be around pretty often . . . Also a film producer who was brushing up on a little late-night business with his secretary, if you know what I'm talking about. Man's won two damned Oscars. Don't know why he can't rent that poor girl a furnished room with a hot plate somewheres."

"And no one came through the gate until the workers arrived this morning?" I asked him.

"That's right," Shadow affirmed. "Except for Shelley, that is."

"At seven-thirty," I said, nodding. "We ran into him when we were leaving."

"No, this was before that," said Shadow. "About six."

"You were here earlier?" I asked Shelley.

"Well, yeah," he replied sheepishly. "We swung by to pick up my car on the way home from the airport. I left it here while we were in New York. I followed Shelley and the kids up to the house and took a shower and then I came back."

"All you did was pick up your car? You didn't come inside?"

"Not me," he said. "Shelley came upstairs. But just for a second."

"Upstairs where?"

"Here, to use my john. She doesn't like public lavatories. A thing she has."

"Ever since she was a little girl," confirmed Bunny. "She'd hold it in for hours until she—"

"Did she know where you kept the negatives?" I asked Shelley.

"Wait one second, Hoagy," he said angrily. "You're not trying to say my wife had anything to do with this, are you?"

"I am not," I said. "Just exploring the possibilities."

Shadow cleared his throat. "If I may explore another one . . ."

"Go ahead, Shadow," said Shelley.

"We do have good security, sir, like you said. But it ain't like we're some kind of strategic military installation. We're mostly set up to protect against people making off with our stuff. The cameras and sound equipment, props, office machines. They need a car for that—that's why we funnel all our traffic through the one gate. But if somebody genuinely wants to get on this or any other film lot undetected, he can do it. Under the fence. Through the fence. There are bound to be soft spots. Local kids, they sneak onto the lot all the time, fool around in Homewood, drink their beer. We chase 'em off, plug up the hole, they just find another one. There's no stopping 'em."

"Shadow's right," Matthew agreed. "I used to get onto the Panorama lot all the time when I was in high school, and they had great security there."

I tugged at my ear. "If someone knew this lot well, Shadow, would they know where those soft spots are? A former employee, perhaps?"

"Possibly, sir."

"Who do you have in mind?" Shelley asked me.

"I can think of two former employees right off," I said. "There's Johnny Forget, who has a personal connection with Zorch of the deepest kind, and then there's Pennyroyal herself."

"Not Pennyroyal," said Matthew, dismissing the idea. "She'd have to be crazy."

"I can think of worse words to call her," muttered Bunny.

Matthew rolled his eyes. "C'mon, Ma, you're being ridiculous."

"Am I?" she fumed.

"Johnny Forget," said Shelley, mulling it over. "Interesting . . ." He shook his finger at me. "You think a lot like a lawyer, Hoagy."

"I don't deserve that," I snapped. "I really don't."

"I meant it as a compliment," he protested.

"Sorry, my mistake."

"Meat's kind of touchy," explained Matthew.

"I heard that," chimed in Sarge, drily.

"So what do I tell the press?" Shelley wondered aloud.

"Tell them you've launched a full-scale investigation and expect to have results very soon," I suggested. "Which is to say—tell them nothing."

"Sold." Shelley glanced at his watch. "I've got a four-thirty doctor's appointment. I'd better run."

"Getting that wrist looked at?" I inquired.

"My colon," he replied, reddening.

"Shelley had polyps a few years ago," disclosed Bunny. "Benign, thank God, but he has to be checked regularly. I have a hair appointment myself," she added, taking to her feet.

"Want me to drop you there, Bun?" Shelley asked his mother-in-law.

"Thank you, no," she replied. "I have a number of other stops to make—it isn't easy keeping food in the house when there's a growing boy around." She smoothed Matthew's hair lovingly, carefully avoiding his bald patch. "Not to mention a little girl." She made kissy noises at Lulu, who moaned softly under me. "She gets to have my tuna surprise tonight," Bunny announced. "It's Sarah and Benjamin's favorite."

The moan was louder now.

"We'll have to take a rain check," I said.

"You're not coming over for dinner?" asked Shelley.

"Can't. Sorry."

Lulu rubbed my foot gratefully with her head. She hadn't done that since the time I first introduced her to caviar.

"How about stopping by for dessert?" pressed Shelley.

"I'll try."

"Wonderful," exclaimed Bunny. "I'll save her some leftovers."

She bustled out, charm bracelet clanging, followed closely by Shelley. Matthew slowly got up and went into his office, shutting the door softly behind him. Sarge watched him, her brow furrowed with concern. Then she sprang up from the floor and strode out the door to her own office.

"There goes one fine-looking woman," observed Shadow wistfully.

"Little young for you, isn't she?" I asked, grinning at him.

He yawned and knuckled his eyes. "Man's got to have his fantasies."

"That he does. I understand she has a fiancé in jail."

Shadow made a face. "He's trash. Don't give a damn about her. She don't love him no more herself. No, sir, there's only one man for Charmaine. Woman don't show a man that kind of devotion without she loves him."

"Does he know?"

He showed me his gold tooth. "She don't even know it herself."

"Then how do you know?"

"The Shadow knows plenty," he replied. "What he don't know is why Mr. Shelley won't bring the police in on this. It's robbery, plain and simple."

"There are two possibilities. One is that he's afraid of the press, like he said."

"And what's the other?" Shadow asked.

"That he knows more about who took Pennyroyal's negatives than he's letting on."

He thought this one over, nodding to himself. "He was wrong about you."

"Was he?"

"You don't think like no lawyer at all. You think more like a man who's been directing his feet to the shady side of the street."

"That can't be helped, I'm afraid," I told him. "The fancier the address the shadier the street. Ask any realtor."

• • •

Abel Zorch's street had plenty of shade.

He lived on Hazen Drive up in the hills north of Sunset off Coldwater Canyon. Cherokee, a steep, winding road, got me there. Lulu rode next to me in the Vette with her shades on, feeling somewhat better after lapping up an Alka-Seltzer. The air was a little cooler and a lot less smoggy up in the hills. It was dusk.

Hazen was narrow and quiet, the houses the usual jarring mix of new and old, gaudy and gaudier. Most were set back from the road behind walls with remote-controlled iron gates. None were small. None would fetch less than two million, no matter what the economy was doing. The entertainment business constantly generates new millionaires. And discards old ones. Zorch's was a fine example of the early mishigothic style of architecture, complete with turrets, stained glass windows, and ivy-covered walls. A cream-colored Rolls Corniche convertible was idling there outside the gate with its top down, unoccupied. His. The man certainly got good service—he already had his new windshield. The driver's door was open. The gate was closed. Zorch was nowhere in sight. I idled there in the road, waiting for him to return. A car came up behind me, wanting to get by. I swung around next to the Rolls in the apron of the driveway so it could, and that's when I saw him.

He was there on the pavement next to the intercom box set in the wall. On his back, staring up at the sky. He'd been shot twice, once in the forehead, once in the groin. For some reason, he had bled very little. Maybe that's just how reptiles are. I got out and went over to him and discovered the Rolls was not unoccupied. Geoffrey with a G lay sprawled across the front seat, minus one side of his head. He had bled a lot. The blood was quite fresh. It had just happened. I found myself unable to move for a second. All I could do was stand there and stare. Slowly, I backed away from the Rolls and got my battered silver flask of calvados out of the glove compartment of the Vette. I drank deeply from it, Lulu whimpering softly next to me. I bent down and stroked her, wondering what Abel Zorch had been so anxious to talk to me about. It was vital, he said. Vital. I took another drink and put the flask away. Then I went for help.

# Chapter Six

L amp didn't notice me there at first. Zorch and Geoffrey with a G hogged his immediate attention. Dead bodies will do that. He stood huddled over Zorch's with three uniforms, asking questions and giving orders. A fourth uniform quizzed the young, muscular Filipino houseboy who had been inside when it happened, and was now standing next to the Rolls, weeping. I lounged across the street against the Vette, arms folded, watching. It wasn't until Lamp pulled aside two of the uniforms and told them to canvass the neighbors that he noticed me there. First he did a startled double take. Then he grinned and waved me over. Lulu came, too.

"Read any good books lately, Lieutenant?" I asked, as I strolled across to him.

"Only when you write them, Hoagy," he exclaimed, pumping my hand vigorously. "Cheese and crackers, it's good to see you." He bent over and scratched Lulu's ears. "And you, too, little gal."

Lieutenant Emil Lamp of the Los Angeles Police Department had handled the trouble when I'd been in town before. He specialized in the big-time show-biz killings. He happened to be uncommonly good at not stepping on famous toes. He happened to be uncommonly good, period. Sharp, determined, thorough, and unfailingly polite. And he couldn't have been more unlikely looking. He was a fresh-scrubbed, bright-eyed, and bushy-tailed little guy with neat blond hair and apple cheeks. He looked like Howdy Doody. He had on a no-iron khaki suit, white button down oxford shirt, striped tie, and nubucks with red rubber soles. "When the heck did you get into town?" he asked brightly.

"Yesterday."

"And already two people are dead." Lamp shook his head in amazement. "I read in the paper you were out here working for Matthew Wax. You could have called me, you unfriendly so-and-so. I'd have bought you a beer."

"They'll sell you beer now?"

"Heck, yeah." He grinned and winked at me. "I have a fake ID."

"Well, I would have called you, Lieutenant, but I had a feeling we'd just bump into each other anyway."

The grin left his lips immediately. He looked over at the bodies. A cop was photographing them now. "What do you know about it?"

"We had a six-thirty appointment to meet here. I just missed whoever did it."

"You didn't notice anybody flying down the hill on your way up, did you?"

"I did not."

At my feet, Lulu whined anxiously for our attention. When she got it, she barked twice.

"Why is she doing that?" asked Lamp curiously.

She barked twice more. Louder.

"Ignore her, Lieutenant. She's just doing her imitation of Jerry Lee, the crime-solving star of *K-9*. Next she'll try to knock you flat on your back and sniff your person for drugs. I was hoping she was over this."

"Maybe she knows something," Lamp suggested eagerly.

"She doesn't. Trust me."

I advised her to shut up. She snuffled and skulked back to the Vette, miffed.

Lamp walked out into the street and faced the Rolls, playing the angles. "They must have fired the shots from their car, then taken off."

"Have to be a pretty good shot, wouldn't they?"

"Fair, certainly."

"Care to guess what they used?"

"I don't like to guess."

"I remember."

He rubbed his smooth chin thoughtfully. "Offhand, though, I'd say it was a Glock nine-millimeter semiautomatic pistol."

"You can tell by the wounds?"

"Partly." He grinned at me. "And one of my colleagues found the murder weapon in the ivy over by the wall."

"Why leave it behind?"

"Why not? Better than being caught with it. Guns are awful easy to come by these days. Easy as scoring a joint."

"The Glock's a popular weapon, I understand."

"Very. Austrian-made. Fires rapidly, accurately, clip holds up to seventeen rounds. Half the P.D.'s in the country use them now instead of the old six-shooter." He opened his coat to reveal the Glock that was holstered there.

"Any chance you'll be able to trace it?"

"There's always a chance," he said doubtfully. "You know, this would be a really good opportunity, Hoagy."

"For what, Lieutenant?"

"For you to confess. Save all of us a lot of trouble, and the taxpayers a lot of their hard-earned money. I'll get you in the end. You know it and I know it. So why don't you just get it off of your chest? You'll get a fair deal from me."

I stared at him. He stared back at me.

"Sorry, Lieutenant. I didn't do it."

He kicked the pavement. "Nerts. You know that speech has *never* worked? Not once?"

"Cheer up, Lieutenant. Maybe you'll get lucky some day."

"Hope I didn't offend you, Hoagy. I had to take a shot."

"Of course you did. No offense taken."

"I know very little about the boyfriend, Geoffrey Brand. Abel Zorch I'm plenty familiar with. Any idea who would want him dead?"

"You mean other than my employer?"

"That thought had crossed my mind," he admitted.

"Lots of people. Abel Zorch had a gift for making enemies."

He glanced at his watch. "Something tells me I'll get more out of having dinner with you than by hanging around here."

"You'll certainly get fed. Chuy's okay?"

"Meet you down there as soon as I can."

I got back in the Vette and started it up, Lulu glowering at me from the passenger seat.

"Great car, Hoagy," observed Lamp, admiring it. "You always know how to live, don't you?"

"Oh, yeah. I've discovered the meaning of life, all right."

We heard the vans before we saw them. The TV news crews —one after another of them roaring up the hill toward the scene of the crime. They pulled up with a screech behind the police cars, next to the police cars, wherever they could. Reporters and cameramen hopped out, jabbering excitedly.

Lamp's face dropped. "Nerts. I hate these guys."

"And they say such nice things about you. Straighten your tie and smile, Lieutenant. It's showtime."

"Nerts."

I got out of there before they'd completely blocked the road.

Chuy's hadn't changed. The decor, mostly plastic potted plants and gaily colored tissue paper, looked like it all came free with a tankful of gas. But Chuy's mom was still there, cranking out those fresh, hot corn tortillas, one by one. I was on my second basket of them and my third bottle of iced Dos Equis when Lamp came bounding in. He sat down across from me and ordered an iced tea. We both went for the chile rellenos.

"I read your second novel over the summer, Hoagy," he informed me, tasting his iced tea. "I thought it was a good job. A real insightful look at a marriage gone sour."

"Why, thank you, Lieutenant."

"How are you and Merilee getting along these days?"

"Couldn't be better. She's fine, I'm fine, we're both—"

"Cheese and crackers, Hoagy," he fumed. "I thought we were friends."

I sipped my beer. "I haven't the slightest idea how she is."

"I'm awful sorry to hear that," he said gently.

"That makes two of us."

Lulu grumbled at me from under the table.

"Correction—three of us. What have you got so far?"

He opened a small notepad and examined it. "Zorch's house-boy, name of Kenji, was very tight-lipped. But he did suggest we may have ourselves a lover scorned."

"You certainly may."

"Seems that Zorch's new friend, Geoffrey Brand, broke it off recently with a bad apple, name of Darren Dust. Big-time art dealer and honorary chairperson of the Westside Little Boys in Handcuffs League. We've had him in twice for aggravated assault. Nothing's ever stuck, though. Seems he and Geoffrey were living together until a couple of weeks ago, when Geoffrey dumped him for Zorch. Zorch did take one right in the groin, which tends to suggest a crime of sexual orientation," he concluded primly. "You already knew about Darren?"

"I did not."

"Then how come when I said, 'We may have ourselves a lover scorned,' you said, 'You certainly may'?"

"I was approaching it from the other end, so to speak."

"You mean Zorch's ex, Johnny Forget?"

I nodded.

"Another neat fit," Lamp acknowledged, chomping on an ice cube. "Has a history of wigging out—tried to kill his own mother last year. According to Kenji he was extremely upset about Zorch taking up with Geoffrey. Even went so far as to shoot out the windows of Zorch's Rolls last night in the Spago parking lot."

"I was there."

He chuckled. "Same old Hoagy. How is it that you're always around when the doo-doo comes down?"

"Near as I can tell, it's a rare combination of good breeding and bad luck."

Our dinners arrived. The chile rellenos were even better than I remembered.

"Think Johnny could have shot them?" asked Lamp, as we attacked them.

"He certainly has a child's capacity for anger," I replied. "But he's not what I'd call overly swift. I'm not sure he could plan something like this."

"What's to plan?" wondered Lamp. "Nice, quiet street. Very little traffic, houses set way back from the road. He waits. He plugs them. He flees."

"I came up Coldwater," I said, "then took Cherokee to Hazen. Is there another way in and out?"

"Alto Cedro. Comes into Hazen just before the top of the hill. Twists around into Loma Vista, which goes down through Trousdale to Sunset. He could have taken off that way and you wouldn't have seen him."

"No one heard the shots?"

"Kenji claims he didn't. He had the air-conditioning on, and a gardener was mowing the lawn next door at the time it happened. I don't know about the other neighbors yet." He dabbed at his mouth with his napkin. "High-powered street, Hazen. Zorch's pal lives right at the top of the hill. Must have some view of the Valley from up there."

"Which pal is that?"

"Norbert Schlom. He drove by on his way home after you left. Saw all of the commotion. Got very upset when he found out what happened."

"Was Mrs. Schlom home at the time?"

"I don't know yet. Why?"

"Just curious."

"What else can you tell me, Hoagy?" Lamp asked. "What do you know?"

"I know Johnny wasn't the only one who had it out with Zorch last night at Spago. Trace Washburn did, too. It seems that Schlom has been sitting on Trace's career, and Zorch could have fixed it for him but wouldn't. They didn't like each other very well. Pennyroyal Brim had words with the man as well. She was none too happy about the way he was handling things. The fanfare, the frenzy. And that was *before* her nude shots leaked out this morning."

"I heard about that on the radio," Lamp acknowledged. "Surprised the heck out of me. Imagine a girl like her ever posing that way. I mean, golly . . ." He got a dreamy look on his face, his eyes aglitter. "She's so pretty and sweet and . . ."

"Why, Lieutenant, if I didn't know you better I'd swear you have the tiniest crush on her."

"No, it's not like that," he said hastily, reddening. "I just . . . well, she's awful attractive, don't you think?"

"Does your mom know you're starting to take an interest in girls?"

"Long as I'm home by eleven it's okay with her," he replied, grinning. "What's Penny like?"

"She's an actress like any other. What you see is what you don't get. She's awfully confused right now. Needs a nice, stable career guy with a good pension to take care of her. You'd make an awfully cute couple, you know."

"Cut it out, will ya?" he objected.

"Sorry, Lieutenant."

"You don't honestly think *she* killed Zorch and Geoffrey, do you?" he wondered.

"I don't know. But I do think it was carefully planned."

Lamp frowned. "Planned how?"

"Why did Zorch stop his car there outside the gate and get out?"

"I wondered about that myself. It wasn't to get the mail—Kenji picks that up about noon. I figured he got out to talk to his killer. I figure they had words before he and Geoffrey got plugged."

"He never opened the gate. Why not?"

"Maybe he didn't want them coming in."

"Or maybe he couldn't get in himself," I suggested. "Maybe Zorch had to get out of the car so he could ring Kenji to open the gate for him. He'd make a perfect target that way, stuck out there in front of that closed gate."

"True," said Lamp. "Except there's a remote control to the gate right there in the Rolls."

"Is it functioning?"

"Haven't tested it," he replied. "Left it for the lab people."

"I wouldn't be surprised if it's been tampered with. Removing the battery would be the simplest way. The only problem with that theory," I admitted, cleaning my plate, "is that the Rolls was in the shop today getting new windows."

"Kenji said the Rolls-Royce agency picked it up early this morning. They provided a chauffeur-driven limo to take Zorch to his office."

"Nice service."

"They ought to provide nice service, the prices they get for those cars. After they fixed it they left it for him in the parking lot of his office building in Century City."

"What time?"

"I don't know. I can find out, if any of this plays." He mulled it over. "They'd have to go to his office garage and disarm the remote. Then go up to his place to wait for him. But it's a possibility. Of course, a lot of things are possibilities at this stage. It could have been random violence. An aborted break-in attempt, a drive-by shooting. We get a lot of those now, even in the best neighborhoods."

"Think that's what it was?"

"No, I don't," he confessed. "Not with it going down the same day as this *Enquirer* business. Zorch was behind that?"

"Shelley Selden seems to think so. I'm not sure. Zorch was a sleaze, but he wasn't dumb. He told me last night that the Murakami people had been leaning on him to cool it. They hate all of this publicity. Might even pull out. He and Schlom seemed genuinely nervous about it. And Zorch definitely sounded nervous on the phone this afternoon."

Our waiter cleared our plates. We ordered coffee.

"I'd love to find out who the *Enquirer* did get them from," muttered Lamp, scratching his chin thoughtfully. "But the press gets real mulish about revealing stuff like that to the police. Heck, they'd go to jail before they'd tell me."

The waiter returned with our coffee, and to tell Lamp there was a phone call for him. He headed off eagerly to take it. He was positively beaming when he came back a few moments later.

"Chalk up one for you, Hoagy," he reported, as he sat. "The remote in Zorch's Rolls was indeed nonfunctioning—no battery. You're getting pretty darned good at this."

"Why, thank you, Lieutenant."

"Just for that you get a prompt, courteous reply to your question—Norbert Schlom's wife, Toy, *was* home at the time Abel Zorch and Geoffrey Brand were shot. Would you believe the Schloms have a fake squad car parked outside their house twenty-four hours a day? He borrowed it from one of the cop shows his studio does. Keeps it there to ward off burglars."

"Can he do that?"

"He's doing it." Lamp consulted his notepad. "Mrs. Schlom says she heard nothing. Her maid and gardener didn't hear anything either. One neighbor down the block thought she might have heard several pops, but she said the canyons are always playing tricks with sounds, so she ignored it." He grinned at me expectantly. There was more.

I tugged at my ear. "A little something else, Lieutenant?"

"A big something else—housekeeper directly across the street from Zorch's has noticed a certain *poco* lurking outside his place off and on for the past several days. She considered calling the police, until she recognized him as *Yonny Forhay*, the famous American movie actor. Did you know Johnny's even bigger in Guatemala than he is here?"

"No, I didn't."

"She said he rides a motorcycle. Big, white one."

"It's a Harley Fat Boy. She saw him today?"

Lamp nodded. "Sitting out there on his bike at about a quarter to six—maybe half an hour before the shooting."

"What was he doing?"

"Smoking a cigarette."

"Did she see him leave?"

"Nope."

"Did she witness the shooting?"

"Nope. But you've got to admit that Johnny looks good for it now. Sure wasn't bright of him to let himself be seen that way."

"Like I said, he's not totally *there*."

"Apparently he's *there* enough to figure out how to take the battery out of a remote."

"Apparently." I thought this over. "So that explains it . . ."

Lamp frowned. "Explains what, Hoagy?"

"The fuss Lulu was making. She smelled Johnny's Patchouli."

"She smelled his what?"

"His cologne. That's what she was trying to tell us."

Lulu sat up and yapped at me. She was waiting for some kind of appreciation.

"Good work, Lulu," I said, patting her. "You were right. I was wrong. I apologize for doubting your sincerity."

That wasn't enough. She barked. People turned to look at her.

"Very good, Lulu. Good girl."

She barked again, her big one. Water glasses shook.

"You can stop now, Lulu."

She wouldn't stop. Not until I'd promised her a certain treat. And told her that if she didn't shut up she'd get nothing but Bunny's cooking for the rest of our stay. That did the trick.

"Any idea where we can find young Johnny?" Lamp inquired.

"He's into spontaneous."

"He's into real trouble, is what he is. Any of the Bedford Falls people know where he is, they'd be wise to help us. They'll be helping him in the long run. Because we *will* find him." He cleared his throat uneasily. "I like you, Hoagy. It's real nice to see you again. But I'd be fibbing if I told you I was happy to have you here in the middle of this."

"Whatever do you mean, Lieutenant?"

"I mean you played it a little too close to the vest last time."

"I seldom wear a vest."

"You put your celebrity's interests ahead of the law's. I understood. I forgave. But try to be a little more open with me this time, okay?"

"I've been totally open with you so far."

"And if I end up having to squeeze your man?"

I drained my coffee and called for the check. "Good luck."

"With what?" he demanded.

"Finding Johnny, of course. What did you think I meant?"

"Gosh knows," he fumed. "I don't know what you mean half the time."

"Don't let it get you down, Lieutenant. I don't know either."


"He didn't do it, Meat. Johnny didn't do it."

"How do you know, Matthew?"

We were sitting in the Seldens' den. We were not alone. Sarah sat on the floor at Uncle Matty's big feet, chomping on popcorn. Benjamin snuggled in Uncle Matty's lap, chomping on his own left thumb. They were watching a tape of their all-time favorite movie on the big screen TV, Uncle Matty's *Dennis the Dinosaur*. The scene where Dennis meets up with Theotis, the jungle bully. Danny De Vito provided his voice.

"How do you know, Matthew?" I repeated.

"I just do," he said stubbornly.

"I'm afraid that won't be good enough."

The press had already started calling. Shelley was on the phone right now in his study with an *L.A. Times* reporter. Lamp had called, too, urging the family to cooperate if Johnny contacted them. Shelley had assured him they would.

The two Shelleys lived in a vast, pueblo-style hacienda tucked into a rural pocket of Brentwood north of San Vicente, by way of Santa Fe. The walls and ceilings were rough, textured stucco, the beams exposed, the floors Spanish quarry tile, the furniture heavy antique Spanish colonial. No shortage of Indian artifacts. Navajo rugs, wall hangings, patterned pillows, and brightly colored ceramic plates were on display everywhere.

There were Zuni totems of stylish rusted iron. There were cacti. There were hand-woven baskets. It was all a bit much, but it was airy and cool. The ceiling fans helped.

"I know Johnny didn't do it," Matthew insisted, "because Johnny was with me when the police say it happened. We were together from maybe six until a little before seven."

"You were?"

"We were."

"Where?"

Before he could answer me, Bunny came bustling out from the kitchen with pound cake and dessert plates. "Later," Matthew whispered.

Sarge followed with a trayful of coffee cups. Mrs. Shelley had the coffee. On the TV, Dennis and Theotis were throwing rocks at each other.

"I'm worried about you, Matty," Bunny fretted, handing him his cake. "You hardly touched your tuna surprise."

"I'm fine, Ma," he said, looking around for a fork.

Sarge was there with one instantly. Sarge was always there.

"There's plenty of it left, Hoagy," Bunny informed me. "You sure Lulu won't have any?"

Lulu gazed at me imploringly from her perch by the screen door to the courtyard.

"Thanks, but she had a big dinner," I replied. To Matthew I said, "If Johnny didn't do it, he should turn himself in."

"He's right, Matthew," Mr. Shelley said, appearing in the doorway. "Hoagy's absolutely right."

"He can't," contended Matthew. "He's totally terrified of the law. He can't handle them."

"He won't have to," Sarge pointed out. "That's what they got lawyers for."

"Where is he now?" I asked Matthew.

"I don't know, and I wouldn't tell you if I did," he replied petulantly.

"Matthew," said Mr. Shelley sternly. "If Johnny's innocent, he has nothing to fear. But if he stays on the run, he'll just be hurting himself. The publicity alone will—"

"They'll railroad him," Matthew blurted out. "They won't believe him. Or me. They'll say I'm covering up for him."

"Are you?" Mrs. Shelley asked him.

"No!"

"What were the two of you doing, kid?" Mr. Shelley asked him gently.

Matthew shot a nervous glance over at Bunny. "Talking," he mumbled.

"About what?" he asked.

Matthew shrugged. "Stuff."

"And you really haven't heard from him since the murder?" he persisted.

"I haven't heard from him!"

"You will," I advised. "Just as soon as he finds out he's a wanted man."

Mr. Shelley went over to Matthew and laid a hand on his shoulder. "When you do, tell him to turn himself in. Will you do that?"

"I can't make him," Matthew declared. "And I won't." He dove into his cake, the matter closed as far as he was concerned.

The two Shelleys exchanged a look of frustration. She gestured for him to join her on the sofa. He did, sitting heavily.

"You were with Johnny until when?" I asked Matthew.

"I already told you," Matthew replied coldly, cramming a huge forkful of cake in his mouth. "A little before seven. I got here about a quarter after."

"Does that sound about right?" I asked Mrs. Shelley.

"I wouldn't know," she replied. "Matthew was the first one here. I was still out with the kids. Twinkle and Sarge and Mom hadn't gotten here either."

"The traffic was murder tonight," said Bunny. "Absolute murder."

"Was your housekeeper here?" I asked Mrs. Shelley.

"We don't have one," she replied. "Just a woman who comes in two days a week to clean. Today wasn't one of them."

"She's all alone now," Matthew said softly, almost to himself. "Penny's all alone. What'll she do?"

"Land on her feet like any alley cat would," sniffed Bunny.

"C'mon, Ma," protested Matthew. "Enough already, will ya?"

"Excuse me," she said curtly. "I didn't mean to interfere."

"What do you want me to say?" Matthew demanded, raising his voice at her. "You want me to say I shouldn't have married her? You want me to say I blew it? Huh? What do you want?"

"I want you to be happy," she said quietly.

"I'm happy, okay? I'm very, very happy!"

"Someone'll find her another lawyer," Mr. Shelley broke in. "Either Schlom or HWA will step in and help her."

"I hate to sound like some sort of ghoul," said Sarge, "but don't this help our cause—Zorch being taken out of the game?"

"No question about it," Shelley acknowledged. "Whoever she hires *won't* be Zorch, and that's a godsend." He shifted uncomfortably on the sofa. "But I know what you mean—I hate to say it, too."

"She must be feeling awfully alone right now," said Matthew, his voice quavering.

"Why don't you call her up?" I suggested.

Mr. Shelley gave me a conspiratorial wink. "Yeah, go ahead and use the phone in my study, kid. I'm sure she'd love to hear from you."

"No, I couldn't." Matthew's voice was choked with emotion. "God, this is Georgie's favorite scene." His eyes were on the TV. The scene where Dennis meets Theotis's kid sister, Althea (voice by Winona Ryder), and falls hopelessly in love with her. I didn't know six-month-old babies could have favorite movie scenes, but there's a lot I don't know about babies. And don't ever intend to find out.

Benjamin began wriggling around in Matthew's lap, his face all scrunched. Matthew noticed, and made a face of his own. "Uh . . . Sis?"

She immediately tensed. "Okay, it's fire drill time."

Mr. Shelley tensed, too. "Right. What do we do?"

"Act relaxed, most importantly," she replied. "It has to seem like a fun thing."

"Fun. Right."

I glanced curiously at Sarge.

"Master Benjamin is experiencing a small difficulty making his transish to big-boy pants," she explained.

"He won't go," confessed Mrs. Shelley. "That's where I was tonight—we had a late appointment with his child psychologist."

Little Sarah made a face. "Ugh. Benjamin smells, Mommy!"

Benjamin began to wail.

Lulu was nowhere to be seen now.

"Now, Sarah," Mrs. Shelley said with forced patience. "Benjamin is your brother and we all love him, just like we all

love you. And if he has a problem we all have a problem together."

"But Mommy, he smells like *poopy!*" she wailed loudly,
though not nearly as loudly as her brother.

"Okay, here we go, big guy," said Mr. Shelley, scooping Benjamin up out of Matthew's lap. "And the operative word here is
*go.*"

"Remember, Twinkle," cautioned Mrs. Shelley. "Relaxed."

"Right." Grimly, father and son trudged off down the hall.

Lulu was still nowhere to be seen.

"Well, Hoagy, I guess you officially qualify as family now,"
said Mrs. Shelley with a chuckle.

I tugged at my ear. "Anything else I should know about?"

"There's more coffee in the kitchen," she offered, getting to
her feet. "How's that?"

"Sounds good. I'll help you."

The kitchen wasn't lacking for counter space. They were
topped with orange and blue Spanish tile. The cupboards were
pickled pine. There was a central work island with a sink and
chopping block. A set of copper pots and pans hung from the
ceiling over it. The stove was a mammoth cast iron four-oven
AGA, blue. Glass doors opened onto the courtyard.

"I guess this won't exactly encourage you to have kids of
your own," Mrs. Shelley ventured wryly.

"Possibly not."

She poured both of us more coffee. "In quiet moments you
do find yourself strangely drawn to them. It's just that there
aren't many quiet moments. Milk?"

"This is fine."

There were stools. I sat on one, so I wouldn't tower over her.
Shelley leaned against the counter, ankles crossed, and sipped
her coffee. She was wearing a coral silk T-shirt, white linen
slacks, and deerskin moccasins. I was struck, once again, by her
comfortable plumpness and warmth. She seemed happy to be
who she was. I so seldom meet people who are.

"Matthew is very pleased with you. He said you're really
helping him get in touch with himself." She laughed. "It didn't
sound quite so seventies when he said it—words to that effect."

"You can be a big help, Shelley."

"Me?" She seemed surprised. Flattered, too. "What can I
do?"

"Fill in a few blanks."

"I'd be happy to, if I can. Like what?"

"Did you do it on purpose?" I asked.

"Did I do what on purpose?"

"Forget him at kindergarten that day."

She ducked her head in defeat. "I honestly can't believe it. He's made such a big thing of that all these years. He even put it in *Dennis*. It makes me feel like the biggest meanie on earth."

"Evidently it made quite an impression on him."

"All I wanted to do was have some fun," she recalled. "Be with my friends, go where they were going. Matthew was my twerpy kid brother. I always had to be responsible for him, since Mom worked. One day I acted up. You know how kids are. But, really, it was nothing personal."

"Was it personal with your father?"

Her dark eyes flashed at me. "You get right to it, don't you?"

"I try to. Why was he good to you and not Matthew?"

She sipped her coffee. "Matthew is somewhat self-centered, as I've found most creative people tend to be. The truth is, Dad wasn't particularly nice to me either. He was just a little less obvious about it, maybe because I was a girl. Dad was a frustrated, unfulfilled man. A failure. It suited him to blame it on us. He insisted he would have made it big if only he hadn't been tied down by a family. A cop-out, but he believed it. He certainly said it enough times."

"Matthew thinks your father hated him."

"Dad hated everyone, Hoagy."

"There wasn't anything special about the way he treated Matthew?"

"There really wasn't, believe me. You might try talking to Mom. Maybe she can shed some more light on it. I never really understood the man myself." She looked up. Her pudgy husband and son were standing in the kitchen doorway, hand in hand. "Well, how did it go?" she asked, smiling at them.

Mr. Shelley smiled back. "Go in and say good night to Grandma, Ben."

The kid toddled off.

"Zilch," Mr. Shelley informed his wife miserably. "He got all tensed up and wouldn't go."

She rolled her eyes in frustration. "I can't stand this anymore."

"Didn't the shrink have *anything* else to suggest?"

"Just patience."

"And for that we pay him a hundred dollars an hour?"

"No, for that we pay him a hundred dollars a half hour," she replied.

"You could try doing what they do at the Four Seasons," I suggested.

They looked at me blankly.

"What's that, Hoagy?" he asked.

"Put a TV in there."

He held out his hands, palms up. "Hey, I'm willing to try anything at this point."

"The bathroom's not wired for cable," she pointed out.

"So we'll wire it. Get the Z Channel. Get Disney. Put one of the damned VCRs in there, too, so he can watch *Dennis*. What the hell." He puffed out his cheeks wearily, then frowned at us. "What's going on in here, anyway? You trying to steal my wife, Hoagy?"

"He's interviewing me, Twinkle," she said proudly. "Just like a real celebrity."

"I'd better leave you to it." He started out.

"Twinkle?"

"Yeah, Cookie?"

"Will Matthew have to make a different movie now? If Johnny's in trouble, I mean."

He lowered his voice. "I don't know," he said gravely. "But I'll tell you the God's honest truth, for our ears only. That would be something of a godsend, too. Not that I want to see Johnny thrown in jail, mind you."

"Matthew will be destroyed if he is," she said.

"I don't think Johnny will fare too well either," I said.

"Hey, I got my own goddamned problems," he snapped, with unexpected vehemence. "And that toxic little turd isn't one of them. Screw him!" With that he left us. I watched him go, wondering just how much more anger was simmering away under his jovial surface.

"What else can I tell you, Hoagy?" Mrs. Shelley asked, unfazed by her husband's outburst. "Not that I've told you anything so far."

"You're doing fine," I assured her. "Matthew got very resistant when we started talking about his days on the Monroe High basketball team. He told me he quit, but I hit a stone wall when I asked him why."

She nodded pensively. "I remember that he refused to tell any of us why. Shelley was quite concerned, since Matthew had worked so hard to make the team, and was so proud he had. Shelley even called the coach to find out what had happened, but he didn't know anything either. He thought Matthew was enjoying the team. He was by no means a star athlete, but he was contributing, making friends with the other boys . . . Until he just walked in one day and quit. Never went back. Never mentioned any of those boys again. Or her, for that matter."

I leaned forward. "Her?" I said carefully.

"He didn't tell you about Mona Schaffer?"

"He denied there was anyone."

"Well, that's basically true. But it's not the whole story."

"I'd like to hear it."

She hesitated, nibbling on her lower lip. "If you don't mind, I think I'll show you something first."

She headed off down the hall. Lulu resurfaced, ambled over to the fridge, and sat there, staring at it. She wanted the treat I'd promised her.

Shelley returned in a moment clutching a high school yearbook. "Is she hungry?" she asked, noticing Lulu.

"She wants a treat."

"I don't have any dog biscuits, I'm afraid."

"That's not the kind of treat she has in mind."

"What kind of treat does she—?"

"An anchovy. Chilled, preferably. Have you any in there?"

"I think so," she said, eyeing Lulu with bemusement and, well, revulsion. "Shall I give it to her?"

"Better let me—you might lose a finger."

I found the jar in the door and dropped a filet Lulu's way. She snapped her jaws on it like Shamu the killer whale, then stretched out contentedly. I sat back down at the counter while Shelley leafed through the Monroe High yearbook. It gave off the same musty smell that all old yearbooks do. And it had that same gallery of stiff portraits in it, too, everyone looking frozen and lacquered and geeky. Particularly Matthew. Actually, he didn't look much different than he did now. I think he was even wearing the same pair of glasses.

"Schaffer, Mona . . . Here she is." Shelley pushed the book toward me so I could get a good look.

It was a photo of Pennyroyal Brim.

Same innocent baby's eyes. Same snub nose. Same dimples. Same blond hair. It was Pennyroyal Brim, America's sweetie pie. Except it wasn't.

"Mona was the Miss Everything of Matthew's class," Shelley recalled. "Head cheerleader. Homecoming queen. She was the girl of Matthew's dreams. He absolutely worshiped her. She was the reason he joined the team. I think he somehow hoped he would win her over if he became a star athlete. When it came time to cast the Debbie Dale role in the first *Badger*, he looked at literally hundreds of girls—known actresses, unknowns, fashion models, amateurs . . . even had his casting director scouring high school drama productions up and down the coast. No one was right. He wasn't satisfied. He kept saying, 'I'll know her when I see her.' And then one day Pennyroyal walked in. He hired her on the spot. Because she looked like Mona. Exactly like Mona. I almost fainted when I saw her. She hasn't the slightest idea, in case you're wondering. Shelley and I decided it wouldn't be fair to show her Mona's picture. We thought it would make her feel too weird, what with Matthew searching for her the way he had, and then making her into a star and then marrying her."

"Whatever happened to Mona?"

"I have no idea."

"I wonder if she'll be at his class reunion."

"If she's anything like she used to be, she's probably organizing it. But Matthew will never go."

"He's going," I assured her. "You knew her?"

"I was friends with one of her sisters. She was a nice girl. Awfully pretty. Nothing at all like Debbie Dale. Of course, no one is."

"Are you and Pennyroyal at all close?"

"I can't say we are," she admitted unhappily. "And that's probably my fault. I've always had trouble thinking of her as anything more than this strange *pet* of Matthew's. I mean, she's practically a child. I couldn't believe it when he married her. We did go target shooting together sometimes when she wasn't working."

"Is she a good shot?"

"Adequate. She hits what she aims at. She was always asking me a million questions about what Matthew was like when he was little. She said he'd never tell her anything. I felt uncomfortable talking to her about it. I thought he should be the one, you know? Maybe she thought I was being standoffish. I don't know. We were never close. She's a glamorous young actress. I'm a middle-aged housewife. When she had Georgie I thought that might bring us closer together. But by then, things were turning sour between her and Matthew." She finished her coffee and put her empty cup in the sink. "Would you like me to contact the reunion committee for you? I can find out about Mona."

"That would be great."

She chuckled softly to herself. "God, I wonder what all of those people will do if he actually shows up. When they knew him he was this big, nerdy lunk. Now he's a world-famous director. That would really be something."

"That pistol range you go to," I said, bringing her my cup. "You mentioned that a lot of the other wives shoot there, too."

She nodded. "Canyon Pistol Range. It's up in the hills, just off Sepulveda Boulevard."

"Is Toy Schlom one of them?"

"Toy's an excellent shot. One of the best." She made a face. "No big surprise she can handle a gun, considering her previous line of employment."

"Is she as good as you are?"

"How do you mean?" she asked, raising an eyebrow at me.

"With a gun."

"No, she's not. But . . ." She hesitated.

"But what?"

Shelley Selden's face broke into a wicked smile. "No one's as good as I am."

"Okay, Matthew, it's later."

"What do you mean, Meat?"

We were standing on the two Shelleys' front porch. He was showing me out. It was hushed outside, the night air balmy and smelling of eucalyptus trees.

"You said you'd tell me later where you and Johnny were at the time of the shooting."

"Oh, right. He called me at about a quarter to six from the

Hamburger Hamlet on Sunset and Doheny. Wanted me to meet him there. He sounded really, really upset. He was sobbing. So I did. I got there about six."

"Made pretty good time from Culver City, didn't you?"

"I was in the Batmobile," he replied, as if that were a logical response. Maybe it was, to him.

"I see. Go on."

He glanced furtively at the front door to make sure we were alone. "See, I really hate Ma's tuna surprise. Always have. And I really love their hamburgers. I had two number elevens with extra onions. Ma would kill me if she knew I spoiled my appetite that way. I mean, she's *fierce*. That's why I couldn't say anything to you about it before—she was in the room."

"Jesus Christ, Matthew. You're a grown man. You can eat whatever you want whenever you want."

"Ma doesn't see it that way," he said.

"Then it's up to you to make her see it that way."

"Now you're starting to sound like Pennyroyal," he said sullenly. "She was always getting on me to stand up to her more. She never did understand—your ma is your ma."

"And Johnny?"

"What about him?"

"You were having two number elevens with extra onions. What was he having?"

"Beer. Johnny was drinking beer. Why, don't you believe me?"

We strolled down the front path to the circular driveway, where the Vette was parked along with Sarge's Land Cruiser, Bunny's Jaguar, and Matthew's Batmobile. A rough stucco wall enclosed the front yard. There was an automatic gate, similar to Zorch's.

"If the two of you were at Hamburger Hamlet when the shooting happened then somebody there should be able to back you up," I said.

"Absolutely," he exclaimed. "Johnny's totally in the clear. The hostess recognized him. So did our waitress. They'll vouch for him."

"And for you," I pointed out.

"Why would they need to vouch for me?" he asked, puzzled.

"Did you tell Lieutenant Lamp all of this?"

"Shelley did. They're checking it out. I'm sure Johnny will be cleared. But he's still going to freak if they try to question him. He has this thing about the police. Uniforms, especially. He's totally paranoid." Matthew glanced out the front gate at the street. Something out there seemed to have caught his gaze. I didn't see anything. Just some parked cars. He opened the door of the Vette for me. Lulu hopped in and curled up in her seat. "Know what I like best about you, Meat?"

"I can't even begin to imagine."

"You haven't tried to sell me anything. Everybody's always trying to sell me something. A script, an idea, a gimmick. Even Shelley. You heard him this morning—he wants me to make that stupid comic strip of his into a movie. I've done that stuff already. I keep telling him. You, on the other hand, haven't tried to sell me a thing. How come? Is it because you're an intellectual?"

"Recovering intellectual," I corrected him. "And I want plenty. You'll see."

He studied me thoughtfully. Then grinned and shut the door. "*Vaya con Dios*, Meat."

I started up the Vette. He entered a code in the security panel by the front door. The gate swung open. He waved and went back in the house and I headed out, the gate closing automatically behind me. As I turned onto the street my lights swept across the cars parked there. That's when I saw what had caught Matthew's eye. A black BMW convertible sat there with its top up and Pennyroyal Brim inside of it watching the house. I pulled over and got out and said hi. She said hi back. Whispered it, more precisely—Little Georgie was there next to her in his car seat, fast asleep, his blond locks tousled, a little bubble of saliva forming on his lips. There was something forlorn and touching and terribly sad about her sitting there like that with her baby on this warm October night.

She looked over at him with motherly concern, then grabbed her cigarettes and lighter and got out, closing the car door softly behind her so as not to wake him. We went over to the Vette. She moved lithely in the streetlights, looking like the world's cutest surfer girl in an oversized man's T-shirt with the sleeves turned up, faded blue jeans, and spotless white Keds.

She lit a cigarette and inhaled it deeply. "I don't like to smoke in front of him," she said in her uncommonly husky voice. "The incidental smoke is bad for him."

"Where's Trace?" I asked.

She leaned against the Vette and tossed her golden head, Lulu watching her every move with suspicion. "Cassie needed to interview him some more. She went out to his place in Trancas. I didn't feel like going."

"What have you been up to?"

"Just driving around in the hills with Georgie, thinking. I had to get out of the house. The reporters and everything. I've been driving for hours. He seems to love riding in the car. He drops right off." She puffed on her cigarette.

"I suppose you've had better days."

She laughed her sad laugh. "No shit. Everyone in America is *positive* that I'm a whore now, just in case they had any doubt. I was seventeen years old, Hoagy. A professional photographer with his own studio told me I had to be photographed with all of my clothes off. Standard procedure, he assured me. The casting agents have to know what kind of goods they're buying. What did I know? I was a senior in high school. Christ, it's not as if I did it for money—*I paid him*."

A Miata drove past, its lights illuminating her face. The resemblance to Mona Schaffer was startling.

"How did you get hooked up with Shambazza anyway?"

"Through Toy Schlom." When she caught me staring she said, "Her name was Toy Barbie then. She lived with Shambazza. Recruited girls for him. Me, I actually thought she was a model's agent. God, that was a lifetime ago." She shivered. "Norbert was the one who told me. About Abel, I mean. He reached me on my car phone when he found out. Said he was driving past Abel's house and there was this huge—"

"You were where?"

"Way up near the top of Mandeville Canyon. I almost cracked up my car when he told me. Maybe that's what I should do—drive off a cliff. Then this would all be over . . . *Jesus* . . . Norbert said he'd find me another lawyer. He said everything will work out. I don't know. I don't know what to do anymore. About anything."

"Nobody does," I said. "You do what you have to do. Sometimes things work out all right for you and most of the time they don't."

Her eyes searched my face. "Don't they?"

"In the real world we just live unhappily ever after."

"They said on the radio they were looking for Johnny." She

stubbed her cigarette out on the pavement and sighed wistfully. "The teen fan magazines decided we were an item after the first movie came out. He actually did ask me out once. We went to see Michael Jackson at the Forum. A limo took us. Afterwards, we made out in the back seat. It was like kissing your boyfriend in kindergarten. So sweet and harmless. He turned gay right after that. I sometimes think I was the one who drove him to it. Poor Johnny, he just can't stay out of trouble."

"He didn't do it. He and Matthew were together at the time."

She swallowed, startled. "Then who did?"

"Excellent question. The cop who's on it will find out. He's an old friend. Good man. Major fan of yours, too. Rising star in the department, real cute. Want to meet him?"

"You're busting me, aren't you? Sorry, I guess I'm not much in the mood for jokes right now." She pushed herself up off the Vette and started back to her own car.

"Why don't you go inside?" I asked, glancing at the two Shelleys' house.

She stopped there in the middle of the street. "What makes you think I want to?"

"Wild guess."

She put her hands on her hips. "Maybe I was waiting here for *you*," she suggested provocatively.

"Now who's busting who?"

She looked at the house. "They hate me," she said softly.

"I'll go in with you," I offered. "Me they like—so far. And they don't hate you."

"Bunny does."

"Okay, Bunny does. What do you say?"

She hesitated a moment. "I have to get Georgie home." She walked back to her car.

I followed. He was still asleep, burbling quietly. "Seems like a very well-behaved little guy," I said as we stood there, looking in at him.

"He's an angel," she said. "I love him to death. Does Matthew . . . does he ever ask about him?"

"He started crying before, just thinking about him. Georgie's favorite scene in *Dennis* came on the TV."

"I know just which one it is," she said. "It's when Dennis meets Althea and he . . . and she . . . and they . . ." The tears came first. Then the sobs, big wrenching ones. And then she hurled herself into my arms and let go completely. I held on tight. She was small and slim, but a sturdy little package, her back ridged with muscle, her clutch pythonlike. When she was all cried out she released me. I gave her my linen handkerchief.

"I—I don't know why I did that," she blubbered, using it.

"You're upset."

"But I hardly know you."

"Think nothing of it. People cry in front of me all the time. I seem to have that effect on them."

"You're awfully nice," she sniffled.

"No, I'm not."

She studied me, her porcelain blue eyes shimmering. "I meant, you're very comforting."

"I'm a good, hot bowl of Cream of Wheat, all right."

"In case you didn't know it, Cassie has a terrible crush on you."

"Don't remind me."

"And she's not the only one who does." She whispered that. I barely heard it. Maybe I never heard it at all. She gave me back my handkerchief. Then she got in and drove off.

I watched the lights of her car disappear down the road . . . *"What makes them so special, Meat?"* . . . I don't believe I'd ever missed Merilee as much as I did right then, standing there in the road, holding my wet hankie. I missed her so much my chest ached. I took a couple of deep breaths in and out. Then I shook myself and climbed into Tod Stiles's Vette and headed back to the dream factory.

The phone was ringing in the Ramon Novarro bungalow when I came in. Merilee. She missed me. She couldn't live without me. Her. It was her. It had to be her.

I lunged for it. "Hello?"

"Gawd, you're such a star."

It wasn't her. "In what sense, Cassandra?"

"I mean, ya get so used to people not living up to their own hype," she gushed. "But you, wham, this thing's already going right through the roof. I'm in awe. No shit—*awe*." She lowered her voice conspiratorially. "Didja steal Penny's negatives yourself? Is that how ya did it? Your secret's safe with me."

"Actually, I rather thought *you* did it."

She let loose her shriek of a laugh. "Me? No way, Jose." She lowered her voice again. "What about Zorch and his boyfriend? Didja kill 'em?"

"What do you think?"

"It occurred to me, I gotta confess, that ya mighta. I mean, you're *so* lucky, and nobody's this lucky, but—nah—you're too classy to shoot down two guys. Ya wouldn't. Ya didn't." She came up for air. "Didja?"

"They were dead when I got there."

"Yeah, yeah, shewa. So listen, I'm out here in Trancas and Penny just called and—"

"Locked in a heavy give-and-take session with Big Steve?"

"Jealous?"

"I don't believe so."

"She said they think maybe Johnny didn't do it."

"Evidently not. What time did you get out there?"

"Me? Hey, forget it, honey. I been here since five. Took a dip in the blue Pacific. Neighbors can vouch for me."

"And Trace? Where was he?"

"Someplace up the beach. He come shambling in about seven-thoity. He has no concept of time. None. He's the reason I'm calling. Penny said you're tight with the cop who's investigating it."

"I wouldn't exactly call it tight."

"Trace wants him to know that the fight he had with Zorch at Spago was just . . . Here, wait, I'll let him tell ya. Trace, wake up! Christ, he's so laid back he's comatose. Hey, honey, wake up! I got Hoagy here, will ya?"

There was a rustling, followed by the heavy breathing thing. "How the hell are you, Buck?"

"Just dandy, Trace."

"I . . . uh . . . I wouldn't want anybody getting the wrong idea about me and Abel. He was a worm, and I hated his fucking guts, but it's not like I'd kill him or anything. What I mean is, I already got enough problems without the cops mixing me up in some fag killing. Half the casting directors in town are fags. They'll cut me dead if they think I had anything to do with it."

"Where were you when it happened, Trace?"

He yawned. "Right here."

"Cassandra just told me you weren't."

"She did? But I was . . . I see what you're saying. I wasn't home, but I was *here*. Up the beach, visiting a sick friend."

"What's her name?"

"Hey, let's not get too carried away here, Buck," Trace warned roughly. "I'm not involved in this thing, remember?"

"What are you doing tomorrow, Trace?"

"Maybe a joint at sunrise," he replied. "Couple of margaritas for breakfast. Care to join me?"

"I thought you'd never ask."

"Come on out. I'll be here all day. Fourth house from the left, one looks like it's ready to fall over. Takes after me."

"I'll be there. Could I speak with Cassandra again?"

She got back on. "So listen, Hoagy, if there's anything I can do . . ."

"Actually, there is."

"Gawd! This is like a dream. My old lady in Bensonhurst won't believe this. Just name it. Anything."

"You used to work for the *Enquirer*. Know anybody here in the L.A. bureau?"

"Yeah, yeah, shewa. Coupla people."

"Think they might tell you how they got hold of the negatives? Off the record, I mean."

"I was wondering about that myself," she admitted. "They may not, since they know I'm woiking for her. But I could try, if ya want me to."

"I want you to."

"Hey, it's done. I'm like Domino's. I deliver—right to your door."

"The phone will be fine, thanks."

"Does this mean we're actually woiking together?" she asked eagerly.

"It means we're cooperating."

"What are you gonna do for me?" she wanted to know.

"I'll let you have my autograph. How's that?"

"Hey, Hoagy?"

"Yes, Cassandra?"

"You're a real douche bag."

"And it's high time you found out."

I hung up. The phone rang again almost immediately. Lamp. He was at the station house. I could hear voices and phones in the background.

"Just wanted to let you know it checked out, Hoagy," he reported crisply. "Johnny and Wax *were* at Hamburger Hamlet.

The waitress and hostess IDed the both of them for the time of the shooting. I'd still like to talk to Johnny though. He may have some ideas."

"I highly doubt that."

"Maybe he saw something when he was hanging around at the scene. Or someone. He's not there at Bedford Falls, is he?"

"Not that I know of."

"If he turns up will you call me?"

"Of course, Lieutenant."

"We've got ourselves one other dead-end road," he informed me. "That ex-boyfriend of Geoffrey Brand's, Darren Dust, has been in Palm Springs for the past three days. Jeepers, who goes to the Springs in the middle of a heat wave? It must be a hundred and thirty there. Anyway, we can cross him off . . . Oh, I got hold of the service manager at the Rolls-Royce dealership. His boys worked on Zorch's car this morning and delivered it to his office on their lunch break. It sat there in the parking lot of Zorch's building until he used it in the late afternoon to go to court. I drove by the building just now. It's all valet parking. They keep them down in the basement, unlocked. Someone easily could have slipped down there and fooled with his remote. We'll check the day men tomorrow, see if they remember noticing anybody." He hesitated a moment. "The heat's on under this one, Hoagy. Zorch was big time. Many powerful friends. You, uh, don't have anything for me, do you?"

As it happened, I had four or five things he could check out that I couldn't. He wrote them down and said he would.

"There is one other thing, Lieutenant," I added.

"What's that, Hoagy?"

"I smoothed the way for you with you-know-who."

"You did what?" he asked, his voice cracking.

"She thinks you sound real nice. Seriously, I think if you play your cards right you and Penny will soon be—"

"Cut that out!" he cried. "Gosh darn it, Hoagy, I mean it!" Then he slammed down the phone, hard. He was getting a little touchy. Must have been the heat.

It was certainly hot in the bungalow. No breeze came in through the windows. I shut them and flicked on the air conditioner. I took Lulu out for a walk while it did its job.

The bungalow courtyard was dark and deserted. Bunny was still at the two Shelleys'. We strolled, Lulu sniffing at the plants,

me sniffing at the day's events. The theft of Pennyroyal's negatives. The murders. It couldn't be a coincidence. They had to
connect. And the same person had to be responsible. But who?
Matthew and Johnny were accounted for. Cassandra, too, apparently. But Trace wasn't. Nor was Pennyroyal. Except that she
wouldn't discredit herself by leaking her own nude shots to the
press. That made no sense. There was Norbert Schlom, whose
multibillion-dollar deal with Murakami was in jeopardy because
of Zorch's gutter tactics. There was Toy Schlom, whose murky
past tied her in with Shambazza and the negatives. And then
there was the Bedford Falls inner circle. The two Shelleys,
Bunny, Sarge. They'd do anything to protect Matthew and his
studio. Had one of them killed for him? Possibly. But why leak
Pennyroyal's negatives? Why drive a deeper wedge between her
and Matthew when reconciliation was Bedford Falls' best hope?
No sense. It made no sense at all.

Perplexed, I found myself up near the front gate. Shadow
was on duty in the guard's booth, browsing through a copy of *The
New England Journal of Medicine*. A small fan blew on the
counter before him.

"Evening, Shadow," I said.

He showed me his gold tooth. "Why, good evening, sir."

"Batman make it back yet?"

"He did."

"Any visitors? Robin, perhaps?"

Shadow hesitated. "No sir. Quiet night. Extremely so."

"Did you really do that to him, Shadow?"

"Do what, sir?"

"Plant coke in his bungalow so he'd have to direct *The Three
Stooges?*"

He shifted uneasily on his seat and looked away. "That happens to be a part of my life I deeply regret. Mr. Schlom, he's an
evil man. Expects his employees to be just as evil as he be. But I
got out of that place, thanks to Matthew. And I've tried as hard as
I know how to make it up to him. I truly have."

"What else do you know, Shadow?"

"Sir?"

"You told me the Shadow knows plenty. What else?"

The old outfielder thumbed his chin thoughtfully, then
crossed his big arms. "I know that Bedford Falls is doomed. I
know that. Yessir."

"How come?"

"Because Miss Ayn Rand was right. She be one smart lady, that gal. Ever read a hefty volume of hers by the name of *Atlas Shrugged?*"

"I have."

"You'll recall she suggests that the true hero of this American land ain't no ballplayer or soldier but the man who creates something, a product, and makes a profit off of it. And that this here creator, he is destined to be destroyed by the moochers and parasites and other various forces of mediocrity who are lurking out there in the tall grass."

"Is that what you think is happening to Matthew?"

"Don't you?"

"I think that's the essence of the movie business. Always has been. Always will be."

Shadow took a handkerchief out of his back pocket and swiped at his thick, muscled neck. "Small fry. We all be small fry here. Don't stand no kind of chance. No sir." He sighed wearily. "Shit, don't be listening to me. I'm just tired and hot. Said on the radio it might finally break tomorrow. Something sure gonna, it don't. You get yourself some rest, sir."

"Good night, Shadow."

We kept walking. Took a turn through Homewood, which almost seemed like a real place in the night. Its business district all buttoned up. Its residents tucked safely into their beds, dreaming nothing but sweet dreams. It gave me the creeps walking through there. Lulu seemed to like it.

We moseyed by Stage One on our way back. I hadn't thought Shadow was being totally straight with me, and I wasn't wrong. Johnny's big white Fat Boy was parked there at the stage door. He was inside visiting Matthew. I thought about going in. I thought about phoning Lamp like I said I would. I didn't do either of those things. I went back to my bungalow and poured myself two fingers of Glenmorangie and put on some Garner. I stretched out on the bed and listened to him play "Body and Soul" like no one else ever has or ever will. I lay there a long time, listening. And remembering how Pennyroyal Brim had felt in my arms.

# Chapter Seven

The heat wave didn't break. It was eighty-six degrees by eight A.M., the weatherman promising it would top a hundred for the fifth day in a row. Pennyroyal's pictures did. The *Enquirer* hit the stands that morning with all of her plastered tastefully across the front page —the headline, "SAY CHEESECAKE, PRETTY PENNY," also serving as a bikini of black ink. She was standing beside a potted plant, wearing a top hat and no tails. She had a dreamy expression on her face, lips parted, as if in rapture. Her face was a bit fuller, but otherwise she hadn't changed much over the past eight years. *Penthouse*, it was announced, had won the bidding war with *Playboy* and would be showing us the X-rated Penny in a few short weeks.

The House of Wax story got plenty of play that morning, what with the murder of Abel Zorch, high-powered Hollywood attorney and former ranking official of the Committee to Re-elect the President. There were expressions of great sadness from the likes of Norbert Schlom, noted paper eater, who called Zorch "a man of vision and clarity who looked into the future and saw how to get there." Executives of the Murakami Corporation of Japan noted him as one "who paid scrupulous attention to the difficult demands of business without ever sacrificing his honor." G. Gordon Liddy, former CRP general counsel turned lecture circuiteer, lauded him as "one tough son of a bleep. Abel took no prisoners." There were no new leads on the killer of Zorch and Geoffrey Brand, age twenty-three, of West Hollywood. Film star Johnny Forget, who had been observed at the scene shortly before the crime, was wanted for questioning but was not considered a suspect, according to Detective Lieutenant Emil Lamp of the L.A.P.D.

I was up early, stropping Grandfather's razor. Time to get out my mukluks. I wore them when I wrote the first novel. I've worn them at the typewriter ever since. There's not much holding them together anymore. In that respect, they're a lot like me. I spent the morning roughing out Matthew's childhood, Lulu dozing under my chair with her head on my foot. I gave him a boyish, earnest voice. I focused on the latchkey kid angle, contrasting the warm, caring family and community life of his Badger movies with Matthew's own solitary childhood of safe places and imaginary gunfights played out in the backyard of his bland suburban ranch house. I wasn't overly happy with it. There was still too much I didn't know. About his father. About the basketball team. But I did cover some ground, and that's what mattered right now—the pressure was on. My drum banger called me that morning from New York in a major dither. Cassandra was already delivering pages to her publisher. Why wasn't I? Cassandra was going to be done by January first. Why wasn't I? Penny's book would be in the stores by the summer. Ours wouldn't be out until fall. Why? Calmly, I pointed out that our deal called for me to deliver in April, not January. Not so calmly, he pointed out that we had to get into the stores while this story was so hot. He suggested this wasn't publishing—this was war. I suggested he find a different, faster warrior, which made him even more agitated. Then I hung up on him. I don't think that made him feel any better, but it worked for me.

Mrs. Shelley called me that morning, too, right after she got off the phone with the Monroe High Alumni Association. The Class of '72 twentieth reunion dinner dance was this coming Saturday night at the Sheraton Panorama City. She had made us a reservation for two. Mona Thayer, née Schaffer, would indeed be in attendance. Mona was a registered nurse, divorced, and the mother of an eight-year-old daughter. She lived in Canoga Park.

Merilee Nash did not call me that morning.

My name was stenciled on my parking space now. I was

somebody. It was obvious. Martin Short, who was writing a script in the bungalow next door, said hello when I passed him on my way to Stage One. Leonard Nimoy smiled at me when he rode by on his bike, and he doesn't even know me. Former angry playwright turned boring director David Mamet rode by me too, only he didn't smile. He does know me. I also saw six little boys dressed up like bumblebees. I couldn't tell you if they were smiling or not.

I ran into Sarge on the way, striding regally along in shorts and running shoes, clipboard clutched to her breast, calves glistening in the sunlight.

"Just the person I was looking for," I said.

She raised an eyebrow at me, amused—I was dribbling the basketball that I'd bought. Today's gift. "Ain't you, like, the wrong color, man?"

"I thought Matthew could show me a few of his moves."

"He hasn't got any." She laughed. "Suffers bad from White Man's Disease—vertical leap's maybe four inches. Pathetic. Why you looking for me?"

"I lost my Waterman pen. Thought maybe I left it in your Land Cruiser."

It was parked nearby in the executive lot. She unlocked it for me and waited while I pretended to search under the seat. A secretary stopped and said hi to her. That's when I snuck a look in the glove compartment.

Her Glock was still in there. She was clear.

Unless, of course, she happened to own two.

"No luck," I reported. "Must have left it at the hotel." We resumed walking. "On your way to see Matthew?"

She nodded. "Got some locations for him to approve. Bachelor pads for Badger. I checked them out yesterday."

"That's where you were at the time of the shooting?"

"Uh-huh." She eyed me coldly. "What, they thinking I did it?"

"I doubt it. But they'll want to know where you were and how well you can handle a gun."

"Why?"

"You have a motive."

"Me? Why'd I want to kill that gee and his little boy?"

"To protect the fort," I replied. "Can you?"

"Can I what, man?" she demanded, flaring her nostrils at me.

"Handle a gun."

"I can handle anything," she said, matter-of-factly.

I don't know about you but I believed her.

The Fat Boy was gone from outside the stage door. Bunny was busy preparing Matthew some Aunt Jemima frozen toaster waffles in the Hayes's kitchen. She wore a *Dennis the Dinosaur* apron over her white designer sweats, and seemed bothered. Matthew was slumped at the table, glumly watching a rerun of *Gilligan's Island* on a portable TV. The one where Gilligan starts picking up radio broadcasts with his teeth. Bunny poured him a glass of milk and placed his waffles before him. Carefully, he cut them into tiny bite-sized pieces. He poured a quart of syrup on them, then began to eat. Bunny watched him, crinkling her nose as he chewed. Lulu watched her warily, afraid she might try to feed her again.

Sarge turned down the TV. "Okay, show 'n' tell time," she declared, all business. She arrayed Polaroid snapshots of houses on the table before Matthew. "We got three possibilities for Badger's home base. One on the left is a beach house in Malibu that—"

"No beach house," said Matthew peevishly. "Badger wouldn't live in one. No."

"Okay, that one's out," she agreed readily, turning over the beach house shots. "This here one's at the top of Laurel Canyon. All glass. Very modern, outstanding views in three directions. Valerie Bertinelli once lived there . . ." She watched him, waiting for his reaction. He had none. She plowed ahead. "Third one's on Stanley Hills Drive, also Laurel Canyon. Spanish-style. Dig, it has a two-story living room with a vaulted ceiling, and this totally outrageous, like, tower, with a room up there. Funky, the realtor called it, if you can believe that. It's a bank foreclosure. Belonged to a network executive. We can rent it for two months, cheap. Want to see it?" She waited for some kind of reaction, any kind of reaction. Nothing. Just glum silence. "Well, I'll go ahead and set something up for this afternoon, in case you do. And don't forget we got more actors coming in at lunch to read for the part of his agent. Okay, I'm outta here." She gathered up her pictures, watching him. "You okay, darling?" she asked him.

"Fine," he grumbled, munching on his waffle. "Why?"

"No reason." She shot a look over at Bunny.

Bunny hastily removed her apron. "We'll leave you two boys to your work. Don't forget to put your plate in the sink, Matty." She hesitated. "You sure you're okay, sweetheart?"

"I'm fine!" he erupted. "Why does everybody keep asking me how I am!"

"Because you seem a little cranky this morning," Bunny replied soothingly. "What time did you get to sleep last—?"

"Stop babying me, will ya?!" cried Matthew. "I hate being babied!"

Bunny whirled and gave me the evil eye, somehow certain this was all my doing. It was an impressive one. I could practically feel the boils forming all over my body.

"We girls seem to be in the way, Charmaine," she said icily. "Come, the boys wish to talk."

Out she bustled, Sarge in tow. Lulu curled up under the table, relieved to see her go.

I tossed Matthew the basketball and poured myself some coffee. "What's going on, Matthew?"

"Been thinking about the script." He began spinning the ball on the tip of his upraised index finger. "You may be right about Debbie Dale. We *do* need to see that she and Badger once had a good thing. Maybe some flashbacks would help . . ." He trailed off, looked up at me, clearing his throat uneasily. "I don't know what it is, Meat. Everybody treats me like a little kid around here. And it bothers me sometimes. Especially since you got here. I don't know why."

"Johnny stay the whole night?"

"What do you mean?" he asked, startled.

"I mean, did he stay or did he go?"

"He left about two-thirty. He was really upset about Zorch. He really loved the guy, I guess."

"Is he going to talk to the police?"

"Today. He won't go into the police station. He's too paranoid. But he's agreed to meet with that detective friend of yours, Lamp, at his agency. Joey Bam Bam is putting it together." He put the ball down and flicked off the TV. "I'm all ready, Meat. Where do we start today?"

"With you telling me about Mona Schaffer."

A weak whimper came from Matthew's throat. He turned pale. Green, almost.

"You're not going to barf again, are you?"

"N-No, I don't think so," he stammered weakly. His fingers found his forelock and started tugging at it.

"What happened to your Silly Putty?"

"It's right here in my pocket." He dug it out and began to work it, his rabbit nose twitching furiously. "She's . . . Mona's not anyone, really. Just this girl I had a crush on. She was . . . I mean, we never dated or anything. I don't even know why you're asking me about her. D-Did my sister mention her or something?"

"Showed me her yearbook picture as well." I sipped my coffee. "Pennyroyal looks somewhat like her. More than somewhat, in fact."

"Same basic type," he admitted, offhanded. "Blond hair, blue eyes, all-American cheerleader. That's my type. Guess that makes me an all-American boy." He forced a chuckle. He sounded like a machine gun running out of zip.

I sat. "Tell me more about your relationship."

"We didn't have one, Meat. I just told you. I was . . . infatuated with her. I memorized her phone number. I followed her around campus. If we had a class together, gee, I'd just stare and stare at her. She was *so* pretty. When she started driving to school, I'd purposely pass through the student parking lot on my way in just so I could touch her car. It was a Skylark, powder blue." He was starting to perspire. He swiped at his forehead with the back of his hand. "Is it getting warm in here or is it just me?"

"I'm cool as a cucumber."

"I even saved her gum," he blurted out.

"You saved her what?"

"She sat in front of me in Spanish one semester, and she'd stick her bubble gum up under her desk every day before class, and leave it there. I'd take it home. Kept it all in my dresser for months. Until I got ants."

"I'm beginning to think less and less of you, Matthew."

"I guess it does sound pretty pathetic," he admitted.

"Did you ever talk to her about how you felt?"

"Not exactly."

"Did you ever talk to her at all?"

"Not exactly. Well, once. Sort of."

"Want to tell me about that?"

He sat there, sweating. His color was not good.

"Does this have anything to do with why you quit the basketball team?"

His mouth tightened. "Why do you keep harping on that?"

"If you'd rather, Matthew, I'll ask her about it at the reunion. It's up to you."

His eyes widened. "She'll be there?"

"She will. She's a nurse now, divorced. Has a daughter."

"Wow, that would be major strange seeing her again. Mona . . ."

"I imagine some of your former teammates will be there, too. I can ask them about why—"

"You're really not going to let this thing go, are you?"

"I'm really not."

He slumped in his chair and sighed. "All right, Meat," he said with glum resignation. "But this does happen to be the single most traumatic moment of my entire life. We're talking major, major wound here." He cleared his throat and took a deep breath. "I was . . . I was trying really hard to be a part of the team. Coach, he encouraged me. Patted me on the back in practice and stuff. But the guys, they never accepted me in the locker room. They weren't nasty to me or anything. They just ignored me. I wasn't one of them. They were all tanned and good-looking and popular. They had girlfriends. Me, I was this pale, clumsy oaf. This goon . . . Our first game was with Taft. They beat us, 58–50. We didn't play well. I only got in for a couple of minutes and didn't do much. Afterward, in the locker room, the guys were pretty down about it. Kip London, who was our best player, and who went steady with Mona, he had a really bad game. Kip was looking to take it out on somebody, I guess. He chose me. Started picking on me when I took off my jersey. Teasing me about how pale I was. He called me Whitey. A bunch of 'em picked up on it. 'Whitey's never had any rays,' they kept saying. 'Let's get Whitey some rays.' And then they *descended* on me. Began stripping me. Playfully, at first. Only they wouldn't stop. I fought them but that only seemed to egg them on. They were like wild animals who'd found a weakling to devour. They stripped me of my shorts, my jock, my shoes, socks. They stripped me naked. 'Let's get Whitey some rays!' they chanted. 'Rays! Rays! Rays!' They started carrying me around the locker room over their heads, like a lynch mob. They carried me right out the door into the gym, stark naked. There were *girls* out there, Meat. Their girlfriends were waiting there for them. *Mona* was waiting for Kip in her little cheer-leader costume. They . . . they dumped me right at her feet. Then they ran back inside, laughing. They left me there at the feet of my dream girl, stark naked. And . . . And that's when she spoke to me. The only words she ever said to me in all of the years I loved her."

"What did she say, Matthew?"

"She said, 'Would you like to borrow my pom-poms, Mar-tin?' *Martin*. Can you believe it? She didn't even know my name!" He trailed off, glaring at me. "What are you doing, Meat?"

"Doing?"

"Are you . . . giggling?"

"I do not giggle. I chortle. Occasionally, I guffaw. But I never—"

"You actually think this *funny!*" he cried, outraged.

"It *is* funny, Matthew. It's excruciating. But, mostly, it's funny. Did you?"

"Did I *what?*"

"Borrow her pom-poms?"

"Yes. Only, I couldn't get back inside. They'd locked the door on me. Somebody had to find a custodian to let me in. I was stuck out there for ten minutes. It was like a nightmare. It still makes me shudder, just thinking about it. I—I could never face any of them again. So I quit the team. And that's the whole ugly story, Meat. Go ahead and laugh some more."

I tugged at my ear. "That would make a great movie scene, in the right hands."

"Whose?" he asked scornfully.

"Yours. I'm surprised you haven't used it, frankly."

He shook his head vehemently. "I could never film that. Never. Much too painful."

"All the more reason for doing it. That's the good stuff gener-ally."

He considered this, slumped there in his chair fingering his Silly Putty.

"Best way to get over it, Matthew, is to come face to face with it," I advised. "Just like going to your reunion."

"I really don't think I can go, Meat."

"She'll be there, Kip'll be there. It's a terrific chance for you, Matthew. You're an idol to these people. They probably tell complete strangers that they once knew you. Hell, they'll be in awe of you. I don't see how you can let a chance like this pass you by. It's your moment of triumph—*Martin Returns: The Sequel*."

"I wonder what she looks like now," he said softly, intrigued.

"How do you want her to look?"

"Just like she did," he said with adolescent longing. He finished his milk, slamming down his glass with fierce determination. "We're going, Meat. We're going to the reunion."

"Good."

"You're pleased?" He seemed anxious for my approval.

"Absolutely. I'd hate to think I brought my dinner jacket all the way out here for nothing."

He picked up the basketball and spun it from his finger again. "Wanna play some Horse out back?"

"I thought you'd never ask."

By out back, of course, he meant the set for the Hayes's driveway. The garage door with the basketball hoop over it. The clothesline. The fence between the Hayeses and the Dales. I half expected Teri Garr to call us inside for brownies.

"Try this, Meat," dared Matthew. He dribbled the ball toward the hoop, leaped, and slam-dunked it mightily. Not that this was any rare physical accomplishment. The basket was a full foot lower than regulation so that Johnny Forget wouldn't look like a midget.

I tried it. I made it. Then I tried a jumper from fifteen feet out. It clanged off the front of the rim.

"Ha!" he exclaimed. "Okay, okay, sucker—try this . . ." He stood ten feet from the basket with his back to it. Blindly, he tossed the ball over his head. Nothing but net. He fired it at me, cackling with glee.

"This is a whole new side of you, Matthew. And it's not pretty."

"Come on, come on," he said impatiently. "Try and make it, sucker."

I couldn't. That meant I had an H. The game was on.

"What did you do with yourself after you quit the team?" I asked.

"I started riding my bike a lot," he recalled. "Especially that summer. Rode for miles and miles. I was too restless to sit around the house watching TV. I guess my hormones were raging. I used to ride all the way to Panorama. It was still a genuine working lot then. They had whole villages, jungles, lakes, tank battalions. It was this fantastic sort of playground. Except there were no other kids around. Just me. I'd ditch my bike in the bushes and wander around all day, watching them film stuff. Sometimes the guards would catch me and throw me out. But I'd just come right back the next day." He dribbled the ball. "Okay, make this one, buttwipe . . ."

" 'Buttwipe'?"

He tried a high, arching hook shot from twenty feet out. All net. "Hah!" he cried triumphantly.

My attempt soared over the backboard, the garage, the whole set. The ball ended up in Badger's bedroom.

"You'd better get it together, Meat," Matthew cackled, retrieving it. "We're talking major blowout here."

Lulu could stand no more. She was too embarrassed for me. She wandered off to the living room.

"There was a TV series they were filming there for ABC," Matthew recalled. "A youth-oriented Western called *The Groovy Seven*. Remember it?"

"Unfortunately."

"The director was this one-eyed B-movie maker from the fifties named Ernst Vinkel. He was Austrian. Had an accent. An eyepatch. Wore his jacket loose over his shoulders, like a cape. I loved watching him work. Especially the action sequences. The precise planning that went into them. The horses, the stunts, the dozens of technicians who had to perform their specialty perfectly in order for the scene to come off. The whole process fascinated me. I'd never realized before just how unimportant the actors were. I mean, when I was watching on TV at home, they were the whole show. But during filming, the real action was all happening behind the scenes. Ernst, he was like a general, and they were his army. He was masterly, the way he ran his set. I hung around watching him in awe. I was there at his elbow so much he assumed I was a summer intern—a gofer. One day he sent me out for sandwiches. He liked chicken salad on white with extra mayonnaise. Since he thought I was an intern, everyone else did, too. Before I knew it, I was. Got a pass onto the lot, a hundred dollars a week, and a front row seat. You know who went out of his way to be nice to me? Trace Washburn. He'd just washed out of the NFL and was working as a stuntman, falling off of horses. One of the producers was a big SC alumnus, and got him the job. Trace treated me like a real teammate. I never forgot that. I remembered him years later when I was casting *To the Moon*. Ernst was real nice, too. Gave me his number at the end of the summer and said if there was ever anything he could do to just call him. From then on, I knew what I wanted to do with my life, Meat. I wanted to make movies . . . Okay, okay, Wilt Chamberlain at the free-throw line . . ." Matthew spread his feet wide at the line, heaved a huge sigh and shot the ball underhanded, two hands. It went in.

So did mine.

"You got lucky," he sneered, unimpressed. "You're still history."

"I was planning to be gentlemanly, Matthew, but you've asked for it, and I'm afraid you're going to get it."

"Get what?" he wondered, amused.

I moved a good thirty feet from the basket, set myself, and aired out the old javelin shoulder. A low line drive that hit nothing but net. A true Howitzer shot.

Matthew stared at the basket in disbelief. "What the heck was that?"

I tossed him the ball. "Let's see you do it."

"Let's see *you* do it again."

"If you wish." I did it again. And again. And again.

Lulu reappeared, tail wagging, man's best fair-weather friend.

"How many in a row can you make?" he wondered, incredulous.

"My record in college was thirty-six."

Matthew swiped at his mouth with the back of his hand. "Gee, I'm kinda thirsty. Let's go make some Bosco, huh?"

"Does this mean you're conceding?"

"I'm conceding, okay?" he said sharply.

"Fine. I just wanted to hear you say it."

We returned to the kitchen. Matthew busied himself with the chocolate milk fixings.

"Had you made a movie yet?" I asked, sitting.

"Nope," he replied. "But that fall I dug my dad's old Super-Eight camera out of the garage. He hadn't used it for years, and didn't much care if I did. He was in and out of the hospital by then, dying. Ma was working at the accounting firm, running to the hospital to see him, running home to take care of Shelley and me. It wasn't easy for her. Plus we were broke. Sis had an academic scholarship to SC, otherwise she'd never have been able to go. She lived at home and worked at Shelley's dad's shoe store in Van Nuys for her pocket money. It was a pretty rough time."

"And this was your way of dealing with it?"

He handed me my glass of Bosco and sat with his. "What do you mean?"

"If you place a camera between you and something horrifying, it makes it less horrifying. You're an observer instead of a participant."

He thought this over, ignoring the chocolate milk moustache on his upper lip. "Gee, Meat, I never made that connection before. So you think I took up making movies as a way of coping with my dad dying?"

"Possibly."

"But we didn't get along," he reminded me.

"That doesn't make the experience any easier. Sometimes it even makes it harder."

He frowned. "Gee, that would mean . . ."

"That would mean what, Matthew?"

"Dad's responsible for all of this," he said, looking around at the sets. "In a weird sort of way . . ."

"Tell me about your first movie. What was it?"

"My own version of a fifties horror movie," he recalled fondly. "I called it *The Dog Who Ate Sepulveda*. I used the neighbor's labrador retriever, Casey, who was always in our yard. Made a bunch of miniature cities out of my old Erector Set and Lincoln Logs, hillsides out of papier mache. Then I let Casey loose to destroy them, just like Godzilla. The Shelleys helped me film it one Sunday afternoon. She shot some of it while he and I tried to zap Casey with ray guns. We had a lot of fun. I'd never had such fun."

"Did the monster die at the end?"

"No, we tamed him. He let us pat him on the belly, and when

we did the mutation process was magically reversed and he became dog-sized again."

"The patented Matthew Wax happy ending."

He grinned at me. "I got it developed at a camera store on Nordhoff, and bought a splicer and glue and put it together. It was eight minutes long. The Shelleys thought I ought to show it to my English class at Monroe or something. But I didn't feel like it."

"But it did get you into SC film school, right?"

He looked at me oddly. "I never went to SC film school."

"I thought you did," I said. "I thought you dropped out to work in TV."

"A common misconception," he acknowledged. "Repeated in article after article. People have always assumed that since I was a young filmmaker and I was going to SC that I was in their film school. But I never was. I never took one film class. I was a political science major."

"You were politically inclined?"

"Not in the least. It never occurred to me that you went to school to learn about anything you were interested in. I hated school. But I had to go—to stay out of the Vietnam draft, and because Ma wanted me to. Her boss, Mr. Ferraro, advanced her the money for my tuition. I drove over the hill every morning to class in Ma's old Falcon. Came straight home. I studied just enough to pass. Never went anywhere near the library. I'm not even sure I knew where it was on campus. I dropped out at the beginning of my sophomore year. By then the war was over." His face darkened. "And my dad was dead."

"What was the funeral like?"

"Small. Just the three of us and Shelley and a couple of Ma's old cousins—the type who always show up at funerals. Mr. Ferraro came, which we thought was nice. No friends or business associates of dad's. Not one." He got up and hunted around in the cupboard and came away with a package of Oreos. He tore into it. "After my freshman year I went back to work at Panorama as a summer intern," he said, chomping. "Ernst put in the word for me. I worked as a gofer on a bunch of different shows. In my spare time, I wrote *Bugged*. All twelve pages of it. It came to me in a nightmare, actually. The idea that you wake up one morning and something's happened to you, and everyone knows it but you. What I did, I had this nerdy high school kid who wakes up looking normal to himself in the mirror. But to every-one else, he's been transformed into this giant, ugly insect. He's a real unpopular kid, the kind who's always wanted the other kids to pay attention to him. Well, now they do . . . Everyone I talked to said I ought to make this one in sixteen-millimeter. The pros wouldn't even bother to look at eight-millimeter. The quality was also much better with sixteen. Only, I needed about seven hundred dollars to rent the equipment and buy the stock. Shelley gave me the money out of his law school savings—no questions asked. That's the kind of guy he is. Whatever else I needed, I begged or borrowed. It didn't hurt that I had the run of the Pan-orama lot."

"Who played the lead?"

"Another intern there. His mom was a costumer. Real nice kid named Steve. I had him narrate it, like the guy did in *The Incredible Shrinking Man*. His friends around the lot filled in the other parts. We filmed it on a bunch of different standing sets during lunch breaks. His house was the house from *The Brady Bunch*. The street he lived on was left over from an old Rock Hudson-Doris Day movie. The bug costume, which I got from Steve's mom, had been used in *Land of The Giants*. It took us about a week to shoot it, and a couple more weeks for me to put it all together. Ernst was nice enough to look at it when I was done."

"I take it he was impressed."

"He thought it was crude but clever. What impressed him was that I knew how to tell a story, a proper story with a begin-ning, middle and end. Most young directors don't."

"Many directors don't, period. How come you did?"

"I can't answer that, Meat. It was instinctive. Maybe it came from watching so many hours of TV when I was a kid."

"And maybe," I suggested "you were just extraordinarily gifted."

He ducked his head bashfully. "I was doing what came natu-rally, that's all. Ernst made an appointment for me to see this guy who was second in command of Panorama's TV production, Nor-bert Schlom. I was surprised that anyone that important would want to see me—I mean, I was nineteen. But Ernst said the stu-dios were totally desperate for young talent that could bridge the generation gap. The man wanted to talk to me. So I went to the Tower. That's what they called the old executive office building. It was only eight stories high, but there was nothing else that tall out there in those days. When I got to the office his door was closed and his secretary was nowhere to be seen. I waited around for fifteen minutes, and then I finally tapped on his door. I heard this groaning and gasping in there. After a minute the door opened and this blonde with giant boobies comes out all flushed, straightens her dress, and sits down at the secretary's desk. I think the two of them were having . . . I mean, I think they were . . ."

"Fucking?"

"Norbert sat there behind his big desk looking like a Detroit gangster. Had on this really loud plaid sport jacket, and a red shirt, and a white tie. He told me to sit down. He called me 'Kid.' He always called me that. He just sat there looking me over for a while, cracking his knuckles, not saying a word. Then he got up and came around the desk. He was wearing a white belt and white shoes. And his fly was open. The tail of his shirt was sticking way out of it. He came over close to me, real close, and started sniffing at me."

"Sniffing at you?"

"Like a dog would—no offense, Lulu. His nose maybe an inch from my armpit. I said to him, 'Is something wrong, Mr. Schlom?' I'm thinking maybe I forgot to put on my Right Guard that morning. And you know what he said to me?"

"I honestly can't imagine."

"He said, and I'll never forget this as long as I live, he said, 'Kid, I know shit from scripts. I know shit from dailies. I know shit from rough cuts. I only know one thing—money. And I smell money on you. I'm putting you to work.' And that's how I became a director."

"Kind of a stirring moment."

"Hey, it happened," Matthew insisted.

"Hey, I believe you."

"What he had in mind for me was this new Saturday morning serial they were doing for CBS based on the Rick Brant books of the forties and fifties. All about the adventures of this teenaged inventor named Rick and his pal, Scotty. A fellow named John Blaine wrote them. Schlom wanted me to break *The Rocket's Shadow* into twelve episodes, with a cliff-hanger every week, and then direct them. For which he offered me a contract paying me five hundred dollars a week. I brought the contract to Shelley. He showed it to one of his law professors, who said it was fair except for this one clause that bound me exclusively to the studio for seven years, at their option. He said we should try to get it reduced to one year, otherwise I'd be signing my life away. The Panorama people said okay. That turned out to be really important later on.''

"I'm surprised they let you reduce it."

"It was a mistake, actually. Norbert fired the guy who made it. They assigned me a line producer, an old pro, and I went to work breaking up the book. Then we cast our leads and I walked out onto the floor and said 'Action' for the first time.''

"What was that like—being in charge of a shoot at age nineteen?"

He sat back in his chair, hands behind his head, a contented smile on his face. This recollection he was enjoying. "Lots of people have asked me that through the years. For me it was no problem. The leads were kids, for one thing. They looked up to me. And the crew, they don't care how old you are. All they care about is whether you're decisive. If you are, you earn their respect. What they can't handle is indecision, tentativeness, vagueness. It makes them freak out. That wasn't a problem for me. From the first day I walked out on the set, I felt I belonged there. I felt at home. And I knew what the show was supposed to be— something fun, *something I would watch*. I can't emphasize that last point enough, Meat. Because that's all I've ever tried to do— entertain myself. It's as simple as that. People in this town, they're always trying to figure out what will or will not work for this or that audience. It's all bull. If it's something you yourself would go see, then it works. That's the only marketing strategy I've ever followed. And, as far as I'm concerned, it's the only one there is." He dug into the package for another Oreo, animated and effusive. "I knew what I wanted. And I knew when I'd gotten it. That made me a director, even if I was only nineteen. We had to work tremendously hard, fourteen hours a day, to grind those episodes out. It was a grueling pace. But they left us alone, which was a real plus. Nobody from the studio interfered, or even paid much attention to what we were doing.''

"How did Bunny feel about all of this?"

"She thought the whole thing was *nuts*," he laughed, smacking the table with delight. "She couldn't believe I was actually directing a real television show. She figured I was selling drugs

or something. She insisted on coming down to the set for a look.
And she *still* didn't like it. Thought it was some kind of fluke. That
I ought to go back to school. She'll deny that now, of course. Say
she was one hundred percent for it. But she wasn't. Although she
did get a bit more supportive when *The Rocket's Shadow* pre-
miered. It did really well in the ratings. The kids responded to it.
The critics loved it. I started getting a few requests for interviews.
At first, I did them, but they made me so uncomfortable I decided
to stop. The press didn't understand that. Still don't. They don't
get that someone might want to be left alone."

"They get it fine," I said. "They just don't care."

"Norbert immediately got me started on another Brant, *One
Hundred Fathoms Under*, which was all about deep sea diving.
We got to use a water tank in that one, which was real neat. It did
even better than the first one. By then my one-year contract with
Panorama was up. The series was hot. Norbert wanted me to
keep going with it. He offered to double my salary to a thousand
a week. But Shelley got an offer that was even better. An independent company offered me the chance to write and direct my
own low-budget feature. Any film I wanted to do. Shelley called
Norbert and told him I was leaving. Norbert hit the ceiling—this
would never have happened if they hadn't screwed up my contract. He basically had to match the offer or lose me. So he went
to the Panorama feature people and talked them into matching it.
And I did *The Boy Who Cried Wolf* for them, with Norbert moving
over into the feature business with me as my supervisor. I ended
up staying there with him for the next twelve years. Eight pictures in all. Panorama was my second home. I had my own playpen there. It was great. Norbert let me make the pictures I
wanted to make, and let me spend what I wanted to spend. Because my pictures made hundreds of millions of dollars for him.
It's funny—Norbert always takes credit for me. Says he made
me. And for a long time I believed that. But the more I look back
on it now, the more I realize that *I* made *him*. He got into the
feature business because of me. He made it all the way to the
Panorama throne because of me. *He* needed *me*. He's always
needed me. That's why he's trying to get me back. Trying to buy
this place. But I'll never work for him again. Never. I'll retire
from the business before I'll make another movie for that man. I
mean it." He grabbed the basketball and jumped to his feet.
"C'mon, I'll play you again."

"You'll just lose again."

"Fat chance," he exclaimed, dribbling the ball out the door. Until suddenly he stopped. "I can't go to the reunion dinner, Meat."

"Why not?"

"It's a fancy dinner dance."

"So?"

"I don't have anything to wear." He fingered his ravaged scalp. "And my hair . . ."

"Leave that to me," I said soothingly. "All part of the service."

He brightened. "Really?"

"Really. One question—do you care how much you spend?"

"I guess not."

"Good answer," I said, rubbing my hands together.

"I still can't go, Meat," he insisted stubbornly.

I sighed. "Why not, Matthew?"

He reddened. "I—I don't know how to dance," he confessed.

"Well, don't look at me, buttwipe. I don't dance with boys."

# Chapter Eight

The brand new headquarters of the Harmon Wright Agency was on Beverly Boulevard, a half block from Cedars-Sinai Medical Center. It was a squat, rather ugly six-story concrete bunker with a flat roof and narrow slits for windows. It reminded me a lot of an Iraqi bomb shelter. Except not quite as cheerful.

Joey Bam Bam met me on the fourth floor at the elevator. "Johnny just got here—he's freshening up," the pint-sized agent informed me brightly. "This is the new Johnny: professional, cooperative, happy to talk. Scared shitless but happy to talk."

"Thanks for including me."

He nodded with a vigor that bordered on the convulsive. "No problem. We're all family here." He lowered his voice. "Besides, I understand you're tight with this Lamp."

"I wouldn't exactly call it tight."

The corridor was long, narrow, and dismal. The walls were bare concrete, the carpeting institutional, the lighting so dim that Lulu, with her shades on, kept bouncing off the walls like a bumper car. I had to remove them for her.

"Great place, huh?" burbled Bam Bam as he bopped along ahead of us. "It really, really sends out the new message: We're here to serve our talent, not ourselves. CAA, they go out and spend millions on themselves. Hire I.M. Pei to design their place. Not us. We're lean and mean.''

"Seems like an awfully grim place to spend eight hours a day," I observed.

He laughed. "Eight hours?! Eight hours is a *morning* around here. Oh, hey, somebody I want you to meet while you're here . . ." He opened the door to a small, windowless conference room. A half dozen baby agents were crammed in there like caged animals waiting for a slab of fresh meat to be thrown in. I was the slab of fresh meat. Quickly, Bam Bam shut the door behind us. "Okay, Stewart Hoag, these guys all know you. Christ, who doesn't? But you haven't met them yet, and are you in for an ultratreat. Say hello to the new team, each of us pulling for the other. From left to right that's Len Levitt, Cuffy Cohen, Moke Mokatoff, Bruce Blick, Patty Plunk and Baby Jane Mandel. The Cuffster here is an ultraintellectual. When you go to his house you'll find hardcover books all over the place."

"I don't think so," I said.

Bam Bam frowned. "You don't think he reads?"

"I don't think I'll be going to his house. Look, kids, this is great, but—"

"We can make you a star," vowed the Cuffster.

"Tried it. Vastly overrated."

"At least let us show you what we can do for you," Bam Bam pleaded.

"Bam Bam is ultraexcited about you," chimed in Patty. Or maybe it was Baby Jane. Or Bruce. They all looked alike—like hamsters in Italian clothing.

"Some other time," I said. "Unless, of course, you're interested in representing a dog act . . ."

Lulu scrambled for the door, moaning, and hurled her body against it, paws first. It was the fastest I'd seen her move since the time she surprised a bat in Merilee's barn. I guess civilian life didn't look so bad to her all of a sudden.

God, I was proud.

Johnny was waiting for us in Bam Bam's office, a drab little cubicle with a steel desk, a sofa, and no art or personal objects of any kind. It was the sort of office that would belong to an assistant professor of economics at a state university—in Gdansk. Johnny sat hunched in one corner of the sofa, smoking a cigarette and trembling. He was pale and drawn, his eyes bloodshot.

He had tied a red bandana over his dreadlocks, and put on a black Bedford Falls T-shirt. His jeans were still torn. He was nervous and jangly, his mouth dry. He kept licking at his lips.

Lulu took one whiff of his Patchouli and went back out in the hall to wait.

"Here's your friend Hoagy, John-John," Bam Bam announced, raising his voice as if we were speaking to a small, slow child. Everyone talked to Johnny that way. Everyone except Matthew.

Johnny hugged his knees and looked up at me vacantly. "I remember you," he said in his soft, little boy's whisper. "We met in Homewood."

"We did," I affirmed, thinking how much he made Homewood sound like a real place. Maybe he thought it was. Maybe he wasn't wrong. Maybe I'd been in L.A. too long already.

"Matthew likes you," he said. "You're Matthew's friend."

"And yours, too," Bam Bam assured him. "We're all friends here. Right, Hoagy?"

"We are."

"Can I get anyone a glass of water?" the little agent offered. I said I was fine.

"How about you, John-John?"

John-John said he was thirsty.

Bam Bam went bound-bounding down the hall for his drink.

I took off my straw boater and sat and smoothed the trousers of my white cotton planter's suit. "Matthew has been telling me all about his early days, Johnny. When he first got started making movies."

Johnny stubbed out his cigarette and immediately lit another one, still trembling. "Where is he?" he wondered.

"Matthew?"

"The cop. Where is the cop?"

"He'll be here soon, pal," said Bam Bam, returning with a paper cup of water.

"I was hoping you'd tell me about when you first met Matthew, Johnny," I said.

Johnny sat there with his water.

"Anything you remember," I added. "It's for his book."

Johnny drained the paper cup and crumpled it and tossed it on the floor. Bam Bam picked it up and put it in the trash.

"The wicked witch," whispered Johnny.

"The wicked witch?"

"She heard about it." He was answering me, in his own way. "That this woman, this casting agent, was looking for a little boy to star in a movie. Only, we couldn't get in to see her. We were new in town. Just got here from Canada . . ."

"The casting agents practically run this fucking business," conceded Bam Bam. "I'd like you to meet ours, Hoagy. She's a terrific—"

"Down, Bam Bam," I commanded.

"I'm down. Not one more word." He clapped his hand over his mouth as proof.

"So what did your mom do, Johnny?" I asked.

Johnny sniffled. "Sent Matthew my picture with a loaf of Wonder bread and a jar of peanut butter and a jar of jelly. And a note that said, 'Let's do lunch.' " He giggled. "And people wonder why I'm so fucked up." He stopped giggling. Now he was sobbing. "Abel," he wailed. "I want Abel."

"Abel's gone, pal," Bam Bam said gently. "How about some more water? You want water?"

Johnny nodded. Bam Bam scurried off to get it.

"And that's how you got the part in *The Boy Who Cried Wolf?*" I asked.

He swiped at his nose with the back of his hand. "He didn't have me read for him or anything. We just played pinball and rode skateboards and talked. He didn't even show me the script. Never did the whole time we were filming. Just pages . . . We filmed it out in Sylmar someplace. I was scared shitless the whole time. I was supposed to be—I saw a murder. I did! And nobody believed me, and they were after me and . . ." He trailed off, his eyes wide with horror. I wasn't sure if he was still talking about *The Boy Who Cried Wolf* or about what had happened last night on Hazen Drive. He swallowed. "Matthew was scared, too. It was his first movie, too. But he looked out for me. Told the wicked witch off. And she couldn't do a thing. It was great . . . Matthew, he really cared about me. The other directors didn't. I did that Stephen King thing in Alaska with Chris Walken and nobody cared. Nobody. I was stuck there for weeks in the trailer with *her*. Screaming at me, hitting me. I wanted to go to school like a real kid. But she wouldn't let me. I was making too much money. She made me work. All those other movies. It sucked, man. All of it. Except for Matthew. I'd be dead without Matthew. We've always been close. I guess because of *them*."

" 'Them?' "

He turned and stared at me. "Huh?"

"Who, Johnny?"

His cigarette had burned down. He flicked it onto the floor. "Our moms."

"What about them?"

"We hate them."

"He hates Bunny?"

Johnny rolled his eyes. "C'mon, man, you shittin' me?"

"Not intentionally."

"She has two hands around his throat, man. She's choking him. He wants to kill her half the time. Make her bleed."

"Like you did?" I suggested.

"The wicked witch got what she deserved," he snarled. "I'm just sorry she didn't die."

Bam Bam returned now with Johnny's water. And with Lamp, who had on an olive poplin suit today, and seemed even more alert and eager than usual. Or maybe that was just in comparison to Johnny.

"Here we are, Lieutenant," declared Bam Bam. "Here's Johnny Forget, as promised. He's anxious to help the department in any way he can. Isn't that right, John-John?"

"Nice to meet you, Johnny," Lamp said warmly, sticking out his hand.

Johnny shrank from him, terrified. "A-Are there uniforms here?"

"No uniforms," Lamp promised. "That was our deal."

Johnny wasn't convinced. "G-Go look, Bam Bam. Go look."

Bam Bam obediently stuck his head out into the hall. "Nope," he reported. "Just Hoagy's pooch."

"I hate uniforms," Johnny whined. "I hate them."

"Sometimes I don't disagree," said Lamp. "But they do serve their purpose. I'm sorry about your friend, Johnny."

"Abel wasn't my friend," he spat. "He was the man I loved."

Lamp nodded grimly and turned to me. "What brings you here?"

"We're all family here. Haven't you heard?"

"I didn't do it!" cried Johnny. "I didn't kill them!"

"No one is saying you did, Johnny," Lamp assured him, calmly and patiently. "No one is accusing you of a crime. You're a free man. I simply want to ask you some questions, okay?" In response, Johnny started weeping again. Lamp tried a different approach. "If it will make you feel more comfortable, you can have an attorney here."

"Present," piped up Bam Bam.

We both turned to him.

"You're an attorney?" asked Lamp.

"Yessir. Third in my class. Harvard, class of '89."

"Did you know that?" Lamp asked me.

"Nothing about Bam Bam surprises me."

"I gotta go to the bathroom," announced Johnny, struggling to his feet. He wavered there unsteadily.

Bam Bam took his arm. "Sure, pal. Come on. I'll go with you. Here we go . . ."

Off they went.

Lamp clucked sympathetically. "Wowie, zowie, what a basket case." He sat on the sofa, posture perfect, hair combed, hands folded neatly on his lap. He looked as if he should have been running a day-care center for the Campbell's Soup kids, not a murder investigation. "I checked out the day parkers at Zorch's garage, Hoagy. They were no help, as I expected. Saw no evil, heard no evil. The murder weapon is no help either. No prints, no registration. Black market gun all the way—they steal them out of the warehouses by the crateload." He took out his notepad. "Per your suggestion, I also did some backtracking on the death of Rajhib Shambazza, a.k.a. Tyrone Johnson. Exactly how does he figure in?"

"He may not."

Lamp raised his chin at me. "Oh, no you don't, Hoagy," he said crossly. "Ix-nay. I'm not doing your legwork for you for nothing. You did this to me before, and I'm not going to let you—"

"He was hooked up with Toy Schlom. She lived with him."

"Norbert Schlom's *wife?*"

"She used to be a hooker."

He shook his head. "I don't understand these people."

"And you're a lot better off for it." I glanced at the notepad. "Okay?"

"Fair enough," he said reluctantly, opening the notepad.

"Our late friend Shambazza liked to pass himself off as a photographer. Even had himself a studio over on Gower Street in Hollywood. In reality he was an all-around bad apple with a long record. Pornography, pimping, drug dealing . . . Especially drug dealing. Big time to the show-biz crowd. Got hauled in on the Belushi thing, though they never nailed him for it. County sheriffs found him in his studio one morning with a couple of thirty-eights pumped into his head. They figured it for a hit, drug-related. Never got anywhere with it." He closed his notepad and leveled his gaze at me. "He the fellow who took Pennyroyal's nude pictures?"

"He was," I confirmed.

"You're thinking his death ties in somehow?"

"I am."

"How come you didn't mention any of this?" he asked sternly.

"I was going to."

"Same way you were going to call me last night if Johnny showed at Bedford Falls?"

"Shadow told me there were no visitors. Go ahead and ask him."

"Jiminy Cricket, Hoagy," he fumed, exasperated. "I asked you not to do this and you're doing it. What is it with you?"

"I never claimed I was a perfect person, Lieutenant. Only gifted."

"That's just not good enough, Hoagy," he snapped. "No siree. Nope. No way. Uh-uh."

"I'm sorry, Lieutenant. I really am."

He weighed this, arms crossed. "Still not good enough. *I'm* sorry, Hoagy. I'm afraid you're on my doo-doo list from here on in."

I tugged at my ear. "What does that mean exactly?"

"It means no more running down leads for you, no more trading. It means I close the iron door on you. That's what it means."

"Oh, dear."

"It's your own fault, Hoagy."

"It generally is. Want me to leave?"

"No, I don't want you to leave!" He seemed even touchier today. Definitely the heat.

John-John and Bam Bam returned. Johnny flopped onto the

sofa and lit another cigarette, head bowed like a child waiting to be scolded.

Bam Bam sat behind his desk. "Okay, Lieutenant, what can my client tell you?"

"You were seen outside of Zorch's house shortly before the murder, Johnny," Lamp began, treading lightly.

Johnny nodded once, briefly.

"How long were you there?"

Johnny shrugged his shoulders. "I'm not into watches, man," he whispered. "An hour, two hours, dunno. I was there. Then I wasn't."

"Why were you there?" asked Lamp.

"I w-wanted to talk to Abel."

"The housekeeper across the street said you'd been there off and on for several days."

"I wanted to talk to Abel. I wanted him back."

"Okay," Lamp agreed easily. "Any reason you left when you did?"

Johnny didn't answer. Just sat there chewing nervously on the inside of his mouth.

"Johnny?" Lamp pressed gently.

"I felt like it," he breathed in reply.

"No other reason?"

"Like what?"

"Like maybe you saw something?" suggested Lamp.

No reaction.

"Or someone . . . ?"

Johnny's eyes widened in terror. He began to shake again. "Who t-told you?" he stammered, teeth chattering.

Lamp leaned forward. "Is that what happened, Johnny? You saw somebody there? Is that why you cut out?"

An unpleasant rattle started coming out of Johnny's throat.

"Who was it, Johnny? Who did you see?"

"Please don't make me tell you," he whined. "Please. I didn't tell. Not even Matthew. I don't wanna get anybody in trouble."

"You won't get anybody in trouble," Lamp promised. "Except for maybe yourself."

"Hold on a minute, Lieutenant," Bam Bam broke in. "I think you'd better clarify that last remark."

"I'm concerned for Johnny's safety, to be frank," explained Lamp. "If Johnny saw somebody there, then that somebody may

have seen him, too. And if that somebody is our killer, then
Johnny's life is in danger. But I can't help him. Not unless—"

"I don't wanna die!" wailed Johnny.

"You won't, pal," Bam Bam assured him. "You won't. The
man's trying to help you. Only, you'd better tell him who you
saw. Go ahead."

"I'm scared," Johnny whispered. "I—I didn't tell anyone.
Not even Matthew."

"Tell *me*," urged Lamp.

Johnny rubbed his hand over his face. He took a gulp of air.
Then he told Lamp who he saw outside of Abel Zorch's house
minutes before the lawyer and his new boyfriend were murdered.

The House of Wax was a salmon-colored Spanish-style mansion
with a tile roof set on a three-acre hillside off Sunset down in
Pacific Palisades. Its previous owners included Barbara Stan-
wyck, Bobby Darin, Xavier Cougat, and Chad Everett. Fifty or so
members of the press were herded outside the gate in the hot sun
with a couple of cops standing watch over them. Inside the gate
there were a lot of lemon trees, very pretty. Also stands of Italian
cypress, fig, and olive. A row of evenly spaced palms rimmed the
circular driveway, where we left our cars.

The front door was hand-carved mahogany. One of those
yellow Post-It memo tags was stuck to it with the word "Door"
written on it, in case there was any doubt. The housekeeper who
answered the bell was young and quite pretty. She wore a crisp
yellow uniform and spoke only Spanish. But she had no trouble
with the word "police." She led us inside, frowning disapprovingly at Lulu.

The entry hall was quite grand. Two stories high, curving
staircase. The living room, where we waited, was grander. Also
two stories high, with a vaulted ceiling and tall leaded windows
offering a panoramic view of the Pacific. The cool, elegant decor
had that *just so* quality that professional decorators tend to leave
behind, like fingerprints. A matched pair of low-slung bone-
colored sofas were set before the fireplace. The coffee table between them was a massive slab of glass set upon four brass urns.
Magazines, books, a bowl of fruit, a pitcher of dried flowers were
arranged artfully on it. A second conversation area was situated
around an ornate backgammon board, which I thought had
stopped being fashionable on or about when the Bee Gees did.

Maybe it was staging a comeback. Still, I doubted whether Matthew or Pennyroyal ever played it. Or the grand piano that was over by the windows. Maybe that was for Georgie, when he got big enough. The only personal touch in the room was the "George Lassos the Moon" needlepoint from *It's a Wonderful Life* over the fireplace. I was surprised Matthew hadn't taken it with him when he moved out. Possibly he was still figuring to move back in.

There were more yellow Post-Its in here. Affixed to just about every object in the room—a word of identification scrawled on each in big letters. There was even one on the tile floor. It said "Floor."

Lamp paced while we waited, nervously smoothing his neat, blond hair and drying his palms on the thighs of his trousers. Lulu watched him curiously.

"Don't worry, Lieutenant," I said. "You look stunning."

"I'm not speaking to you," he muttered, scowling at me.

"Is that part of being on your doo-doo list?"

He wouldn't answer me.

"Here . . ." I went over and straightened the knot in his tie for him. "There you are. Now you'll knock her dead."

"I'll get you for this, Hoagy," he vowed, reddening.

"That's the spirit. Fiery. Women like that. And don't forget to smile—you have nice teeth."

"You're succotash, Hoagy. Succotash."

The housekeeper returned and led us out through the French doors to a brick terrace, where there was a weathered teak dining table and chairs and a built-in barbecue grill. A faint breeze was coming off of the ocean. A flight of steps took us down to the pool, which was set off from the rest of the yard by a privet hedge. Rosebushes and camellias had been planted in front of it for color. The mistress of the house was in the pool, swimming laps with a steady, determined crawl. Cassandra sat at a round table under a bright green market umbrella watching Georgie, who was wriggling around in his playpen in the shade next to her. Cassandra wore a white tank top, hot pink leggings, gold gladiator sandals, and her usual shocked expression. Her bare arms and ankles were unnaturally pale, almost waxen. She had no yellow tag stuck to her, but there was one stuck to the table. It said "Table."

Pennyroyal waved to us and swam over to the edge and

pulled herself up out of the water, sleek and shiny as a porpoise. I could hear Lamp draw in his breath. He stopped breathing completely thereafter. She had on the tiniest of white string bikinis. Her body was magnificent—slender, shapely, smoothly muscled, ripe, firm. There was no hint of spread in her haunches, no sag to her breasts. Her skin was golden and flawless. She shook the water from her hair, then went over to the table and got a towel, moving nimbly and gracefully on her dainty bare feet. She dabbed at herself with the towel and then showed Lamp her two-million-dollar dimples. "Pleased to meet you, Lieutenant," she said huskily.

He nodded dumbly, said nothing.

Cassandra looked him up and down. "You're cute. Ya really a cop?"

He nodded again.

"I could just eat ya up," she said, flirting.

"And she would, too," I pointed out.

Cassandra treated me to her upraised middle finger.

"We've been working and trying to pretend we're not prisoners here," Pennyroyal informed us. "Would you guys care for some iced tea?"

I said that would be fine. I said it for the both of us—Lamp seemed incapable of speech.

She turned to her housekeeper. "Maria, could you get us two more glasses, please?"

Maria frowned, not comprehending.

Pennyroyal held up a glass and two fingers. "Glasses, *por favor.*"

Maria nodded eagerly. *"Si, señora."* She went off to the house to get them.

"She's wonderful, but she's only been in the country two weeks," explained Pennyroyal. "That's what all of the yellow tags are for—I'm trying to teach her English."

"Ah."

"Georgie just loves her," she added, scooping him up out of his playpen. "Don't you sweetie? Huh?" She nuzzled him and cooed at him playfully until he giggled with delight. Then she sat in a chair with him, cradling him in the crook of her arm. He had her porcelain blue eyes and blond hair. Otherwise, I thought he looked like Sydney Greenstreet. She looked up at Lamp and smiled. To me she said, "Is he okay?"

The lieutenant was frozen there, staring, his mouth slightly open.

"He's fine. Just a huge fan of yours." I raised my voice. "Exhale, Lieutenant. You're turning blue."

He did, his chest heaving. "Lovely home you have here, Miss Brim," he got out, weakly.

"Why, thank you. Won't you sit down?"

We sat. Lulu gave Cassandra a disdainful sniff just to throw a scare into her, then curled up under me in the shade, immensely pleased with herself. Maria came back with our glasses and filled them with iced tea from the pitcher on the table. Then she retreated.

Lamp drank deeply from his, recovering his composure. Both women watched him carefully. He put his glass down and looked at Pennyroyal, then at Cassandra. Then back at Pennyroyal. "You know, this would be a real good opportunity, Miss Brim," he said, his voice firm and earnest.

"For what, Lieutenant?" she asked.

"For you to confess."

"Gawd!" shrieked Cassandra, goggle-eyed.

"You'll save all of us a lot of trouble. And the taxpayers a lot of their hard-earned money. I'll get you in the end. You know it and I know it. So why don't you just get it off of your ch-ch-chest. You'll get a fair deal from me."

"Gawd, I don't believe this!"

Pennyroyal was silent. Her beautiful face gave away nothing.

"We know you were at Abel Zorch's house at around the time of the murders, Miss Brim," he went on. "We have an eyewitness who can testify to that. So you may as well just—"

"Johnny told you, didn't he?" she said coolly.

"He did," Lamp affirmed. "He saw you. And I take it you saw him."

"You were really there?" cried Cassandra.

"Yes," Pennyroyal said quietly.

"Why didn't you step forward and tell us about this, Miss Brim?" Lamp inquired.

Georgie wriggled a bit in her arms. She stroked him soothingly and leveled her innocent blue eyes at Lamp. "It would have been the right thing to do, Lieutenant," she admitted. "I know that. Honest I do. But you already knew about Johnny being there. And I just . . . I didn't want to get involved. I've had so much terrible publicity already. The last thing I need is more. You can understand that, can't you?"

Lamp pitched right over onto his back, four paws up in the air. "Oh, sure," he said, a sickly grin on his face. "Sure thing. This business with the photos—it must be pretty awful for you."

"Pretty awful," she agreed unhappily, rocking Georgie gently back and forth.

"And I'm not accusing you or anything," he said. "Heck no. I just want you to tell me what you know."

"Anything, Lieutenant," she said. "I'll tell you anything I can."

"Good." He grinned at her some more, and kept on grinning until he turned to me helplessly and said, "Where was I?"

"You were going to ask her what she was doing at Zorch's," I said.

He nodded. "What were you?" he asked.

"I'd been driving around," she replied. "I was upset about everything, and I needed to think. I've already told Hoagy all of this."

Lamp looked at me with a pained expression.

"It's true, Lieutenant. She did."

"I wanted to talk to Abel about my pictures," she continued. "Why he did it."

"You think Abel's the one who leaked them?" I asked her.

"I'm sure he was," she replied. "I was planning to fire him because of it. I couldn't take any more of his tactics. I tried calling him at his office earlier, only his secretary said he was in court. I think he may have been ducking me—he knew I was furious. Anyway, while I was driving around I decided to stop and see if he was home yet."

"What time was this?" asked Lamp.

She considered this. "Sometime between five-thirty and a quarter to six, I think. I rang the bell at the gate. His houseboy told me Abel wasn't home and he didn't know when he would be. He didn't invite me in to wait."

"I wonder why Kenji didn't mention this to me?" mused Lamp aloud.

"He probably didn't think it was important," she offered.

"Still," countered Lamp. "We *are* investigating his boss's murder. You'd think he'd want to be more candid."

"No, you wouldn't, Lieutenant," she argued politely. "People like Kenji are trained to be discreet. They don't volunteer infor-mation to anyone. Especially if they work for someone like Abel."

Lamp nodded, unconvinced. "Could be. He didn't give us anything about Johnny either. We had to get that from the house-keeper across the street. Go on, Miss Brim."

"When I was backing away from the house, I noticed Johnny sitting there across the street on his motorcycle, looking so sad. Before I could pull over to say hello, he bolted. Took off like a scared little boy."

"Then what happened?" asked Lamp.

"I drove around in the hills some more, like I told Hoagy. And that's all there is to it, Lieutenant." She leveled her blue eyes at him again. "Please believe me—it's the truth."

Lamp cleared his throat. "That's all there is?"

"That's all there is," she swore.

He put away his pad and pencil. "Okay, Miss Brim. I'm satis-fied. For now. But if you remember anything else, please call me. Work with me, trust me. I can keep you out of the papers."

"Nobody can do that, Lieutenant," she said bitterly.

"Maybe you're right," he conceded, getting to his feet. "Sorry to bother you."

"It was no bother at all, Lieutenant. You've been very kind."

He blushed. "Nice meeting you, Miss Dee."

"Yeah, yeah, shewa," said Cassandra. "Any time, honey."

"Coming, Hoagy?" asked Lamp.

I stayed put. "I have some more questions, strictly book-related. If you don't mind, Pennyroyal."

"Of course not. Stick around." She stood up with Georgie. "But this does mean you have to babysit," she said, plopping him down in my lap.

"Oh, no, it doesn't."

"Just while I show the Lieutenant out, Hoagy. Please?"

Before I could mount a successful argument she went pad-ding off toward the house with Lamp, asking him how long he'd been a cop and if he enjoyed it.

Georgie squirmed around in my lap, gurgling, then nestled against my chest and gazed up at me with awe and wonder. And he hadn't even read my novels yet. I asked him what he thought of the new Don DeLillo. He drooled in response. At least he had some taste. I offered him my linen handkerchief, which he clutched tightly in his tiny fist. Lulu watched all of this carefully, a noise coming from her throat that makes her sound like an asthmatic Hereford. This was her being jealous.

"How's Big Steve?" I asked Cassandra.

"Fuck you," she replied shortly.

"Aren't we the touchy one today."

"You'd be touchy, too, if ya had my morning."

"Having trouble with her?" I asked.

"No shit. She's such an appallingly sweet person. I can't get her to say a single bad woid about anyone, especially Matthew. This is a goil's woist nightmare, I'm telling ya."

Georgie began to doze. He seemed very relaxed. I guess he didn't have a lot on his mind.

"She's already dished plenty in the newspapers," I pointed out.

"She says that all came from Zorch and she don't wanna use it. I mean, hey, she's *gotta* dish. I just got our publisher on the phone to remind her of that. It's a fight, I'm telling ya. I gotta push, push, push. But if I push her too hard, I swear she'll pull out of the whole deal, leaving me high and dry. I'm getting bad vibes about her, I'm telling ya. I don't think she's tough enough to carry this off." She took a gulp of her iced tea. "Oh, hey, I had an early breakfast with one of my pals at the *Enquirer.*"

"And?"

"Nuttin'. The negatives were the proverbial gift horse. Somebody just left 'em there under the office door in a plain envelope. They found 'em when they opened up for the day, about nine. They got no idea who it was—no name, no address, no note, no nuttin'. Whoever did it, it shewa wasn't money they was after—none changed hands."

"I see. Well, thanks for checking."

"Hey, we're in this together, like I keep telling ya."

"If we're in this together then how about holding Georgie for a while?"

But that wasn't necessary. America's cutest mom was already making her way back toward us around the pool, moving with loose-limbed, provocative grace in her bikini. She didn't flounce. She didn't preen. She was utterly natural. Most uncommon.

She smiled at the sight of Georgie dozing there in my lap. "I think he likes you, Hoagy."

"No, he doesn't."

"You seem very at home with a baby."

"No, I don't."

Amused, she lifted him up and laid him down gently in his playpen. Then she curled up in a chair with one bare, shapely leg under her. "Now, what is it you wanted to ask?"

"Before we go any further," Cassandra interjected, "I wanna go on record as saying I'm totally opposed to this."

Pennyroyal looked at her curiously. "Opposed to what, Cassie?"

"Collaborating with the enemy," she replied sharply.

"What happened to 'We're in this together'?" I asked.

"Whatever ya tell him," she went on, ignoring me, "he's gonna put in Matthew's book. That defeats the whole point of what we're trying to do here. Our publisher is *not* gonna like this, believe me."

"Fine," said Pennyroyal, bristling. "I'll give him his money back."

Cassandra panicked. "Whoa, honey, now let's not lose our—"

"I'm writing this book to set the record straight," Pennyroyal said firmly. "That's all I care about. If talking to Hoagy will help me do that, then I'll talk to Hoagy. Is that understood?"

"Yeah, yeah, shewa," muttered Cassandra unhappily. "Dense I'm not."

Pennyroyal shook her head at her. "God, Cassie, you're such a pit bull sometimes. Chill out. And why don't you sit out in the sun for a few minutes? You're pale as a ghost."

"I boin."

"I have sun block," Pennyroyal offered.

"It makes me break out," Cassandra said stubbornly.

Pennyroyal rolled her eyes. "Would you rather not sit in on this?"

"Just try and get me out of here," Cassandra dared her.

"Okay, okay, fine," she said wearily.

"Besides, this is a major privilege for me," Cassandra added. "Getting to watch the master at woik. Where's your tape recorder, huh?"

"Didn't bring it."

"Gawd, ya keep it all in your head? How?"

"That's no problem—it swells to meet any occasion."

"I'm in awe."

Pennyroyal poured us some more iced tea and told me to go ahead.

I did. "You mentioned that Mrs. Wax doesn't much care for you."

She nodded. "Not much."

"How come?"

She sipped her tea. "I'm not completely sure. Bunny just always treated me like an intruder. From the second Matthew and I started going out." She gazed out at her view of the ocean, her tousled blond hair drying in the breeze. A wisp of it fluttered across her eyes. She brushed it away. "He took me go-cart racing on our first date. A place out in Northridge called Malibu Grand Prix."

"He still goes there," I said.

"Does he?" Her eyes turned soft. She swallowed and reached for her cigarettes. "It took him forever to ask me out. He kept staring at me on the set. But he could barely talk to me, he was so painfully shy. I couldn't believe it. I mean, I was nobody and he was this world-famous director. . . . He actually had Johnny ask me if I'd go out with him. You know, like a junior high go-between. He was incredibly nervous that first night. It took him three or four dates before he started to relax."

"Yet you kept going out with him."

She showed me her dimples. "I thought he was cute. And sweet. And before I knew it, I was in love with him. It was all straight out of a storybook or an Archie comic. It was like being a kid again, innocent and happy and clean. Christ, the man didn't even try to kiss me until we'd gone out five times. That sort of thing just doesn't happen. Not to me." She shook a cigarette out of the pack and lit it thoughtfully. "But, yeah, from the beginning Bunny didn't approve. I guess she thought I wasn't good enough for her precious little Matty."

"Because she knew you'd had an abortion?"

Cassandra screamed. Big one. The birds flew for the trees. Lulu scurried for cover. Georgie woke up, wailing. *"Gawd, Penny!"* Cassandra cried in shock and fury. *"Gaaaawd!"*

Pennyroyal's eyes avoided her collaborator's. "I was going to tell you about it, Cassie," she said hastily. "I was, honest. I—I was working my way up to it, that's all. I guess I just feel funny talking about it."

"How d'ya think *I* feel?" Cassandra demanded angrily. "Having to find out something like this from my bitterest rival?"

"What happened to 'colleague'?" I inquired, tugging at my ear.

"I was going to tell you," Pennyroyal insisted. "Now just cut me some slack, okay?" She stubbed out her cigarette and went over to Georgie and quieted him down. She seemed a good mother—calm, attentive, loving. "In answer to your question, Hoagy—yes, that didn't help me with Bunny. She thought I was a tramp. The public, meanwhile, thought I was a goody-goody. I'm not either of those things, and never have been. I'm just me, Pennyroyal."

"That's our title," Cassandra said proudly.

"Catchy."

"I've never slept around," Pennyroyal said. "Not in high school, not now, not ever. I go out with one guy, and I give it my best. Until it runs its course. I always hope it won't, but it always does. I don't know, maybe it's me . . ." She glanced down at Georgie. He was slipping back to sleep. She came back and sat down. "I was a typical Valley girl. I partied a little, smoked and drank a little. I went to Taft High. I was a cheerleader. Craig, my boyfriend—my only boyfriend—was a soccer player. We started having sex when I was fifteen. He was seventeen. We'd gone out for six months before we did. One night when my parents were out we got careless—which is to say, he told me not to worry, and I believed him."

"Shithead," muttered Cassandra.

"No, that's not fair," said Pennyroyal. "He stuck by me through the whole thing. He was a nice boy."

Cassandra shook her head in disgust. "See what I'm up against, Hoagy?"

"My mom knew all about it," Penny continued. "My dad still doesn't know. He'll freak out when he reads my book."

"And Craig? Whatever happened to him?"

She smiled wistfully. "He went off to Berkeley. Dumped me for a college girl. I never heard from him again."

She reached for a tortoise-shell comb on the table and began to gently comb out her long, lustrous, golden hair. I watched her, remembering all those times I'd brushed out Merilee's, brushed it until it shimmered in the flickering light of the candle beside our bed. I watched her. And I found her watching me back, her innocent blue eyes holding mine, weighing mine, inviting mine . . . *"What makes them so special, Meat? . . ."*

"When I was hired to play Debbie Dale," she went on, her voice low and throaty, "Shelley asked me straight out if I had any skeletons in my closet. I told him all about it. And about the photographs, too."

"This is cool," said Cassandra, backing off. "This I know all about."

Penny set down the comb and reached for her iced tea. "I was working at the Gap in the Galleria Mall," she recalled, sipping it. "Toy came in one day, real elegant and well tailored, and told me she was an agent who represented fashion models. She asked me if I'd ever considered doing any modeling myself. Hoagy, every teenaged girl in the world dreams of some woman coming up to her and asking her that question. She gave me her card and suggested I think it over. I didn't have to for very long. I phoned her the next day. She seemed pleased to hear from me. For starters, she said I'd need to put together a book. She gave me the address of a photographer in Hollywood and told me to meet her there and to bring a bikini and two hundred dollars. That was my whole savings. But she said that's how much a good set of professional shots cost. I didn't tell my parents about it. I didn't tell anyone . . ." She lit another cigarette. Her eyes were on the ocean now, her voice flat and unemotional. "He was a black man, the photographer. Very handsome and charming. He and Toy were lovers, which sort of surprised me. He kept telling me how pretty I was, but I was real tense. So he gave me some weed to relax me. The three of us smoked it together. He took some shots of me in my bathing suit. And then he wanted to take some shots of me *out* of my bathing suit. I freaked, naturally. Said no way. He got real pissed at me. Told Toy he was tired of dealing with amateurs. She explained to me that professional models all have to do full nude shots for their portfolios, like it or not. She was real nice about it. Even told me I could have my money back if I wasn't into it. She was so nice I decided to go ahead and do it. My teeth were clenched the whole time. I felt like I was being X-rayed for some terrible lump at the doctor's office. When it was over she hugged me and told me she'd call as soon as she had something for me. I went home and waited by

the phone, positive I was going to be the next Christie Brinkley."
She laughed to herself sadly. "I was pretty naive."

"She didn't call you?" I asked.

"Oh, she called me, all right," Pennyroyal said. "But not
with any kind of modeling assignment, per se. She kept wanting
me to go out to dinner with these men. One was an advertising
executive. Another was a producer. They were always older men,
men who she told me could do my modeling career a lot of good.
I kept telling her I wasn't interested, and she kept on calling.
Finally, it dawned on me what I'd suckered myself into—
Shambazza was really a pimp, and she recruited teenaged girls
like me for him. I guess I was pretty slow. But she was so low-key
and oblique about it all. I mean, she never came out and said it.
Or even made any dark hints. It was more like . . . it was simply
*there* for me, if I wanted it. The parties, the cruises, attending to
certain men. Making little movies for them, with them. It's a
whole little world, Hoagy, an ugly little world, and a girl with
looks can make a good deal of money in it. Even convince herself
she's helping her career. There *are* a couple of pretty big actresses who got started that way." She cited as example one of
the biggest prime-time soap opera stars of the 1980s. "But it
certainly wasn't for me, and I told Toy so. She was very good
about it. Said to call her if I ever changed my mind. But I never
did. And she never contacted me again. They made their two
hundred bucks off me and moved on. I was never paid to model
in the nude, Hoagy. I never made a dirty movie. I was never a
paid escort or a hooker or whatever else you want to call it."

"Did you ever go by a different name?"

"When Shambazza was shooting me, he and Toy mentioned
that they didn't think the name Pennyroyal Brim sounded sexy.
They thought the name Carla Pettibone did. But I never used it. I
never had the opportunity to." She sighed. "And that's the whole,
sordid story, Hoagy. My life as a bad girl."

"That's as far as it went?"

She raised an eyebrow at me. "Don't you believe me?"

"It's nothing personal. I don't believe anyone."

"That's as far as it went," she stated. "Just a stupid school-
girl mistake, really. But it made Shelley crazy when I told him
about it. Debbie Dale . . . Debbie Dale would not model in the
nude. I guess he had visions of Shambazza trying to peddle the

shots to a magazine. So he got hold of him and bought the negatives. Just to play it safe."

"Shambazza was murdered a few weeks after he was paid
off. Did you know that?"

"I read about it in the paper," she acknowledged.

"He dealt drugs, I understand."

"That part came as news to me. He had a little weed around,
but nothing that indicated he was a big-time dealer."

"Toy lived with him, you said."

"Uh-huh." She coughed and cleared her throat. She was getting a bit fidgety. Her bare foot tapped the pavement.

"Must have been odd for you to come across her again," I
suggested. "Married to Norbert Schlom, I mean."

"Extremely odd," she agreed. "But that's the movie business
—people are constantly reinventing themselves. You get used to
it. She and I are not close friends, if that was going to be your
next question."

"It wasn't. But I'll try to remember it next time I throw a
dinner party."

"You can be terribly caustic sometimes," she said softly.

"I can be," I admitted. "It's best to wash thoroughly with
strong soap if you get exposed to me. I'm liable to leave burns."

She gave me an up-from-under look. "Should I consider
wearing rubber gloves?"

"That depends."

"On what?"

"On how you're planning to use me."

"*What* are youse two going on about?" Cassandra demanded, bewildered. "I mean, does somebody wanna tell me?"

"Sorry," I said. "We got off the subject."

"Or onto it." Pennyroyal moistened her lips with the tip of
her pink tongue. "Depending on how you look at it."

This one roused Lulu, my fierce protector, who got up and
moved halfway between Pennyroyal and myself, the better to
watch over me.

"My next question," I continued, "was going to be about
how you got discovered."

"After high school I enrolled at USC, where I was fortunate
enough to become a member of the cheerleading squad," she
replied mechanically. She'd obviously undergone this particular
Q&A in a thousand interviews. "They happen to do a lot of pro-

motional things for the school—calendars, posters. The SC cheerleaders are very popular. Anyway, Matthew had been looking for a blond cheerleader type to play Debbie Dale, and I guess he was really starting to scrape the bottom of the barrel because—"

"Don't put yourself down, honey," cautioned Cassandra.

"Correction—they were searching for a new face," Pennyroyal said tartly. "Anyway, his casting agent sent him some of our group shots. Legend has it that Matthew pointed right to me and said 'That's Debbie Dale.' I had zero acting experience. He didn't care. He wanted me. And he got me."

"Did he give you much direction?" I asked.

"He just kept telling me to be myself," she replied. "Because I *was* Debbie. That's what he kept saying: 'You *are* Debbie.' What I was was petrified. My knees shook. I was nineteen, for God's sake. I still am. Frightened, I mean. I'm positive that everybody's finally going to wake up one of these mornings and realize that I'm a complete fraud. I'm no movie star. I'm just lucky, that's all."

"I'll let you in on a little secret," I said. "Every star in the business feels that way."

"Even Merilee Nash?" she asked.

"Especially Merilee Nash. There are mornings when she's so convinced she's a fake that she almost convinces me."

Her eyes searched my face. "But she doesn't?"

"Not a chance."

"That must be nice," she said longingly. "Having someone who believes in you that way. That's a real relationship. Not like what I had. All I had were the highlights. A second Badger movie. A twenty-first birthday party. A wedding. A third movie. Georgie. I had everything but the relationship in between."

"I'd like to hear about the wedding," I said.

"It was very exciting," she recalled, brightening. "Sinful, almost. We just ran off to Las Vegas one weekend and did it, totally spur of the moment. Told no one. Neither of us had ever been to Vegas before. We had fun there. That was our honeymoon. We had to be back first thing Monday morning—he was in postproduction on *Badger Two*. The Shelleys, they were really happy for us. Threw a small party for us at their house. Bunny, she just kept glowering at me, *willing* me to drop dead on the spot." She looked around at her yard. "We bought this place the following weekend. Spent a lot of our time fixing it up. We never did get to have a real honeymoon. I'd like to have one someday."

"Possibly you and Trace . . . ?"

Cassandra leaned forward.

"No," said Pennyroyal regretfully. "Trace was always a friend. A good friend. And then he was a strong shoulder to cry on when things went sour with Matthew. But I think we've gone sour, too. It sure doesn't take long, does it?"

"Not in this weather. Where did you and Matthew go wrong?"

She tossed her head, considering her reply a moment. "I honestly don't think Matthew has the slightest idea who I am. I'm not Debbie—I'm a human being. He was totally shocked to discover that I get my period and shave my legs and have bad breath in the morning. And I'm not Little Miss Sunshine, either. I can be moody and stupid and a real bitch. I throw things. That shocked him, too. Matthew . . . Matthew doesn't understand adults. It shows in his movies. They're a child's view of the world. No grown-up love scenes. Our marriage was exactly like that— strictly 'Fade-out to the next morning.' Because that's how it's done in the movies and TV shows he worships. He has no other frame of reference to draw upon. His parents weren't close, I gather. He even insisted we sleep in twin beds. I hated those beds. I have a big bed up there now. . . . He never knew how to behave after the fade-out. He hasn't the slightest concept of sharing, confiding. He never, ever opened up to me. As for the sex itself, I don't feel very comfortable talking about that. Let's just say it was consistent with the rest. There was no closeness or intimacy. It was always kind of . . . furtive."

"And before the fade-out? What was he like then?"

"He smothered me," she replied flatly. "He couldn't stand me having other friends or interests. He wanted my whole life to be *him*. And when I got offered other parts, he freaked. I was offered good parts, Hoagy—*Pretty Woman*, *Ghost*, Maid Marian in *Robin Hood*. I had to turn all of them down. He forbade me to work for other directors. He was so jealous and insecure. So immature. I tried to help him grow. Become more social, get out more to concerts and plays, maybe dress a little nicer. Neither of us have ever been to Europe. I thought it would be fun to have someone come here a couple of evenings a week to teach us French. I thought we could go to France for a month. Learn about the culture, the food, the wine. He refused. He wouldn't do it. All he ever wanted to do was sit in the den and watch old movies, over and over again. To me, a relationship is growing together. To Matthew, it's hiding together. Matthew Wax is a shut-in. That's what he is. And that's what did us in." She sat back and puffed out her cheeks. She'd spoken her piece.

"Sounds like you've given it a lot of thought," I observed.

"Damned right I have," she said.

"For what it's worth, he is making more of an effort now."

"Because I left him or because the critics did?" she wanted to know.

"Because he's lost his way."

The breeze picked up a bit. She shivered, goose bumps on her arms. "Maybe you'll have better luck with him than I did."

"I might. It's easier for me."

"Why?" she wondered.

"I don't love him."

"I'll always love him," she admitted, her eyes filling with tears. "It's true."

"Gawd, this is so *sad*," whined Cassandra.

"Don't tell me you're just figuring that out." I reached for my boater. Lulu stirred. "I want to thank you, Pennyroyal. You've been very helpful. I appreciate it."

She didn't seem to be listening anymore. She was gazing out at the Pacific.

"I do have one more question," I said.

"Of course," she said hoarsely, wiping her eyes. "Anything."

"If all of this were happening to Debbie Dale—the breakup, the bad publicity, the nude shots . . ."

"Yes?"

"How would she handle it? What would she do?"

She let out a short laugh. "Seriously?"

"Seriously."

"The answer to that question," she replied, "is that none of this would ever, ever happen to Debbie Dale."

Norbert Schlom had reportedly plunked down $275 million on Panorama City's new Yeti-inspired office tower, a thirty-two-story postmodern Himalayan peak complete with crags, escarpments and snowy peaks. It looked a little like the Matterhorn with windows. An open-air arcade connected it to the Panorama City Convention Center and the adjoining Sheraton Hotel complex, which was situated directly across a man-made lake from the grand entrance to the Panorama City Studio Tour.

It wasn't a place to make movies anymore. No wonder he needed Bedford Falls.

He was looking at dailies in one of the few remaining bungalows, which was located across an alley from one of the few remaining soundstages. Inside was a quaintly old-fashioned screening room. Oversized red velvet armchairs with individual cigarette stands and phones were positioned six across, a dozen or so rows deep. Schlom's bulky, intimidating self was parked in the middle surrounded by a coterie of development boys and girls and the director of what was up on screen. They were watching Panorama City's hottest new chop 'n' sock star, Sylvie, a sexy Norwegian kung fu mistress whose low-budget debut had grossed $120 million. Right now she was busy grabbing two Japanese thugs by the lapels, conking their heads together, and hurling them bodily through a plate glass window.

"What the *fuck* is this?!" Schlom erupted. "Hold it! Stop! Cut it!" The lights came up. "What the fuck you doing to me?" he demanded of the director. "Is this some kind of joke?"

The director, a thin kid with a see-through mustache, cleared his throat nervously. "I—I don't think so, Norbert. What's the problem?"

"What's the *problem*?!" he raged, turning purple. "You got two Japs chattering away like monkeys and then getting thrown out a window like a couple sacks of *shit*! How do you think that's gonna make 'em feel?!"

"Who, Norbert?"

"Who the fuck do you think?" he bellowed.

"But you approved the script."

"Get rid of it, putz! Cut it! Jesus, this is all I need right now!" He spotted me standing there by the door, hat in hand. "Okay, all of you get outta here. Scram. Beat it. I got another meeting." Angrily, he stuffed a piece of note paper in his mouth and began chomping on it.

They quickly filed out, pale and tight-lipped. The director was muttering under his breath, though not too loud. Lulu watched them go. I don't think she was regretting her decision to stay out of the business.

"Hiya, Norb," I said pleasantly, as I strolled down the aisle toward him. "Eat any good books lately?"

"Shit for brains, all of 'em," he grunted sourly. "Idiots. Punks. Not like Kid. Kid was smart."

"Still is, I believe."

"Take a seat, Hoag," he said, turning genial. He wore a white shirt, red tie, and navy blue tropical suit. His white hair was beautifully coiffed. His manicure gleamed. His eyes were still yellow.

I sat. The armchair swung back on me, like a recliner. I yanked it upright, my balmorals set firmly on the floor.

He checked the Philippe Patek on his thick, hairy wrist. "I can only give you a few minutes, and wouldn't even do that if it weren't for Kid. I don't want no ill will between him and me. But I'm telling you straight off if you changed your mind about that stock offer you're too late. Your deal was with Abel, not me. Me, I'd just as soon crap on you. I remember you from before, see. Harmon Wright told me all about you. He said you were a total fucking pain."

"That's me, all right. And the stock isn't why I called."

"I'm running this show now," he declared, stabbing his chest with his thumb. "And I got a different agenda than Abel. The Murakami people, they've had it with nudie pictures and killings. Enough already. From now on everything is strictly dignity and class. I've hired Pennyroyal a new lawyer, Kinsley Usher."

"The former senator?"

"Dignity and class," he growled with pride. "Top-notch Beverly Hills firm. Excellent contacts in Washington and Sacramento. The man's high road, all the way."

"Aside from his indictment for accepting illegal company contributions," I mentioned.

Schlom scowled at me. "That was all a misunderstanding. He was fully cleared. Look, we want this thing off the front page, Hoag. We want a nice, civilized, low-key settlement. Strictly business. Abel just didn't understand that."

"You didn't approve of his methods?"

"Abel Zorch, God rest his soul, was a schmuck," he replied, inspecting his manicure. "I mean that in the kindest sense."

"I wasn't aware it had one."

"So today you learned something," he retorted. "Abel played by his own rules, and he played for keeps. Guys like that rub most people the wrong way. Me, I admire 'em. It's easy to go along with the flow. It's hard to go against it. You gotta be tough and you gotta be a little crazy." He looked me over with his rat's eyes. "I see a little of him in you."

"Do you?"

"Yeah, I do," he observed, sticking out his thick, liverish lower lip. "You don't give a fuck. You make it very clear."

"And all along I thought I was being subtle."

"Toy and me are throwing a big memorial thing for him up at the house Saturday night. Chance for everybody in the film community to pay their respects. Also to meet the president of Murakami, Mr. Hiroshi Nakamura, who's flying in from Tokyo. Usher's making sure the better elements are on hand—Jack Valenti, Chuck Heston, Greg Peck, the Reagans . . ."

"Dignity and class?" I observed.

"East meets West," he said, helping himself to another piece of crisp white notepaper. "In fact, it's gonna be a Wild West theme. Couple of tons of ribs on the barbeque, everybody dressing like cowboys. Toy's very creative that way. She wants you to come."

"I'll be happy to."

"Good," he grunted. "Everybody'll be there."

"Even Trace Washburn?"

He stopped chewing.

"How come you won't let him work here?" I asked.

He shifted in his armchair, swiped at the lint on his trousers with one of his thick, blunt hands. "Trace is used up," he said gruffly. "He's too old, he drinks too much, and his price is too high. Kid was the only director in town who'd still hire him, and just to show you how smart Trace is he goes out and shtups the man's wife."

"There's no other reason why he can't work here?"

"Like what?" he wondered, narrowing his eyes at me.

"Something personal, perhaps."

"I don't believe in personal," he said shortly. "Strictly business." He glanced at his watch.

"Just a few more questions—what made you decide to hire a nineteen-year-old kid to direct for you?"

"What did he tell you?" he shot back.

"That you smelled money on him."

"I did," he affirmed, a rare smile crossing his pitted, ugly face. "Some people reek of it. You, for instance . . ."

"What about me?"

"You don't."

"Thanks. That's something I've always wondered."

"I seen a million of them film school bright boys," he said. "They all come strutting into my office spouting John Ford and Preston fucking Sturges. They know *Citizen Kane* shot for shot, *Casablanca* line for line. They know it all. If they're lucky, they end up directing commercials for toilet bowl cleaners. Kid, he had his *own* ideas. That's why I gave him a job, and that's why he made millions for this studio and himself."

"Shelley Selden claims you stole many of those millions from him. They still haven't seen a penny from the net proceeds of *Yeti*, for example."

"Aw, you're not falling for that old ploy, are you?" he blustered.

"Which old ploy is that?"

"All of 'em pull that shit on us—claim we cheated 'em. Then they hold a gun to our head and demand gross points, or else. They're ruining the business. The talent is ruining this business. We're the ones who make the movies, not them. We take the financial risk, not them. A movie flops, we're the ones who have to eat it, not them. They never offer to give us any of their salary back. Hell no, a movie flops, that's *our* problem. But when it's a hit, suddenly we're stealing from them. You wanna talk about *Yeti*? I gave Kid an unlimited budget. I never said no to him. He had to shoot in fucking Katmandu, fine. He had to have cheeseburgers and tapes of the fucking Dodgers flown in daily, fine. I gave him whatever he asked for. *And* I gave him a million dollars in salary. Now don't you think that's enough?"

"That's not the issue."

"What is?"

"Whether or not you cheated him out of his share of the profits."

"I treated him like a son," he insisted. "Invited him into my home. He never came, but I invited him. He was my ace. Why would I want to cheat him, huh? Why would I?"

"For money."

He stared at me a second with his rat's eyes. "Our books are always open. I told them. I'm telling you. You wanna run an audit, go ahead. You won't find a fucking nickel."

"Of course not. Your accountants could hide a herd of elephants in a Porta Potti. About *The Three Stooges*—"

"What about it?" he demanded, tensing.

"Matthew says he never wanted to direct it."

Schlom laughed harshly. "They always say that about their flops."

"Did you force him into it by planting cocaine in his bungalow?"

"That's bullshit, pal. Put it in his book and I'll sue your fucking asses."

"I'll rephrase it: Did you have someone plant cocaine in his bungalow?"

He reached for another sheet of notepaper. Carefully, he worked it into a small ball. "I'm gonna tell you the God's honest truth," he reflected, popping the paper in his mouth. "So you'll know the real story. And why I blew the other night at Spago when you brought it up. See, I heard he was having problems. There were rumors before the picture even went before the cameras. That he was using heavy."

"Matthew?"

"Kid," he affirmed sadly. "Why do you think the movie sucked? He was stoned on coke the whole time. I was told he even had drugs on the set. I don't go in for that. I run a clean studio. This is a family environment. So I said something to him. I said it to him as a friend, as a mentor, whatever I was to him. I cared about him. I wanted him to get help. I wasn't worried about the movie—fuck the movie. I was worried about *him*. This was his life we're talking about." Schlom shook his head. "He got pissed at me. I guess he was in what they call the denial stage. That's why he left Panorama—because I was hassling him to clean up his act. I hear he has. I hope so. I do. For his sake, and his family's. But I'm angry and I'm hurt that he'd try to blame me for what happened. I've heard that story before, that I planted stuff on him. He made it up. The truth is, it was all his own fault."

I could only stare. I was in the presence of greatness. Norbert Schlom was the most brilliant liar I'd ever come across, capable of sounding caring, benevolent and even a tiny bit bruised while in the midst of dishing out slander of the most malicious sort. They can't teach you how to lie like that. It's a gift you're born with, a gift that had taken him all the way to the pinnacle of Hollywood success, and kept him there.

"Does the name Shambazza mean anything to you?" I asked.

He mulled it over. "Character in *Star Wars*, wasn't he? Furry fellow who tried to shtup the princess?"

"He was a drug dealer and pimp."

"I don't know from pimps and drug dealers," he growled.

"Toy knew him quite well. She lived with him. Before somebody shot him in the head, that is."

He grinned at me crookedly. "Trying to piss me off, aren't ya?"

"I am not."

"Toy and me made a pact when we got together," Schlom said easily. "No past. I don't ask her about hers. She don't ask me about mine. That way nobody gets upset."

"I see. What about her and Abel Zorch?"

"What about them?"

"Were they close?"

"Ask her," he suggested. "Nicely."

"I always ask nicely."

"Toy is a fine, lovely woman. I care about her more than anyone in the world. You hassle her about her background, you make her feel crummy and you'll go back to New York pissing blood, Hoag. Is there anything else? I got people waiting."

"One more thing. Now that Pennyroyal has herself a kinder, gentler lawyer, will she be changing her settlement demands? Or does she still want half of Bedford Falls?"

"She wants it and she'll get it."

"It bothers you that Matthew got away from you, doesn't it? You want him back, firmly planted under your thumb. You won't be happy until he is."

"I told you, I don't believe in personal," he said impatiently. "This ain't a vendetta. It's business. She wants to produce her own pictures. Be a player. I'm willing to give her the shot."

"In exchange for her half-interest in Bedford Falls," I pointed out.

"What's wrong with that? It's a straightforward arrangement. Good for her, good for me."

"What about what's good for Bedford Falls?"

"I gotta have Bedford Falls," he insisted. "I need it."

"Matthew won't ever sell you his half, Norb."

"He'll sell," he said with utter certainty. "He'll see he has no choice but to sell."

"How?"

"I'll make him see," he responded darkly.

"Can you be a little more specific?"

Norbert Schlom gazed up at the blank screen in front of us, savoring his reply. "Let's just say, it'll be like a guy getting his dick lopped off with an ax—he'll know it when it happens."

I got out to Trancas around sunset. I took Topanga Canyon, which was brown and dry as chalk in the late season heat. The sun was dropping bright orange into the ocean when I hit Malibu. Trancas is another half hour or so up the coast from there. There's not much to it. Just some houses crowded shoulder-to-shoulder on the narrow ribbon of sand between the pounding surf and Pacific Coast Highway. Many were extravagant Bauhaus sand castles of glass and bleached wood. Trace Washburn's wasn't one of those. The fourth house from the left was a rickety beachcomber's shack on stilts, tar roof patched, clapboard siding warped and peeling, redwood deck rotted out. His neighbors probably wanted to nuke it. I rather liked it.

I left the Vette in the narrow alley out back. Wood steps led up to the deck. A clothesline was stretched between two of the deck posts. T-shirts, jeans and beach towels were drying on it. A surfboard was propped against the side of the house. I made my way around to the front, the entire house shuddering with each step I took. Lulu followed me, stepping gingerly around the gaps in the deck where planks were missing. Sliding glass doors faced the water. A few sailboats were out. The tide was receding. Lulu excused herself and headed down to the water's edge to sniff at shells. I tapped on one of the doors, and went inside.

The living room, dining room, and kitchen were one large room. The decor was early dude ranch, but of an uncommonly high order—log furniture made in the 1940's by the Shoshone Furniture Company of Cody, Wyoming, under the guiding hand of Thomas Molesworth, the Stickley of the Wild West. Two massive Molesworth wing chairs, their leather arms topped with moose antlers, were parked around a Franklin stove along with a pair of his fringed leather armchairs. The dining table, upon which Cassandra Dee had first been formally introduced to Big Steve, was a massive slab of honey-colored fir. Six matching Molesworth dining chairs were set around it, their backs ornamented with the silhouette of a bow-legged gunfighter. Trace was not a tidy housekeeper. Empty beer bottles were everywhere. Sand crunched underfoot on the whitewashed wooden floor. Dirty dishes were piled high in the kitchen, where a chubby, sunburned teenaged girl in a T-shirt and nothing else stood aimlessly stirring a pot of chili on the stove, a look of bovine torpor on her face. It was a plain face. Her hair was stringy, her ankles thick and not particularly clean. It took her a while to notice me standing there.

When she did she gave me a sleepy, sated grin. "He's asleep. You a friend of his?"

I said I was.

"Want me to wake him?"

I said I did.

She clumped off toward the bedroom. I heard murmuring in there, followed by some playful giggling. A slap and some more playful giggling. Then he came shambling out, yawning, big and brown and naked except for the faded blue jean cutoffs he was buttoning. His shaggy blond hair was rumpled, his deep-set eyes bleary, his two-day growth of beard flecked with gray. He was tanned and weatherbeaten all over. His hide was like old leather. Nothing but rope underneath. His shoulders were broad, his belly flat and hard. There were long, jagged surgical scars on both knees and one on his right shoulder. He moved slowly and stiffly, like the wounded. Most of his toenails were black and dead looking.

He limped over to the refrigerator, pulled out a six-pack of Corona longnecks, and started his heavy breathing thing. "Guess I dropped off. That there Rosie—she plum wore Big Steve out. Found her at the market this morning. Never know what you'll find there." He tasted his chili, poured a jolt of Wild Turkey into it, and himself. Then he looked me up and down. "Want a pair of trunks or something?"

"I'm fine."

"Then c'mon, Buck."

Steep, wooden stairs took us down to the sand. It was much cooler down there with the spray coming off of the water. A pair of rickety lounge chairs were half buried in the sand by the water's edge, where Lulu was having a grand time nosing around at the assorted sea life, paws and ears all wet and sandy. She snuffled happily at our arrival and bounded over to say hello. We sat. Trace opened two Coronas and handed me one. Most of the sun had dropped into the ocean now. The sky was turning from red to purple.

"See that thin gray line out along the horizon?" he said, squinting out at it. "Heat wave'll break tonight. Be cold and foggy in the morning. I grew up around here. Surfed these beaches for almost forty years. You get to know the signs." He shifted in his chair, wincing. "The old aches don't lie, neither."

"Get kicked by a lot of horses?" I asked.

"Horses, blitzing linebackers, and crazy ladies." He took a swig of his beer and scratched at the wiry stubble on his cheeks. "I had nothing to do with shooting Abel."

"So you said. Can someone vouch for you?"

"That part's a little tricky."

"I'm not the law."

"But you talk to them."

"If I have to. When I do, I choose my words carefully. Have they questioned you yet?"

He nodded. "Came out this afternoon."

"Was it Lamp?"

"He a black guy?"

"No."

"I told him I was swimming. He talked to some of my neighbors, then split. He wasn't satisfied, but he did split."

"They'll be back. You can count on it, Trace. And you can't duck it."

"Well, shit." His chest rose and fell. "Maybe you can impress upon him how touchy this is."

"Maybe." I sipped my beer. "But I have to know who you're protecting."

He told me. She happened to be one of the three biggest box office names in the world. Bigger than Pennyroyal. Bigger than Merilee. Her husband ran one of the major studios. They were, without question, Hollywood's most glittering duo.

"I thought they were happily married," I said.

"They are," he assured me. "She just gets a little wild sometimes, comes looking for a jab from Big Steve. Hell, better me than some guy'd try to take advantage of her. I was with her. No lie. That's their place over there." He pointed down the beach to one of the grander sand castles. "I'd surely hate for this to get out. It'd hurt her bad. Wouldn't do me much good either. Angry husbands don't go out of their way to hire me. I haven't worked in a year. I'll lose this place soon if I don't. Ain't much, but it's all I got."

"I'll see what I can do," I said. "No promises."

He shook his head sadly. "Big Steve just gets me into one scrape after another. He can't turn a girl down. And I can't make him. I figure I owe it to them. They deserve something sweet to remember in their old age, something that'll put a smile on their pretty little face. Hell, that's what I'm here for. Dumb, I guess."

"I wouldn't call it smart getting mixed up with Pennyroyal. As a career move, I mean."

"You're right," he admitted readily. "Smoked me with Matthew. I knew that going in, too."

"So to speak."

He gave me a sleepy grin, crossed his scarred, knobby legs. "She's a nice kid, Penny. Sweet little body, great skin. Awful serious. She don't laugh much. I like to laugh. We're real different that way." He was silent a moment. "She also has a future. I don't. But I'm crazy about that little girl. She's one worth holding onto. Wish I knew how." He glanced over at me. "You and Merilee been together a long time."

"Off and on," I said.

"She's an impressive woman."

"Only if you're impressed by perfection."

"I'm impressed by you. You must be all man."

"I wouldn't go that far."

"What's your secret then?"

"My secret?"

"How do you manage it?"

"You wouldn't, per chance, be yanking my frank, would you?"

"Hell, no," he insisted. "Holding on to 'em is something I never learned how to do. I envy anyone who can. No lie."

"There's no real secret," I informed him. "She just gives me plenty of room to be myself, and I give her plenty of room to be herselves."

He scratched his stomach with a big brown hand. "And that works?"

"Not right now it doesn't."

"How come?"

"How about if I ask the questions?"

"Sure, sure," he said easily, draining his Corona. "Go on."

"Has Pennyroyal ever talked to you about her past?"

"What past? She's twenty-five years old."

"Those nude shots of hers."

He shrugged, eyes on the ocean. "These things happen. Everybody gets used."

"She said it was Toy who did the using—back when Toy was a pro."

"That I didn't know," he said, surprised. "But I reckon Toy's boned and fileted plenty of folks. Ol' Toy's a hard number. People who get what they want tend to be."

A long, lovely young redhead in a blue spandex unitard went jogging past us on the hard sand. She blew Trace a kiss. He blew one back and watched her disappear down the beach, a hungry look on his chiseled, weatherbeaten face. "Gentle now, Big Steve," he murmured. "Gentle, boy."

"What does Norbert Schlom have against you?" I asked.

"Ask him."

"I did."

He looked at me. "What did he say?"

"You drink too much, you cost too much, and you're too old. He said you're used up."

He laughed. "That pretty much covers everything—except for the real reason."

"Is Toy the real reason?"

"Aw, hell no," he said, shaking his head. "She's got nothing to do with it. I've had her, sure. But that's the sort of thing Norb gets off on, knowing that someone like me is fucking his wife. He's into pain and humiliation. They both are. Hell, Harmon Wright used to pay her to take dumps on his chest. He got off on it. Norb does, too. Or so she says."

"Did she and Abel Zorch have any kind of relationship?"

"She used to get him girls in the old days."

"For what?"

"His parties. Abel was very big that way. Brought politicians and money men together from all over—Washington, Japan, the Middle East. Lots of deals got struck at Abel's parties, while the liquor and the girls were flowing."

"Would Toy have wanted him dead?"

"I wouldn't know about that."

"What's the real reason, Trace?"

"Real reason?"

"Why won't Schlom hire you?"

He turned chilly on me. "You like all the dirty details, don't you, Buck?"

"Not particularly."

"You get off on this? Go home and jerk off?"

"I go home and write. Pretty much the same thing."

"Why you do this shit?"

"Pays the bills. And helps keep me insane."

He tossed his empty beer bottle aside and opened us both fresh ones. He took a gulp and squinted out at the surf, breathing in and out. "It happened seven, eight years ago, when we was shooting the interiors for *Yeti II* at Panorama. Norb was still married to his first wife, Elaine, who looked remarkably like a sheep. His kid, Toby, took to hanging around the set over summer vacation. He'd just graduated from one of them eastern prep schools. Was off to Princeton in the fall. He was a good kid, especially when you considered who his old man was. Funny, in a quiet sort of way. Liked to party, too. Snort, drink, listen to heavy metal. One day, he turns eighteen. Damned if Norb don't give him a red Lamborghini Countach. Sucker cost more than a hundred grand. Me, I decided to get him laid. Figured it was the least I could do for the little fucker. Had him out here for a little party. Some women I knew came over. We all got ourselves ripped on coke, and into a sandwich. That kid was laughing and grabbing and groaning and sucking. You never saw a hornier kid. He fucked four different women in a half an hour. He fucked like there was no tomorrow." Trace paused. "Which there wasn't. He went flying out of here about four in the morning, happy as can be, and crunched his Countach on Sunset. Don't know if he fell asleep behind the wheel or what. It was a one-car accident. No skid marks . . . I felt like shit . . . Norb went berserk when they found the coke in his body. And when they found out where Toby'd been that evening . . ." Trace whistled softly. "Norb kept it all out of the papers, out of respect for Toby. Didn't send the law after me. But he made sure he nailed ol' Trace to the barn door. No studio in town would use me after that. They all stick together, y'know. He also managed to get me audited by the IRS.

They cleaned me out of every penny I owned. I didn't work for two whole years. Matthew rescued me with the Badger pictures. He was the only guy in town who'd give me a job. Now I can't work for him either. I'm on my ass. Norb, he just won't let me get back up. I've paid, man. I surely have. But Norb is not one to forgive and forget. Neither was Abel. I begged him. You heard me beg him. That wasn't easy for ol' Trace. But it was no use. He wouldn't help me. People in this business, they delight in kicking a man when he's down."

"Zorch seemed to take a special delight in it. He told me he'd hated you for a long, long time. Why is that?"

Trace thumbed his chin ruefully. "How much you know about the movie business?"

"More than I care to."

"I'm just a dumb ol' football player," he drawled, "but it's been my experience that this whole crazy fucking business can be reduced to one simple little word. One word explains it all. I'm gonna give you the benefit of my experience and share that word with you, Buck. It's *revenge*."

"Revenge?"

"There was a time at SC, long ago, when I was what they called a big man on campus. I was the golden boy. The quarterback, the campus hero. I got the girls. I got the glory. I got it all. Abel Zorch, he was an unpopular little weasel. A twerp."

"You knew him?"

"Never so much as met him. But he knew me. And envied me. And hated me—for being everything he wasn't. That hate is what drove him to the top. Gave him his greatest ambition in life, which was to someday, somehow, *own* me. Me and every other golden boy and girl like me. This business, Buck, is run by dozens of little Abel Zorchs. Them studio execs, agents, producers—they're all sweaty, unpopular, bitter little fucks. And now it's their turn. They get to make all of us golden boys and girls jump through hoops. They decide who's popular and who isn't. Who's pretty and who isn't. Who gets their phone calls returned and who doesn't. They make us grovel, submit, suck up to 'em. . . . They're getting back at us, man. It means more to them than the money, the fame, the glamour. Having power over guys like me, girls like Penny, it's what they live for. Penny, she's trying to fight it. But it'll never happen. Norb's just telling her what she wants to hear so she'll hand over her half of Bedford Falls. You don't really think he's gonna let her have any clout, do you? No way, man. She's fooling herself big time, you ask me. But that's part of this business, too. Big part."

"Who do you think killed Abel?"

He yawned. "Shelley Selden."

"Mister or Missus?"

"Mister. He's Matthew's protector, keeper, stooge. He's devoted his whole life to the guy. If somebody got in that boy's way, he wouldn't hesitate to take him out—especially if Bedford Falls was at stake."

"He hardly seems the type," I observed.

"Don't be fooled. That there teddy bear can turn into a real grizzly. He beat the shit out of some guy Johnny's mom was living with one time when the guy got outta line. I seen him coldcock a caterer on the *Badger* set with my own eyes. Guy got lippy and, *pow*, Shelley punched his lights out. He can definitely blow."

"That's very interesting," I said, thinking about the bandage Shelley had been wearing around his wrist. Had he tripped, like he said? "Let's talk about Matthew. You've made more movies with him than anyone."

"Seven, if you can believe that. First time I met him he was a pimply kid fetching coffee. Next time I saw him he was a pimply kid directing his own sci-fi film, and I was starring in it. If you're looking for me to dump on him, I won't. I got nothing but respect for Matthew. And gratitude. He made me star of five of the top grossing movies in history. Pretty amazing, when you think about it. I mean, shit, Bob De Niro I ain't. Matthew's the most single-minded man I've ever met. And that includes head football coaches. The man lives, breathes, eats, and sleeps his movies. I can't honestly say I know him well. It ain't like we ever raised hell together. He doesn't do that sort of thing. And he likes to keep his distance from his actors."

"He and Johnny seem close."

"That's really more of a father-daughter thing," he said. "Any actor needs hand-holding on the set is dead meat with Matthew. He doesn't like to rehearse, doesn't like actors offering their input. I think that's one of the reasons he always liked me— I did what he told me to. Actors, we're props to him. I'll give you an example: When we was looping *To the Moon* he added all kinds of sound effects to my big fight scene with the mutant—

when I pull the dude's arm out at the socket—so it's real grue-some sounding. We're sitting there watching it one morning and there's this look of childlike bliss on his face. 'No one's ever done that before, Trace,' he says to me. 'Done what, Boss?' I says, thinking he's making an observation about my performance. 'The bones,' he says. 'You can hear them break.' Action stuff's what he lives for, and he's a master. Storyboards everything. Has it all laid out in advance, like a big, live-action cartoon. *Yeti* was his greatest achievement, in my opinion. Shit, that picture was Oper-ation Desert Storm. Planes flew us from Katmandu to a dirt air-strip at Lukla, this Sherpa village about nine thousand feet up. From there it was three whole days by trail up to our location. All the cameras, equipment, people, supplies, everything had to be taken up by these animals they call *dzoms*, which are half yak, half cow. We're up there eight weeks at nineteen thousand feet, living in tents. It's fifty below, wind's howling, Olivier's half dead. Me, I got frostbite in half my toes. Finally, I says, 'Hey, Boss, why can't we just shoot this fucker on a nice warm sound-stage somewhere!?' He says to me 'No, Trace, that's what was wrong with the original movie. You knew they weren't really in the Himalayas.' I says, 'How?' He says, 'You couldn't see their breath.' My attitude was, hey, who gives a fuck? It's just a movie. But to him, it's more than that. He spent millions on the ava-lanche. He was obsessed with making it look authentic. Drove the Sherpas crazy. Kept telling 'em he wanted to bring all of this snow down on top of their village. They kept telling him hey, you can't—you'll bring down the whole mountain. And he's like, hey, so what? I've seen it done in a million movies. But in those mov-ies it was *fake*. In a studio. This was a real mountain. Real snow. Real village. He almost didn't seem to realize that. Never was satisfied with that avalanche. He wanted to bring the mountain down, and they wouldn't let him.'' He laughed. ''Whatever he's doing, it's always in his own head. Nobody else knows what he's thinking. Even the *Badger* movies, which had very little action, it was strictly his spin on things that made 'em work.'' He cleared his throat. ''I hear there's no part for me in the new one.''

''You hear right.'' I drained my beer. The sky was purple now. Lights were twinkling down the coast in Malibu. ''Will you be sorry if he loses Bedford Falls?''

''I don't concern myself with that stuff,'' he responded. ''I'm just an old surf bum, Buck. I ride the waves. Climb on my board, ride the big ones in, hope that there board don't conk me in the head when I wipe out. That's about as far as I take it." He breathed heavily a few times in the darkness. "Maybe I'm down right now. But I'll get back up. I'm a star. A fucking star. They can't keep me down. They never have and they never will." He struggled up out of his lounge chair, bones creaking. "How's your stomach?"

"Compared to what?"

"Want to try some of my chili?"

"I would."

"Then let's do it. Got me some major bug killer we can wash it down with."

"Bug killer?"

"Tequila, Buck. Only we'd better get one thing straight—Big Steve always gets the worm."

"And who am I to stand in his way?"

It was past ten by the time I left Trancas, comfortably lit by Trace Washburn's chili and bug killer. Trace downed three shots for every one of mine. Even pulled out a guitar and serenaded me with a somewhat diseased rendition of "I'm an Old Cowhand." His phone rang constantly—women wanting him. At some point a pair of aging brown surfers named Rip and Corky came by with news of a party. The three of them went staggering off down the beach together. I headed back to Bedford Falls. I had business. I drove the Vette hard, enjoying the open road. I thought about Merilee and how much I wished she were riding next to me with Lulu in her lap, the wind blowing her golden hair. I wondered if she missed me. I wondered if we were through. I wondered. Bug killer does that to me.

The reporters were still on the gate. So was Shadow, sweating before the fan in his guard's booth as he browsed through *Beyond Good and Evil* by Mr. Friedrich Nietzsche.

"I have it on good authority that the heat wave will break by morning," I informed him solemnly.

He showed me his gold tooth. "You been out enjoying yourself some fine mash, haven't you, sir?"

"The finest. Matthew at home?"

"Yessir. He and Shelley and Sarge be working on some preproduction details up in the main building."

"And Bunny?" It was Bunny who was my business.

"No, sir. She still be out."

I glanced at Grandfather's Rolex. It was nearly midnight. "She often stay out this late?"

"She's got her friends," he replied, swiping at his brow with his handkerchief. "You know how it is with them widows. They play their cards, drink their coffee, gossip til all hours."

"Does she ever stay out all night?"

He peered at me, amused. "Little bit old for you, isn't she?"

"Idle curiosity."

"Ain't nothing about you that's idle." He folded the hanky carefully and set it aside. "She always makes it back. The Shadow'll tell her you was asking for her."

"Thank you, Shadow. About that coke you planted in Matthew's bungalow at Panorama . . ."

His face dropped. "Yessir?"

"Who gave it to you?"

He frowned. "Gave it to me?"

"Where did it come from?"

"I bought it, sir," he said uncomfortably. "Mr. Schlom give me the money, some five thousand dollars it was. And the name of a certain individual known to be a reliable and discreet supplier. You seem inordinately interested in that sad episode, if the Shadow may say so."

"What was the dealer's name?"

He took off his cap and scratched his head. "Tyrone Johnson. African-American gentleman. Preferred to call himself—"

"Shambazza."

His eyes flickered. "Yessir."

"He died."

Shadow shrugged. "Happens to the best of us. And the worst."

"Someone shot him. Not long after you bought that coke from him, actually. Did you know that?"

"No, sir, I didn't," he said coldly. "But I'd let that particular sleeping dog lie if I was you. Might bite your hand clean off."

"Thanks for the warning, Shadow."

"You're most welcome, sir. Goodnight."

I drove on in, glancing at him in my rearview mirror. He was watching me. And he wasn't showing me any gold tooth.

There were two phone messages under my door, both from Lamp. There were no messages from Merilee Nash. My bungalow was hot and stuffy. I put on the air and took a shower and slipped into my silk dressing gown. Then I padded out to the phone to call Lamp.

Only the bungalow had changed. The desk light was off, a candle flickering in its place. A leather tote bag lay on the desk, two bottles of Dom Perignon inside, chilled. Our drink. I heard the toaster pop in the outer office. Toast meant caviar. Our favorite bedtime snack. She was here. She was really here. Heart pounding, I dashed into the other room.

She wasn't here. It was America's sweetie pie who stood there bribing Lulu with a wedge of Beluga-laden toast. The little mercenary won't growl at other women when they do that.

I stood there staring at her. Because this was Pennyroyal Brim like I'd never seen her before. She had on the tiniest of black leather minidresses, strapless and skin tight. Cut very low in front, cut even lower in back. She wore black spiked heels with no stockings. Her golden hair was up. There were diamonds in her ears, some red on her lips. She looked nothing like Debbie Dale, girl next door. She looked glamorous and radiant and outrageously seductive.

"Ah, there you are," she said, voice low and throaty, her eyes blue and innocent. "I was just getting out the ice. Care to help?"

# Chapter Nine

"One doesn't generally serve Dom Perignon on the rocks."

"It's not for the champagne, you silly-willy," she said, favoring me with her sunniest smile. "It's for me—I worked up quite some sweat getting here."

"Shadow glad to see you?"

"I didn't use the gate. Think I want everyone in the world to know I'm here?"

"I don't think."

"I parked around the corner and came through the fence like a burglar," she revealed proudly. "There's a break in it behind a bunch of overgrown bamboo out by the prop warehouse. It's been there for years. Johnny showed it to me when we were making *Badger One*. He used it to slip out on his mom."

There were two ice trays in my little freezer. I cracked the cubes into a bowl. She carried it into the other room with the caviar and toast, swaying slightly on her high heels. It was a nice kind of sway. She knew it. I knew it. She knew I knew it, and I knew she knew I knew it. Lulu followed her. All she was interested in was the caviar.

She came back with the champagne and two long-stemmed

glasses. She put one bottle in the fridge. The other she handed to me. "Will you do the honors?"

"All right."

I removed the foil and slowly worked the cork out. She drifted back into the other room. After I'd filled our glasses I joined her. She was seated on the edge of the sofa bed in front of the air conditioner, slooooowly rubbing an ice cube up and down her bare legs. They were lovely legs. Tanned, smooth, gently swelled at the calf, finely tapered at the ankle. The beads of moisture glistened on them in the candlelight.

"Shall I get you a towel?" I asked. "Or do you just want me to wipe you off with my tongue?"

"You really should do screenplays. Your dialogue's outrageous."

"The problem is finding someone who can say it as well as I can."

I handed her a glass. We drank.

"Say something else witty," she commanded airily.

"Sorry. I've punched out for the night."

"No, you haven't."

"Haven't I?"

"No."

She helped herself to caviar and gave some more to Lulu. Then she kicked off her shoes and sat back on the bed, pillows propped behind her, wiggling her little pink toes. She drank, watching me over her glass. I watched her watching me. Everyone, Grandfather once told me, is selling something. What was Pretty Penny selling?

"Where's Georgie?" I asked, sampling the caviar. I wasn't disappointed.

"He almost always sleeps through the night," she replied. "Maria has your direct number here if he needs me. Cassie gave it to me."

"Does Cassie know you're here?"

"No one knows I'm here." She cleared her throat. She seemed nervous now. Extremely so. "See, there was something more that I . . ." She trailed off, lit a cigarette, and pulled deeply on it. "Something I wanted to tell you this morning that I didn't want to say in front of Cassie."

I pulled the chair out from behind the desk and sat. "She's your collaborator. You shouldn't keep secrets from her."

"Screw Cassie. Screw the book. What matters is that I lied to *you*." She leveled her porcelain blue eyes at me. "I don't ever want us to do that to each other."

Outside, I heard footsteps in the courtyard. A door opened and closed. Bunny was home.

I sipped my champagne. "Go on."

"I told you I never took Toy up on any of her invitations. You know, to meet those men?"

"And you did?"

"Once," she said, her voice quavering. "Once was . . . *plenty*. She invited me to a party up at this movie big shot's house in Trousdale. She said I'd meet a lot of important people there. Like I told you, Hoagy, I was naive."

"You believed her."

Her glass was empty. She held it out to me. Our fingers touched. Hers were cold. I filled her glass and handed it back to her. She was trembling.

"I expected there'd be all these cars there," she said, gulping at her champagne. "But there weren't—no people at all. Just Toy and this guy. She said everybody was at a screening that had run long, but they were on their way. He gave me some wine to drink and showed me around. He told me he and his wife had just separated. He seemed nice enough. I—I thought the wine tasted a little funny, but it wasn't like I knew a whole lot about wine."

"They drugged you?"

"I *was* the party, Hoagy. Me. Nobody else. W-When I came to I was lying spread-eagled on this bed, naked, my wrists and ankles tied by stockings to the bedposts. There was a plastic sheet under me. I've always remembered that. I don't know why. Toy and this guy . . . they were naked, too."

"How does Norb look with his clothes off?"

She stared at me. "How did you know it was him?"

"Wild guess."

"She hurt me, Hoagy. She burned me. She stuck sharp things inside me. When I started to scream she stuffed my panties in my mouth. He sat there watching her do it to me and growing more and more aroused. And then . . . and when he was good and ready, h-he raped me. My insides . . . I thought they were going to burst open. It went on for hours. Just for fun, he gave it to her while he watched her use a soldering iron on me. I passed out from the pain. When I came to he was all over me again, like an animal. When he'd had his fill he p-peed all over me. Then they untied me and left me there. I-I couldn't even move a muscle for a while. Finally, I crawled into the bathroom, bleeding, sobbing, vomiting. I washed myself as best I could, put my clothes back on. I thought about calling the police, only—"

"It would be your word against theirs," I said. "You were there willingly. You accepted the drink."

She nodded. "Exactly. They were sitting out there in the living room in bathrobes, friendly as can be. They even invited me to join them for a snack. I couldn't believe it. I'd been tortured, violated, debased . . . and they were offering me a sandwich. He also offered me money—five hundred dollars."

"Did you take it?"

"I earned it, didn't I?" She said this defiantly. "Toy called me a few times after that. I just hung up on her soon as I heard her voice. Pretty soon she stopped calling. Next time I saw her, she and Norb were husband and wife. And I was Debbie Dale. She was happy to see me again. They both were. Like we were old friends. I suppose they thought we were, since the three of us had so much fun together . . . I'm probably one of a hundred little girls that he's peed on. Just a coincidence that I ended up being discovered by Matthew, his former protégé . . ." She bit down on her lower lip. She was fighting back tears. "Anyway, now y-you know the truth, Hoagy. The whole ugly truth." Timidly, she watched for my reaction.

"That abortion you had—Schlom wasn't the father, was he?"

"God, no. That was all true about Craig."

"One thing I don't get—how can you even consider going into business with the man?"

"Better the devil you know," she replied simply. "Face it, there's nothing he can do to me that he hasn't already done."

"That's true," I admitted.

"You don't think I should?"

"It's not too late to back out."

She shook her head. "We have a deal."

"Which Norb would bust in a second if it suited him."

"Maybe. But I'm not like that."

I had some more caviar, as did Lulu. "Does Matthew know about this?" I asked, munching.

"No one knows about it. Except for Norbert and Toy, of course."

"Why tell me?"

Her eyes shone at me in the candlelight. "I thought that was kind of obvious," she said huskily.

I opened the other bottle of Dom Perignon. When I returned with it she was back up on her feet, shoes on. Lulu was busy with the rest of the caviar.

"Do me a small favor?" she asked shyly, gazing up at me.

"What is it?"

"Dance with me?"

"I don't hear any music."

She'd brought her own. The cassette was in her tote bag. She popped it into my player. I could tell after one note what it was—Ray Charles's version of *Georgia on My Mind*. Our song, the one we danced to over and over again that first night, when we drank up peppery vodka—and each other—at the Polish Seaman's Club on First Avenue and Ninth Street. When we knew.

"This song belongs to Merilee," I said, my chest aching.

"I know. I read about it in *People*. Also about the champagne and caviar."

"There are no secrets anymore, are there?"

"Not for people like us." She held her arms out wide. "Shall we?"

"I'm afraid not. Sacreligious."

"But I thought she . . . I mean, aren't the two of you—?"

"We're not through. And it's still our song."

"Oh." She dropped her arms, disappointed.

"I do have some Garner," I offered.

She brightened. "He doesn't belong to her?"

"He belongs to no one."

I put the Elf on. He played *Penthouse Serenade*. We danced. She felt young and eager in my arms, her bare back electric velvet to my touch. She swayed against me, her leather hips undulating gently. She smelled of rosewater. We danced. The tape was over before we knew it. She stayed right there in my arms. I let her stay there.

Slowly she raised her face up to mine. There was a slight smile on her lips. Her eyes were dreamy. I felt myself getting lost in them.

"What happens now?" she murmured.

"We could stand here like this for a few more hours."

She laughed. "And then?"

"We could finish the champagne."

She lowered her eyes. "And then?"

"And then you go home."

Her forehead creased. "I do?"

"You do."

She swallowed. "I'd make you happy, Hoagy. I'd work real hard to make you happy."

"It's not going to happen, Penny."

"Because of Matthew?"

"Matthew doesn't even enter into it. So to speak."

She looked up at me curiously. "She must be incredible."

"She is."

"Would you . . . ?"

"Would I what?"

"Kiss me just once?"

Her mouth was soft and warm and friendly, as was she. It was, well, not a quick peck. It went on for quite some time, her body pressed tightly against mine. I was the one who ended it. I expect some credit for that. We stayed right where we were, too out of breath to move.

"That wasn't like kindergarten," she gasped.

"Certainly not like any kindergarten I ever went to. You don't, by the way."

"Don't what?"

"Taste like a grasping, airhead megabitch. I thought you'd want to know."

"Thanks. I did. What do I taste like?" She was gazing up at me.

"I was just trying to figure that out." I was getting lost in her blue eyes again. Really lost. They were a bottomless pool. I felt myself falling into them . . . Falling . . . *"What makes them so special, Meat?"*

The pounding saved me. Someone was pounding at my door, yelling for me. I went and opened it while Pennyroyal hid in the bathroom.

It was Bunny, standing out there in a quilted robe and running shoes, her hair in curlers. "Hurry, Hoagy," she cried. "It's Homewood!"

"What about it?"

"It's burning down!"

I heard the sirens now, the rumbling of fire trucks.

"I'll catch up with you," I said, closing the door on her.

Pennyroyal stood in the bathroom doorway, wide-eyed. "I'd better go."

"You'd better," I agreed. I threw on some clothes. Then I took off after Bunny, Lulu by my side as the fire trucks roared past us toward the flames that were shooting high into the midnight sky.

I've never liked the way newspeople use the word *spectacular* to describe a blaze. It makes it sound like something wonderfully terrific. But spectacular was the only word to describe the Homewood fire. Because a whole town was going up in flames all at once. The shops on Main Street. The Bijou Theatre. The courthouse. Badger's house on Elm, Debbie Dale's house next door, all of it. A dozen fire trucks were on hand, a hundred men fighting to save it. Only there was nothing to save. No buildings. Just flimsy wooden facades. Tinder. It was only a matter of minutes before they fell away from their steel pylons and crashed to the ground. And were gone. Nothing left. Nothing *there*. All the fire people could do was douse the rubble and keep it from spreading to the rest of the studio. A helicopter hovered overhead, bathing it with a huge white spotlight. The TV news crews were there, too, getting it all on videotape. It was a strange scene, kind of like watching a reenactment of the burning of Atlanta in *Gone with the Wind*. It was spectacular.

I found the family huddled together on the town green, watching in horror. Bunny and Mrs. Shelley both had their arms around Matthew.

"I'm all gone, Meat," he babbled at me, wild-eyed. "I'm gone."

"Why won't they leave us alone, huh?" Mr. Shelley moaned. "Why can't we be left the fuck alone?"

Sarge and Shadow watched in grim silence, arms crossed.

I watched with them, feeling the heat from the flames as the hometown of Matthew Wax's imagination went up in smoke. Lulu crouched at my feet. I thought about what Norbert Schlom had said to me when I'd insisted Matthew would never sell out to him. He'll see that he has no choice, Schlom said. *I'll make him see.*

It took them about an hour to put it out. Only the steepled congregational church was left standing. It was situated across the town green from the rest of the sets. A fireman stomping through the wet, smoldering remains of the malt shop found the one-gallon gasoline cans. A pair of them. Whoever did it didn't even try to make it look like anything but what it was—arson. Unless you wanted to consider it murder. Certainly a piece of Matthew Wax died that night in those flames.

Emil Lamp, boy detective, showed up looking like a high school tennis star in a white polo shirt, white shorts and sneakers. He had cute legs.

"Nothing like a small, tasteful bonfire to bring the citizens out," I said.

"Heard it come over the radio," he explained. "Not my turf, but I thought it might tie in with the rest somehow."

"Good thought."

He gazed up at the church, hands in his back pockets. "Jeepers, I was just thinking how it was spared because God had blessed it, only it's not a real church, is it?"

"Welcome to show business, Lieutenant," I said.

He nodded. Then he asked me if there was someplace where we could talk.

We found a twenty-four-hour coffee shop on Culver Boulevard over near the freeway, deserted. Lamp ordered tapioca pudding and a large skim milk. I ordered coffee. Lulu stayed outside, napping in the front seat of Lamp's car. It was past her bedtime.

"Any chance they'll catch who did this?" I asked, sipping my coffee.

"Culver City will track it best they can," he replied. "Get assistance from the county if they need it. Only . . ."

"Only?"

"I doubt they've left any footprints. We're not dealing here with someone stupid." He sampled his pudding. "Nerts, this isn't tapioca," he said, making a face. "It's instant vanilla with lumps in it."

"I'm sorry, Lieutenant. Life is full of these small disappointments."

Disgusted, he pushed it away. "You get my messages?"

"I did. I was just about to call you. What did you—?"

"I've decided to give you one more chance," he announced decisively.

"At getting off your doo-doo list? That's very generous of you."

"The quality of mercy is very important in law enforcement."

"Are you making any progress?"

"You bet. Picked up a whole lot of neat stuff today."

"Such as?"

He stuck out his chin. "Nope. No way. You go first. That's the deal."

"How come?"

"Because it's my investigation, that's how come. Heck, I don't even have to talk to you at all. Only reason I am is—"

"You like me?"

"No."

"You don't like me?"

"No, I *do* like you, Hoagy, and stop sparring with me, gosh darn it."

"No offense, Lieutenant, but you're a bit crankier than you used to be."

He took a sip of his milk, sat back in the booth. "The chief called me personally today to do some heavyweight leaning," he confessed wearily. "This is big-time stuff, Hoagy. Hammer time."

"I'm sorry, Lieutenant," I said sympathetically.

"Thanks, Hoagy. But you still go first. Give."

I gave him that Schlom had planted coke on Matthew to force him into doing *The Three Stooges*, that Shadow Williams had done the planting, and that he had bought the stuff from our late friend Shambazza.

"Interesting," said Lamp, mulling this over. "Could be Shadow went back and shot the guy, too. Neat and clean that way."

"Perhaps shot Zorch and Geoffrey as well," I suggested. "He was off duty at the time."

"Motive?" asked Lamp.

"To save the studio. To make up for what he did to Matthew."

"Why shoot Zorch in the groin?"

"To throw you off."

Lamp considered this, tugging on his lower lip. "He's an interesting candidate. As chief of security he'd certainly have the means to steal Pennyroyal's negatives out of Selden's desk. And to start this fire."

"Means, yes," I agreed. "Motive, no. Those are both acts of sabotage. I can't see him doing either of them. He wouldn't hurt Matthew."

Our waitress came by and refilled my coffee cup. Lamp asked her to please remove the so-called tapioca. She did, without comment.

"I keep going back to Shambazza's murder," I mused aloud. "Break it open and you've got wires going off in two different directions. One wire leads to Seldon Selden. Shelley admits he paid off Shambazza for Penny's negatives. Maybe Shambazza wasn't satisfied with the one payment. Maybe he had another set of negatives. Who knows? Then there's the other wire, which leads to Mr. and Mrs. Norbert Schlom, acting either alone or in tandem. Shambazza was her lover in a previous life. Maybe she eliminated him so as to eliminate her past. Norbert, meanwhile, had *two* conceivable reasons for wanting Shambazza dead—his wife's past involvement with him, and his own. He bought dope from the guy. He also bought women. He happens to like his play on the rough side. Maybe he got a little too rough one time. Maybe he was paying Shambazza hush money. I don't know. I do know he looks good for killing Zorch, too. The Japanese didn't like the way Pennyroyal's divorce was being handled. They were leaning on Schlom to do something about it. If he believed Zorch was responsible for stealing Pennyroyal's negatives, then maybe he decided the man had to be eliminated."

"Schlom has no alibi for the time of the shooting," Lamp revealed. "According to his secretary, he left his office at Panorama City at a quarter to six. When he stopped at the scene on his way home it was past seven. Could be he got stuck in traffic. Could be he's our shooter."

"He happens to look very good for this fire, too," I pointed out. "He wants Bedford Falls, and he intends to get it. What happened tonight certainly qualifies as giving them the message."

Lamp nodded. "Interesting . . . Okay, Hoagy, that's one wire. Now let's follow that other one—to Selden. Let's say he shoots Shambazza because he's blackmailing him over Pennyroyal's pictures. And he shoots Zorch for trying to bring down his studio. Okay so far?"

"So far," I agreed. "Was he anywhere near Hazen Drive when it happened?"

Lamp looked through his notes. "Selden had a four-thirty appointment in Beverly Hills with a Dr. David Kaminsky, proctologist to the stars. The doctor was a bit backed up that afternoon . . ."

"So to speak."

"Selden didn't get in until five, at which time he was examined, had various tests taken . . ."

"I don't need to hear about those."

Lamp grinned. "He got out of there about six. Arrived at his home in Brentwood sometime past seven. Traffic could account for that. It's brutal on that side of town at rush hour."

"Then again . . ."

"He *could* have taken a detour up to Zorch's house," Lamp suggested. "Arrived there after Pennyroyal and Johnny were gone. Shot Zorch and Geoffrey, then took off for home. The timing's tight, but it works."

I sipped my coffee. "Except for one thing—how would he know he'd find Zorch stranded there in his driveway at exactly that time?"

"I asked myself the same question," acknowledged Lamp.

"Oh, God."

"What's wrong, Hoagy?"

"I'm starting to think like a cop."

"That's not such a bad thing, you know. We have orderly, efficient minds."

"Don't make me feel any worse, Lieutenant."

"I did check with Zorch's secretary to see if he'd scheduled another appointment at the house besides the one he had with you. At, say, six. He says no."

"Zorch could have made an appointment with Shelley without his secretary knowing it."

"True. Apparently, he was out of the office in the late afternoon. That jibes with what Pennyroyal says she was told when she called him. By the way, I checked back with the houseboy, Kenji. He confirmed what she told us. She was there when she says she was. He saw her drive away. Her and Johnny both."

"You didn't believe her?"

"Just making sure. Okay, let's say Zorch did make an appointment on his own with Selden. Let's say Selden plugged him, okay? How does he fit for the rest of it? Would he torch Home-wood? Doubtful, it seems to me."

"Not necessarily, Lieutenant. He doesn't want Matthew to make this new Badger film. He thinks it's a loser. Maybe this was his way of discouraging him."

"Pretty expensive way, don't you think?"

"I assume they're insured."

"And Pennyroyal's negatives? Would he leak those?"

"No," I contended. "He wants to get the two of them back together. He wouldn't have done it."

Lamp glanced down at his notepad thoughtfully. "It could be that the negatives don't figure at all."

"Meaning?"

"Maybe the *Enquirer* got them on their own. Or a second party stole them, someone who doesn't figure in this at all." He considered this idea a moment, then moved on. "Tell me about Trace Washburn."

"What about him?"

"He's being most vague about his whereabouts at the time of the shooting. Said something about going for a long swim. You know anything more about it?"

"Yes."

Lamp leaned forward. "Well, where was he?"

"With a married lady who lives down the beach. Rather famous one."

"Who?"

"If you need to know, I'll tell you."

"I need to know."

"No, you don't."

"Hoagy, I'm up to my ears in this thing," Lamp protested. "If I don't produce some hard evidence soon I'm—"

"You have to handle this personally. Her husband mustn't know."

"You have my word. Who is she?"

I told him.

He was shocked. "I thought she was happily married."

"She is."

"I don't understand these people."

"And you're a lot better off."

"That writer friend of yours, Cassandra Dee, claimed she was in Trancas at the time, too. Also swimming."

"It was a hot day."

"Only when we canvassed Trace's neighbors, nobody re-members seeing her."

I tugged at my ear. "Interesting. I've always liked her for stealing Pennyroyal's negatives. Anything to up the ante for her book. Killing Zorch would certainly qualify. As would the fire."

"She connect up with Shambazza at all?"

"Not that I know of."

"Any idea where she was this evening when Homewood was getting torched?"

"Nope."

"What about Pennyroyal? Pick up anything more from her this afternoon after I left?"

"Nope."

He frowned at me. "Why are you suddenly giving me the Gary Cooper routine?"

"Because I'm doing all the giving and you're doing all the taking."

He thought this over. "Fair enough. You done good, Hoagy."

"Am I off of your you-know-what list now?"

"Let's say you're on probation." Lamp leafed through his notepad. "Mrs. Shelley Selden . . . Now she's real interesting. Seems young Benjamin had a five o'clock appointment in Century City with one Robert Isaacs, child psychologist. Sara went along. They left his office around six. Didn't get home until after seven."

"Traffic again?"

"And the market. Vicente Foods on San Vicente. Still . . ."

"I understand she's not terrible with a gun."

"Awesome is more like it," he said. "The instructors at the range she goes to call her Annie Oakley. They're trying to get her to compete nationally. She's that good. Trouble is, she had the two kids with her. The three-year-old might not pay it much mind, but, cheese and crackers, the older one would have to notice Mommy gunning down two guys in the street. Television hasn't numbed them that much, has it?"

"Don't ask me. I'm not Mister Rogers, and that's not my neighborhood. What else have you got?"

He beamed at me. "I was saving the best for last—potentially our most interesting candidate."

"Who?"

"Bunny Wax. She had her hair done that afternoon. Place called Guillaume's on Wilshire and Barrington. She was there from four until five."

"What about after that?"

"Excellent question, Hoagy," he exclaimed approvingly.

"You're making me feel worse and worse, Lieutenant."

"She *says* she was running errands. Only she's very foggy about the details. She stopped at a drug store, but she can't remember which one or what she purchased. She went to a ladies' shop in Century City to shop for a blouse but she didn't buy one and nobody at the store remembers her. None of it scans, Hoagy. Her whereabouts are a blank from five until she arrived at the Selden house at seven-thirty. What do you think? Could she be our shooter?"

"I know she's fiercely protective of Matthew. I know she despises Pennyroyal. Whoever leaked her negatives to the *Enquirer* was certainly no friend. I know that much."

"And I know she's hiding something. Any idea what it could be?"

"Perhaps."

"Want to share it with me?"

"Eventually."

Lamp narrowed his eyes at me. "Who do you like for it, Hoagy?"

"Schlom."

"Because it points to him, or because you want it to?"

"Because I want it to."

"It doesn't work that way with the law."

"I'm not the law."

"I am."

"I know. Don't remind me."

He chuckled. "No offense, but you've gotten a bit cranky yourself, Hoagy."

"Correction, Lieutenant—I was *always* cranky."

Bunny's light was still on. Her TV glowed blue in the window. I knocked. It took her a minute to answer. She had her robe on, her glasses off. She seemed somewhat fuzzy. Clearly, she'd been dozing in front of the set.

"Oh, it's you, Hoagy," she said, blinking at me.

"Expecting someone else?"

"Sometimes Charmaine looks in on me. Makes sure I go to bed. Except I can't sleep once I do. Only when I watch the TV." She yawned. "Did you want to come in, sweetheart?"

"I wanted to tell you something."

"Tell me something?" She was more alert now. "What?"

"I know where you were tonight. And I know where you were when Abel Zorch was shot. I know all of it."

Bunny's mouth tightened. "Who told you?"

"Matthew has to know, Bunny. If you don't tell him, I will."

"You bastard," she spat. "You no good trouble-making bastard. I knew it the second I laid eyes on you!"

"He has to know, Bunny."

She grabbed me urgently by the shirt. "He can't know. He can't."

"I'm going to tell him. And you can't stop me."

She couldn't. Not without killing me. There was always that chance, of course. But I had to take it. There was no other play.

She couldn't stop me. All she could do was slam the door in my face—which she did. Hard enough to shake the whole bungalow.

The Ramon Novarro bungalow was quiet. Pennyroyal had cleared out. She was an extremely neat little guest. She'd taken the empty champagne bottles and glasses with her. Caviar, candles, crumbs, she'd taken it all. She left no note behind. Nothing behind. Not even the scent of her rose water. The air conditioner got rid of that.

It was as if she had never been there at all. Maybe she hadn't been. Everything was possible.

And nothing was real.

# Chapter Ten

The old surf bum called it. Morning dawned foggy and blessedly cool. I threw open my windows and let in the damp air. It smelled of the ocean and the charred remains of Homewood. Most of the front page of the *Times* was given over to a photo of the blaze, which authorities were labeling as man-made in origin. Sheldon Selden, president of Bedford Falls, stated: "A piece of movie history has been destroyed. But Homewood will live on. We will rebuild as soon as humanly possible." Mr. Selden said it was too soon to estimate the cost of the damage. He also said he had no idea why anyone would want to do such a thing.

Matthew Wax could not be reached for comment.

No new developments were reported in the police investigation of the Hazen Drive shootings.

I awoke paying for the sin of mixing champagne with high-octane bug killer. My head had a Spalding Top-Flite II caroming around inside of it. A pot of coffee and three extra-strength Excedrins managed to lodge it snugly behind my right eye but, as Robert Benchley once wrote, the only real cure for a hangover is death. I pulled on my old sweatshirt of gray cashmere and my mukluks and spent the morning at my Olympia. I worked my way through Matthew's crush on Mona Schaffer, his brief, humiliating fling with high school hoops, his discovery of the Panorama back lot. The work went smoothly. But I wasn't pleased. Gloomy was more like it. Part of it was all of this murder and mayhem I'd gotten myself into. I wanted it to make sense. It didn't. Part of it was Merilee. I wanted her to call. She hadn't. Part of it was Pennyroyal. I wanted to kiss her again. I couldn't. And part of it I couldn't put my finger on. Whatever it was, Lulu was feeling it, too. She was sulky and restless all morning. I think she'd had it with Hollywood. I think she wanted to go home. I think I did, too.

It was Saturday, and the lot was quiet. I strolled over to Stage One by way of Homewood. Lulu stayed behind in the bungalow. She wanted to be alone. She gets that way sometimes. From being around me, I imagine. Insurance and fire department investigators were sifting through the ashes. Sheldon Selden stood there with them, chubby hands on his chubby hips. A few studio employees had stopped by on their day off for a glimpse at movie history. One of them, an elderly woman, was taking pictures. When Shelley noticed this he wigged out.

"What the fuck do you think this is?!" he screamed at her, veins popping from his neck. "A fucking amusement park?!" He stormed over to the frightened woman, snatched the camera from her and hurled it to the ground. Then he stomped on it until he'd destroyed it. Only then did he calm down. And become aware that everyone was watching him in horror. "Jesus," he gasped, his chest heaving. "I—I'm sorry, Maureen. I don't know what got into me. I'll replace it right away. Jesus . . ." He rubbed his hand over his face, and spotted me there. "Whoa, I'm losing it, Hoagy," he moaned, shaking his head. "I'm genuinely losing it."

"Perhaps you've been under a bit of pressure," I suggested.

"That's no excuse." He forced a smile. "I was on my way over to talk to you, guy," he said, putting his arm around me. "Would you do me a huge favor?"

"How huge?"

"Talk him out of it, will you?"

"Out of what?"

"Just try, okay?" he pleaded, gripping me tightly by the shoulder. "I'd be forever in your debt. I mean it." Then he released me and went back to watching the fire inspectors.

I found Matthew and Sarge having lunch in the Hayes's liv-

ing room. A cheeseburger and fries for him, a salad for her. He
was talking basketball. She was writing it down.

"I want real teams in a real gym," he declared forcefully. "I
want authentic all the way. See if Monroe will let us film one of
their games. That would be great. We could use their fans, their
cheerleaders—we'll stick our people in with 'em. Ask them about
their locker room, too. Maybe they'll let us use it on the week-
ends. If not, I want an exact duplicate built here. Everything the
same. Okay?"

"I'll get right on it," she assured him briskly.

"How's the book coming, Meat?" he exclaimed, taking a
huge, starved bite of his cheeseburger.

"It's coming," I replied, surprised by how up he was.

"Same here," he gushed. "I was up half the night writing.
Got a whole new angle on Badger, and I've got you to thank for
it."

"You do?" I glanced over at Sarge. She wouldn't look at me.
She seemed very uncomfortable.

"I'm gonna use it, Meat," he informed me. "That whole humiliating nude scene. Just like you suggested. As a flashback to
when Badger was on the Homewood High team and Debbie was
head cheerleader. See, that was when he thought he'd totally
blown it with her. Only it turns out that's when she *knew*."

"Knew what, Matthew?"

"That she loved him," he replied earnestly. "And always
would. And get this—it's their ten-year high school reunion,
okay?"

"Okay . . ."

"And each one goes, figuring the other one won't. She's left
him, remember? So there they both are at the reunion, together,
and they *have* to confront their feelings for each other."

"Which are?"

"I don't know that part yet," he confessed. "It's still un-
folding."

I tugged at my ear. "How are you planning to film all of
this?"

"What do you mean?"

"Last I heard, Pennyroyal wasn't planning to be in the
movie. How can you do it without her?"

"Oh, I wouldn't worry about that," he said, dismissing it

airily. "Worst case scenario we can use a different actress. But it won't even come to that. You'll see."

Again I looked at Sarge, and again she looked away. Because she knew what I knew—Matthew genuinely believed that if he was excited about this, Pennyroyal would be, too. And she would want to be in it. And he would win her back. And everyone would live happily ever after again in the land of Bedford Falls.

I crossed to the easy chair by the fireplace and sat, my head spinning.

Matthew frowned at me. "I thought you'd be all excited, Meat."

"I am. I just have a strange way of showing it." I closed my eyes a second. When I opened them things had stopped spinning. The room was back to normal. Except, of course, it *wasn't* a room. It was a set. Home. I wanted to go home. "So you intend to go ahead?"

"Oh, absolutely. The fire won't slow me down one bit. In fact, I'm getting a crew together tomorrow to film the wreckage before they cart it away. I'm thinking it'll serve as a great image for what's happening in Badger's head. You know, a burning of the bridges to his past. Nice, huh?"

I said nothing. My head was spinning again.

He popped a french fry in his mouth. "Everything's cool—as long as Johnny's fine, and he is. He's sober, he's feeling good. We talked this morning."

"Where is he?" I asked.

"We moved him into that house Sarge rented for Badger up in Laurel Canyon. He needed a place to stay. Figured we may as well put it to good use."

"When did he move in?" I asked her.

"Last night," she replied. "About nine, nine-thirty. He spent the night there."

"Alone?"

"Why you asking me?" she demanded.

Matthew's eyes widened behind his mangled glasses. "Hey, you're not thinking *he* started the fire, are you, Meat?"

"Who do you think started it, Matthew?" I asked.

"I honestly can't imagine," he replied. "Homewood stood for everything that's clean and decent and good in this world. Why anyone would ever want to destroy it . . . They'd have to be *sick*."

"Have you spoken to Bunny today?" I asked him.

He shook his head. "Today's her golf day. She leaves at dawn. Why?"

The phone rang.

Sarge grabbed it. "Sarge talking, go . . . Uh-huh . . . Hold it, lemme check my list." She reached for her clipboard. "Okay . . ."

"Do you really hate Bunny, Matthew?" I asked.

"Hate her?" He stared at me in amazement. "How could you think something like that?"

"Johnny told me you do."

"Oh, sure, I get it now," he said, nodding. "See, Johnny hates his mother. Always has. I told him I hated mine, too, to make him feel more at ease. But I don't. I'm crazy about Ma."

"Even though she treats you like a little boy?"

"I try to be a good son," he said defensively. "Is that so terrible?"

"I don't know. You tell me."

Sarge hung up the phone and sprang to her feet. "Okay, Hoagy, your posse's at the front gate. I'm gonna go fetch 'em. They got a whole load of shit with 'em."

"Posse?" asked Matthew. "What posse?"

"You left it up to me, Matthew, remember?" I said.

"I left what up to you?" he asked, bewildered.

Sarge strode off into the darkness.

We sat there in silence.

Matthew began to fidget. "Why this sudden interest in Ma?"

"It's not sudden. It's been building for a long time."

"Well, just leave it alone, okay?"

I shrugged. "It's your life."

"That's right, it is."

"And everybody takes care of it for you—Bunny, Sarge, Shelley. That must be nice. That must be terribly fucking nice."

"You got something bothering you, Meat?"

"I do, Matthew. And I've just put my finger on what it is. No one in this business has a memory. One day somebody rapes you, the next day you go into business together. A lawyer gets murdered? You just hire a new one. A town burns down? No problem. You just rewrite the movie. It's not as if it was a real town, after all. Tired of being a thug? How would you like to be a distinguished corporate president instead? Don't want to be a hooker anymore? How about being a society matron? No problem. Not any of it. This whole place—it's one giant Winky Dink magic TV kit."

Matthew brightened. "Wow, I had one of those! It was this clear plastic overlay. And you'd place it over the TV screen and draw a picture on it. Like a ladder, if Winky needed one."

"Exactly. And if you wanted to draw a new picture all you had to do was lift the overlay away from the screen and the ladder would disappear. Like it was never there. Nothing leaves a mark, Matthew. No memory. No outrage. No nothing."

He shook his head. "That's not true, Meat. The movies—they leave a mark."

"Do they?"

"Of course," he replied emphatically. "They make people happy. That's what it's all about. Gee, you sure woke up on the wrong side of the bed today."

"I woke up on the wrong side of the continent today."

"It's gonna be okay, Meat. I know it will. Don't ask me how —I just do. You wait and see. Things'll turn out for the best. You have to have faith, that's all."

It was a good little speech. Also a familiar one. Badger had delivered it to his dad in *Badger Hayes, All-American Boy* when Mr. Hayes feared he'd be ousted as chief of Homewood's volunteer fire department for losing the doughnut money.

Home. I wanted to go home.

Almost as much as I wanted to go to Fiji.

Sarge returned now with my posse. Nearly a dozen of them altogether, chattering excitedly. A stagehand yanked open one of the big stage doors. The truck with all of their stuff came rolling in with them and pulled up in front of Badger's bedroom. Two men began unloading it.

A man can accomplish a lot in twenty-four hours if he has taste, breeding, an unlimited budget and the Bedford Falls jet, gassed up and ready to fly. I'd had it flown over the pole to London, where it picked up Nigel of Turnbull and Asser, Jermyn Street, Mr. Tricker of Strickland's, Savile Row—along with three of his finest tailors—and Tim of Maxwell's, where I have my shoes made. It had stopped off in New York on the way back to pick up world-champion hair stylist Sal Fodera of the St. Regis Hotel, as well as his best manicurist, and half the staff of Leonard's Opticians on West 55th Street.

Sal went right for Matthew, the better to inspect his bald patch. I'd warned him. He circled Matthew slowly, appraising it. "Hoagy, I'm glad you didn't call anyone else," Sal confided. "I don't think anyone else could save this head."

"Can you?"

"He'll look *fantastic*," vowed Sal, removing Matthew's glasses. The opticians took them from him and scurried off. They already knew Matthew's prescription—Sarge had it on file.

Mr. Tricker, who was under the greatest time pressure, ordered Hollywood's most successful director to stand up on a small platform so his tailors could begin taking measurements. While they did he and I went through the bolts of suiting he'd brought. There were blues, grays, browns. Glen plaids, pin stripes, houndstooths. I chose a fine, midweight navy blue flannel. Single-breasted jacket. Pleated trousers with cuffs.

"And will Mr. Wax be wearing braces, sir?" Mr. Ticker inquired.

"He most certainly will."

"What are braces, Meat?" Matthew wondered, blinking at me myopically from the platform.

"Suspenders, Matthew."

"Who, me? No way."

"We'll get right on it, sir," Mr. Tricker said. "Will he be needing a topcoat today?"

"That won't be necessary."

"Spread or straight-collared shirt, Mr. Hoag?" asked Nigel, stepping forward.

"Spread. White broadcloth. French cuffs."

We picked him out a paisley tie of burgundy silk to go with it. I left the braces and other accessories up to Nigel. For shoes Tim and I decided on Maxwell's cap toe balmoral, cordovan. Matthew Wax wore a size 16 shoe, D width, in case you're interested.

Sarge watched all of this activity with a smile. It amused her to see her general being pushed and prodded this way.

"I'm going back to my typewriter now, Matthew," I announced. "You're in excellent hands. By the way, did you take care of that other matter we discussed?"

"What other matter, Meat?" he asked, as Nigel took his collar measurement.

"You know which one," I said, glancing over at Sarge.

He followed my glance. "Oh," he said, reddening. "I kind of forgot, I guess."

"Ask her, Matthew," I commanded. "I won't do it for you."

"Ask me what?" she demanded, suspicious.

Matthew cleared his throat uncomfortably. "I—I just wondered if you might have a little free time later this afternoon."

"I was gonna play some racquetball," she said. "But, like, if it's important I can—"

"Can you teach me to dance?" he blurted out.

She drew herself up, a panther ready to pounce. "Say *what?*"

"I can't dance. Will you teach me?"

"Why me?" she demanded, nostrils flaring. "Think it's, like, in my blood or something? Got them happy feet?"

"No, no," Matthew insisted. "It's just that Meat doesn't dance with boys and—"

"And Arthur Murray's dead," I said.

She weighed this. "Fast or slow?"

"Slow will have to do," I said. "I don't think he has enough time to master the fine points of hip-hop."

"You got that right."

"I have some tapes in my bungalow if you—"

"Get outta here," she whooped. "I got my own sounds."

"Then you'll do it?" asked Matthew bashfully.

"I'll do what I can," she muttered. "But I'm making no promises. Ain't like I got a whole lotta natural talent here to work with."

I left them to it. Spent the rest of the afternoon at the typewriter, doing the job I was being paid to do. The drum-banger called again, this time from his posh weekend home in posh Sag Harbor, which is where publishing people go to get away from everything and everyone—except each other.

"I just came from a cocktail party at Jason Epstein's." He was greatly agitated. "Pennyroyal's editor already has her first five chapters. Cassandra faxes him pages every night to his apartment. He was telling everyone at the party all about it. I didn't know *what* to say about how ours is going."

"I'm already writing Matthew Wax's material," I said. "I can't write yours as well."

"But I don't have *anything*," he complained. "What do I *tell* people?"

"I'm sure you'll think of something. Somebody told me you're the smartest editor in publishing. Oh, I know who it was— it was you."

"But this is the hottest story in—"

"I'll deliver it when I said I'd deliver it. Now is there anything else?"

There wasn't, so I hung up on him. I was starting to enjoy that.

At six I dressed. My double-breasted ivory dinner jacket and pleated black evening trousers with the black satin stripe. My starched white broadcloth tuxedo shirt with ten-pleat bib front and wing collar. My black silk bow tie. Grandfather's pearl cuff links and studs.

Lulu perked up noticeably. She likes parties. People are cheerful, and there is generally seafood. She wore a white silk scarf around her throat and the beret Merilee got her in Paris. Most sassy, provided you weren't downwind from her.

Bunny was outside her bungalow unloading her golf bag from the trunk of her Jaguar. She had on a golf skirt and a cardigan sweater. The bag was big. I asked her if I could help. She didn't answer. Just gave me as hateful a look as a five-foot-tall senior citizen could give a man. It was as hateful a look as this man has ever gotten, and I've gotten plenty. What she really wanted to do was mash me over the head with her mashie. Instead she pulled her bag out of the trunk, slammed it shut, and stomped off toward her bungalow. She'd warned me when we met that I wouldn't want her for an enemy. Well, I had her for an enemy now.

If only I could make friends so easily.

Alberta Hunter was singing "Old Fashioned Love" slow and gentle on Stage One, Fred and Ginger swaying to her in the Hayes's living room. Lulu and I stood in the darkness, watching. They made some pair. Her in her tube top, spandex shorts, and cross-training shoes, murmuring sweet one-two, one-two-threes into his ear. Him staying doggedly in step, holding her as if she were made of china. Sal had given him a stylish high and tight brush cut that completely masked his bald patch, with the help of a little grease. He had a clean shave for the first time since we'd met, manicured nails, and gleaming new gold-framed glasses. His navy blue suit hugged his long, ungainly frame like only the finest material and custom tailoring can.

His fresh white shirt sparkled. His shoes shone. He was every inch the gentleman of distinction. It was quite some transformation.

Something else had changed, too. The way he was looking at Sarge. I think he'd finally realized she was alive. Alberta Hunter and a new suit will do that to a growing boy. He stared at her as she counted. And kept staring.

"Why you looking at me like that?" she finally demanded, fiercely.

"Like what?" he asked, swallowing.

"Don't like this no better than you do," she huffed, as she maneuvered him around the dance floor. "Next thing I'll be coming in and scrubbing your damned back for you."

He was still staring. She was staring back now, her eyes soft and very wary. Shadow knew plenty, all right.

I applauded them when the song was over. Startled, they jumped apart as if I'd caught them doing something dirty.

"What do you think, Meat?" Matthew wondered, bashfully modeling his new self for me.

"I'm not disappointed."

"That's high praise from him," he told Sarge.

"Your posse's on their way home, Hoagy," she reported. "Pockets bulging."

"It was worth it," declared Matthew.

I deepened the dimple in his tie for him. "Glad you think so."

"He looks okay," Sarge acknowledged. "I was afraid they was gonna make him look like some bank president. But I guess ain't nobody can do *that*." She gave me the once-over. "Don't look so bad yourself."

"For a tall, skinny white boy?"

She smiled. "Just plain period."

"And how would you rate your dancing pupil?"

"He'll get by on the slow stuff alright," she replied. "But if turns up-tempo, get his ass off the floor."

"I'll do my best."

"Thanks for the lesson, Teach," he said to her.

"That's okay," she said. "Hard to find anyone to dance slow with. Without it turning into some kind of vertical body rub, I mean."

"What are you doing tonight?" he asked her.

"Working," she barked angrily. "What the hell else would I be doing?"

"I just wondered," he barked back. "You don't have to bite my head off."

She busied herself gathering up her tapes. Alberta was singing "Sweet Georgia Brown" now.

"Ever see her in person?" I asked Sarge.

"I wish," she replied. "You?"

"At the Cookery in the Village, about fifteen years ago. She was in her eighties. Never sounded better. Let's hit the road, Matthew." We started out, his eyes fastened on Sarge's broad, muscular back.

"Hey, Matthew?" she called after him.

"Yes, Sarge?" he said anxiously.

Her face broke into a warm smile. "Knock 'em dead, hear?"

We took the Batmobile, and I didn't much care for the way it handled. Strictly a show car. It took us forever to get there. The traffic was slow. I also had to pull over twice so Matthew could throw up. Still, we turned a few heads when we came zooming into the parking lot of the Sheraton Panorama City. And Matthew turned more than a few when we strolled through the lobby, Lulu in tow. Conversations stopped cold. People gaped. The man was Page One.

There was a big banner over the door to the Blue Room welcoming members of the James Monroe High Class of '72. Three young women were handing out name tags at a table outside the door.

Matthew panicked ten feet short of them. "I can't do it, Meat," he said, wiping his clammy palms on his trousers. "I can't." He was quite pale.

"You can, Matthew."

"Can't."

"All you have to remember is one thing—*they're* going to be afraid of *you*."

"But why?" he wondered, baffled.

"Because you're famous."

"But—"

"Let's go, Matthew," I ordered. *"Action."*

"Hey, that's my line," he protested, grinning at me. Then we got our name tags and waded in.

It was a big room, big enough for two dozen banquet tables, a dance floor, and a stage, where a lite 'n' easy rock trio was listlessly knocking out a medley of early seventies nonfavorites. A bar and hot hors d'oeuvres buffet were set up against one wall, where about three hundred people were laughing and hugging and gaily getting reacquainted. The gaiety was more than a little forced. It generally is at reunions. This was most decidedly not a gathering of balding, beefy plumbers and their girdled wives. It was a Yushie crowd, a veritable hive of the Young Urban Shitheads. The men looked like personal injury lawyers who did a lot of sit-ups. The women were slim, attractive, and stylish. Several wore sequined minidresses. A few were decked out in Calvin's stunningly expensive, stunningly stupid military tunic. Things changed noticeably when they caught sight of their illustrious classmate in the doorway. Eyes widened. Jaws dropped. A respectful hush fell over the entire room. I'm used to showing up at places with Merilee. I know the effect a star can have on a room. This was different. This was like showing up at a party with Moses.

Lulu caught a whiff of crab puffs and headed straight for the buffet table.

"What do we do now, Meat?" Matthew gulped, a frozen grin on his face.

"Not a thing," I replied. "Just wait for them to come to you."

And they did. First to approach was a short, powerfully built guy with a jagged scar across his forehead. His wife was tiny, perky, and frizzy-haired. "Mr. Wax?" he said nervously. "You won't remember me in a million years, but I used to live next door to you when we were kids. Neal Bricker."

"I sure do," said Matthew, awestruck.

He did indeed. This was the bully he'd nailed in the head with the rock. Neal still wore the scar.

"I'd like you to say hello to my wife, Phyllis," said Neal, surprised and flattered that Matthew Wax remembered him. "She's a big fan of yours. We run a pet supplies outlet together in Glendora."

"Pleased to meet you, Phyllis," Matthew said pleasantly.

I headed off to the bar to fetch us some champagne. By the time I got there he had been engulfed. His classmates clustered around him, paying their respects, shaking his hand, proudly introducing him to their husbands and wives. Some took snapshots of him. Others asked for his autograph. At first, he seemed genuinely stunned by all of it. But then he started enjoying it. His eyes shone brightly. He was laughing. He was lapping it up. And why not? He'd always wanted these people to like him. And now they did. It had taken Matthew Wax twenty years, but he wasn't a goon anymore. He was one of them. He was home. And loving every minute of it.

It didn't take me long to find her. She was standing over by the edge of the dance floor exchanging kiddie photos with three other women. She was taller than I expected, much taller than Pennyroyal. And the resemblance had faded some over the years. Her features were more pronounced than Penny's, nose longer, chin more square. Age lines crinkled at her eyes. She was not a great beauty. But she was a striking, handsome woman. She wore a white silk blouse, suede skirt, and black boots. She looked weary. Single mothers tend to. When the other women drifted away, I moved in.

"Mona, isn't it?" I asked.

She smiled, flushing slightly. "Wait, don't tell me, let me guess." She looked me over carefully. "Don't tell me. . . . I'll get it. . . ." She finally gave up, squinting at my name tag. "Stewart Hoag. Wow, the memory's really starting to go."

"It's not, Mona. I never went to Monroe. I'm here with a friend who did—Matthew Wax."

She gasped girlishly. "Matthew Wax *came?* God, my daughter will die when I tell her. She adores *Dennis*. Watches it over and over again."

"He'd like to say hello to you."

Mona brought her hand up to her mouth. "To me?"

"Yes."

She shook her head at me. "No, he must be thinking of somebody else. We hardly knew each other."

"He specifically mentioned you."

"Are you sure about this?"

"Quite sure." I offered her my arm. "Shall we?"

She hesitated, then took my arm. We started across the room toward him. She stopped. "Wait, is this some kind of prank?"

"Prank?"

"They pull all kinds of stuff at these things to embarrass people."

"It's no prank," I assured her.

She bit her lower lip nervously. "Look, let me go comb my hair first, okay? I'll find you."

"Mona, there is one other thing—would you dance with him?"

"*Dance* with him?"

"If he asks. Will you say yes?"

"Well, sure." She was mystified. "Why wouldn't I?"

"No reason. No reason at all."

She headed off to the ladies' room. I went back to Matthew, who was chatting away with a tanned, athletic couple he introduced to me as the Kip Londons.

"Kip played basketball with me, Meat," he informed me, with a sly wink.

"You bet," said Kip, pumping my hand. "I've been telling Andrea for years how we played on the team together."

"I'll bet you guys had your share of laughs," I suggested.

"More than our share," Kip affirmed heartily. "You in motion pictures, too, Stewart?"

"I am not. What do you do, Kip?"

"Manage a Wendy's franchise over on Lankershim for my father-in-law," he replied. "We had your sixteen-ounce cups, Matt. Your *Yeti* cups. Sold a million of them."

After he told Matthew how very, very much they enjoyed his pictures they moved along. Matthew and I were alone.

"This is great," exclaimed Matthew, beaming happily. "Just great. I mean, *they're* the ones who are nervous. I don't know why I was dreading it so much."

"I don't either," I said, watching Mona approach him shyly.

"Hello, Matthew," she said, tapping him on the shoulder. "Remember me?"

He froze, his eyes bulging out of his head.

"Mona Schaffer," she said. "Mona Thayer, now."

He tried to speak but all that came out was a faint whimper. His throat seemed obstructed. "Sure, sure," he managed to stammer, shaking her hand. "Sure you are. Sure." He kept on shaking her hand. She looked at him oddly, wondering if he was ever going to stop. He did, finally. "Sure you are. Sure." He was starting to perspire.

"My daughter just loves your movies."

"Really? How old is he?"

"She."

"I meant she," he said hurriedly, his teeth chattering.

"Eight."

"I—I have a little boy myself. Six months old."

She laughed. "No kidding. I only read about him every day in the paper."

"You do?" He seemed surprised at this.

"Of course, Matthew. We all do."

He stared at her, glassy-eyed. He'd run out of things to say. That helpless whimper came from his throat again.

"I understand you're a nurse, Mona," I said, stepping in.

She nodded. "At the Kaiser Permanente in Woodland Hills. I'm in pulmonary intensive care."

"I—I direct movies," Matthew volunteered.

She laughed again. "He's really funny, isn't he?" she said to me.

"I think so."

Up on stage, the band segued into a perfectly repulsive rendition of *Desperado*, the old Eagles' song. It was, however, slow. A few couples were dancing. I nudged Matthew with my elbow. He looked at me inquiringly. I shot a look over at the dance floor. He nodded grimly.

"W-Would you like to dance, Mona?" he asked her, his voice cracking just like Badger's did when he asked Debbie to the prom. Debbie said yes but got the mumps, so Badger took his mom, who was voted prom queen.

Mona said, "I'd love to dance, Matthew."

"Great." He heaved a sigh of relief. "Will you excuse us, Meat?"

"I have to cut out now, Matthew."

"But we just got here," he protested. "Where are you going?"

"It's business. I'll see you back at Bedford Falls later."

"Okay, Meat, if you say so. Hey, wait—how am I gonna get home?"

"Improvise."

Parked cars lined both sides of Hazen Drive all the way down the hill, well past the gate where I'd found the bodies of Abel Zorch and Geoffrey with a G. Paparazzi were crowded outside the Schloms' gate. A police cruiser was parked there with two uniformed cops inside it. Then again, maybe it was only Norb's bogus car. And maybe they were only actors pretending to be cops. No telling. I only knew that it was definitely time to get out of town.

I left the Batmobile with a male model in a red jacket and strolled up the driveway. It was steep and curved around behind another house before it arrived at a 1940's reproduction of a Provencal stone cottage, not small. It sat on top of the hill, the lights of the San Fernando Valley spread out below. There was a tennis court, a pool, and a large floodlit patio. That's where the activity was. Two hundred or so celebrities had come to pay their last respects to Abel Zorch and their first to Mr. Hiroshi Nakamura of the Murakami Corporation, Wild West style. The old guard was on hand—the Jimmy Stewarts, John Gavins, Charlton Hestons. The new guard was on hand—Tom Cruise and Nicole Kidman, Demi Moore and Bruce Willis, Alec Baldwin and Kim Basinger, Sly Stallone and bimbo. They were all there, costumed in their ten-gallon hats, fringed buckskin jackets and stonewashed jeans, their deerskin vests, elkhide boots and duster coats, their leather chaps, string ties, and calico shirts. They were all there, chewing on their plates of barbecue and cole slaw and spitting the remains into their bandana napkins. A pig was roasting on a spit over an open fire. A country western band was playing—Willie Nelson, in fact. Approved society page photographers and the *Entertainment Tonight* puff crew were on hand to capture all the fun. The earplug brigade was there too, meaning Ronnie and Nancy were about somewhere as well.

Lulu took it all in, awestruck. A relapse, I'm afraid. It was quite some crowd. But a brief relapse, happily. After a moment she shook herself, like she does after a bath, and went scampering off in search of the sushi bar I'd promised her. A small lie on my part. She wouldn't have left the reunion otherwise.

Toy Schlom, elegant society matron, spotted me quickly, her violet eyes sparkling. She seemed gay and at ease amidst all of this. Also lithe and ageless. Not an ounce of fat on her. She wore a black suede vaquero hat, a faded denim shirt open to the navel, and skin-tight white jeans tucked into black snakeskin Tony Lamas. I noticed again how unusually smooth and shiny her skin was. Watching her move across the patio toward me I decided she wasn't coated in polyurethane at all. No, the entire lady was made of durable space-age polymers.

"Why, you've not worn a costume, Mr. Hoag," she observed in her Locust Valley lockjaw. "I should be very cross with you."

"Not to fear, Toy. On the inside I'm still a rootin', tootin', six-shootin' buckaroo."

She laughed and took my arm, guiding me toward the house. "You are an interesting man. I may have to adopt you for the evening. There are *so* few interesting people here." She was skilled at this, all poise and flattery. "You must eat, of course. But first you must say hello to Norbert and our guest of honor."

She took me inside through the French doors. Very Provencal in here as well. Stone floors. Whitewashed walls. Rough, country antiques. There was an upstairs, and wings going off in both directions.

"Not a terrible house," I said.

"I've just finished decorating it," she said. "It *is* nice, is it not? Especially for a tear-down."

"You're tearing it down?"

"On Monday," she confirmed. "We need more space. A ballroom, a dining room that can seat more than two dozen. We love the location, so we have decided to build on it. An exact duplicate of the villa in Tuscany Norbert and I stayed in on our honeymoon. It will be very authentic, very bold. And it will have *space*. My new closets, I assure you, will make Candy Spelling's closets look like—"

"Closets?"

"We're renting down the block while the construction takes place. Abel's house, actually. We've made arrangements with his estate."

"I've been wanting to talk to you about Abel," I said.

"Why, certainly," she said brightly. "After I've greeted my guests, and you've eaten. Shall I look for you in the study?"

"That'll be fine."

They were in the living room, posed stiffly before the stone fireplace like heads of state at a summit conference. On the left was Schlom, the thug with the yellow rat's eyes. On the right was Nakamura, who was a pretty tough-looking customer himself. The man from Murakami was in his sixties and built of solid oak, with slicked-down black hair and steel-framed glasses. The Reagans were with them right now, both of them looking like they'd paid a recent visit to a good, professional taxidermist. So were

the national TV news crews and a crew from Tokyo, lights blazing, cameras rolling. Flanking Nakamura was the Japanese am-
bassador to the United States, who'd flown in from Washington
for the occasion. Flanking Schlom was Kinsley Usher, the tall,
silver-haired ex-senator from the state of California who was every inch Hollywood's vision of a statesman. The man was so distinguished he made Lloyd Bentsen look like Buddy Hackett.
None of these people were in Western wear, though I suspected
Ronnie wanted to be.

After the cameras had stopped rolling and the former President and Nancy had been carted away, Toy led me up to her
husband.

"Darling, here is Mr. Hoag," she sang out.

"Glad to see ya, Hoag," he growled, shaking my hand. "Say
hello to Mr. Nakamura. This is Stu Hoag, Hiroshi. He's helping
us bring this Bedford Falls thing to a conclusion."

"I suppose that's one way of describing what I'm doing," I
said.

Nakamura's eyes flickered at the mention of Bedford Falls. A
brief flicker. Nothing more. He bowed, then shook my hand. His
grip made my fingers tingle. He said he was pleased to meet me,
and happy that the heat wave had broken. He spoke fluent English, or seemed to. He was cordial. Still, I wouldn't have wanted
to get in a fight with him. Next to him, Schlom was Cuddles
Sakall.

I moved over and let Usher dazzle me with his smile.

"I've just been in contact with Sheldon Selden, Mr. Hoag,"
he informed me in his rich, resonant voice. He talked as if the
cameras were still rolling. "I was attempting to impress upon
him how crucial it is for both sides to pour oil on these troubled
waters. I suggested we all sit down together tomorrow morning
like responsible adults."

"A novel concept, Senator," I said. "I like it."

"I hope you'll join us."

"I don't believe I qualify."

"That isn't so, sir," he insisted. "I understand you've become
a trusted family adviser."

"That's not what I meant."

He frowned. "What did you mean?"

"I meant I'm not a responsible adult."

I left him to ponder this and moved on outside. A cowpoke

waiter handed me a frosted mug of beer. I found Pennyroyal and Cassandra standing by the pool polishing off their vittles. Pennyroyal wore a starched calico prairie dress unbuttoned up to midthigh, white boots, and a suede cowboy hat held on with a chin strap. She was unquestionably the cutest little cowgirl there. Possibly the cutest in the history of the West. Or maybe it was just the way she was looking at me.

"You're *here*," she said, her eyes soft and expectant.

"You can't keep Stewart Hoag away from a hootenanny. Ask anyone."

"I'm so glad you made it, Hoagy," she said, resting her hand on my arm.

"I'm glad you're glad," I said, grinning at Cassandra, who had on her denim jacket, jeans, and no hat.

"Gawd," she cried, giving me a buggy-eyed once-over. "Ya look unreal in evening clothes. I mean, gawd!"

"It is a pretty awe-inspiring sight."

"Where's your cute little friend?" she asked.

"She's off playing seek the sashimi."

"I mean the Lieutenant."

"I let him have his Saturday nights to himself, provided he's back for bed check."

"Have you eaten yet, Hoagy?" Pennyroyal wondered, gazing up at me.

"I have not."

"Let me get you something."

"Not necessary. I'll get it myself."

"Please," she insisted. "What can I get you?"

"I want it all," I replied. "While a select few of my organs still function."

Off she went to fetch it.

Cassandra watched her, nodding to herself. "Yeah, yeah, shewa—it all makes sense now," she commented tartly.

"I seriously doubt that."

"All day she's like a love-struck schoolgoil, completely useless to me. Stars in her eyes she has. I figure, hey, Pretty Penny's getting dicked by someone new. Shewa enough, this afternoon she calls up Trace and breaks it off with him *cold*. So I *know* there's somebody else. I shoulda figured, y'know? I really shoulda." She shook her head ruefully. "Wow, I never had a chance with ya, did I? You're waaaay outta my league."

I heard a low growl at my feet. Lulu. She'd discovered I fibbed about the sushi.

"It looks mad," observed Cassandra warily.

"Appearances are not deceiving."

She showed me her teeth. Lulu, that is.

I showed her mine. And said, "I never claimed to be a perfect father."

Grudgingly, she went off to mingle, but not until she'd *hmpht*ed at me, something she got from Merilee.

"Christ, you're smooth. I actually *believed* all that shit ya told me about being loyal to Merilee. So what are ya gonna do if she takes ya back? Dick 'em both?"

"Cassandra, I hate to disappoint you, but I spent last evening in Trancas with Trace. Then I went to the fireworks show at Homewood. I did not, as you so eloquently put it, dick Pennyroyal."

"I don't believe ya."

"Where were you last night?"

"Me? Cranking out pages in my room. Faxed ten more to our editor. How many pages youse guys done, huh?"

"This is not a track meet, Cassandra."

"Don't kid yourself, honey. There's a finish line, and I'm getting there foist." She glanced across the patio. "Christ, look at her, will ya?"

Our little cowgirl was working her way back to us through the crowd with my dinner, a shy doe smile on her face.

"What about her?" I said.

"She's gone. I know women, and that woman is *gone*. I shewa hope ya know what you're doing."

"I seldom know what I'm doing."

"Here you go, Hoagy," Pennyroyal said, somewhat breathlessly.

I took the plate from her. There was barbecue, beans, cole slaw, corn bread. "Thanks. Doesn't look terrible."

"I hope you like it."

"I'm sure I will," I said, tasting the barbeque.

"How is it?" she wondered anxiously.

"Excellent."

"Oh, good," she said, relieved.

"Gawd, I'm outta here," announced Cassandra, rolling her eyes. "This is waaaay too sickening for me."

After she'd gone I said, "She thinks you've fallen for me."

Pennyroyal's baby blue eyes searched my face. "And what do you think?"

"I think the skies are cloudy and the forecast calls for pain."

Her forehead creased fretfully. "I still can't believe what happened to Homewood. I saw the flames when I was leaving. Who would want to do that, Hoagy?"

"Too many people."

"I didn't think it would be smart for me to stick around," she said. "What with the way the family feels about me. I mean, the last thing I need right now is to be caught in your bungalow late at night drinking champagne with no underwear on. . . ."

I tasted the slaw. It was interesting slaw. It had raisins in it, carrots, a hint of onion. Green, I believe . . ."You weren't wearing any underwear?"

She shook her head, slowly and gravely.

"Are you wearing any now?"

She shook her head again, her eyes locked onto mine.

I drained my beer. I was thirsty all of a sudden. "You're not making this easy for me."

"I'm not trying to make it easy," she purred, leaning in to me. I could feel her breath on my neck. "I'm trying to make it hard."

"And you're succeeding admirably."

She laughed. A wicked, delicious laugh. Debbie Dale never laughed like that. She leaned in closer. "Will you come home with me tonight, Hoagy?" she whispered. "I want you. I really, really want you."

"I thought we went through this last night."

"And I thought we got past it."

"It can't happen, Pennyroyal."

"But it will," she vowed. "It has to."

"No, it doesn't. Maybe in a movie. But not in real life. In real life, there's a tomorrow after the fade-out. There are consequences. Hearts get stepped on."

She gazed up at me, a faint, mocking smile on her lips. "You really should write movies. Such a good speech. So noble and honorable and mature. Henry Fonda could have said it. There's only one problem with it."

"What's that?"

"You're full of shit."

"And it's high time you found out."

"Has she called you?"

"No."

"Has she written you?"

"No."

"Have you heard one word from the woman since she left you?"

"She hasn't left me."

"How do you know?"

"I know."

"*How?* What are you going on?"

"Faith."

"That's not much," she sniffed.

"Don't kid yourself. That's everything."

Cassandra came rushing up to us excitedly. "You'll never guess who's trying to crash the party!"

"Elvis?" I ventured hopefully.

"Trace. He's outside the gate, bombed and howling like a wolf. He's calling for ya, honey. He keeps saying, 'Big Steve wants his pretty baby back.'"

"Damn him," Pennyroyal cursed angrily. "Just what I need right now—another 'Penny the Whore' headline."

"Maybe ya oughta go calm him down, huh?" Cassandra suggested. "The guards can't get rid of him."

"And humiliate myself in front of the most important people in the movie business?" Pennyroyal raged. "No way."

"But he's fallin' down drunk. Might get himself arrested."

"Good," Penny said coldly. "I hope they haul him away and throw him in jail. I'm going inside until he's gone. Excuse me." With that she fled for the house. She did not look back.

Cassandra watched her, amazed. "Wow, when that girl breaks it off, she breaks it off."

"So it would appear."

"WHERE'S MY PRETTY PENNY?! WHERE IS SHE?!"

"Oh, gawd."

He had fought his way inside. Two security guards were all over him, but they couldn't bring down the old quarterback. He was red-faced and wild-eyed, arms flailing, shirt torn. "WHERE'S PENNY?! BIG STEVE IS CALLING YOU!"

It got very quiet. The celebrity party-goers watched Trace

with utter disdain. Not because he was drunk or because he was making an ass of himself, but because he so obviously reeked of failure. That's one perfume everyone in Hollywood is allergic to.

"COME TO BIG STEVE, BABY!"

"Possibly you should see about getting the man home," I mentioned to Cassandra.

"Why me?"

"You wanted to be a big-time ghost—this is part of it."

"COME ON, PRETTY BABY!"

"Why don't *you* do it?"

"I only clean up after my own elephant."

"Huh?"

"He's *your* celebrity's mess, Cassandra, not mine."

"BIG STEVE NEEDS YOUR SWEET LITTLE PUSSY, PENNY!"

Reluctantly, she nodded. "Yeah, yeah, shewa." Then she went over to try and calm him down. Guts she had plenty of.

I went inside to find Toy. She was in the living room, chatting with the John Forsyths. She nodded at me and gestured toward the hallway off the dining room. I strolled that way. Past a powder room. Past a spare bedroom, which was being used as a coatroom. A hat check girl sat in there reading the current issue of *People*, the one with Pennyroyal and Georgie on the cover, and the headline "IT'S JUST THE TWO OF US NOW." At the end of the hall was a small, paneled study with shuttered windows. There was a French provincial cherry writing table, a couple of deep leather armchairs, a wet bar. Norb's inner sanctum. The place where he came to be alone with his deepest, vilest thoughts. On the walls were framed pictures of him with Harmon Wright, with Anwar Sadat, Menachem Begin, with Boris Yeltsin, Lech Walesa, Michael Jackson, Bob Hope. There was even a picture of him with Matthew Wax on the set of *To The Moon*, inscribed *Thanks for all of these neat toys, pop. Love, Matthew.* I searched through his liquor stock for a single malt. Finding none, I poured myself a calvados in a Baccarat crystal glass and sat down in one of the leather armchairs.

Toy breezed in a moment later. She left the door open. You don't close doors at Hollywood parties. People will think you're snorting or fucking in there. "Such a lovely party, isn't it?" she said gaily. "Abel would have adored it so. He loved the glitter, the lights, the laughter." She took a seat behind the writing table. "I understand our friend Trace has made his usual drunken scene. And the poor dear wonders why no one will give him a job."

"No, he doesn't," I said. "He knows perfectly well why no one will."

She glanced at my drink. "Fix me one of those, would you, dear?" Then she sat back with a weary sigh and massaged her cheeks. "People have no idea how exhausting it is to smile and be charming for hours at a stretch. No idea at all." Relaxed, she looked closer to fifty than forty, which she probably was.

I poured her a calvados. Her eyes caught and held mine when I handed it to her. There was nothing but confidence and determination in them. I couldn't hurt her. She wanted me to know that. I sat. She took a sip and plopped her Tony Lamas down on her husband's two-hundred-year-old writing table. "Okay, let's have it, honey," she said harshly.

I leaned forward. "Could you repeat that?"

"You heard me the first time."

I tugged at my ear. "Tennessee?"

She nodded, impressed. "Murfreesboro. Been there?"

"Passed through once."

"Don't bother going back. I never did. Ran away when I was thirteen. Believe me, it's nicer here." She looked around at Norb's den. "Much nicer." She sat up straight and rolled up her sleeves like a shitkicker getting ready to arm-wrestle someone, which I suppose she was. Her wrists were thin but looked strong. So did her hands. Her nails were painted plum-colored. She waited.

"I was wondering how close you and Abel were."

"We both loved to gossip," she replied. "Something we didn't really discover about ourselves until we became neighbors. He'd stop over for coffee the morning after a party and just dish away. He loved dirt more than anyone I've ever known. It made him positively giddy with laughter."

"And before you became neighbors?"

"What about it?" she asked.

"Trace mentioned you used to provide Abel with girls for his parties. Back in your career days."

She sipped her drink and said nothing.

"Is that so?"

"Consider your source, why don't you?" she said.

"Meaning Trace made it up?"

Again she said nothing. Gabby she wasn't.

"It would be a mistake for you not to talk to me."

She crossed her arms in front of her chest. "You're the one who's making a mistake, honey."

"Is that a threat, Toy?"

"Let's just say Norbert has been known to get very upset at anyone who offends me."

"Am I offending you?"

"You're working on it."

"I could come back tomorrow morning with Lieutenant Lamp, and he could do the asking. Only, it'll go public that way."

She raised an eyebrow. "And it won't if it's just you and me?"

"My interest is in Matthew Wax. Exposing you doesn't interest me at all."

"*Exposing* me? You make it sound like I've got something I want to hide."

"Doesn't everyone?"

She stared at me. "You're a sleazy, horrible little man, aren't you?"

"I'm not all that little."

She stared at me some more. "Okay, so I set Abel up with some girls," she said reluctantly. "So what?"

"Was Pennyroyal Brim one of them?"

"Pennyroyal Brim?!" she cried in shock. Or a pretty good imitation of it. "Where on earth would you get such a crazy idea?"

"From her. She told me the two of you worked together, briefly. She told me a nice, vivid horror story all about how Norb and you raped her."

Her eyes froze. Something deep inside going snap-crackle-pop. I didn't know what, or what to make of it. "Rape? Is that what she called it?"

"What do you call it?"

She raised her chin at me. "Exactly what did she tell you, honey?"

"That you got her involved with Shambazza under false pre-tenses. That you lured her to Norb's house, drugged her, and did an array of unspeakable things to her. How do you remember it, Toy?"

She was silent a long time. A vein in her right temple began to throb. She massaged it. "I misjudged her, okay? I thought she wanted the work, and knew what she was getting into. It turned out she didn't. She didn't have what it takes, either."

"Not like you, huh?"

"Don't sit there judging me," she snapped hotly.

"I could stand if you prefer."

"It was just a mistake, that's all. These things happen. I made sure she was well compensated for her trouble. And I left her alone after that. Crossed her off my list." She poked at her glass with a fingernail. "She and I get alone fine now. It's not as if the little girl hasn't done alright for herself."

"Did Abel know about this?"

"Abel knew about everything." She stood up abruptly. "Now, if you'll excuse me, I have guests."

"I'm not through."

"What else is there to talk about?"

"Shambazza. Tell me about him. You knew him."

"Everybody in the film industry knew him," she said, parking a lean flank on the desk. "Drug use was totally out in the open until a couple of years ago. Studio executives snorted coke around the conference table. Offered it around like coffee or a cold drink. He supplied them with a lot of it. Also with a lot of the girls they needed. To round out their parties, to cozy up to foreign investors. That was how he made his money. But his real interest was film. He was a serious artist. He wanted to direct. Only none of the studio people would let him. They'd buy his dope, but they wouldn't give him a job. He begged Norbert for a chance. A lousy TV episode, anything. But Norbert wouldn't hire him. That made him bitter." She lowered her eyes. "I loved the man. He was kind and funny and brilliant. We were close once. And then we weren't. He became so bitter and nasty. He slept around on me. Beat me up. So I got out. I had to."

"You've done all right for yourself, too," I suggested.

She picked up her drink and finished it. She said no to a refill. Then she said, "Norbert and I understand each other. We're both survivors. We're very happy. I know I am."

"Somebody murdered Shambazza shortly after you left him."

"Yes. I was sorry when I heard about it."

"Even though you hated him?"

"I didn't hate him. I just got out, that's all. I didn't want him dead."

"Who did?"

"He moved huge quantities of dope. That brought him in contact with some very dangerous people. I assumed it was one of them."

"So did the police."

She frowned at me. "You don't agree?"

"I don't believe in coincidences," I replied.

"What kind of coincidences, dear?" She was putting on the poise and polish again.

"The kind where you dump your bad-ass boyfriend, latch onto a big-league Hollywood power guy, and your bad-ass boyfriend suddenly gets erased. That kind."

"My background has never been a secret to anyone who knows us," she said, looking me right in the eye.

"Still, it would have been a teeny bit awkward, wouldn't it? Having this black drug dealer, this pimp, hanging around. Showing up at inopportune moments. Like tonight, say, with Ronnie and Nancy here. I mean, it would be in such bad taste, wouldn't it, dear?"

She threw her glass at me. Missed. It hit the wall and shattered.

"I thought you said you didn't want a refill," I countered.

She grabbed a heavy crystal ashtray and hurled that at me. Missed again.

"Thanks, but I don't smoke."

She charged around the desk at me, eyes blazing. "Why don't you just come out and say it, huh?"

"Okay," I said easily. "I think you killed the guy. Buried him and your past with him."

She slapped my face. A hard, ringing slap that sounded a lot worse than it felt. It brought Norb—on the run. He stopped in the doorway, barrel chest heaving, heavy fists clenched. He looked at the broken glass. He looked at me. He looked at his wife. "Tell me what he said, honey," he growled menacingly. Smoke wasn't coming out of his ears, but it may as well have been.

She brushed past him without answering. Left him there in the doorway glowering at me, his thick neck bulging with blood above the collar of his white shirt. He looked like a man who wanted to murder me with his bare hands. And could.

He closed the door behind him. I guess he didn't care if people thought we were snorting or fucking in there. That's clout. He tried to pour himself a brandy, only his hands were shaking so much he couldn't get it in the glass.

"Want me to do that for you, Norb?"

"What'd you say to my wife, punk? I wanna know."

I poured his brandy for him and held it out for him. He wouldn't take it. I put it down, topped off my calvados. "We were just discussing her late friend Shambazza."

Schlom made a face, as if he'd just smelled something bad. Couldn't have been me. I was wearing Floris. "What about him?"

"Actually, I should be very cross with you, Norb," I said, sipping my drink.

He let out a short, harsh laugh. "You've got a pair of 'em, kid. I'll give you that. You sure as hell do. Okay, I'll bite. How come?"

"You lied to me yesterday. You told me you never heard of Shambazza. Toy says different. She says he begged you to let him direct."

He stared at me with his malevolent eyes.

"So how come you lied to me, Norb?"

He went over to the writing table, tore off a sheet of crisp, white notepaper, and rolled it between his thumb and index finger. "Because," he said, popping it into his mouth, "you're not worth bothering to be honest to."

"Honesty's no bother. Honesty's free."

"Nothing's free," he grunted.

"Bedford Falls certainly isn't," I acknowledged. "You *were* honest with me about that. You told me Matthew would have to sell. You told me he'd get the message. I'd certainly call last night an impressive message."

"What the fuck are you talking about?"

"The fire, Norb. What else?"

He rubbed the back of his hand over his fleshy nose. His rat's eyes narrowed. "You're a lucky guy, you know that?"

"Not as lucky as I used to be."

"No, no. You're lucky. Plenty lucky. Because I got important people here right now. If I didn't I know just what I'd do with you. I'd take that pig out there off its spit and I'd put you on it and listen to you scream as you turned round and round over that nice, hot open fire. And then when you was good and crisp

I'd cut you up into little pieces and feed you to the coyotes. But I can't do any of that because I got people here."

"And because you're a gent."

"You're fucking right I am." He picked up his untouched brandy and downed it in one gulp. Then he whirled and drove his heavy right fist directly into my left kidney. I'd never felt anything quite like it—it was like getting hit by a wrecking ball. My entire body went into spasm, breathing out of the question. As I began to fold up in agony he drove his knee upward into my other kidney. An animal groan came out of me this time. Then he kicked me savagely in the back of my left knee. I went down in a heap, gasping.

"I warned ya," he snarled. "I told ya you'd piss blood. I warned ya." For good measure he hocked and spat on me. His saliva landed on my neck and lay there in a slimy blob. I'm still not sure I've completely washed it out. He left me there.

I blacked out. I don't know for how long. Lulu licking my face brought me around. Her breath is more bracing than any spirits of ammonia. I opened my eyes and groaned at her. She yapped, tail thumping. She's always liked me best when I'm down on her level, slithering along the floor. It took me a good five minutes before I could get up onto my feet, knee pulsing, insides feeling like I'd just gone twelve rounds with a Jeep Cherokee. Then I hobbled out of there, and headed home to the fort.

Shadow wasn't on the gate. The guard who was told me that Mr. Wax had returned a half hour ago. I found him comfortably sprawled on the Hayes' living room sofa with his jacket off and his tie loosened, dunking Fig Newtons in a glass of milk and watching an old *Addams Family*, the flashback episode where Gomez and Morticia first meet and she introduces him to her collection of headless dolls.

"Christ, Meat, you look like total shit," Matthew cried, when I came limping in out of the darkness.

"Don't kid yourself. I feel like it, too."

"You're positively gray. You sick or something?"

I lowered myself slowly into the easy chair, trying not to wince from the pain. Failed, I'm afraid. "Or something."

Lulu climbed into my lap and gently spread herself across me. Her impersonation of a heating pad. One of her best.

Matthew flicked off the TV. "What happened?"

"I poked a sharp stick around in Norb's cage to see if I could get a rise out of him."

"And?"

"And I did."

Matthew frowned. "Not too smart, Meat."

"I never claimed to be smart. Just gifted."

"But what was the point?"

"When people get upset they tend to drop their guard. That's when they reveal themselves."

"What did Norbert reveal about himself?"

"A brutal right hand."

"You sure you're all right?"

"I haven't been all right for a long time. How's Bunny?"

"Fine. She just went to bed. Why do you keep asking me about Ma?"

"No particular reason. And how did the reunion go?"

He munched on a Fig Newton thoughtfully. He seemed uncommonly relaxed, much more so than at any time since we'd met. "To tell you the truth, I didn't stick around long. Mona and me both thought it was kind of boring, so we left."

"Well, well. You rascal."

He blushed. "It wasn't like that, Meat. She wanted to go and I didn't have any other way of getting home since *you* took the car."

"Where did you end up? No, wait, let me guess—Malibu Grand Prix."

His eyes widened. "You followed us?"

"I did not."

"She drove pretty well once she got the hang of her car. A little tentative, but not bad for a novice."

"And then?"

"We went to Dupars for pie."

"How was that?"

"Not as good as it used to be. I don't think they use real lemon in the meringue anymore."

"I meant you and Mona."

"I knew that." He grinned at me. "Guess I been hanging around with you too much."

"I have been known to have a negative environmental impact."

"It was . . . weird," he said, turning serious. "She seems like a perfectly nice person, only . . ."

"Only what, Matthew?"

"All she did was sit there like a lump waiting for me to say something. And when I did she'd agree with it—without ever really understanding what I meant. I really don't think she *got* anything I said all evening. About myself, my work, anything. It was weird. Like talking to somebody from another planet. I mean, what is that, Meat?"

"They call it dating."

"I didn't like it," he confessed. "I don't know what I expected, but—"

"You expected the Mona of your imagination—a larger-than-life character named Debbie Dale. That's not who she is. She's a nurse with an eight-year-old girl and sore feet. Did you ask her about the time you got pantsed?"

"I sure did," he replied. "She remembers it, all right. Only not the way I remember it. It's funny, she thought *I* was pulling a prank on *her.* You know, that it was something I was in on with the other guys. She didn't realize I was the victim. I guess . . . I guess everybody thinks they're the victim." He loosened his tie and took it off over his head and looked at it. "It really wasn't any big deal, was it? No big deal at all. And it was so long ago. Seeing all those people tonight made me realize just how long." He shook his head. "You're wrong, Meat."

"About what?"

"You *are* smart."

"Of course I am. I was just being modest. Makes for a pleasant change of pace."

"Thanks for pushing me into going."

"Hey, that's why you're paying me the big bucks."

"So that's why."

"Will you be seeing her again?"

"I honestly don't think so," he replied earnestly. "She's a nice person, but we don't have anything in common."

"No spark?"

"None. Want to watch the rest of *The Addams Family* with me? It's a good one."

"No, thanks. I'm going to hit the hay." I nudged Lulu. She got down. I was struggling up out of the chair when the phone on the coffee table rang.

Matthew picked it up. "Hello? . . . Wait, speak up, Johnny. I can't hear you. . . . What's wrong?"

There was another phone on the end table next to me. He pointed to it. I picked up.

Johnny was sobbing. "I'm scared, Matthew. I'm scared. . . ."

"Why, Johnny?" Matthew said patiently. "Why are you scared?"

"Somebody's here," he whispered urgently. "Out in the back yard. I *hear* them. They tried the *door*."

"Is it locked?" Matthew asked.

"Yeah, but I'm *scared*. Matthew, help me."

"This is Hoagy, Johnny," I said. "Call the police. Call them right now. If you've got a prowler they'll get there much faster than we will."

"No!" gasped Johnny, panicking. "No cops!"

Matthew and I exchanged a plaintive look.

"All right, Johnny," Matthew said. "Stay put—we'll be right there."

"Matthew?" whispered Johnny.

"Yes, Johnny?"

"What's my attitude?"

"You're strong," he told him. "You're strong because you know you're going to be okay. Got it?"

"Hurry, Matthew."

We streaked up La Cienega in the Batmobile, running every red light on the way. It was well past midnight, and Gotham City was tucked in for the night. No cops spotted us. If they had I'm sure they'd merely have saluted and said "Follow us, Batman." The Caped Crusader was behind the wheel. I played Robin. Lulu was curled up in my lap.

La Cienega ended at Sunset, which took us to Laurel Canyon. Stanley Hills Drive was a few miles up in the hills, a winding road, dark and quiet. Scruffy cottages were tucked behind overgrown hedges. The Badger house was a miniature Spanish castle, with tower. Looked like it was made out of papier-mâché. The lights were on inside. So was the porch light. Johnny's Harley was parked in the driveway. Matthew pulled in next to it with a screech and jumped out. He got to the front door first—he was moving a lot faster than I was—and rang the bell. Johnny didn't answer. The door was locked. The front windows were open, the drapes shut. Music was playing inside. Loud.

Matthew pounded on the door. "JOHNNY?!" he called through the window. "IT'S MATTHEW! IT'S OKAY—OPEN UP!"

Nothing. Just the steady thudding of the music.

"What do we do now, Meat?" Matthew wondered anxiously.

There were decorative wrought iron bars on the windows for security. No going in that way.

"We go around back," I replied.

"What if somebody's still back there?" He was frightened.

"Want to wait in the car?" I asked gently.

He stuck out his snow-shovel jaw. "I want to help. Johnny's my friend."

"Then come on."

"Wait." He stopped at the flower bed by the front steps and scratched around in the soil. He grabbed onto something, hefted it in his hand. A rock to throw. It had worked the last time he'd been in a fight—with Neal Bricker. It would work now. "Okay, Meat, let's go," he said with grim determination.

There was a gate at the side of the house. A narrow brick path led to the back. I opened the gate and waited for Lulu to go first. She looked up at me, waiting for me to go first. I sighed and hobbled in.

The side drapes were open. The lights inside fell on empty rooms. No furniture. No people.

"Who else knows he's staying here?" I asked Matthew, as we worked our way back.

"I really don't know, Meat. He only moved in last night. Didn't need any help. Just grabbed his sleeping bag and moved right in."

The backyard was floodlit. It was a small yard, most of it brick patio. There was a hot tub, unoccupied. French doors led inside to the kitchen, also unoccupied. The music was louder back here. I could recognize it now. Fats Domino.

"JOHNNY?!" Matthew called out, clutching his rock. "IT'S MATTHEW, JOHNNY!"

A neighbor's dog barked. There was no other response.

Matthew looked around uncertainly. "Should we call the police?"

I tried the French doors. They were unlocked. "Stay out here, Matthew."

Lulu wanted to stay out there with him. But she tagged along with me, after some heavy coaxing.

It was an old-fashioned kitchen. Salmon-colored tile on the counters, pea-green linoleum on the floor. The stove and fridge were from the fifties. A boom box sat on top of the fridge. The Fat Man was singing "Blueberry Hill," his rich, boozy boogie-woogie pouring over the house like heavy syrup. A swinging door led into the dining room, which was L-shaped and completely bare, except for a beer bottle which lay broken in a puddle on the floor. I bent down and stuck a finger in the puddle. Still cold. I moved on, Lulu at my side.

Nothing at all in the living room. A short hallway off it led to two bedrooms, one empty. The other had a sleeping bag spread out on the hard wooden floor. An overturned carton served as a nightstand. The phone was on it, an ashtray and an AK47 assault rifle. I bent over and sniffed it. It hadn't been fired recently. I didn't touch it. I moved on, Lulu at my side.

There was a bathroom. I went in, hoping the shower curtain was wide open. I wasn't feeling very nervy.

It was closed. I stared at it, heart pounding. I looked down at Lulu. She was looking up at me. It wasn't as if she'd never seen *Psycho*. I looked at her pleadingly. Grudgingly, she poked her large black nose in there. A contented snuffle followed. I yanked the curtain open. Nothing.

I went back in the living room. The Fat Man was still singing about Blueberry Hill, Clarence Ford's mournful alto sax alongside him. My eyes fell on the steep, narrow staircase up to the tower. Somehow, I'd known it would be the tower. A vague memory of an anthropology professor telling me that people often climb when they're cornered, even if it offers them no means of escape. An instinct that goes back to our cave-dwelling days, when trees were our only refuge from predators in open country.

I started up the stairs. Lulu stayed right where she was. It was the tower, all right.

He was wedged just inside the doorway, shirtless and shoeless, blood splattered over the floor and on the wall behind him. He lay face up, eyes wide open. No question what his attitude was—he was dead, and selling it hard. One shot had been to his head. His yellow dreadlocks were soaked with blood. The other shot was to the groin. The Zorch killing, all over again.

I heard footsteps on the stairs behind me.

"Find anything yet, Meat?" Matthew called out. And then he came in. A strangled sob came out of him. "Oh, God, no! No, no, no!"

"Go back outside, Matthew."

"Where does this end?" he moaned. "Where, Meat? Where?"

I could answer that one now. It would end right here. Part of it would anyway. Because there would be no *Badger Goes to Hollywood* or *Badger All Alone* or whatever the hell he was going to call it. Badger was no more. Someone had made absolutely sure of it. But I said nothing. I just led Matthew back outside and took his rock away from him and tossed it into the shrubbery. Then I called Lamp.

They still had the best chili dogs in town at Pinks, an aging, somewhat grungy stand down on La Brea and Melrose. Particularly if you loaded them down with cheese, onions, and jalapeño peppers. We devoured two of them apiece in the front seat of Lamp's car, the wrappers spread across our laps and Lulu sniffing at us disagreeably. There was a time, not so long ago, when finding somebody dead would make me sick. Now it made me ravenous. This was not something I liked about myself.

Sheldon Selden and Sarge had been home in their beds when I phoned. They tore up to the Stanley Hills Drive house right away to see to Matthew, who couldn't seem to stop crying. The poor guy was shattered. Shelley and Sarge seemed more stunned than anything else. Joey Bam Bam arrived soon after they did, followed by the endless chain of TV news vans. Bam Bam did the talking to the cameras. He was the only one who wanted to.

Lamp sucked on his orange soda through a straw and took a bite of his chili dog. "The thing I don't understand," he said, munching, "is that the kid has an assault weapon sitting right there by his phone."

"Loaded?"

"You bet your sweet patootie it was loaded. He hears what he thinks is a prowler. He's frightened, he's paranoid. Why the heck doesn't he use it?"

"I wondered about that myself," I said, polishing off my second chili dog. "It must have been someone he felt he had no reason to fear. Were the neighbors any help?"

"None," replied Lamp.

"How about the murder weapon? Was it left behind again?"

"We haven't found it yet. Could be out in the bushes somewhere." Lamp wiped his fingers with a napkin. "Who worked you over tonight, Hoagy?"

"What makes you think someone worked me over, Lieutenant?"

"The way you move around."

"Just a natural part of the aging process," I assured him, massaging my throbbing knee. "It'll happen to you one of these days."

He stared at me.

"It was nothing," I said. "And you?"

"What about me?"

"Saturday night in the big town. Single, good-looking guy—what were you up to?"

"Volunteer counseling at a youth center," he replied. "Saturday's the toughest night of the week for a lot of them, staying away from the drugs and the gangs and stuff."

It was my turn to stare.

"Well, heck," he said, reddening. "Somebody has to give a tinker's whoosis about them."

I reached over and touched his arm.

"What was that for?" he asked.

"Just making sure you're real. I have my doubts sometimes."

He grinned at me and started up the car. "Guess I'd better run you home."

"I happen to be a million miles from nowhere, Lieutenant," I said gloomily. "And that's a long, long way from home."

"You sound like you need some sleep."

"I need something."

La Brea was deserted and quiet. Lamp drove with both hands on the wheel and observed all speed limits. "Like who, Hoagy?" he said, his eyes on the road. "Who would Johnny feel he had no reason to fear?"

"Anyone from the Bedford Falls family, for starters."

"What about Norbert Schlom? Would he have let him in?"

"Possibly. Schlom was tight with Zorch, whom Johnny

loved. Norb could have talked his way in. Told him he had something for him. Sure. Was the roundup at the Schlom corral over
with?"

"Good and over with. Cops on the gate cleared out by
twelve."

"They were real ones?"

"Who?"

"Nothing. Don't mind me."

"Understand Trace Washburn made quite some scene
there," he said.

"He did. Evidently, Pennyroyal broke it off with him."

Lamp made a right onto Washington Boulevard and took
that into Culver City. "Aren't you going to say something clever,
Hoagy?"

"Clever?"

"Like 'Good chance for you to move in on her, Lieutenant,
har-har.' That sort of thing."

"No, I'm not," I said heavily.

He shot me a worried look. "No offense, but I didn't like the
sound of that."

"No offense, but that makes two of us."

He clucked at me disapprovingly. "You're getting mixed up
with her, aren't you?"

"Let's say I'm doing my best not to, and . . ."

"And?"

"And I sure as hell wish Merilee would call. One little call."

"Why don't you call her?" he suggested.

"That wasn't the deal."

"Want me to call her for you?"

"And say what?"

"That you're in trouble. That you need to talk to her. Heck, I
don't know."

"Thanks, Lieutenant, but it's her call to make."

He shook his head. "Cheese and crackers, you're stubborn."

"Everyone ought to be good at something."

We rode in silence a while, Lulu snoring softly in my lap.

"What happened to Washburn after his little scene?" Lamp
asked.

"Cassandra took him home, I imagine."

"To his shack in Trancas?"

"More likely to her bed in the Four Seasons."

"She's involved with him?" he asked, surprised.

"I wouldn't exactly call it involved."

"I hear he was three sheets to the wind."

"Appeared to be."

"Too wrecked to take out Johnny?"

"That's hard to say, Lieutenant," I replied. "He *is* an actor, let's not forget."

"You mean he could have been faking?"

"Could have been. Although I'm not sure Johnny would have rushed to let him in. I don't believe the two of them were particularly—" I stopped short.

"Were particularly what, Hoagy?"

"Trace played Johnny's father in the three Badger movies. I hadn't considered that before. I don't know why."

All was quiet at the Bedford Falls gate. The pack of reporters was still up at the death house on Stanley Hills Drive. The guard waved us on through. Lamp eased his car slowly through the darkened lot toward my bungalow.

"Try and think like a cop now, Hoagy," he commanded.

"Must I, Lieutenant?"

"What can we learn from Johnny's murder? What can we conclude? Ask yourself—Why kill Johnny?"

"To stop Matthew's new movie in its tracks," I replied. "No better way to do that than to kill the star."

"Is that what this has been about? Stopping a movie?"

"It's been about stopping Matthew. Stop him and you stop Bedford Falls. Whoever is behind all of this wants the studio. The fire was a warning, but it didn't deter him. So stronger measures were called for."

Lamp scratched his chin. "Johnny was killed the same exact way as Zorch. One shot to the head, one to the groin. There's a definite sexual message here. Toss in Geoffrey Brand and we've got ourselves three dead gays. Are we looking at someone who can't stand gays?"

"Shambazza wasn't gay," I pointed out.

"That's true," he admitted. "Still think it's Schlom?"

"Has to be. He wants Bedford Falls, and he doesn't care how he gets it. It's Schlom."

"What about Selden?" he countered. "He was against this movie, wasn't he?"

"He was. In fact, he begged me this morning to try to talk Matthew out of it. But you're overlooking one vital point."

"Which is?"

"Schlom is scum."

He grinned at me. "You really want him, don't you?"

"I really want him."

"He the one who beat you up tonight?"

That one I left alone.

There was an empty parking space behind my bungalow next to the Vette. Lamp pulled into it and shut off the engine.

"That sure is some neat car," he said, gazing at the Vette wistfully.

Lulu stirred. I opened my door. She hopped out.

"Go after him, Lieutenant."

"I can't, Hoagy. I have no case against the man. No evidence, no nothing."

"He's scum, Lieutenant. He brutalizes. He rapes. He eats wood. God knows what he alone has done to deplete the Brazilian rain forest."

"Hoagy, will you listen to yourself?"

"I try not to, as a rule."

"Look, I know Schlom's not a very nice guy. But that's simply not enough to go on."

"Why, because he's a respected pillar of the community?"

Lamp's jaw muscles tensed. "I don't deserve that," he said softly. He was hurt.

"You're right, you don't. I'm sorry, Lieutenant. It's just that, hell, this is the movie business. When in doubt as to who is getting fucked by whom you need only ask yourself who stands to profit the most. Therein lies your fucker. And Schlom is our fucker—to the tune of over three hundred million dollars."

"That may be, Hoagy. But I still can't grab a rope and go find the nearest tree. The law is the law. There's no evidence against him. We get some, he'll go down for it. You have my word on it. But until we do, I have to leave him be."

We sat there in silence.

"Boy, I sure do hate this case," Lamp confessed wearily.

"Any particular reason?"

"Think about it, Hoagy. Schlom and Selden talk real good for it. But who in the heck doesn't? Charmaine Harris? She's got the same motives and opportunities as Selden right on down the line. Bunny Wax does, too. And then there's Toy to consider. . . ." He shook his head. "I'm pulling the handle on a big slot machine, Hoagy. I'm standing in a Las Vegas casino watching those tumblers spin round and round, waiting for the lemons to line up so it'll all go click and the coins will spill out. Only they won't. They just keep spinning round and round and . . ."

Only something did go click all of a sudden. In my brain. Of course. Why hadn't I seen it before? It had been there all along. Right there before my eyes. "You're a genius, Lieutenant."

He frowned. "Why, what did I say?"

I climbed out of the car unsteadily. My head was doing the spinning now.

"Are you okay, Hoagy?"

"Yes and no."

"What does that mean?"

"It means good night, Lieutenant."

Lulu was curled up outside the door of the bungalow waiting for me. I unlocked it and staggered in after her.

The phone was ringing. Her. It was finally her. It had to be her. I picked it up.

"Hoagy?"

It wasn't her. "Hello, Pennyroyal."

"I just heard, Hoagy," she cried hoarsely, her voice choked with emotion. "Poor Johnny. Poor, scared little Johnny . . . and *Matthew*. God, it must be so *horrible* for him. Will you tell him I called, Hoagy? Will you? I want him to know how very sorry I am."

"I'll tell him."

She sniffled into the phone. "You disappeared tonight. I looked everywhere for you. When I asked Toy where you'd gone she said the vilest things about you."

"I guess I must be doing something right after all."

"W-Was it me, Hoagy? Did you leave the party on account of me?"

*What makes them so special, Meat?*

"No, I didn't."

Her voice turned intimate. "Are you in bed yet?"

"Not yet."

"I am. I'm lying here under the comforter feeling so totally alone. I'm *afraid*, Hoagy. What if they try to kill me, too? What if I'm next?"

"You're not next, Pennyroyal. Believe me—you're not."

"God, you sound so sure. I wish you were here with your arms around me, Hoagy. Holding me tight. I wish . . ." Her breath caught. "I wish you were *inside* of me. Right now. This instant." She groaned. "Oh, God, Hoagy. Will you catch me?"

"Catch you?"

"I'm falling."

I took a deep breath and let it out slowly. "Good night, Pennyroyal."

"Sleep tight, my darling."

I undressed and got into bed and lay there in the dark. It didn't help one bit. My head was still spinning. Everything was spinning.

# Chapter Eleven

At ten o'clock the next morning, a Sunday, we all sat down like responsible adults in Sheldon Selden's office.

It was a bright, fresh morning. The two Shelleys arrived early bearing lox and bagels, pickled herring and Danish. Bunny laid everything out. Sarge hooked up the coffee maker. Shadow Williams set up a dozen or so chairs around the conference table. Me, I had my own setting up to do.

Matthew sat slumped in a chair beside Shelley's desk, dazed, his fingers absently worrying the short, bristly hairs in his crew cut. He had bounced right back from losing Homewood. Not from losing Johnny. Not this. But he hadn't wanted to call off the meeting. He had simply said, "Let's get it over with." And so we were.

Sarge watched him with concern. I watched her watching him. She seemed unusually hyper and jumpy to me. I moseyed over to the coffee pot and asked her if she was okay.

"Fine," she said brusquely.

"You don't seem fine."

She glared at me. "I was up too fucking late. Didn't get my morning road work in either. Now just get outta my face, will ya?" With that she brushed past me.

"Best to stay away from that gal today," suggested Shadow. "Or she'll bite your head clean off."

"So I noticed."

And hers was a warmer reception than I got from Bunny. Bunny wouldn't talk to me at all. She wouldn't even give Lulu any herring.

Only Mrs. Shelley was happy to see me. So happy she commanded me to bend down so she could plant a kiss on my forehead.

"And what was that for?" I asked.

"Starting my son on the road to normalcy," she informed me proudly. "We moved the VCR into his bathroom, put *Dennis* on when it was poopy time, and—"

"That actually worked?"

"Like a dream. He looks forward to making poopy now. The only problem is we can't get him out of there."

"I'll have to work on that one."

She smiled at me. "You'd really make an excellent father, Hoagy."

"No, I really wouldn't."

Joey Bam Bam arrived wearing a polo shirt, tailored slacks, and tasseled loafers. A pastel-colored cotton sweater was tied loosely around his throat. "Thanks for including me in this," he gushed, pumping Mr. Shelley's hand, then mine. "I'm ultra-ultra flattered."

"Johnny was part of the Bedford Falls family," Shelley explained, munching on a Danish. "As his representative, you have a stake in what happens here today."

Actually, he didn't. But I'd asked Shelley to invite him. I wanted him there.

"Just got off the phone with that buggy old lady of his," Bam Bam said, rocking back and forth on his heels. "She wants him buried in Canada with the rest of her family. Body's gonna be flown up there when the police are done with it. Poor little fucker —even dead he can't get away from her."

The Schloms arrived next with Kinsley Usher. Both Norb and the former senator wore polo shirts, tailored slacks, and tasseled loafers. Pastel-colored cotton sweaters were tied loosely around their throats. I guess it was the official Sunday morning responsible adults Hollywood wardrobe. I wore my camel's hair blazer with a white carnation in the lapel, a cream-colored cash-

mere cardigan, and gray flannels. Toy wore a white cotton jump-
suit unzipped to her navel. She refused to look at me. She asked
Bunny if she could help her lay things out. Bunny merely curled
her lip at her.

Usher approached Matthew slowly, a solicitous expression
on his tanned face. "We certainly do appreciate your sharing this
time with us, Matthew," he intoned solemnly, his hands clasped
before him like a supplicant. "We all share in your grief. All of us.
It's a terrible business."

"Terrible, kid," growled Schlom in agreement, laying a
meaty paw on Matthew's shoulder. "Johnny, he had nothing but
pain and confusion in his life. Now he's free of all that. Maybe
he's better off. Who knows, huh?"

Mr. Shelley watched Schlom's fatherly performance carefully, not liking it. He went for another Danish. Mrs. Shelley
watched him, not liking that.

Schlom came over to me next, a satisfied grin on his ugly
face. "Hey, Hoag," he sneered, faking a kidney punch at me. The
crazy kidder. I wish I could say I didn't flinch. "How ya feeling
this morning?"

I felt like shit. My knee wouldn't bend. My kidneys ached.
"Never better, Norb."

"I guess you didn't look in the toilet bowl then."

"I generally try to set my sights a bit higher."

Cassandra Dee arrived with Trace Washburn in tow. Trace
looked extremely shaky and hungover. Contrite, too, when he
saw that the Schloms were present.

"What's that scumbag doing here?" Schlom muttered
sourly.

"The senator suggested we *all* sit down together," I reminded him.

Schlom made a face and reached for a napkin and tore off a
piece. He chewed on it, glowering. "Who else you invite?"

"Just one other person."

Cassandra got Trace coffee. He slurped it gratefully, then
sidled uneasily over to Matthew. Wanting to say hello to him.
Wanting Matthew to speak to him. Matthew hadn't, not since
Trace had started sleeping with his wife. And he didn't now. Just
sat there tugging at his scalp, oblivious to him.

Cassandra looked even more pale than usual. There were
dark blue circles under her goggle eyes.

"Big night with Big Steve?" I asked her.

"Whatta we all doing here?" she asked me back, nasally.

"It was the senator's idea."

"Big waste of time, honey."

"Don't be so sure, Cassandra."

"Ya got something in mind?"

"Always. That's the secret to my success."

"You know what I think about that?" she said challengingly, hands on her hips. "I think I faxed two more chapters to my editor last night while Trace was passed out on my bed." She grinned at me. "Better hurry up, honey, or youse'll be left behind at the gate."

"I keep telling you, Cassandra—this is not a race."

"Oh, yeah? Better tell your editor that. I hear he's talkin' about dumpin' ya for somebody faster." She shook her head at me. "I got nuttin' but admiration for ya, Hoagy, y'know? So's I'm giving ya the straight shit—get it in gear."

"I'll do my best."

Pennyroyal kept us waiting another half hour. Actresses are always at least a half hour late. On purpose. They do it so everybody will wonder where they are. They do it so they can make a grand entrance. They do it so everybody will make a fuss over them. They do it because they are actresses.

She was done up like the world's cutest little housepainter that morning in a pair of white bib overalls. She did not arrive alone. She brought little Georgie with her. Everyone got quiet, staring as she bent down and gently picked him up out of his stroller.

Everyone except for Sarge, who suddenly got busy rattling the coffee pot. I was wrong about her. She wasn't acting jumpy at all. She was being territorial and pissy about Pennyroyal coming around. I'm a little slower than I think sometimes.

Matthew came to life at the sight of his son. Sat up straight in his chair, face aglow, hands eager to hold him. Pennyroyal carried him shyly over to him.

"Hello, Matthew," she said hoarsely, struggling a bit with Georgie. "Whew, he's getting *big*."

"Hullo." He swallowed, his eyes on the baby.

"I like what you've done with your hair," she said.

He ducked his head, blushing. "Thanks."

"I'm so sorry about Johnny. I feel so bad."

Matthew nodded, tears welling up in his eyes. "Can I . . . ?"

"Yes, Matthew?"

"Can I hold him a minute?"

"Of course you can."

She handed him over. Matthew hugged him tightly, hungrily kissed his fingers, his arms, his face. Tears began to stream down his own face. Pennyroyal began to cry herself as she watched the two of them. So did the Seldens. Actually, there were very few dry eyes in the house, if you must know.

She left Georgie with him and got herself some coffee.

"That was nice of you," I said to her.

"What was, Hoagy?" she asked, dabbing at her eyes with a tissue.

"Bringing Georgie along."

"Matthew's his father," she said, glancing over at the two of them. "A boy should grow up knowing who his father is, don't you think?"

"I do. That way he knows from the outset who to hate."

She frowned at me over the edge of her cup. "You say the strangest things sometimes. I'm not sure if it's your way of being funny or what. I'm not even sure if you believe half of them."

"Let me know if you figure that one out. I'd like to know."

"So would I," she said softly, gazing up at me. "I'd like to know everything about you."

I had no comeback for that one. I went and got myself a large plate of herring. I don't even like herring. Lulu stared at me. I told her to mind her own business.

We took our seats around the conference table. I sat with Cassandra on one side of me and Mrs. Shelley on the other. Pennyroyal was directly across from me, Georgie gurgling contentedly in her lap. He seemed very relaxed and happy there wrapped in his blue blanket. No one else at the table seemed to be. Not Bam Bam. Not Trace. Not Toy. Not Norb. Not Matthew. Mr. Shelley and Usher were at the heads of the table. One empty seat remained. Sarge, Shadow, and Bunny sat on the sofa, arms crossed, stone-faced.

The senator began. "It is my belief," he stated firmly and unequivocally, "that we are all reasonable people here. And that reasonable people act reasonably." He paused, waiting for someone to refute that. Not me—I was planning to needlepoint it on a throw pillow. "We believe that we are taking an entirely *reasonable* position, given the California statutes governing the distribution of community property, given the absence of a prenuptial agreement, given the presence of a child that the mother intends to raise as a single parent, and given the tremendous career sacrifices she has already made at her husband's insistence. What we have asked for, and are asking for, is one half of Mr. Wax's assets, including Bedford Falls. And that is *reasonable*." Usher sat back and sipped his coffee. "Mr. Selden?"

"Reasonable is a good choice of words," began Shelley Selden, adopting a booming, authoritative voice I'd not heard him use before. They teach it to them at law school. "That's precisely how we feel we're being toward your client." He glanced at Pennyroyal, who flushed slightly, her eyes on the table before her. "We're talking here about a young woman who had no acting experience of any kind before she was plucked out of obscurity by my client five years ago. She was a student. He made her a star. Her employability has skyrocketed as a direct result of her association with my client. She had no career before she met him. Now she has one." He reached for another Danish. Mrs. Shelley pushed the plate away from him so he couldn't get at it. "Let's talk about what we've offered her as a settlement. A cash sum of ten million dollars—and we're prepared this morning to raise that sum to fifteen million. The house in Pacific Palisades, which has been appraised at seven point five million, as well as twenty-five thousand per month for expenses and child support. Now, we feel this is a more than *reasonable* return for her two years of marriage to my client. We feel it is extremely generous, and that to ask for anything more smacks of greed."

"I resent that choice of word, sir," objected Usher.

Before he could object any further, the door to Shelley's office opened and Lieutenant Emil Lamp came rushing in, out of breath. "Sorry I'm late. Minister ran way long this morning."

"Pull up a chair, Lieutenant," I said. "I think you know everyone here, except for Kinsley Usher."

Lamp shook the politician's hand respectfully, then sat in the one remaining empty chair.

Pennyroyal smiled at him sweetly. "Nice to see you again, Lieutenant."

"Thank you, miss," he said, blushing furiously.

"As I was saying," Usher continued, "all my client wants is what she is entitled to—community property, which includes one half of this studio."

"Impossible," snapped Shelley. "She's already made clear what she'll do with her half, and we are not going to let that happen. We are not going to jeopardize the future of this studio. Frankly, I don't hear you coming in with anything new, Senator. You're saying the same words Abel Zorch did. You're just saying them quieter."

Usher's face tightened. He turned to Schlom.

Norb cleared his throat. "You're treating me like the Big Bad Wolf or something. So you get me as a partner. I'm a business-man, you're a businessman. What's the big deal?"

"The Murakami deal is the big deal," Shelley said flatly. "As you well know."

Schlom shrugged his heavy shoulders. "New capital. New markets. It's the future."

"Not for us it isn't," Shelley fired back. "We're independent, and we intend to stay that way. I'm sorry, gentlemen. As long as Pennyroyal sticks to this position we're headed for court. I see no other way to resolve this."

"If I may jump in here—" I said.

"You I don't wanna hear from," grumbled Schlom.

"Let Meat talk," Matthew spoke up. "I want him to."

Shelley nodded at me to go ahead.

"I believe we should all try a little harder to understand Pen-nyroyal's side," I said. "After all, she's made a number of sacri-fices. Not just lately, but throughout her career."

Matthew frowned at me, perplexed.

Shelley exchanged an equally perplexed look with his wife. "Wait a second—whose side are you—?"

"Shaddup," barked Schlom. "This I wanna hear."

Pennyroyal gazed at me adoringly from across the table, bathing me in her warm glow.

I sipped my coffee. "To reach this point in her career, Penny has had to do things no one else in this office would even con-sider doing. But she's done them. No matter how unpleasant they were. No matter how unpopular they were. Attention must be paid. Maybe not one half of Bedford Falls, but certainly atten-tion."

And I had everyone's attention. Everyone except Georgie, who was too busy drooling on Pennyroyal's overalls. Even Lulu under my chair was all ears, so to speak.

"This was never a complicated case at all," I began. "It was simple. Painfully so. I was saying to Lieutenant Lamp just last night that when in doubt about who in Hollywood is fucking over who, all you have to do is follow the dollar. Four people have been murdered. Negatives have been stolen out of this office. Homewood has been torched. All for money. That's what it's been about all along. Nothing more. Nothing less. So let's take a cold, clear look at it, shall we? Let's ask ourselves who stands to gain the most from all of this. Norbert Schlom and his lovely wife, Toy?" They both gave me frosty glares. "No way. Sure, Norb stands to clean up when the Murakami deal comes through. But he's already a multimillionaire. As is Toy, thanks to community property. No, they've got theirs. So have Shelley and Shelley Selden. And Matthew. And Bunny. They've all got theirs. These are rich people. Even if they lose Bedford Falls to Norb and Murakami, their pockets will still be full of money. Which eliminates all of them. And which brings us to the people who aren't so rich." I looked around the room at them. "Trace Washburn? He stands to lose no matter whether Bedford Falls stays independent or not." Trace shrugged with bleary-eyed resignation. "Sarge Harris?" She stiffened, flaring her nostrils at me. "She'll have a job either way. As long as Matthew works, she'll work. She has no great financial stake in the outcome of this. Nor does Shadow Williams. Nor does Joey Bam Bam. True, he's lost Johnny Forget. But he'll always get another client. Someone hotter probably."

"That's ultra-ultra true," Bam Bam piped up. "In fact, as of nine o'clock this morning I've signed—"

"Shaddup," growled Schlom.

"Yessir," responded Bam Bam crisply.

"Cassandra Dee?" I continued. "She wins either way. No matter what happens to Bedford Falls, her book makes money, and she moves on to bigger projects. All of which brings us to the one person who does stand to gain the most and always has— Pennyroyal Brim—the self-proclaimed victim of this ugly war, the sweet young thing who five years ago was a starry-eyed cheerleader with pompoms and who today is on the brink of owning a half interest in a major independent studio, a half interest she intends to sell to Panorama City Communications for a reported one hundred and fifty million dollars, plus a production unit to call her very own. Not too shabby. I'd certainly call it worth the trouble."

"Now wait just a minute here, Mr. Hoag," Usher interjected. "I don't see exactly what you're getting at but—"

"You could have made out fine without much of a fuss," I said to Penny. "We've all heard what Shelley just offered you. Plus you're a successful young actress. You'd continue to work. Perhaps meet and marry another heavyweight. But that's not enough for you. That's chicken feed. You so much as told me so at Spago my first night in town. You told me you were tired of being patted on the head like all of the other pretty little girls. You told me you wanted clout. So you've clawed, chewed, sucked, fucked, schemed, manipulated, and murdered your way all the way to the top. Just about, anyway. You almost made it, Penny. But not quite. You came up just a little bit short."

Pennyroyal gazed across the table at me, her face a blank. We might have been discussing the European Community.

"Gaaawd!" gasped Cassandra. "Say something, Penny, will ya!?"

"Is it true, Penny?" Matthew whispered at her in shock and dismay. "Is it?"

"Of course it is," snapped Bunny, a mean glint of triumph in her eyes. "She did it all. I knew it."

"I suggest you say no more, Mr. Hoag," Usher said sternly. "As Miss Brim's legal advisor I must inform you that given the nature of the accusation you appear to be leveling, and the fact that you are leveling it in front of several influential members of the film community, not to mention a representative of the Los Angeles Police Department as well as—"

"Speak English for Chrissakes, will ya?" Schlom hollered at him.

"You're leaving yourself wide open to a slander suit, kiddo," warned Usher. "Stop right now. Or be prepared to face the consequences."

"He's right, Hoagy," Lamp agreed. "Don't do this."

I tugged at my ear. "Thank you for the warning—both of you. I appreciate your concern. Now, if I may continue . . . ?"

"Go ahead," ordered Schlom, anxiously moistening his liver lips. "I wanna hear more."

Usher shook his head. "Norbert, I'd advise you to—"

"I'd advise you to shut the fuck up!" roared Schlom.

Usher reddened. "Let's go, Miss Brim. We needn't listen to any more of this."

Pennyroyal stayed right where she was, her face still a blank. She had not said one word. Georgie dozed in her lap.

"If we're going to discuss your career in detail, Penny," I went on, "we have to go back farther than five years. All the way back to high school." I glanced over at Cassandra, who was scribbling madly in a notepad. "Getting all of this, Cassandra?"

"Gaaawd!"

"Back to that summer before your senior year, when you were first recruited at the Galleria Mall by your soon-to-be partner in crime, Toy Schlom, known then as Toy Barbie."

Schlom whirled on his wife. "*You're* mixed up in this?!"

"No, Norb!" she cried, with such terror I wondered just what manner of body blows he administered to her in the privacy of their own tear-down home. "I'm not! I swear!"

"She's not, Norb," I assured him. "She just happens to know Pennyroyal from their old playground days."

"That's all, Norb," Toy insisted, clutching at his hand with hers. "I knew nothing. *Nothing.*"

"Until last night, that is," I pointed out. "When you and I were talking in Norb's study, Toy. Sure, you backed up Penny's PG-rated version of her past. What are old friends for, right? But something strange happened to you when I bounced that rape story of hers off of you. Something went click. That's when you knew, wasn't it?"

Toy lowered her eyes. "Yes," she said quietly.

"Knew what?" demanded Mr. Shelley.

"That Pennyroyal was choreographing this whole thing," I replied. "Pitting the two sides against each other. Raising the stakes higher and higher. All of it carefully calculated. All of it to her own advantage. You're shrewd, Penny. Much shrewder than anyone has ever given you credit for. Except for Bunny. She never thought you were the girl you made yourself out to be, and she was right. You're also a hell of an actress. Your whole life is one Oscar-caliber performance." I glanced back at Toy. "Penny's been pulling all of the strings. That's what went click in your eyes last night, Toy. But I didn't catch on. Not until later in the evening. It was something the lieutenant said."

"Me?" Lamp spoke up, puzzled. "What did I say?"

"Las Vegas," I replied. "You said Las Vegas."

He scratched his head. "So?"

"So that triggered something in my mind. A slip that you made, Penny."

"What slip?" asked Schlom.

Penny still hadn't said one word. She just gazed at me steadily.

"A small one, really. But you've been so careful all along, so very, very careful, that it stuck out all the more. You were telling me about when you and Matthew got married."

"I remember that," said Cassandra. "I was there."

"You'll recall she said the two of them ran off to Vegas like a couple of kids—kids who had never been to the place before."

"Yeah?" said Cassandra, doubtfully.

"Matthew told it differently. He said Pennyroyal showed him all the sights. He said that she knew the town well."

"She did," whispered Matthew, wide-eyed, as if we were all seated around a campfire telling scary stories.

"Of course she did, Matthew," I said. "Because she'd put in many long hours there under the name of Carla Pettibone, working girl. It was all bullshit, wasn't it, Penny? About how you didn't know what you were getting into when you posed nude for Shambazza. About how when you found out you pulled out. A nice, sweet story. And total bullshit. I sort of knew it. And you sort of knew I knew it. So you came to me in my bungalow with a new, improved version. About that one, horrifying little rape party with Toy and Norb. Another nice story. And more bullshit. Because the truth is you willingly became part of Shambazza's stable from the day Toy first recruited you. He was your pimp for three years. You made good money, certainly more than most high school girls with part-time jobs. You got to wear nice clothes, eat in fancy restaurants. There were trips to Vegas, excursions on big yachts, parties. It was plenty glamorous—you could even convince yourself you were getting into show biz, just like you told me. All you had to do in exchange was—well, we all know what you had to do in exchange. But you did it. You performed. And you're a good, hard-working little performer. They all told you you'd be a star someday. Only, they didn't come through for you, did they? Not any of them. Toy, she hooked herself a big one. All you got was pregnant. That part of your story was really touching, by the way. All about your true-blue soccer player. What was his name? Craig? Touching. And more bullshit. You got pregnant on the job. You got yourself an abortion, and you got out. Amazing, really, how none of it left a mark on you. You're as sweet and clean as the day you were born. On the outside anyway. You left no footprints in the sand either. This is a town with no memory. And you were smart enough to stay out of the porn movies and the magazines. Of course, there *was* the matter of those photographs Shambazza took of you, and wouldn't give back. Those became a real problem later on. But I'm getting ahead of myself, aren't I?"

"Tell me if it's true, Penny," Matthew pleaded, his face torn with pain. "Is it? Tell me! I have to know!"

She sat there holding Georgie. Finally, she shivered and broke her silence. "I did it for the contacts," she began, her voice flat and detached. Mechanical, almost. "There's nothing so unusual about that. Lots of young actresses willingly do it—and they don't even get paid for it. At least I got paid. I wasn't that stupid. But I was wrong. I thought it'd do my career some good. It didn't. They just led me on and wiped the floor with me. So I quit. Carla Pettibone went bye-bye. My high school grades got me into SC. I'd heard that a lot of alumni networking went on there. I took some theater arts classes, and I became a cheerleader. Posed for school calendars, posters. Got my face on TV during games. I thought it might lead to some modeling assignments or TV spots. It seemed like it was worth a shot."

"And it was," I said. "Because it was your turn to get lucky. Even luckier than Toy did. You happened to bear an amazing resemblance to one Mona Schaffer, a girl Matthew Wax had a crush on when he was a kid. Because of that he made you Debbie Dale. You walked in the door and the part was yours. You're not stupid. You knew that the press has a way of finding out things about a star's past. And let's face it—Carla Pettibone, prostitute, and Debbie Dale, America's sweetie pie, didn't exactly fit together. So you went to Shelley Selden with a carefully sanitized version of the facts. You admitted you'd had an abortion when you were in high school, since they might be able to trace that. And you told him all about that mean man Shambazza who took those nude photographs of you. You had to tell him. You couldn't take a chance on them surfacing. Shelley, being a careful man, approached Shambazza and bought the negatives from him, satisfied that he was nipping any potential problem in the bud. Only Shambazza wasn't satisfied, was he?"

"I was still one of his girls," Pennyroyal confirmed bitterly. "That's what he told me. I was his property and always would be. He threatened me. Said he'd slash my face with a razor if I didn't pay up."

"You and Toy both, I imagine," I suggested.

Toy closed her eyes and nodded faintly. "He was free-basing. Horribly strung out. More of a nuisance than a menace, really. Norbert paid him so he'd stop pestering us. And he probably would have continued to pay him if someone hadn't . . ." She trailed off, her violet eyes on Pennyroyal. There was horror in them.

"The police dismissed it as a drug killing," I said. "Only it wasn't. It was you, Penny. You'd worked too hard to get this far. That man wasn't going to threaten what lay ahead of you. No one was."

"It wasn't like that at all!" Pennyroyal objected heatedly. This was the first rise I'd gotten out of her. "I was afraid of what he might do to me! You didn't know him—he was mean!"

I nodded. "So you went up to his studio and shot him dead— the no-more-fears formula. With that you became a star. And you became Mrs. Matthew Wax." Matthew's head was bowed. He looked very pale. "He was a shy, sweet, naive guy. And putty in your hands. You succeeded where so many women before you had failed. You swept the great Matthew Wax off of his feet. Now you had it all. Stardom. A husband who was rich and famous. And, soon, a baby with which to secure your lifelong financial claim. But that still wasn't enough, was it? Not for you. So, after two years of living with the man, two years of pretending to be in love with him, you calmly announced that you wanted out. You felt stifled. You needed your independence. And with that you set out to turn your divorce into the richest, gaudiest breakup in show business history. You hired the most inflammatory high-stakes lawyer in town, Abel Zorch, who also happened to be tight with Norbert Schlom. Zorch assured you he could get you half of Bedford Falls as part of your settlement if you fought hard enough. You knew that Norb was in the process of putting to-gether the sale to Murakami. You also knew he desperately wanted Bedford Falls as part of it. None of this was a secret. So you three cooked up a nice, cozy deal between friends—you would give Norb your half interest in Bedford Falls in exchange for the one thing you really wanted, the one thing every performer in the business wants. *Clout.* A major chunk of Panorama City Communications stock. Your own production company. Your own financing. Whatever you wanted. You'd be a player. And to hell with Bedford Falls. Norb, he'd figure out how to wrest the other half away from the family. That would be a walk in the park for him. You and he shook hands on it. Then you set out to turn up the heat. You *wanted* publicity, the more outrageous the better. You *wanted* to put the House of Wax on page one."

Mr. Shelley shook his head at this. "I don't understand why. What was the point?"

"Because what she didn't want," I replied, "was any kind of peaceful, amicable compromise. Or worst of all, a trial separation. That would blow the whole deal. She needed an outright war, and she made sure she got one." I turned back to her. She was watching me with those innocent blue eyes of hers. "You took up with Trace Washburn right away, knowing it would set off a major scandal. And knowing that Big Steve would be willing."

Trace stirred and went into his heavy breathing thing. "He tries to please," he acknowledged. "Be a sin for him to leave 'em itchy, wouldn't it?"

"You gave Abel Zorch tons of sleazy dirt about your marriage," I continued, "which he promptly and gleefully leaked to the papers. Meanwhile, you set yourself up as the poor victim, the good little mother who had somehow gotten caught in the middle of this mean, vicious studio war. You made everyone think you were being used by Abel. Not so. You were in the driver's seat all the way. You landed yourself a big-time book deal and hired the most hard-nosed ghost you could find, Cassandra, knowing that the prospect of a juicy, tell-all memoir would force Matthew into writing one of his own. Dueling memoirs. What more could a gal ask for? Lots of noise. Lots of ill will. Plus the chance to get down on paper the authorized, utterly fabricated story of your life, a lie that Cassandra has unwittingly been cranking out for you, night after night."

"I been boned," cried Cassandra, aghast. "She's been boning me all along!"

"Welcome to the big time," I said, patting her hand. "This is about where I came in. My first night in town you showed up at

Spago, complaining to Abel that the press was treating you like a whore. You begged him to cool it. Strictly a performance for the benefit of anyone who happened to be listening, particularly me. You figured I could be of use to you, what with being privy to the family secrets and all, so you pulled me aside and unloaded on me. Told me there was no one you could trust. Told me everyone was trying to use you, hurt you. It was quite some performance, considering that it was you who was doing the using and the hurting. You who stole your own negatives out of this office in the middle of the night. You knew how to sneak onto the lot undetected. Johnny showed you how to."

"How did you know where the negatives were?" Mr. Shelley asked her.

"I overheard you tell Sarge, years ago," she replied coolly.

"But how'd you get into the office?" Sarge wondered.

"I still have keys to everything. Hard as it is to believe, I was actually a member of this family once."

Bunny muttered something under her breath.

"What did you say, you old bitch?" sneered Pennyroyal.

"I couldn't repeat it in polite company," Bunny huffed.

"You've always hated me, haven't you?" Pennyroyal charged. "Well, guess what? It's mutual."

"I can't tell you how glad I am to hear that," Bunny fired back.

"When you say, miss, that you possess keys to everything," Shadow interjected, "would that be with the possible exception of Mr. Selden's desk?"

Pennyroyal admitted this was so. "I had to use a pry bar to get the drawer open."

Shadow nodded, satisfied.

"Negatives in hand," I continued, "you slipped out the way you came and dropped them off at the *Enquirer* in a plain envelope. Then you sat back and watched both sides yell at each other while you sobbed over the cruelty and injustice of it all. The Bedford Falls people figured it for a Zorch gambit. Zorch figured they did it to discredit you. Me, I didn't think it made sense for either side to have done it. Neither side did—it was strictly you escalating the war. Zorch phoned me, wanting to discuss it. He was upset. This was, after all, just the sort of noisy public spectacle Murakami was pressuring him to avoid."

"I screamed bloody murder at him," Schlom confirmed.

"He swore to me he didn't do it. You wanna know the truth, I wasn't sure myself whether to believe the guy or not."

"Did he know you did it?" I asked Pennyroyal.

"He knew *he* hadn't," she replied. "And he didn't think Shelley Selden was the type. That left me. He gave me a bunch of shit about it. Called me names. Suggested I may have blown the whole Murakami deal. Then he told me he was going to advise Norbert to forget about Bedford Falls for the time being. Too hot to handle. He actually wanted to go back to Murakami and attempt to restructure the deal without it. He figured if they were patient Bedford Falls would eventually go under on its own anyway." Shelley Selden reddened at this. "He thought Norbert would go along with the idea. Which was well and good for them. But what about me? Where did that leave me?"

"Out in the cold," I said. "You and Abel quarreled, and you came to the conclusion that it was time to dump him as your lawyer, like you told the lieutenant and me. Only you had a different reason for dumping him than you gave us, and a rather stronger definition of job termination in mind. You had already killed one man who threatened to stand in your way. Now it was time to kill another. Abel, he would always be a threat to you. He knew too much about the real you. He might try to use it against you in the future. Besides, his murder would be an excellent way of escalating the war even further. Certainly no shortage of people around who would want him dead. All you had to do was plan it right. Did you already have the gun?"

"I've always kept a couple of guns around," she replied. "Shambazza gave them to me."

"You ducked out on Cassandra at some point in the afternoon," I suggested.

"Yeah, yeah, shewa," Cassandra confirmed. "She said she had to pick up a script."

"You went to Zorch's building in Century City and removed the battery from the remote control in his car. You've got a remote-controlled gate just like it at your house. Later that afternoon you called Abel's office to set something up. He was in court, but he called you back from the courthouse and suggested you meet him at his house at, say, six?" She nodded. "You and Georgie got there early, five-thirty, so you could—"

"Georgie was with you?" cried Matthew, greatly disturbed. "Georgie was *there*?"

"You wanted to be good and ready to ambush him at the gate," I went on. "There was, however, a small, unforeseen problem—Johnny. Sitting there across the street on his Fat Boy with his broken heart. I expect this threw you somewhat."

"I wasn't sure what to do about him," she acknowledged. "But I stayed calm. I rang the bell at the gate. Kenji came out and told me how pleasant it was to see me but that Abel wasn't home. He didn't invite me in. Apparently, Abel hadn't told him I was expected, or he would have. I thanked him and then I—"

"You improvised," I suggested. "Turned Johnny's presence there into a bonus. He'd already tried to kill his own mother. He'd even shot out the windows of Zorch's Rolls just the night before. And if the police happened to ask you, you'd have to admit that, yes, you did see him lurking outside Zorch's house just moments before the killing. Johnny was perfect for it. He was easy. And just think of the publicity: '*Badger Hayes, All-American Killer.*' You waved good-bye to Kenji, then you approached Johnny. He panicked and took off like the paranoid little boy he was. This suited you. You didn't want him around. You drove away. Kenji saw you leave. He saw both of you leave. What he didn't see was that you turned around and came right back. No one saw you that time. Zorch showed up a few minutes later. He was even nice enough to bring his new boyfriend, Geoffrey with a G. That made Johnny look even better for it. You shot them both, Zorch once in the groin, figuring a sexual twist would place it right at Johnny's feet. Then you took off. You used the less popular way out, Alto Cedro, in case anyone, such as me, was on the way up. Then you drove around in the hills like you said you did. You've already acknowledged you have no alibi for the time of the killings. No one to vouch for you except Georgie, and he's not very talkative. Johnny looked ideal for it. A neighbor's housekeeper even IDed him as someone who'd been hanging around outside Zorch's house for days. It all worked to perfection. Except for one problem: Johnny managed to get himself an alibi. He streaked down the hill to the Hamburger Hamlet on Sunset and Doheny, went inside, and phoned Matthew. He was sitting there with Matthew when it happened. That let him off the hook. A shame, but no great loss for you. You still did what you intended to do—you got rid of Abel Zorch. And no one suspected you. You were America's Sweetie Pie. How could anyone in their right mind believe *you* would do something so horrible? The whole thing looked more and more like a war over the future of Bedford Falls. You made sure of that the very next night. You sneaked onto the lot once again, this time dressed to kill in diamonds and black leather, and toting two cans of gasoline, which you splashed about over the false fronts of Homewood. Then you hightailed it over to my bungalow smelling of rosewater, which covered the aroma of gasoline. It took a while before the place caught fire. How did you manage that?"

"I lit a long piece of string, like a fuse."

Matthew sat up. "Hey, I used that in *Badger and His Chemistry Set*, when he blew up the old Applegate place!"

She smiled at him. "Of course. Where do you think I got the idea, Matthew?"

"When you got to my place," I went on, "you sobbingly revealed that you'd been raped and tortured by none other than Norbert Schlom. Now this was quite some performance. Possibly your best to date. You figured this would remove any lingering doubts I might have about your past association with Toy."

"You seemed so skeptical," she conceded.

"I generally am. And with good reason, I'm sorry to say. You also figured I'd eventually leak it to the press. What ghost wouldn't? It was such a lovely yarn. And such a lovely way to escalate the war. You're very shrewd, Penny. And careful. You also tried to seduce me that evening, figuring that as long as I was besotted by you I wouldn't suspect you. You came prepared. Candles, champagne, caviar . . . You were extremely persuasive."

"That part wasn't so hard," she said softly.

"Thank you. I'm flattered. But let's not forget that your primary mission that evening was to burn Homewood to the ground. You wanted the Bedford Falls people to think Schlom was behind it. You wanted them calling each other more dirty names in the paper. It made for one outstanding photo opportunity, too. Page one all the way. Is that about right?"

She was silent a moment. "Not really."

I stared at her. "Then why did you do it?"

Georgie wriggled in her lap. She shifted him, stroking his blond hair with motherly tenderness. That tenderness is something I still think about at 4 A.M., when I can't sleep. "I did it to stop Matthew from making his new movie," she replied. "I don't want him making it."

"Why not?" Matthew demanded.

"Because she's not in it," Mr. Shelley figured. "She's pissed off about it."

Pennyroyal snorted derisively.

"Why?" I asked.

Everyone leaned forward, awaiting her reply.

"Because it sucks," she said.

"Because it sucks," I repeated.

"Everyone knows it," she insisted. "The script's a total piece of shit. A born flop. It'll cost us millions."

Mr. Shelley frowned at her. " 'Us'?"

"This studio is half mine," she said firmly. "Or it soon will be. I have a right to be involved in the decision-making process."

"I admire your idea of creative participation," I said.

"Hey, it's not as if they'd actually pay attention to me, would they?" she demanded hotly. "I hoped Matthew would get the message and back off. But he didn't, so I had to take more drastic measures."

"Johnny," I suggested.

She nodded. "He was so weak. A lost little boy. I went to his place directly from Toy and Norbert's party."

"How'd you know where he was staying?" Sarge wondered. "We only just took the place."

"From me," Joey Bam Bam murmured, a sickly expression on his face. "I told her."

"You told Cassie," Pennyroyal explained. "She wanted to interview him. I got the address from her. Not that she had anything to do with it. She's innocent as an angel."

"Thanks loads," said Cassandra sourly.

"Don't be so bitchy," Penny scolded. "You wouldn't have wanted to know, would you?"

"You're absolutely right," Cassandra said sarcastically. "My mistake."

"It was a really dark, quiet street," Pennyroyal said. "But his porch light was on. I couldn't take a chance on a neighbor recognizing me, so I went around back. He let me in. He was real scared until he realized it was me. He put some music on. Popped open a beer. We talked about Abel, and how much he missed him."

"Did he realize that you had killed him?" Lamp asked.

"Johnny wasn't coherent enough to realize anything," she

replied. "You know what he said to me? He said that I should be in the new Badger movie with him. He said it wasn't right, my not being in it. He was so sweet. I think that was the last thing he said before I killed him. . . . I made it look sexual again to distract people. And to make it more lurid and sensational for the papers." She lowered her eyes. "I hated to do it. I always liked Johnny. But I had to stop this movie. The only other way was to kill Matthew, and I couldn't—Matthew's the studio's biggest asset. This place is worth zero without him. Johnny . . . Johnny was expendable."

"My God!" erupted Mrs. Shelley. "You killed him to stop a *movie* from being made!? He was your *friend* and you *killed* him and you don't even *care!*"

"Don't look down your nose at me, you little bitch!" Pennyroyal snarled. "What have you ever done in life except grow up in the same house with *him?!*"

Mrs. Shelley looked at her brother with great sadness. "I've loved him," she replied. "Which is more than you ever did."

It turned quiet now. Everyone in the room was staring at Pennyroyal, taking in the sublime horror of her. Or trying to.

She colored slightly. "Why are you all looking at me like that?" she demanded.

Usher cleared his throat. "Forgive us, Miss Brim. We're making an effort to understand you. I'm afraid it isn't easy."

"And it's not so hard either, Senator," I countered. "Penny said it best herself: A woman has to go to extraordinary lengths to be a power in this business. And she has."

"That's right," she affirmed eagerly. "Hoagy understands. All I've ever wanted was my share."

"Your *share?*" roared Schlom. "What share are you talking about, you crazy, twisted broad?!"

"The share you'd never let me have, Norbert," she answered. "You and all the other shitheads who run this business. I'm one of the pretty little girls. A disposable commodity. I get hot, I get cold, I get fucked. You'd never, ever let me have any of your precious clout. Well, I wanted some. And I worked for it, damned hard. You think you're tough? Let's see *you* go down on all those fat, smelly old slobs night after night. Let's see *you* swallow their come and pretend to like it. Let's see *you* marry a socially retarded goon who won't cut his toenails. Let's see *you* bear him a child and pretend to be happy about it every minute of every damned day, three hundred and sixty-five damned days a year. I'm tougher than you, Norbert. I had to be tougher. And I had to be more ruthless, too. If it meant killing, I killed. Whatever I had to do to get my share, I did it. This was my chance. My only chance. That doesn't make what I did right. Or wrong. Just necessary. That's what matters. That's all that matters. Don't pretend otherwise. And don't go moral on me either, because if I had to do it all over again, I would. *And so would you.*"

There wasn't much to add after that. I certainly couldn't think of anything. Except to turn to Lamp and say, "I believe it's time for your speech, Lieutenant."

He nodded grimly. "You may as well come along with me, Miss Brim. You'll save all of us a lot of trouble. And the taxpayers a lot of their hard-earned—"

"Wait, you're not actually planning to arrest me, are you?" She seemed genuinely surprised.

"I most certainly am," Lamp assured her.

"But you have no case against me," she argued. "No evidence. Nothing."

"We've all heard you confess, Penny," Mr. Shelley pointed out.

"So what?" she said mockingly. "I'll deny I said any of it. It's just my word against yours. And wait until you see me go to work on a jury. I'll cry real tears. They'll never believe you. You're wasting your time, Lieutenant. The law can't touch me. Isn't that right, Kinsley?"

Usher hesitated, stroking his chin thoughtfully. "I'm not certain that the district attorney would feel he has enough hard evidence at this stage, Lieutenant," he conceded.

"Even with this?" I reached under my chair and produced my tape recorder. It was still recording. I laid it on the conference table and gazed across it at Pennyroyal. "I happen to have this entire meeting on tape. A full confession."

She reached down into the folds of little Georgie's blanket and pulled out a Glock semiautomatic pistol and pointed it directly at me. "And I happen to have this," she said calmly. Shadow started to reach for his own gun. "Don't even think about it, Shadow," she ordered, her beautiful eyes never leaving mine. "Or you, Lieutenant."

"My gun is in my car, miss," he said quietly. "That the weapon you used on Johnny?"

"It is," she affirmed. "And it has plenty of slugs left in it, if that's what you're wondering." She continued to point it right at me, her eyes cool and determined. Until, slowly, she turned it on Georgie. Pointed it right at his small, blond head.

"Not Georgie!" protested Matthew. "Leave him out of this."

The baby was asleep there in her lap, blissfully unaware of any danger.

"I want that tape, Hoagy," she said. "Give it to me."

"Now let's all stay calm," said Mr. Shelley, who sounded more than a little rattled.

"I'm perfectly calm," she said. And she was. "But I want that tape."

"Let her have it, Hoagy," said Lamp.

I popped the cassette out of the recorder and pushed it across the conference table to her. She pocketed it in her overalls, the Glock never leaving Georgie's temple.

"Thanks," she said tartly.

"You're most welcome."

"I'm going to leave now," she announced. "Don't anyone try to stop me."

"We won't," Lamp said.

"Leave Georgie here," Matthew begged. "Please, Penny. Leave him."

"No way—he's my only chance." She got to her feet, cradling him in the crook of her left arm, her right hand still holding the Glock against his temple. Slowly, she backed away from the table toward the door. No one else moved. She didn't bother with Georgie's stroller. When she got to the door she stopped. And said "One question, Hoagy."

"All right."

"When did you know?"

"Last night, like I said."

She narrowed her eyes at me. "You knew when I phoned you from my bedroom? You knew then?"

"Of course. That's how come I was so positive you wouldn't be the next victim."

She thought this over. "God, you're cold-blooded."

"If I'm cold-blooded, what does that make you?"

"A player." She said this proudly, defiantly. Then she vanished out the door with Georgie.

● ● ●

She ran. Not for her car, but for the charred ruins of Homewood. She couldn't move too fast, clutching Georgie. I couldn't move too fast myself, on my gimpy knee. But Sarge, the world-class middle-distance runner, was plenty fast. Fast enough to sprint to her Land Cruiser, grab her Glock from the glove compartment, and tear across the lot after Pennyroyal, stride fluid, knees high. The lady could run. She overtook Pennyroyal before she'd even reached the soundstages. Would have tackled her to the ground, too, if Pennyroyal hadn't shot her. Put one right in Sarge's left thigh. Sarge went straight down with a yelp and stayed down, clutching at her leg. Bunny stayed behind with her. The rest of us followed Pretty Penny from a good, safe distance as she made her way into Homewood. Down Elm Street, where the Hayes and Dale houses had stood. There was only charred remains now. Nothing more, except for the pylons. To the town square, where Matthew's camera crew was busy filming the wreckage. A great image for what's happening in Badger's head, he'd called it. I couldn't imagine why he was bothering to film it. Possibly he was planning to recast the lead. Or bring Johnny back from the dead. As a cyborg. She ran directly for the one set that was still standing there amid the rubble, Homewood's steepled white congregational church. She didn't go inside. There was no inside. But there was a bell tower, the tower where Dale and Badger exchanged their very first kiss. A portable metal staircase like they use on airport runways led up to it. The fire inspectors had been using it. Not that it was a real bell tower. Merely a facade with a catwalk running behind it. Johnny and Penny had stood on this to film their love scene. She climbed the metal steps, clutching Georgie.

"Where's that crazy broad going?" Norbert Schlom wondered, panting.

I considered sharing my tree-climbing theory with him, but decided not to bother.

Matthew didn't have to tell his crew to turn their cameras on her. They already had. They knew a climax when they saw one.

She reached the bell tower, still holding the Glock to Georgie's temple. Only he wasn't asleep anymore. He was wailing, his arms and legs flailing about. He was not a happy baby. I couldn't blame him.

We all gathered down below on the town green, looking up at her. Except for Lamp, who was calling for help. Shadow had his Glock out, but there was no way to shoot her without hitting the baby. Possibly a sharpshooter could pull it off, but even he wouldn't try it with Penny holding a loaded gun at Georgie's head.

"Stay where you are!" she commanded, as the cameras rolled. "All of you!"

We stayed where we were, all of us. I looked around for Lulu, but I seemed to have lost her. Under a bench somewhere, no doubt. There had, after all, been gunfire.

"Come on down from there, Penny!" cried Cassandra. "You're just making things woise for yourself!"

"I'll shoot him if you don't stay back!" Pennyroyal vowed. "I mean it!"

"Leave him out of it, honey—he's got nuttin' to do with it!"

"Talk to her, Toy," growled Schlom. "She's your friend."

"Cassie's right, Penny!" Toy called. "You don't want Little Georgie to come to any harm, do you?"

"Why the hell not?" Pennyroyal cried savagely. "I never wanted him! I *hate* him! Do you have any idea how horrible it was, having him grow inside me?! *His* baby? What do I care what happens to him?"

"She doesn't mean any of that, Matthew," Mrs. Shelley said, clutching her brother's arm. "She's totally out of her head."

Matthew shook his head. "She means all of it," he said hoarsely.

"She loves that baby," Mrs. Shelley insisted. "She'd never hurt him."

"I wouldn't test her," I said. "I really wouldn't."

Trace eased on over to Matthew. "Boss?" he breathed, squinting up at the tower.

Matthew looked at him uneasily. This was the first they'd spoken. "Yes, Trace?"

"I could maybe hook a rope to that thar pylon where the courthouse was," he offered. "Swing on in from the side and kick the gun clean out of her hand. She'd never see me until the last second."

It was a movie stunt. Worthy of Captain Blood or Indiana Jones or Duke Jardine, fearless hero of *Yeti*.

Matthew considered it as the cameras rolled. "I don't think so, Trace," he responded gravely. "It'd be a major gag, but it's too dangerous."

"Fuck it—I don't care about myself," Trace insisted. "It's the little guy I'm thinking about."

"So am I, Trace. She might shoot him if you miss her. We can't take that chance." He swallowed. His eyes filled with tears. "But thanks. It m-means a lot to me—that you'd do that for me."

Trace put a big arm around Matthew's bony shoulders. "Hell, Boss, you and me been through too much to let that little girl come between us. She used me same as she used you. We're in the same deep shit together, just like always. Don't you worry —we'll get him back."

Lamp drove up now in his unmarked sedan and hopped out. "Okay, everyone just relax," he said briskly. "The experts are on their way." He looked up at Pennyroyal. "Is there something I can get you, Miss Brim?" he called out, his tone solicitous and respectful. "Anything at all?"

"You mean like a cold drink?" she asked, sneering down at him.

"I mean like transportation," he offered pleasantly.

She mulled this over, biting on her lower lip as Georgie squirmed in the crook of her arm. "I want my car."

"What the hell for?" Schlom muttered. "She ain't going no-where."

"Hush," whispered Shadow. "He's trying to calm her."

"That's fine," Lamp said, nodding to her. "I think we can manage that. Where do you want it?"

"Right here," she replied. "With a full tank of gas."

"Where are the keys?" Lamp asked her.

"The keys? I have them here in my—" She started to reach for them, froze. "You're trying to trick me, aren't you?!" she said nastily.

"No, I'm not," Lamp assured her. "I'm honestly not that crafty, Miss Brim. But it's okay—we'll come back to that. What else do you want?"

She stood there thinking it over. I heard sirens now off in the distance. And I then heard something else. I heard . . .

I heard Lulu. Barking ferociously. She was up there. She was actually up there on the catwalk with Pennyroyal and Georgie. No more than ten feet from them. Barking ferociously. And then charging. Charging Pennyroyal Brim like a wild beast, teeth bared, a basset hound possessed. Pennyroyal whirled to fire at her. When she did her own body became a human shield between

Georgie and us. For an instant. In that instant Mrs. Shelley Sel-den, the Annie Oakley of the Canyon Pistol Range, snatched Shadow's Glock from his hand and swiftly and surely drilled a nine-millimeter slug through her sister-in-law's right ear. Dead center. Pennyroyal never got off a shot. Slowly, she crumpled to her knees, still holding on to her baby.

Lamp was the first one up the stairway. I was right behind him, bad knee or not. The others stayed where they were.

Pennyroyal Brim lay there on the narrow catwalk, stone dead, hugging Georgie to her chest protectively with both arms. I guess she had some maternal instinct for him after all, deep down inside. Lulu stood over them, tail thumping as she licked Georgie's face. Georgie was giggling with delight. Evidently he hadn't developed a keen sense of smell yet.

Lamp pulled him from out of his mother's death clutch and held him. "Cheese and crackers, Lulu," he exclaimed, looking down at her with awe. "You're a genuine hero."

She was indeed. It was the most fearless display of animal behavior I'd ever seen from her. In fact, it was the only fearless display of animal behavior I'd ever seen from her.

She came over to me a bit shyly. I knelt and patted her and said a few things I won't bother to repeat here, though the words caviar for life did come up. "And to think she actually fooled me into believing she was over it."

"Over what, Hoagy?" asked Lamp, as Georgie wriggled around in his arms.

"The bug," I replied.

"Bug? What bug?"

"The acting bug. This was vintage Rin Tin Tin, Lieutenant. Pure hamming. She was strictly angling for a part in the picture, the little vamp."

"What picture?"

"The one she thinks is being made right now. Don't you see, Lieutenant? This is a movie set. The cameras are rolling. The director and a bunch of studio bigwigs are standing down there. Pennyroyal is, or I should say, was an actress. Lulu thinks this has all been fake. She doesn't realize those were real bullets. And that Pennyroyal is really dead. And that she herself just about was, too. Believe me, I know her well. It'll all sink in in a moment. And when it does, well, I can tell you exactly what will happen. . . ."

She was starting to notice that Pennyroyal wasn't getting up. She ambled over and peered at her. Then peered up at me. Then back down at Pennyroyal. Then back up at me. Then her eyes rolled back in her head and she let out a low moan and slowly tumbled over onto the catwalk. She landed with a thud.

"See, Lieutenant? That's my girl."

"Son of a gun. I've never seen a dog faint before."

"It's one of the things she does best."

I picked her up and squeezed her large black nose between my thumb and forefinger. She snuffled and began to stir. I stood there with her, looking down at Pennyroyal. Her eyes were closed. There wasn't much blood. She was even a cute corpse, if you can believe it. The world's cutest. Lamp looked down at her, too, Georgie gurgling contentedly in his arms.

"So pretty and sweet," he said softly. "And such a monster."

"Straight out of a horror film," I said. "The kind that keeps you awake, night after night."

"I still can't believe it. I was so wrong about her."

"So was I, Lieutenant."

He looked at me. "You were?"

"I was." I yanked the carnation out of my lapel and placed it gently in her hand, its petals fluttering in the breeze. "She *was* the next victim."

We went down the staircase. Matthew immediately took his son from Lamp and went and sat on the town green bench with him, hugging him tightly. Mr. Shelley stood with his arms around Mrs. Shelley, who couldn't seem to stop shaking.

"That, Mrs. Selden, took a lot of nerve," I said to her.

"I—I didn't even think," she mumbled, her lips quivering. "I just did it. It was like an impulse. I—I can't explain it. I don't even know why I did it."

"To save Georgie, cookie," Mr. Shelley said, smiling at her. "You did it to save Georgie. They're the strong ones, Hoagy. Women are the strong ones. They run this world."

"And it's high time you found out."

Shadow Williams was still staring up at the bell tower in shock and disbelief. He continued to stare for a long time.

I sat on the bench next to Matthew. He was so preoccupied with his son he didn't notice me for a while.

"I think I've figured it out, Matthew," I said, when he did.

"What, Meat?" he asked hoarsely.

"What makes them so special."

"Who?"

"Actresses."

"Tell me, Meat. I want to know."

"Guys like you and me, we go off in our own little worlds. Worlds we invent. Actresses know how to go there with us. They even know how to go one step farther than we do. Deeper into it. Beyond anything we can possibly imagine."

Matthew's hand reached for his scalp, then dropped. "This . . . this was never part of my world."

"It was. You just didn't know it. Now you do. And for that I'm sorry, Matthew. Very sorry."

Later, after she'd been taken away, we sat in the front seat of Lamp's car looking up at the Homewood Congregational Church. Everyone else was gone. Sarge was going to be fine, the emergency medical people said. The bullet didn't strike a bone. They were keeping her in the hospital overnight.

Lulu lay on my lap, still woozy. She usually is after a fainting spell.

Lamp sat stiffly, hands gripping the wheel tight enough to make his knuckles white. "I wish you had told me."

"Told you what, Lieutenant?"

"That you knew it was her."

"I didn't."

He drew his breath in. Then he said, very slowly, "You were bluffing?"

"I figured it was her. It had to be. That was the only way it made any sense. But I had no proof. She was too smart for that. Confronting her in front of the others seemed like the only way to play it."

"I wish you had told me," he repeated. "I would have been armed, gosh darn it. I would have stationed someone outside the office to grab her when she ran. There are ways professionals do these things, Hoagy. Procedures we follow. Safeguards we employ so as to avoid this sort of high-risk situation. Wowie, zowie, if a cop had pulled such a reckless play he'd be torn limb from—"

"I'm not a cop, Lieutenant. I keep trying to tell you."

"Well, you'll have to start thinking like one," he said sternly.

"I can't. Something to do with my brain synapses."

"Succotash, Hoagy! You boxed me into a no-win situation. I

couldn't have made that shot in a million years. I'm not that good with a gun. If Mrs. Selden hadn't been standing there, Georgie would be dead right now. And so would Lulu. And it would be your fault."

Lulu stirred, a low moan coming from her throat.

"And I'm not happy about that, Lieutenant. I don't enjoy getting caught in the middle of any of this. Believe me, I don't. Maybe what I did was reckless. But you would never have gotten that confession out of her. Never have put her behind bars. Your procedures and safeguards would have done you no good. She'd be a free woman, instead of a dead one. And I don't see how that makes you right and me wrong."

"Because you took the law into your own hands."

"It was the only way."

"I wish you had warned me," he said stubbornly.

"Next time I will, okay?"

He sat there in brittle silence a moment. "Next time I don't think I'll be happy to see you coming, Hoagy."

"Not even a little bit happy?"

"Nope."

"Not even a teeny, weeny bit happy?"

He scowled at me. Then he sighed and reached over and opened up the glove compartment. A copy of the second novel was inside. "I've been carrying this darned thing around for days," he muttered. "Was hoping you'd autograph it."

"My pleasure, Lieutenant." I uncapped my Waterman and signed it: *To Emil Lamp—When are you going to find a nice girl and settle down?*

We sat there looking at the church a while longer. Until Lamp started up the car and said, "Let's head down to the beach and drink some beer, okay?"

"It's a deal, provided we take the Vette. You drive."

His eyes widened. "Jeepers, can I?!"

"You most certainly can." I tossed him the keys. "Let's ride, Buz."

# Chapter Twelve

---

The heat wave returned in the night. That morning's *Times* was chock full of dire pronouncements about global warming and drought and the death of The California Dream as we all know and love it. It was almost enough to crowd Pennyroyal Brim's death off page one. But not quite. There was so much to tell. How she had murdered her way to the top. How she had held her own infant son hostage at gunpoint. How little Georgie had been so dramatically rescued. The reports were somewhat fuzzy as to who actually fired the fatal shot. The shooter was merely identified by police as a "sharpshooter." That was how the Seldens wanted it. As a result, most of the attention went elsewhere. To Lulu the Wonder Dog, if you must know. That's what everyone started calling her. It seems the network news people got hold of the film Matthew's crew had shot of the rescue. Lulu's brave deed was all over the air waves, coast to coast. This was it—her fifteen minutes of fame. She got pretty hot, too. My phone rang constantly that morning. Arsenio Hall wanted her to come on and get busy. A dog chow company wanted her to give them her paw on an endorsement deal. CBS called about her doing a *Lassie*-type Saturday morning thing. ABC wanted to do a rescue docudrama. Disney wanted to sign her to an exclusive three-picture deal. Joey Bam Bam called, saying he would consider it an ultra-ultra privilege to represent her. Everyone called. Everyone except Merilee Nash. Merilee did not call. That much didn't change.

I told Lulu I wouldn't stand in her way if she wanted to cash in. But she wasn't interested. In any of it. All she wanted to do was forget the whole ugly business and go home. She even started tugging my empty suitcase out the closet with her teeth.

But I couldn't go. Not yet. I wasn't done.

Bunny was on her Nordic Track when I knocked on her door.

"I'm taking Matthew for a drive, Bunny," I announced. "You can come or not come. It's up to you. But I'm taking him."

"Wait, Hoagy," she begged. "Please." She climbed down off the machine and wiped her forehead with a *Dennis the Dinosaur* towel, then heaved a sigh of resignation. "Give me a minute, okay?

I could hear her dialing the phone as I went out the door. I waited for her on a bench in the courtyard. She emerged a few minutes later dressed in a short-sleeved blouse and shorts, her bunny rabbit charm bracelet clanging on her wrist. She looked meek. She looked scared.

Matthew was sprawled on the sofa in his office, furiously scribbling on a yellow legal pad. A vacant office next to Sarge's had been converted to a nursery. Georgie was in there swatting gleefully at toys in his playpen, his own full-time nurse and two secretaries cooing over him. Sarge hobbled around in gym shorts on a pair of crutches, her thigh heavily bandaged. She refused to stay home.

"Let's go, Matthew," I commanded him from the doorway.

"Where, Meat?" he wondered, still far away in his thoughts.

"Something Bunny wants to show you."

He frowned. "What is it, Ma?"

Bunny said nothing.

"I'm kind of busy right now," he said, tapping at the pad with his pen. "Can we do this later?"

"No, we can't."

We took Bunny's Jaguar, air conditioner blasting. Lulu the Wonder Dog and I sat in back. Bunny drove, gripping the wheel firmly with her small, brown hands.

Matthew was talkative. And full of plans. "I'm selling the house first thing," he revealed. "It's from the past—my old life. I'm buying a new one for me and Georgie. And I'm gonna strike the Badger sets on Stage One. That whole thing is over. History. It's time to move on." He turned and glanced at Bunny. "What's this all about, Ma?"

Bunny said nothing. Just drove. Over the hill into the valley. She got off at Roscoe Boulevard and steered us through the dried, searing flats of Northridge to Reseda Boulevard. She took that for a few blocks before turning off onto a side street of faded, two-story apartment houses. She pulled up in front of a pumpkin-colored, eight-unit building and parked there. Then she got out and started inside.

"What is this, Ma?" Matthew called after her. "Where are we going?"

We were going upstairs. There were two doors at the top of the stairs. Bunny used a key on one of them and opened it. Inside was a plainly furnished living room cooled by a window air conditioner. A white-haired man in his seventies sat on the sofa watching a soap opera on TV. He was a big man, paunchy. Wore a knit shirt buttoned to the neck, dark brown slacks, and Hush Puppies. He and Bunny stared at each other. He got up and turned off the TV, nervously rubbing his hands together. He stood there in awkward silence. We all did.

Matthew's face broke out into a grin. "Sure, sure," he exclaimed, shaking a finger at him. "I remember you—you're Mr. Ferraro, Ma's old boss at the accounting firm. You came to Dad's funeral."

"Nice to see you again, Matthew," he said, his voice quavering slightly as they shook hands. "And it's Carlo."

"So what's this all about, Ma?" asked Matthew.

Bunny eyed the carpet. Carlo cleared his throat but said nothing. That left it up to me.

So I was the one who broke it to him. I said, "Matthew, Carlo is your father."

"The love had gone out of our marriage by the time your sister was born, Matty. If you can even call it love."

Bunny spoke in a soft, halting voice. She was seated on the sofa, Carlo beside her with his arm around her. Matthew and I were in chairs across the coffee table from them. Matthew clutched the arms of his tightly, as if he were afraid it might throw him.

"I don't believe I ever loved Joe Wax," she went on. "Joe was a cold, selfish, bitter man. Whatever I felt for him, it wasn't love. Because I didn't know what love was. Not until I met this dear, lovely man here. This man who I spent eight hours with every day. And who I have loved for forty years, just as he loves me. It wasn't something either of us wanted. We both resisted. It was shameful. But when we were together, it wasn't shameful, Matty. It was pure and wonderful. It was love. Our secret love. Carlo is a devout Catholic. A man with a wife and four healthy, beautiful daughters. Divorce has always been out of the question. I could never come between a man and his faith. . . . We felt shame. But we swallowed our shame. We didn't want to keep meeting in some cheap motel, so Carlo rented us a small, furnished apartment in Encino. We saw each other there after work. Mostly when Joe was out of town. And then I—I got pregnant, Matthew. With you. I didn't know what to do. Carlo didn't believe in abortion. Neither did I. But Joe would know it wasn't his. He hadn't laid a hand on me in years. I was so sick about it I even considered suicide. Carlo had to talk me out of it. Finally, I told Joe. I had no other choice. I thought he'd kill both of us. But he didn't. He merely accepted my unfaithfulness as his miserable lot in life. It fed his bitterness. The three of us decided that for the good of the baby, and of both our families, that Joe and I would simply raise you as our own. And that's what we did. Carlo, Joe, and I are the only ones who have ever known that Joe wasn't your real dad. Shelley doesn't know. Carlo's wife, Mary, doesn't know. Joe tried at first to treat you the same as Shelley. But he just couldn't. You were a constant reminder to him of his own failure as a husband. So he took it out on you. Treated you with nothing but hate, no matter how much I begged him not to. It was never you, sweetheart. He never hated you. It was what you represented."

Matthew stared at her in amazement. "All these years, Ma," he cried. "All these years of thinking there was something wrong with me. Why didn't you ever *tell* me?"

"When you were little I was afraid you wouldn't understand. . . ."

"But what about after he died?" Matthew protested. "I was in college, for chrissakes!"

"I wanted to, Matty. So many times. But I was ashamed, don't you see? I didn't want you thinking I was . . . I didn't want you thinking less of me. Maybe it was wrong of me to keep silent. But I did what I thought was best." She glanced uneasily at Carlo. He took her hand and held it. "That's all a person can do, sweetheart. What they think is best. Gradually, Carlo and I grew accustomed to our little snatches of life together. We rented a number of apartments together through the years. We've had this one for about ten. Carlo was always there for you, even though you never knew it. He helped us out when Joe was having business trouble. A little something extra in my paycheck. And when you needed money for college, he provided it. We called it a loan. After you became such a big success, you wondered why I kept working for him. You wanted me to relax and enjoy myself. I *was* enjoying myself. I was with the man I loved all day long. I stayed with him until the day he retired."

"I have a good, steady income from my investments," Carlo said. "I'm not rich, but I'm comfortable. My house is paid off. My girls are all married. Would you like to see their pictures?" He pulled out his wallet and handed it over to Matthew, who leafed slowly through a collection of color snapshots, his eyes glazing over.

"We still spend as much of our time together as we can," Bunny said. "We talk, eat, watch television. Every time I told you I was out playing golf I was here. I've never been on a golf course in my life. I put the clubs in the car. I take them out of the car. I was here when Mr. Zorch was shot. I—I couldn't tell the police that, for fear it would get back to you. So I was vague with them. They got suspicious. I was afraid I would have to tell them the truth. But I didn't. Your friend Hoagy, he insisted I tell you. He was going to do it if I didn't." She patted Carlo's knee. "I feel as if a huge burden has been lifted from my shoulders."

"Only because it has been," I observed.

She gave me a hard, cold look. "Yes, I suppose it has," she admitted, thawing a few degrees. "I'll make us some coffee, Carlo."

"Fine, dear," said Carlo, beaming at her. "I picked up some of that decaf you like. I had a coupon—saved seventy-five cents. It's in the cupboard over the sink."

"Thank you, dear."

She went bustling off to the kitchen to make it, Matthew observing their little snippet of domestic routine in stunned silence.

Carlo shifted on the sofa and looked at his famous son warily. I was starting to notice the resemblance now. The snow-shovel jaw. The gawky arms and legs. The small, freckled hands. "I've always been proud of you, Matthew," he said. "Not just because of what you've accomplished as a film director, but because of the way you've always taken care of your mother and sister. Your family is all you've got in this world. A man who takes care of his family is a man I respect—even if he only digs ditches for a living." Matthew nodded dumbly at this. I'm not sure he heard any of it. "I know I can never be a father to you. It's much too late for that. But now that we've finally broken the ice, I hope we can be friends."

Matthew looked at me. His eyes were really glazed over now, as if he were coming on to a tab of orange sunshine. "How, Meat?" he wondered. "How did you know?"

"Certain things are a little more obvious to an outsider than they are to a member of the family. That's why they invented family counselors and therapists and—"

"And people like you?" asked Matthew.

"Not exactly, Matthew. I invented myself."

The House of Wax story didn't exactly die with Pennyroyal Brim. It just got bigger and uglier. The police, under considerable media pressure, released the transcript of my tape recording of her confession. *People* devoted an entire issue to it. The cover said simply, "HER OWN WORDS." The tabloids, meanwhile, dug into Dirty Penny's childhood with a zeal that crossed over into the truly sick. The *Enquirer* found a girlhood friend who swore that when Penny was ten years old she'd savagely murdered several neighborhood dogs and mutilated their corpses—strictly for kicks. Lulu didn't care for that one at all. The *Star* found a male cousin who claimed to have been raped by her at age twelve. Toy Schlom, her old running mate, was pursued relentlessly for gory details about their nasty days together. The press even camped out in front of the Schlom's swank tear-down on Hazen Drive, forcing her into seclusion at the exclusive Golden Door Spa in Escondido.

People were utterly fascinated by Pennyroyal Brim. They couldn't get enough of her story. And they couldn't stop asking that same question—how could someone so pretty do such monstrous things?

I don't know how. I don't want to know. I know what she tasted like. I don't need to know anything more.

Cassandra Dee truly lucked out. She alone had Penny's authorized story. The public was clamoring for it. Her publisher was rushing it into print. She stopped by my bungalow a few days later. I was at my Olympia, working on a new first chapter.

"I've had offers like ya wouldn't believe, Hoagy," she informed me in a surprisingly quiet, somber voice. "Six figures for the exclusive story of our last days together. *Good Morning, America* wants me on, *Today, Tonight* . . ." She flopped glumly down onto my sofa bed. Lulu growled at her from under my chair. She jumped back up. "I guess you been through this shit. I never have. I never been this hot before. Not ever. I'm *made*, Hoagy."

"Congratulations."

"So how come I'm not happy?" she complained mournfully. "I mean, why am I not happy?"

I took a good look at her. She wasn't wearing her usual Betty Boop makeup that day. She seemed younger and more vulnerable without it. She also seemed profoundly depressed—she hadn't tried to sneak so much as one glance at the manuscript pages stacked on my desk. "I don't know, Cassandra. Why don't you think you're happy?"

"I guess on account of the whole time I was woiking with her I had no fucking idea what was going on. I mean, not a *clue*. So what kinda reporter does that make me, huh? I'm a damned good one, Hoagy. At least I always thought so. Now I don't know. I mean, I blew this story. Totally." She shook her head at me. "I can't get no satisfaction from any of this—the bucks, the heat. I gotta earn it. I gotta be satisfied with myself as a professional. And I ain't."

I went over to her and kissed her full on the mouth.

"Gaaaawd, Hoagy," she cried, shuddering. "A shiver just went through my whole body."

"You earned that."

"Does this mean you're proud of me?" she asked, coyly, nasally.

"It means there's hope for you, Cassandra."

"I hope we get a chance to woik together again," she said, her goggle eyes gleaming at me hungrily.

"I told you—we're not working together. We just happen to be on the same story."

"So maybe we'll be on the same story again, huh?"

"There is always that possibility."

She went to the door and opened it. "Gimme a call when you're back in New York. After ya finally get over it, I mean."

"Get over what?"

"Merilee dumping ya, silly."

"She didn't dump me," I insisted.

"Yeah, yeah, shewa." And then Cassandra Dee went out the door, cackling.

But how could I think otherwise? I still hadn't heard from her. Not one word. Even Lulu the Wonder Dog hadn't heard from her. It was over. It was really over. I didn't know why. I didn't know how. But it was over. For good.

And I couldn't get used to that. I didn't want to get used to that.

I wish I could tell you that Norbert Schlom was ousted as president of Panorama City Communications and was now selling rug shampoos door to door. Not so. The sale of Panorama to Murakami went through. Final sale price: five point eight billion. Schlom, it was estimated, personally cleared three hundred million. And this without Bedford Falls as part of the package. Schlom was in no position to include it. Pennyroyal's claim to one half of the studio died with her. The studio was all Matthew's, and Matthew wasn't selling. Bedford Falls was safe and snug once again, provided the studio was able to right itself financially.

And Sheldon Selden vowed that it would.

"Now that the management situation is stable the top creative people will want back in," he explained to me confidently over family dinner at Casa Selden, "We're still here. We still treat people like human beings. We're still their best hope. I'll be green-lighting quality projects before you know it."

Dinner was red snapper that Mrs. Shelley grilled on the barbecue and topped with salsa. We ate out on the patio at a weathered teak table. Matthew, Bunny, and Sarge were there, too. The kids were inside watching TV with Georgie and his nurse. The atmosphere was strained. Matthew and his sister were still rocked by the news that their mother had been leading a double life for the past forty years. It was a bit much to take on top of everything else that had gone on. This one would be the hardest to come to grips with. It would take all of them a long time.

"Besides," Mr. Shelley added, grinning at Matthew, "we've still got our ace in the hole, right?"

"I've decided to take a long trip," Matthew announced, as he carefully cut his snapper into small, bite-sized pieces. "Soon as Meat and me finish. Before I do anything else."

Sarge glanced at him sharply. Clearly, he hadn't told her about this.

"A trip to where, kid?" Mr. Shelley asked, frowning. Clearly, this wasn't part of his plan—he wanted Matthew back in production immediately.

"I've been living inside my own head for too long," Matthew explained intently. "I want to expose myself to new places and new people. I want to go to France. I want to go to Italy, Greece—"

"For how long?" Mr. Shelley wanted to know.

"Six months," Matthew replied. "A year maybe. However long I feel like. I think it'll be good for me. What do you think, Meat?"

"I think it will be great for you."

"Sure, sure," Mr. Shelley agreed, jumping on board. "Take some time off. Do you good to get away from all of this. If anybody deserves a vacation, it's you. Go have yourself a good time."

"And don't worry a bit about Georgie," Mrs. Shelley chimed in enthusiastically. "We'll be more than happy to have him here while you're away."

"Oh, no, no, no," Matthew countered vehemently. "Georgie's coming with me. Absolutely. He's a big part of why I'm going. I want to expose him to the world right from the start. I want him to see things. Experience things. I don't want him to grow up in the dark the way I did."

Bunny's mouth tightened. She said nothing.

"But will you be able to handle him all by yourself?" Mrs. Shelley asked gently. "He does need a lot of attention and care."

"I'll take somebody," he promised, turning to Sarge. "Wanna come?"

"What you doin' on me, man?" she growled.

"I want you to come with us," Matthew said earnestly. "You'll be on full salary. I'll pay for everything. Come on. It'll be neat."

"No, thanks," she said, eyes on her plate. Her back was very stiff.

Matthew seemed genuinely astonished. "Why not?"

"Because changin' diapers ain't part of my job description. And I got too much to do here as it is. And it'll look like you and me are . . . It's just no, that's all. Forget it. No." She threw down her napkin and started clearing the table. She no longer needed crutches, but was still hobbling.

"Sit, Charmaine," Bunny commanded. "I can do that."

"I'll do it," she barked. "Doc said not to favor it."

"But what happens if I have to take care of some business while I'm over there?" Matthew persisted.

She snatched his plate away from him. "You'll take care of it," she replied curtly.

"What if I get an idea for my new script?"

"You'll write it down."

"I want you to come," he said stubbornly.

"Just drop it, Matthew," she huffed. "I ain't comin' wit' you!"

"Please?"

"What the fuck is your problem, man!?" she demanded. "What do you care if I go or if I don't go?! Huh?! What do you care?"

Matthew reddened. "Because I don't think I could stand to be away from you for that long," he said forthrightly. "I'm totally lost without you." His voice didn't even crack a bit. God, I was proud.

She softened, her eyes shining like wet stones. "I don't know what you're talking about. Does anybody know what he's talking about?"

"Maybe you two would like to be alone," I suggested, getting up from the table. The others started to do the same.

Matthew waved us off. "No, no. Sit. Please. Everybody."

"Charmaine?" Bunny spoke up. "I know this is none of my business, but if I might be allowed . . ."

Sarge nodded. "Go ahead."

"Don't worry about how it might look. Or about what people might think. No good ever comes of that. Just listen to your heart —that's the only truth there is."

Sarge was silent a moment. "Mind if I think it over?" she asked Matthew, her voice husky.

"Not as long as you end up saying yes."

"Probably will," she murmured.

"Good," he said happily.

They gazed across the table at each other, glowing.

"This new script of yours," I said to him. "What will it be about?"

"Me," he answered promptly. "A guy who discovers at middle-age that he has a father he never knew. It forces him into this amazing new relationship, and also forces him to reflect back on his life. His relationships with his family, with women, with his dog . . ."

I tugged at my ear. "His dog?"

"I was thinking of making his best friend a basset hound," Matthew said, his eyes twinkling at me brightly.

Beneath me, Lulu stirred and made small, litigious noises.

"The lead part's perfect for Trace," he added enthusiastically. "I'm gonna make him this ex-jock who's down on his luck. A guy who was somebody once, and now's just sort of a beach bum. It's *him*. I really miss Trace. He's my man. And so are you, Meat. I want you to write this script with me. I want you by my side."

"Sorry, Matthew," I said. "I move on after our business is done."

"To do what?" he wondered unhappily.

"My own stuff, for better or worse."

"Will you at least read my first draft?" he asked. "Tell me what you think?"

He awaited my reply anxiously. So did the others. It meant a lot to Matthew, therefore it meant a lot to them. This much hadn't changed. Never would.

I reached for my wine glass. "Just send it to me in a plain brown envelope—marked personal."

I was spending long days and nights at the typewriter now, pausing only to walk with Lulu through the studio to clear my head. Usually we walked late at night, when it was quiet. The charred ruins of Homewood were gone. So was the church, which had been taken apart section by section and carted off to a warehouse. There were no more benches in the town green. No more town green. The bushes had been removed. Even the grass had been rolled up and trucked away. It was simply a vacant space now. A place to build new dreams. Matthew's dreams and the dreams of others who sought refuge here inside the gate of the fort. Norbert Schlom couldn't touch them here. I suppose I could take some small satisfaction in that. But I didn't. I was too busy wondering where I was going from here. The first and only stop on my itinerary appeared to be nowhere. Back to a novel that wouldn't yield to my touch. Back to that drafty fifth-floor walk-up on West Ninety-third Street. Back to the worst kind of aloneness —the kind without Merilee.

I couldn't remember the last time my life seemed so barren and hopeless.

I was at the typewriter working on the first time Matthew Wax met Pennyroyal Brim when the phone rang. I glanced at Grandfather's Rolex. It was three o'clock in the morning. It rang some more. I stared at it. It wasn't her. It wasn't ever going to be her. I picked it up.

It was the drum banger. He was depressed.

"Oh, who cares, Hoag?" he moaned, when I assured him I was hard at work. "What difference does it make? Can you tell me that?"

Here was one of the big changes in modern publishing. It used to be that editors were paid to hold writers' hands. Now it's the other way around.

"What seems to be the problem?" I inquired pleasantly. After all, he was paying me a lot of money. And knowing that he was miserable was already making me feel better.

"The problem," he replied glumly, "is that I get paid righteous bucks. You know I'm the second highest paid editor in all of publishing? Only Michael Korda makes more than I do, and everyone knows he's a dickhead."

"And?"

"And I fucked up. Pennyroyal's book is *the* hot property of the decade. The Literary Guild just paid more for it than any book in the history of publishing. Me, I'm sitting on Matthew fucking Wax." He sighed heavily. "I'm shook, Hoag. Nothing like this has ever happened to me before. I look like an idiot."

"We'll make out just fine," I assured him soothingly. "Matthew still happens to be the most successful director of all time. And I've got major stuff about his father."

"Oh, who gives a shit about his father?"

"The guy *was* married to her," I pointed out.

"That's true," he conceded grudgingly. "Could you maybe do more on her? Deemphasize him?"

"It's his book."

"It's my reputation."

"I'll do what I can." A meaningless phrase, but it always makes them feel better.

"Good man," he said, brightening. "Have you got a sexy title?"

"I was planning to call it 'The Boy Who Never Grew Up.' "

Long silence from his end. Plus another heavy sigh. "Oh, well, there's still time. . . ."

I hung up on him. Lulu looked up at me anxiously, hoping it was finally time to get the suitcases out. I shook my head. She went back to sleep. The phone rang again. I snatched it off the cradle.

"Now what do you want?" I snapped.

"Merciful heavens, Mister Hoagy. It took me thirty-eight calls on two different coasts to track you down and *this* is the hello I get?"

My heart started pounding, which it always does when I hear that feathery teenaged girl's voice that is hers and hers alone. The connection was fuzzy, and there was an echo. But it was her. It was really her.

"How are you, Merilee?" I asked casually.

"Forget about me—what on earth is going on there, you son of a sea cook?"

"I've missed your quaint little expressions."

"Never you mind, mister. Our assistant costumer just flew in with all the appalling news. Pennyroyal Brim and Matthew Wax and *Lulu*. My Lord! When did you go to work for him, anyway?"

"You didn't get my letter?"

"I did not. I hadn't the slightest idea you were in L.A. I've been calling your apartment, my apartment, the farm . . . I'm completely in the dark, don't you see? We're on Wakaya Island, completely cut off from civilization. No television. No phones. No mail. That's how the director wants it. I had to charter a plane to Viti Levu so I could call you. I've been sitting here in the airport for the past three hours trying to reach you. Now tell me everything, you gherkin. At once."

I did, while Lulu the Wonder Dog stared at the phone and whimpered. She always knows when it's her mommy. Don't ask me how. "You would have been proud of her, Merilee."

"My brave little sweetness," she exclaimed. "What possessed her?"

"She got the bug, I'm afraid."

"That happened the last time she traveled. Put her on a high-fiber diet and bottled water. She prefers Evian."

"The acting bug."

"Never. I forbid it."

"Not to worry. It's out of her system for good now."

Merilee was silent a moment. "I almost feel for Pennyroyal, you know that? There's no excusing what she did, of course. But why she did it . . . Believe me, it's awful being someone like her. One of the sweetie pies. I know. I was once one myself."

"You still are."

"Hoagy, I happen to be playing a middle-aged nun with pronounced butch tendencies. I am no one's sweetie pie anymore."

"How is it coming?"

"God knows."

"How is Michelle?"

"Skinny."

"And how is Merilee?"

"Ready to talk," she informed me gravely.

Here it was. Our good-bye scene. "Okay," I said, taking a deep breath. "I'm ready to listen."

"First I want to say I'm sorry I left you in the lurch the way I did. I needed to—"

"Get in character, I know."

"You don't know," she said sharply. "You don't know a thing. It has nothing to do with this stupid movie."

"What does it have to do with?"

"A woman's body."

"Any particular woman's body?"

"Mine. It so happens I'm forty years old and—"

"I'm well aware of how old you—"

"I'm pregnant, Hoagy," she blurted out. She waited for me to say something. Anything. "Are you still there, Hoagy?"

I cleared my throat and managed to say I was.

"I realize this comes as a bit of a surprise."

"You knew before you left?"

"I did."

"Why on earth didn't you say something, Merilee?"

"Because I needed to make up my own mind about it. Now hush up and let me say what I have to say, okay? I want a baby. I've been wanting one for a while. I haven't pressured you about it because I know how much you hate them. What is it you call them? Midget human life forms? I understand your feelings perfectly. I honestly do. But I've decided to have this baby. I have to. I can't put it off any longer. Now, before you go into complete cardiac arrest, let me assure you that you are absolutely, positively under no obligation. It's my baby. I will raise it on my own, and provided we're both mature, sensible adults—"

"What's your second choice?"

"I see no reason why this should have any effect on our non-relationship. We'll go on as we have, or haven't. The only difference is I'll now be toting a small child along with me."

"You seem to have it all figured out," I observed.

"Yes, I believe I do. And I feel good about it. I feel happy and wonderful, and I just hope to God we finish up here before I begin to show. It would *not* do for Sister Mary Catherine to be overtly preggers. Hoagy, I think you should finish that book here. I miss thee somethin' arful. I've my own little thatched beach hut —they call them bures here. Nothing but white sand a mile in each direction. Sunshine, fresh air, fresh fish for sweetness. And wait until you see me in a grass skirt."

"I'd rather see you out of it."

"You'll join me?"

"You know I will, Merilee. And you know you can count on me. Who knows? Maybe this is the best thing that could have happened to us. Maybe it's what we've been needing all along. And maybe fatherhood is something I'll actually take to. Stranger things have happened. After all this isn't going to be just any midget human life form. It's going to be *our* midget human—"

"Oh, dear, I'm afraid I've made a total mess of this. I thought you understood, darling."

"What's to understand, Merilee? All that matters is that we love each other and that we stick together and we—"

"You're not the father, Hoagy."

She said it gently. She was very gentle about all of it. Classy, too, I must admit. But, hey, so was I. I didn't even try to find out just who the father was. That wouldn't be gentlemanly, and I'm always the perfect gentleman. Ask anyone. After I hung up I sat there staring at the carpet for a while. There were cigarette burns in it I hadn't noticed before. My chest ached. I got up and poured myself three fingers of Glenmorangie and drank it down. It didn't help. It didn't hurt either. I poured myself another and drank that down. Then I sat on the bed. Then I broke the news to Lulu.